Blood Road:

Milliseconds to Murder

Bryce Anderson

Sugarbush Studios
Atlanta
www.sugarbushstudios.com

ISBN 978-1-7329965-3-3

CHAPTER 1

When my phone rings, someone's usually had a messy death.

The crash scene was typical. Squad cars from the Oak Ridge Police Department and the Anderson County Sheriff's Department were still on-scene. The edges and lines of the police cars were drawn into sharp focus as they were lined up on both shoulders, blue lights flashing.

The afternoon sun cast harsh, pure light on the bleached gray asphalt of the rural two-lane road and the heat-burned greenish-yellow grass on both sides of it.

Edward Hopper could have painted this, I decided, as I walked toward the crashed Nissan Maxima on the westbound side of the road. The sunlight washed over the white police cars and the roadway just like *Second Story Sunlight* washed over those white houses in Hopper's painting.

The wrecked Maxima was at rest in the grass, right front corner up against the berm of the hillside that began about twenty feet from the edge of the pavement. It had been traveling in the same direction as I was walking, heading towards Oak Ridge National Laboratory.

Matted grass from rolling tires revealed the path of the car as it had transitioned from the roadway and onto the grassy shoulder. The car had been steered into the grass in a tight arc.

A yellow flatbed dual-axle utility trailer with a long neck was at rest in the middle of the road, just across from the Maxima. Debris and broken parts littered the space between them.

There was usually important information in the broken pieces. The same was true for people's lives in general. But unlike people, I knew how to read broken car parts.

The deputy who had escorted me into the scene, the same one who'd called me earlier, cleared his throat and pointed. "The pick-up truck was pulling that trailer. He was heading east, out of the national laboratory and back into town. Said he was doing about sixty."

I turned to face him. He was young, maybe twenty-two years old. Eager brown eyes and a medium build. His black uniform was absorbing the July sun's heat, and it showed. Sweat beaded on his upper lip. The nametag under the badge said LARKIN.

Larkin was pointing behind us at a white Ford F-350 dually. It was parked on the eastbound shoulder of the road, sandwiched by police cars.

"Is that where he stopped when he saw he lost his trailer?" I asked Larkin.

Larkin nodded. "That's what he told us. Witness confirmed it." He turned back and pointed in front of us. "The Maxima was heading west, toward the lab." Larkin gestured to the car. "The bodies are still in the car. Jordan said to wait for you. "

"Polite of him." I resumed walking toward the Maxima and the trailer.

The trailer was a one-ton model with a long steel neck designed for a tight turning radius. Medium duty, not tractor-trailer sized. It was sitting in the middle of the road pointing west, back towards the national laboratory, opposite of the way it had been pulled.

The right front corner of the Maxima had dug into the earthen berm that paralleled the road. This is where the car's number came up, along with the driver and the right rear-seat occupant. The front passenger had made it out without injury. Physically, that is. He'd have some nightmares for a while.

The fire department, also known as the Evidence Eradication Team, had cut off the entire roof to extricate the surviving occupant. A white sheet covered the car where the roof had been.

"I'll need to pull that off," I said.

"Sure thing," Larkin said.

We walked toward the car. I dropped my camera bag next to the left front wheel, then reached into it.

"Gloves," I said, and handed Larkin a pair of latex gloves, then pulled some onto my own hands.

"Thanks." Larkin went to the passenger side.

I went to the driver's door. We pulled the sheet off and draped it on the berm in front of the Maxima. The white fabric billowed out like a sail and floated onto the parched grass.

"Gericault," I said, looking over the dead occupants. His still life drawings of severed limbs, done near the end. This car was definitely a Gericault.

I pictured the vehicles approaching each other on the road, prior to impact. The pickup truck and trailer had been heading east. The Maxima had been heading west. The long-necked trailer had somehow detached from the pick-up truck and veered into oncoming traffic. The Nissan Maxima was the unlucky car that happened to meet it. The equally unlucky driver jerked to the right just before impact. It was a purely instinctive reaction, but it also killed him and the guy in back. Instead of hitting the front of the car, where the engine and front structure of the Nissan would have stopped it, the trailer neck went in through the driver's door.

"Damn," Larkin said.

The trailer's long neck had punched through the driver's door at a slight angle. It then severed the driver's left thigh in half at the linea aspera, broken the head of the femur out of the pelvic girdle socket, and then continued through the driver's torso and through his seatback.

The driver was smashed against his seatback. His head was tilted back, face towards the sky. His mouth had frozen into a large O. His skin was pale white. His right hand was locked onto the steering wheel in a true death grip. His left arm was severed at the distal brachioradialis, just below the elbow.

"His left arm is in the road." Larkin jerked a thumb over his shoulder. "But how did it get both his leg and his arm?"

I studied the driver, mentally reconstructing the trajectory of the trailer neck. "He lifted his left leg and pulled his left arm down."

"Why would he do that?"

"He saw it coming. It was reflexive, just like steering to the right to try to avoid it. But the trailer was turning in an arc, too, and they ended up converging."

I pointed to a reddish-pink blob on the rear seat. "That's his stomach." It was resting against the right thigh of the dead guy in the back seat.

Larkin turned pale. He looked away, then forced himself to look back. "What's that underneath it?"

I walked to the rear door and pulled the handle. It swung open easily without the weight of the window glass or window frame on top of it.

"It's his upper lumbar vertebrae. Part of it, anyway." The spiny column of delta-shaped bones was twisted on the seat under the stomach. Cerebrospinal fluid leaked from both severed ends. But that didn't compare to the rear footwells.

The right-rear passenger in the backseat had been slouching, so the steel trailer neck had rammed though his chest. Both he and the driver had hemorrhaged out in the car. Their blood and other body fluids had pooled in the rear footwells at least an inch deep. The driver's intestines had roped out through the seatback and coiled partially in the footwell, torn and lacerated.

The smell of blood iron, pulped adipose tissue, and feces hung in the air. It's different from decomp, and it's a smell you never get used to, no matter how many times you're exposed to it.

I reached out and put my hand on the right rear passenger's shoulder. He was still warm, and his blue eyes were still open. I pulled him gently forward. Blood poured out of his open mouth.

The long trailer neck had exited through his upper back. It had penetrated his rear seatback, too. A fist-sized piece of muscle was crammed in the hole.

"That's his heart," I said. "Would you mind..."

I looked up. Larkin had dropped his head and turned away. Then he threw up.

"You okay? Larkin?" I kept the dead guy forward.

"Mm-hm." Larkin had turned away, but he held up his hand and waved me off.

The shredded heart filled most of the hole. I couldn't reach far enough into the car to move the heart.

I gently put the guy back against the seat. "I'm so sorry." I said it quietly, out of Larkin's hearing.

"What?" Larkin coughed, straightening up. He spit on the ground.

"I'm going to look at the trailer," I said. "These can be tagged and bagged."

Larkin gave me a thumbs-up. "Will do, boss."

I studied the roadway as I walked towards the trailer. The Maxima hadn't left any braking marks. Even with anti-lock brakes, if the driver had gotten on them hard, the tires would have left faintly visible rubber patches on the road as the wheel locked and unlocked to achieve the highest possible friction. So he'd made the decision to turn instead of brake. No surprise there. When faced with a head-on collision, drivers usually steered first, then braked. This guy had been too dead to get to the braking.

The trailer used hydraulic brakes, not air brakes, but it still should have had an emergency system to lock up the wheels if it disconnected from the pickup truck.

I scanned the roadway. *There.*

A skidmark from one of the left side trailer tires began at the centerline of the two-lane road. The skidmark strayed into the oncoming lane for about thirty feet, eventually reaching about halfway into the oncoming westbound lane, then disappeared.

A matching skidmark from one of the trailer's right side tires was mirrored on the eastbound travel lane and curved toward the centerline, converging slightly toward the left skidmark as the trailer had started rotating when the neck impaled the Maxima.

The trailer brakes had activated when the trailer disconnected from the pickup truck, but the single set of skidmarks showed that the brakes were only on one axle, and at around sixty miles per hour, they had not slowed the trailer much before it impacted the Maxima. The end of the trailer skidmarks showed me where the trailer had impacted the car. This was the area of impact, or AOI.

There were more tiremarks from the trailer in a crazy swirl at the area of impact, but these weren't from braking.

This was where the trailer had danced macabre with the Maxima, then had separated and come to rest pointing backwards.

The Maxima had more momentum than the unloaded trailer, so it continued forward after the impact, still turning to the right from the death grip of the now-deceased driver. This caused the trailer, stuck into the Maxima like a harpoon, to spin counter-clockwise, yanking the long steel neck back out of the Maxima and the occupants inside it, spraying blood and tissue all over the tan leather interior of the car. The trailer had some angular momentum from the Maxima and kept rotating as it separated, finally pointing back towards Oak Ridge and at its final rest into the middle of the road.

I continued my slow walk to the trailer, focused on the asphalt in front of me.

A black plastic cube, battered and scraped, was lying in the westbound lane next to the centerline, near the area of impact. It was about the size of a tissue box. I picked it up. Wires dangled from the top. It was the battery for the trailer's emergency braking system, which explained why there weren't any braking skidmarks from the trailer as it traveled to final rest in the center of the road. The impact had ripped the battery off, and without the battery to keep the brakes on, the wheels were free to roll.

The trailer had dual axles, so the neck was pointing straight out, not resting on the ground. I knelt and studied the yellow-painted square steel tubing of the neck. It was scratched and gouged from penetrating the Maxima. I paid close attention to the coupler on the end, the part that locks onto the ball hitch of the pick-up truck.

It was a Husky Class IV straight coupler, rated for more than ten thousand pounds. Blood and tissue obscured most of the surface. What surprised me, though, was what *wasn't* there to be seen: the locking lever was gone. This was the lever on top of the coupler that pivots down on top of the coupler to secure it to the truck's ball. And it was missing.

A missing lever would certainly explain a detached trailer.

The locking pin was gone, too. The small diameter cable that had held the pin was frayed at the end. It had obviously been ripped off in the crash, but the relevant issue was whether it had been in the hole of the locking lever, or dangling free, prior to coming off the truck.

Where were the missing latch pieces?

Something else was odd. Normally a trailer will have dedicated safety chains bolted to the neck, one on each side. The chains should have been crossed under the hitch as they hooked into holes on each side of the truck's hitch. That way, if the trailer jumps off the ball, it's caught by the crossed chains.

It's a last-ditch safety measure to prevent this kind of accident from happening.

On this trailer, there were two large threaded holes on either side of the trailer neck. Each of the holes should have had a bolt threaded into it that secured the end of that side's chain from the opposite side of the pickup's hitch.

The hole on the right side of the trailer neck only had the threaded body, or shank, of the bolt in it. The head had broken off.

The left side hole was empty. No bolt on the left side.

I peered closer at the broken body of the bolt on the right side. A cellphone can be used as a magnifying glass, and I pulled mine out, selected camera mode, then zoomed in on the top of the bolt body, where the head had snapped off.

I studied the fractured area closely.

Cold fractures on hardened steel have a very specific appearance. The edge of the area that begins to fail first will elongate a little, like hard taffy. Then, as the forces exceed the yield strength of the steel and the metal breaks, the rest of the fractured surface looks like the surface of a rock. It's roughly flat, but the surface texture is grainy, with small peaks and valleys. The underside of the missing bolt head would match up to it perfectly, if it could be found.

The surface I was looking at appeared normal...except for one part, where the broken surface abruptly stopped and dropped down a fraction of an inch, creating a notch that extended about a quarter-inch into the diameter of the bolt. Curved striations ran along the bottom of this notch, as well as reflecting a faint rainbow pattern in the sunlight.

A chill began at my neck, then radiated down my spine. My body shivered in spite of the July heat.

I took several photos with my phone, then turned and walked to the pick-up truck.

It was a late-model Ford F-350 Super Duty with dual wheels on the rear axle. No damage anywhere. I studied the ball hitch. It was a 2 $^{5}/_{16}$ inch ball, the largest available. That ruled out an undersized ball inside an oversized receiver.

The safety chains were still hooked into the holes on each side of the receiver hitch. I knelt down and inspected the forged steel links of the chain.

Only the safety chain on the left side of the hitch showed evidence of use. Small scratches on the last link, called witness marks, matched up to where it had been bolted to the right side of the trailer. Some of the yellow trailer paint had rubbed off onto the dull silver chain.

The obvious conclusion was that the left side bolt on the trailer had somehow come loose, with the resulting vibration and rattling of the chain causing it to unscrew completely out of the hole. Possible, but unlikely.

Then, if the trailer happened to jump off the ball, which it obviously did, only the safety chain on the right side of the trailer neck connected the trailer to the left side of the hitch on the truck. The forces acting on that single chain then yanked the trailer to the left, towards oncoming traffic, while also exceeding the strength of the right side bolt on the trailer, which caused the head to snap off.

There were two problems with that scenario. First, there would have been a slight imprint (another witness mark) on the last chain link from the underside of the bolt head as it broke off, but none was evident on the link.

Second, that single hardened steel bolt should have been strong enough to drag the trailer down the road by the chain alone. Breaking it would have required a force of about fifty thousand pounds. The force of pulling the empty trailer would have been a few thousand pounds, maximum.

The chain from the left side of the trailer had some marks on it as well, but no yellow paint. None of the marks corresponded to the side of the trailer neck around the bolt hole, either.

It had never been tightened against this trailer neck. Or bolted to it in the first place.

The chill hit me again.

Think.

If the chains had been properly crossed under the hitch, and the chain running from the right passenger side of the truck had somehow disconnected from the left side of the trailer neck, then only the chain running diagonally from the driver's side of the pickup would still be bolted to the right side of the trailer neck.

When the trailer jumped off the ball hitch, the unbalanced force of the single chain yanked the trailer to the left, hard, which would yanked the chain on the bolt head. That shouldn't have been a problem for a hardened ¾ inch bolt. But this one had been weakened by that tiny circular notch I'd observed.

So the bolt head snapped, and freed the trailer from the pick-up truck. Straight into oncoming traffic.

But none of this should have happened if the trailer latch was locked down.

I walked back to the trailer. I pulled my little flashlight from my right rear pocket and used the intense beam of light to inspect the slot where the locking lever would have been attached. Blood and tissue were all over the top of the coupler, but jagged metal edges reflected the light.

Interesting.

The locking lever had broken off in cold shear.

I heard someone approaching. It was Larkin.

"Anything?" he asked.

"The locking lever is gone. It was sheared off in the impact. What did the pickup driver say?" I pocketed my flashlight.

Larkin shook his head. "He's an eighteen-year-old kid working a summer job. Said he showed up for work at the dealership this morning and his boss told him to deliver a trench digger out to the Spallation Neutron facility at ORNL."

I looked down the road towards the lab. "Yeah, I know that place. It's only about a mile. Not far."

"You worked out at ORNL?"

"Yeah. Master of science research. I designed bullets at X-10 for the Department of Defense."

Larkin furrowed his brow. "How'd you end up doing this recon stuff?"

"I got tired of designing things to hurt people. Bullets are small things moving fast, cars are heavy things moving slow. The physics are the same, so now I'm doing this for my doctorate." I looked back at the trailer neck. "Did the kid personally hook up the trailer before he left the dealership?"

"No. He said it was already hooked up and loaded." Larkin shrugged. "But hell, that's what they all say. Same old SODDI as always."

Some Other Dude Did It. A common excuse.

"I need to find that trailer latch," I said.

Larkin looked around the roadway. "It could be anywhere."

"It's not on the road." I started toward the Maxima. "It's in the car."

Gotta find the trailer latch. Something about this wreck was making my skin crawl.

If the latch was locked down, then it was likely that some*thing* had broken, and my fear from what I'd seen so far was probably just paranoia.

If it was unlocked, then some*one* had killed- no, murdered- two people. It was my job to discover which. And then understand why.

Then I could get back to the university and resume working on my doctorate before my funding ran out. Funding is always a nail-biter in graduate school. I needed two more semesters to finish writing my dissertation and graduate, and the chairperson of my doctoral committee had assured me that my funding application would be approved. That was one positive thing in my life, and I was grateful for it.

Larkin ran to catch up with me. "You mean in the trunk? We checked it already. Nothing there."

"No, not in the trunk. Probably caught in the rear bulkhead or the steel mesh frame that supports the rear seatback foam. The latch would have acted like a hook and broken off as the neck was being pulled back out when the vehicles separated."

We walked past the bodies as they were being zipped up. The driver's leg had been inserted upside down, and the shoe was where the femur would have connected to the pelvic girdle. The guy's penis was jammed between the shoe heel and his pelvis.

I winced.

One of the cops saw me looking. He held up the driver's left arm. "Takes a licking and keeps on ticking," he said, pointing to the watch on the wrist.

I nodded, lips tight, but didn't rebuke him. Graveyard humor was a coping device for many people in the forensic field, even if they weren't self-aware of the reason they needed it.

"Why did Jordan want me on this crash so badly?" I asked Larkin. "Any of the reconstructionists in your department could have handled this."

There were three officers in Jordan's department who were certified crash reconstructionists. He could also call one of the best recons I'd ever met, Bobby Jones, who had retired from the force a few years earlier.

"Chief said the victims used to be with the department. He knew them."

"Oak Ridge PD?"

Larkin nodded. "They left to work for Wackenhut. Guarding nuclear warheads at Oak Ridge National Lab paid a little more. Better benefits, too."

The last time Jordan called me about a crash, I'd told him that my research had to come first. I'd turned down low-paying consulting work to focus on finishing my doctorate. This job was a double-whammy because I didn't run the meter when it came to helping law enforcement.

"Bobby could have handled this." I stripped off my soiled latex gloves and fished around in my camera bag. Damn. No plastic bags.

"Jordan said he wanted you here." Larkin shrugged. "I'd sure like to make the Traffic Division someday. Do recon, like you do." He wiped his forehead with the back of his hand.

"How many of these have you seen?"

"A couple. Not this bad, though." Brief smile, then he quickly dumped his face back into a serious frown. "Can I help?"

Most police officers told me the same story. The Hollywood CSI shows have made the forensic reconstruction field glamorous. Cops are people too, and they're drawn to drama just like everyone else. That's one reason so many officers respond to a bad motor vehicle accident (MVA) call. It's also why so many younger officers want to be a reconstructionist.

Then they see too many broken bodies of young kids in the middle of a highway, or too many seventeen-year-old girls with heads rolling awkwardly off of broken necks, and they usually transfer back out. Reconstructing crashes didn't start out with baggage. You picked it up along the way.

This car added more images I'd never forget. From this day on, I'd never be able to look at a Nissan Maxima without picturing these dead men in my mind.

"Plastic bags," I said, looking up.

Larkin turned his head. "Huh?"

"Plastic bags. For my boots. If you can find some." This was going to be messy, and my car was parked outside the police perimeter.

"Okay. Yeah, we got that." He headed toward one of the police cars.

"And tape, please," I yelled after him.

Despite being deputized by Jordan a while back, I'm not a police officer, I'm a scientist. They don't seek out my help on every crash, but Jordan calls me on the bad ones. He asks me for help because I have an uncanny knack for figuring out accidents. Not just the *how*, which is usually straightforward, but the *why*. And that's the more important part.

It's my job to seek the truth about why a crash has happened. In this case, that meant finding the latch. Which, in turn, meant digging through the exploded remains of two human beings.

While Larkin scrounged the bags and tape, I checked my e-mail on my phone. And promptly received a kick in the gut from the assistant dean of the graduate school at the university regarding my latest application for funding.

> Dear Soren Graves:
>
> We regret to inform you that your application for funding to complete your doctoral research has been denied.
>
> Also, in reviewing our records of your academic program here at the University, it has come to our attention that you have reached the maximum allowed duration for the completion of your doctoral degree. If graduation requirements have not been met by the end of the semester, including passing the final dissertation defense, submitting your dissertation for publication and paying the graduation fee, you will be required to formally reapply to the program and to retake the majority of your coursework and submit a new research proposal. Your current fee of $22,923

is required at the Bursar's Office by November 1st in order to meet the graduation deadline.

We encourage you to seek out student loans which are available from both the Federal government and private financial institutions.

Thank you for choosing to study at the University of Tennessee. We truly hope that you will contribute to the University through the Alumni Donation Fund after you have left our institution.

Sincerely,

Gayle Reed, Ph.D.

Assistant Dean of Graduate Studies

Had Dr. Reed checked my financial profile, she would have seen that I'd reached my borrowing limit last semester.

I cursed under my breath.

To reach this point in my education and career, I'd already fought through a grueling undergraduate engineering program with an eighty-percent attrition rate while working as a painter in a body shop fixing wrecked cars to pay for it, then fought my way through a three-year master of science program in engineering dynamics while working for the Department of Defense designing deadlier bullets for them, and was now nearly at the finish line after fighting my way through seven years of doctoral research studying forensic reconstruction of motor vehicle crashes.

Currently, I have a teaching assistantship through the university that pays me $900 each month with no benefits, no retirement, and no tuition waiver. I don't even get a staff parking permit. That money barely covers rent.

To feed myself for the past several years of graduate school, I'd been taking on part-time consulting work reconstructing motor vehicle crashes for attorneys and insurance companies, but that part-time income wasn't enough to pay for school and my research. Without funding, I was dead in the water.

Adding to it all, today I was doing Chief Chuck Jordan a favor and working for free, instead of being back at the university, frantically asking why my funding had been denied. And racing to beat the now-accelerated clock.

My head began aching. I resisted the urge to hurl the phone into the asphalt roadway.

In the distance, a gleaming new silver Mercedes E63 pulled off the road and parked next to my own old, high-mileage, dark red Mercedes S420.

I recognized the car, and the profile of the man who climbed out of it.

The throb behind my forehead intensified.

Larkin saw my expression change. "You know him?"

"Yeah. Wayne Richards. Plaintiff attorney."

"Bad guy?"

"No. One of the good guys. But he's going to clash with Jordan about who can use me as their expert."

Since Jordan had contacted me first, my obligation was to help him with a possible criminal case, which was looking likely. But Wayne would want me to be his expert on the civil case.

The problem is that there's the appearance of a conflict of interest in being the testifying expert to jail a bad guy, which is the responsibility of the State of Tennessee, and recovering monetary damages for the families of the victims, which would be paid consulting work. A police officer could do both lines of work, but not on the same case.

Of course, I wasn't a police offer, just a deputized civilian. There's a big difference.

My deputy status with Jordan was a grey area. He could probably order me to testify through the DA, but that would be a foolish move if he wanted my help on future cases.

Wayne Richards was a client of mine in past cases, and also a friend. His presence here would make things complicated and uneasy with Jordan.

I liked Wayne. He was sharp. My best friend Ken Frazier joked that Wayne had been born with a dorsal fin on his back. Wayne took his doctorate of jurisprudence from Vanderbilt, and being groomed by his dad for a career in law since childhood didn't hurt. His father had been gracious enough to give me work when I first began consulting on the side.

Wayne's father had succumbed to cancer last year, but Wayne began hiring me as well. He'd been using my services ever since, even in cases when my opinion wasn't favorable for him. I was grateful that he never pressured me to sway the truth. I don't work for clients that do.

Most people didn't understand that Wayne was successful because he was smart *and* honest. None of the usual lawyer jokes he liked to tell applied to him. And the fact that he resembled actor Jerry O'Connell didn't hurt his appeal to juries, either.

A woman was exiting the passenger side of Wayne's car. Sunlight reflected off her long blond hair. The woman was Cynthia Carter, Wayne's paralegal.

Cynthia had been a minor league supermodel who'd quit the glamour business to take a job with the State Department to try to help make the world a better place. After ten years in Belgium, she'd had enough adventure and settled back down in her hometown. She and Wayne made a killer team, but it was all professional. Wayne's wife had nothing to worry about. I did. Cynthia's crosshairs were on me every time we met. An expert witness should never get involved with clients, but in my case it went deeper than that. It's hard for me to get involved with anyone.

Wayne and Linda were intercepted by an officer at the perimeter. That would keep them busy long enough for me to search the car.

Larkin was running back towards me. White plastic Wal-mart bags and a roll of black cotton duck tape were in his right hand.

"It's all we got." He handed them to me.

"That's fine." I took the bags and tape, then fluffed open one of the bags. The yellow Wal-mart smiley face grinned up at me.

"This is a good time to double-bag," I muttered.

"Did you start out in LE?" Larkin asked. Law Enforcement.

"No." I pulled a bag over my boot and up my calf and zipped the tape around it. "Long story."

"They said you were deputized."

I ripped off a piece of tape and grabbed another bag. "I am. Just didn't start out that way."

"Oh."

He waited for more, but I changed the subject. "I need you to shoot me."

"What?"

"With my camera. You know how to work a digital camera?"

He brightened. "Sure do."

I retrieved my Canon single-lens-reflex from the bag. He took it delicately.

"It's ready to go," I said. "Just point, turn the barrel to zoom in or out, and push the button."

"Got it."

I pulled on a fresh pair of latex gloves, then checked them for tears.

Being July, I hadn't had a long-sleeved shirt on me when Larkin had called. The gloves stopped above the wrist. My arms were bare. I prayed these guys had led clean lives. HIV and hepatitis C were valid concerns when you're rolling around in freshly blood-soaked broken glass and jagged metal.

The plastic bags over my boots swished on the roadway with each step. Sharp edges of the body pillars framed the right rear passenger doorway. I studied the footwell for the best place to plant my boot.

I do not enjoy this part of the job. Actually, I don't enjoy most parts of this work. But I was good at it.

I placed my hand on the top of the rear seat to steady myself. The tan leather seats of the Maxima triggered an old memory.

My mother's body, slumped in the front passenger seat of our old Bonneville. Her head turned towards my sister and me in the backseat, her eyes unfocused just like the dead men from this car.

"You okay? Mr. Graves?" Larkin's voice reached me. "You look like you seen a ghost."

I shook my head again. "Yeah," I said. "I'm fine."

The old Bonneville had been tan cloth, but it was similar enough to my decades-old memory to freeze me for a moment.

I stepped into the footwell. The blood was slick and viscous. I centered my weight so I wouldn't slip. The congealed blood and tissue pushed against my boot. I moved it around, hoping to bump into the latch. Nothing.

Before exploring the rear seatback hole, I checked the easy-to-reach places first.

The blood was more shallow near the front seats. My fingers pushed into the muck. The torn metal of the latch would be sharp. Probably broken into smaller pieces, too. I probed delicately. No latch under the driver's seat. Passenger side was zilch as well. I pushed my hand between the driver's seat and center console. A plastic pouch brushed my thumb. I pulled it out.

Trojan's finest. Ribbed for her pleasure. Great.

The passenger side yielded a dime and two pennies. I tossed them onto the front passenger seat. My payday would come from Wayne in civil court. And whatever marker I called in on Jordan.

Sides of the front seats? Nothing there.

Between the rear seats and the doors? Non, rien.

The hole in the driver's seatback?

I bent, trying to see inside. There was something just inside the hole. It bulged the backside of the leather. My fingers circled the ragged edge. Small chunks of yellow foam floated down like diseased snowflakes, swirling into the bloody gore of the footwell. It couldn't be this easy, I thought. Life is much harder than this.

Then I touched it. My pessimism was confirmed. It wasn't the latch.

A finger. Ring finger, by the size of it. Gold band confirmed it. Of course, it didn't look like a finger. More like a fat hot dog, some of it purple. The ring was barely visible in the swollen flesh. White trabecular bone peeked out from the center.

Sometimes it happens. I didn't fault the first responders. Hard to get everything the first time around.

I swiveled behind me, reached over the cut rear window, and gently put the finger on the trunk lid. Finished searching the seatback. Still zero.

I brushed a clump of bloody tissue off the top of the back seat, clearing a space to anchor my right hand. My left hand reached into the hole. Sharp wire ends pressed on my arm. I poked around gently, searching with my fingertips. Tiny little pieces of *something* in there. Tactile clues told me it was human bone, probably rib or vertebra. I pulled them out, then placed them onto the rear decklid. Next to the finger.

My hand went back in the hole. The phone on my hip rang.

High pitched whine next to my ear. Mosquito. I shook my head, trying to drive it away. A drop of sweat splatted on the bloody leather. The mosquitoes and flies were starting to find the car and me.

Another chime. Voicemail.

Still no latch pieces.

I reached in further. My head was now intimately close to the blood-spattered leather seat. I tried to keep my face from touching it and extended my arm farther. My cheek brushed the blood on the seat, putrid and coagulating from baking in the sun.

Something was there. Small and slick, but heavy. Not bone. I pressed harder, stretched a little more. Finally got my fingers around it. I pulled the slippery piece of metal back through the seat cushion wires carefully. The sharp edges and the weight told me it was part of the latch.

In the sunlight it was just a clump of bloody red and black tissue.

I wiped away part of the gore. Yellow paint.

The broken edges were bent to one side.

The chill hit me again, even stronger than before.

"Hey, Larkin," I called.

"You find it?"

"Yeah. Come on over and get some shots of it."

At ten feet from the car he abruptly stopped. Then he belched.

I glanced over. He wasn't looking too good. My $3000 camera dangled in his hands. In front of him. In the flight path of what remained of his partially digested lunch.

"Larkin, please don't puke on my camera."

Pause. "Yes sir."

"Breathe through your mouth."

"Okay."

"There's some mints in my bag."

"I'm all right." He still didn't move.

"You sure?"

"Yeah, I'm okay." He straightened up, brought the camera to his eye.

"Take some overall shots and then zoom in on the object in my hand."

The camera clicked. I held the clump out, then laid it on the decklid.

"Is that it?" Larkin asked.

"Part of it. Not all of it."

"Good Lord," he said. He retreated out of the smell.

I turned back to the hole. One more time.

My left arm snaked back in.

I moved my arm upwards, managing to keep my cheek off the seat leather this time. There, near the top. Something stuck in the seat wires. More sweat dropped from my brow. Another tug and it came free, almost dropping out of my hand.

Again, through the hole and into the light. It was big, and it was heavy. Should be the last piece.

"One more time, Larkin." I looked back at him. "You up for it?"

He jammed three mints in his mouth. Nodded. He snapped off more shots, came closer.

I dropped that piece on the decklid next to the other one. I shook the blood and tissue off my hand, then wiped it on a clean piece of the leather seat. I braced myself to move out of the footwell. As I moved my foot, my boot touched something hard in the blood of the footwell. I'd missed it earlier.

I bent slightly, just enough to dip my fingers in the blood and feces and body fluids. The smell was stronger down here. I breathed through my mouth, wishing I had a mint of my own, and fished around the gore with my fingers. I moved the intestines to the side.

My fingers touched metal. Something narrow, long, and cylindrical, like a bolt. I pulled it up. It was the locking pin. I placed it on the trunk lid next to the other metal parts.

Blood and tissue sucked at the plastic bags as I exited the car. I walked around to the rear and studied the pieces I'd retrieved.

Larkin came around the car from the upwind side. He stopped several feet away. "Can you tell anything yet?"

My answer was interrupted by more footsteps.

"Doctor Graves." Wayne's voice. He came near me, into the burgeoning smell of decomposition.

"Not a doctor yet, Wayne."

"What, couple of semesters? That's a technicality." Wayne started to reach for my hand, then dropped his when he saw the mess on my gloves. "Soren, that's...disgusting."

"Sorry." I dropped my hands low, out of view. "You're out here fast. Got some interns hanging around the emergency room?"

"One victim's sister called me a few minutes ago. Friend of a friend of Margaret's." He surveyed the roofless Nissan. "Bad one. How'd the trailer come off?"

"Don't know yet. But I can tell you that only the right side trailer chain was attached to the truck. And the bolt head was weakened on that side so that it would break and veer into oncoming traffic if it came unhitched."

"What does that mean?" Wayne asked. Larkin stepped closer.

"I think it was intentional."

Their eyes widened. "Are you sure?" Wayne asked.

"There's a barely noticeable grinding mark under the head of the right side bolt that secured the chain to the trailer neck. The left chain doesn't show any evidence of being bolted to the left side of the neck. It also appears the latch was left up to let it disconnect. And when the trailer did jump off the ball, the force from the right chain is what caused the trailer to swing into oncoming traffic. If only the left chain had been attached, it would have swung toward the shoulder."

"Is it possible that was just carelessness?"

"Wayne, the probability of all of these things happening at once is astronomical."

"If that's true, then this kid deserves jail time," Larkin said. "That's enough for us to arrest him and keep him off the road."

"It may not be this kid's fault." I picked up the latch pieces. "Let's go clean these up."

Larkin held open a paper bag. I dropped the pieces in it. The finger went in a separate pouch. He folded the paper bag shut. "You all know how to get to the department from here?"

"Yes," I answered. Wayne nodded.

Larkin walked to his police car, leaving me with the finger.

I stripped off my gloves and threw them in the open Maxima. "I shouldn't have said that in front of you or Larkin. Please keep it confidential."

Wayne nodded. "You've got my word. But if it's the truth, then it needs to come out."

"Yeah. But Jordan knew these men, so he's emotionally invested in this. Now Jordan will arrest the kid, and they'll think the case is closed." I shook my head. "And something still doesn't feel right."

"How so?"

I looked at Wayne. "Because if the kid driving the truck didn't do it, it's going to happen again."

~~~

It was a short drive to the Oak Ridge Police Department.

"Such an awful wreck." Cynthia met me in the hallway. "And you had to dig through it."

"Occupational hazard." I wiped my brow on my bare forearm. Sweat was still beading on my forehead.

"You've got something on your cheek." Cynthia looked at me with concern. "Did you cut yourself?"

I reached up. Dried blood flaked onto my fingers. "I'll get it later." I didn't tell her it wasn't mine.

"Still looking good," she said, smiling. "You spend more time in the weight room than your office, don't you?"

"I wish. Rec sports is free at the university. If I didn't take time to work out, I'd die from stress." I smiled. "You look good too, Cyn."

We walked into the conference room. Larkin and Wayne were already seated. I'd been delayed removing the plastic bags from my boots at the scene.

"Did Jordan say you could be here?" I asked Wayne.

"Hell, no." Wayne smiled like the Cheshire Cat. "But the DA owes me a favor, and he told Jordan to let me sit in on this meeting."

Cynthia took a chair and crossed her long legs and smoothed her skirt.

"Any luck identifying who hitched the trailer?" Wayne asked her.

She smiled back at me, then grabbed the legal pad in front of her. "The supervisor of the dealership says it was the kid's responsibility."
~~~

"Told you," Larkin said, looking at me. "That's all there is to it."

"Soren and I can look into it later." Wayne gestured to me. "Doesn't matter until we know how the trailer came off."

"No, I'm okay." I held out the pouch. "Wayne, I'm giving you the finger."

Cynthia blanched.

"You're awful," Wayne said.

"No, I wasn't trying...just take it to the medical examiner's office." I handed the pouch to Wayne, then looked at Larkin. "Where can I wash the latch?"

"Use the locker room. Follow me."

I followed Larkin, carrying the bagged latch pieces. He pushed open the door. A large institutional sink was against one wall.

I carefully placed the parts in the sink. I'd deposited my soiled gloves and plastic bags in the Maxima before leaving the scene. I washed my hands and face. New gloves went on my hands.

The water wasn't getting the crevices clear. "You got a small brush?"

Larkin glanced around the room. He grabbed a toothbrush on one of the lockers.

"You sure?" It was a fancy model with different-sized bristles and an angled neck.

"Yeah, it's okay."

The brush worked great. Wonderful opportunity for a product endorsement. I handed it back to Larkin, who placed it back in the locker.

"No," I said. "Trash."

"Oh, yeah." He tossed it in the trash bin.

"Larkin, it's biohazard. You'll need to throw it and the paper bag in a biohazard bin."

"Oh, right." He dug the brush out, dropped it in the used paper bag, and left the locker room.

I put the parts aside and began on my arms. The blood had dried dull black.

The sight of dried blood froze me again.

I leaned forward, placing my head against the mirror in front of me. My breath caught.

It took me a minute.

I pulled myself back from the mirror, caught a glance of moisture on my cheek mixing in with the dried blood.

The water was still running. I scrubbed like hell to get the blood off my skin, careful not to break the dermis.

My body had almost stopped sweating. I needed water. There was a refrigerator in the break room just down the hall. As I walked, I checked the voicemail on my phone.

"Soren. Hi. It's Judith Warner. I sent you an email but I wanted to call you, too. We need your help with something. My nephew was in a car crash a few weeks ago...out in Clinton..." Her voice pitched high and cracked. "He was killed." Long pause. "There's so much that isn't right about it. No one is telling us the truth about how it happened. I hate to bother you but please call me back if you get a chance. Please. It's destroying our family."

She left her number and the message ended.

It pained me, but I tried to forget Judith's voice as I made it back to the conference room. There simply wasn't time for me to do it. I was already fighting off an anxiety attack about my funding being cut and trying to finish up my dissertation by November.

"Everything's here." I placed the parts on the table. Chairs scraped floor tiles as Wayne and Larkin stood up to see the parts better.

"Cold shear, like I said. The edges of the metal are stretched where the lever portion of the latch has been sheared off." I took a sip from the water bottle in my left hand.

I moved the pieces around. Like a puzzle, the broken parts fit together only one way.

"It was up when it hit the car," I said.

"You're certain?" Wayne asked. "Why wouldn't it just fold down?"

"It's bent over on the side. It can't rotate back down into the locked position. The bend to the side occurred first. Likely when the trailer first hit the car door."

I paused and drank more water, reflecting on it again. "It was definitely up and unlatched when it hit the car. After it was bent to the side, which weakened it, it acted like the barb on a fishhook. The sheet metal of the rear seatback caught the hooked end and broke it off as the trailer spun out of the car. The parts got caught up in the seat cushion wires."

"My God," Cynthia whispered. She shifted her focus back to the legal pad.

"So he didn't latch it down when he picked up the trencher?" Larkin asked.

"I don't know that. All I can say is the latch was up when it hit the car." I turned it over. "See the locking pin holes? No sign of elongation."

I picked up the locking pin. "There's no witness marks on the pin at all." I handed it to Larkin.

Larkin studied it. "Jordan and the district attorney will push for a homicide charge now. Especially if it was intentional." He placed it back on the table.

"Let's not rush to judgment," Wayne said.

I knew what Wayne was thinking. It would be easier for him to show negligence on the kid, but he could get a higher settlement if he could prove someone else from the business knew about it before the kid drove out to the Lab. The business wouldn't be able to place all the blame on the kid, so they'd share more of the guilt, and be liable for more money.

Wayne shot me a glance. I sucked down some more water.

Loud footsteps echoed in the hallway. Chuck Jordan, chief of the Oak Ridge Police Department, entered the room. "Soren, thanks for coming out on this."

"You owe me. And this needs to be the last time, at least until I graduate." I reached for his hand. He pushed a card into it. "What's this?"

"Read it." Jordan shook Wayne's hand, nodded to Cynthia.

It was a small orange card. Picture of a guy in a striped jumpsuit jumping out a cage.

"You gave me a Monopoly card?"

"Not just any card. Get out of jail free card. I even signed it."

"Funny. Thanks. I'm sure the Tennessee Highway Patrol will honor it."

"Probably not. They're still mighty hot about you. But if you need help on any of your other cases with law enforcement, show 'em that card."

I put the card in my wallet. "You're not off the hook."

"If I had pull with THP, I'd try to smooth their feathers." Jordan sat down. "Larkin called and told me you thought the latch was unlocked. And he said that you thought it was intentional."

"I think it was." I pulled out my phone and opened the photos of the sheared bolt. I zoomed in on the quarter-inch notch, then turned the phone to Jordan.

"This is the bolt?"

"Yes. The striations are from a cutting wheel. The cut was made just deep enough to pass cursory inspection and even tightening a little. The rainbow coloring is where the heat of the cutting annealed the metal, weakening it."

Jordan pursed his lips. "This is a serious allegation for an eighteen-year-old kid. He could go to jail for life, because I'll go after him with both barrels." He pushed the phone back to me with his finger. "Trailers sometimes jump off hitches. Hell, there was one that killed a lady out in Maryville last year. Are you sure you're not looking for something that ain't there?"

"I'm not saying it was the kid."

"The business owner says the kid hooked it up."

"The kid says he didn't."

Jordan looked up from the latch to focus on me. "People lie. You know that."

He looked at Wayne. "Why shouldn't I tell the prosecutor to press a homicide charge on this kid?"

Wayne nodded. "You could. But you might be going after the wrong guy. One, we're not certain he hooked up the truck. Two, he might not have known it was unlatched."

"Two good men are dead." Jordan picked up the latch, turned it over. "I hate to say it, but it had to be him. The trailer stayed on the truck all the way from Knoxville, which means it was probably latched when he left."

My mind raced. *Think.*

I jumped in. "Not necessarily. The weight of the trencher would have kept it on the ball of the truck without being latched."

Jordan pursed his lips, then nodded. "True. But then that trailer would have jumped off the ball when he offloaded the trencher, wouldn't it?" Jordan turned his gaze to me. "It's looking intentional, just like you said."

Damn, I regretted saying that in front of Larkin. Now they were focused on punishment and retribution instead of the truth. It happened constantly. Foolish tribal human behavior.

I thought about it some more. "Did he back the trailer in to unload the trencher?" I asked.

"What does it matter?" Jordan pushed the latch back to me.

"If he backed it in, it would have forced the latch housing against the ball. Trailer wouldn't have jumped."

We all looked at Larkin.

Larkin cleared his throat. "He said he backed it in, yeah. But maybe he knew if he didn't, someone would get wise to what he was doing."

Wayne cleared his throat. "Look, my job is to recover for the family of the deceased. The value of the case goes up if I can prove negligence on the part of the business and not just the kid." Meaning, more money from the insurance company who would be footing the settlement. The business that delivered the trencher wouldn't pay. Their insurance company would, and that's where the big money was.

Jordan shook his head. "I know their wives. Their kids. When I see them, I'll be thinking about how the person who killed those men wasn't punished for it. You want to trade justice for money. And don't bullshit me. You get a third of whatever settlement you finagle."

"Would you rather hang the kid, even if he didn't hook up the truck?" Wayne asked.

Jordan shook his head. "He was *driving* the truck. And Dr. Graves said the latch was up. The kid driving the truck is the most likely suspect."

"Guys, I'm not a doctor yet. Me. Right here." I waved my hand.

"Who is Soren going to testify for?" Cynthia asked.

"Whoa," I said. "That's a good question. Who am I working for here?"

"Me," Wayne and Chuck Jordan said at the same time.

"Larkin can handle the criminal side," Wayne said. "I need Soren for the civil case."

Larkin beamed.

Jordan shook his head. "Wayne, I called Soren out here. He's already conflicted out from working for you."

"Chief, don't you want the families to recover on this? I thought you said you cared about them."

"Damn right I do. And someone needs to go to jail over this."

Wayne nodded. "I agree. And I'm sure their wives and children will think of that every time they get an overdue draft notice or an unpaid bill that leads to a collection agency harassing them because they've had to file for bankruptcy without their husband's income."

"Guys," I said. "Look, Larkin can handle the criminal side. He was with the me the entire time, and the criminal side will be a fait accompli. I can handle the civil side. You both know that the insurance company for the dealership will hire the best attorney they can to limit their payout on this, and that's where I'll be needed."

"A fet what?" Jordan asked.

"A slam dunk," I said.

"Dr. Graves has an excellent point," Wayne said.

Jordan grimaced at Wayne. "You know the criminal defense is going to hire the best expert money can buy. None of my recon-certified officers have a science and engineering background. On this one, I need someone who does. I need someone who can beat the other side. And that's Dr. Graves." He pointed at me.

My fist hit the table. "Damn it, I'm not a doctor yet!"

They went silent.

I rubbed my forehead. "Sorry...I received a stressful e-mail about school earlier. Look, I'm not a damned gladiator. Chuck, you wanted me to find out how it happened. I did. You've got three certified reconstructionists in the traffic division. One of them can handle the crash reconstruction with Larkin. Now let Wayne pay me for the time it will take to figure out why it happened. I need the money for school more than you can imagine."

Jordan ran his fingers through his gray hair, thinking it over. "On account of you being out here as a favor, Soren, here's what I'll do. I'll pull Bobby Jones out of retirement to handle the recon."

"I know him. He's excellent. He'll do a fantastic job."

"You find out the facts, and discuss them with Bobby. Then he and Larkin can testify on the criminal side. Meanwhile, if that kid didn't hook it up, find out who did." Jordan pushed his chair back and stood up. "Thanks for coming out on this. We'd have never found that latch, or known how it broke off."

I shook his hand. "Yeah, you would have. But this is it until I graduate. I don't have the time."

"I know. That's why I'm giving you two weeks before we arrest the kid and I tell the DA to file the homicide charge." He clapped me on the shoulder. "Tell Rob I said hello. And ask him when the hell he's coming back to his old job on the force. I still can't find anyone good enough to replace him."

~~~

I was dialing Dr. Peckem's number before I was out the door of the conference room. Peckem's cellphone voicemail was full. Next up was the Engineering Department.

"Shirley, it's Soren. Sorry to bother you, but is Dr. Peckem in his office?"

"Soren! There was a woman looking for you here a few hours ago. Did she call you?"

"Who?"

"Jill...Judy..."

"Judith Warner. She did. Thanks for telling me. About Dr. Peckem..."

"Haven't seen him. Want to leave a message for him? I know he never responds to student voicemails, so I can put a post-it on his door."

"That would be wonderful. It's about my funding. Denied by the assistant dean."

"Honey, I am so sorry. I'll put the note at the top of all the other ones. Hopefully he'll see it first."

"Seeing it is one thing. Doing something about it is another." I punched my free hand against the concrete wall. "Thanks."
~~~

CHAPTER 2

The bamboo stick screamed through the air toward my head. My right hand brought my own stick over my cranium in an umbrella block. My left hand slammed into his forearm. His stick impacted mine and jarred my wrist to the bone. I ignored the sting and followed through in an arc, swinging my own stick around in a watik, jerking back at the last moment as he took the bait. He pivoted towards my faux threat. I switched direction and swung the bamboo stick around, angle two, to his midsection. The stick caught him in the side harder than I intended.

The air left his lungs in a grunt. We stopped. Rob coughed. “Fifty percent, damn it.”

“Like your fifty percent?” I pointed to the welt on my right forearm that he’d inflicted moments earlier. It was turning an ugly purple already.

“Okay, we’re even,” Rob said. Robert Wallace, formerly of the Fifth Special Forces Group, Chief Warrant Officer (Retired), modern-day Viking turned graduate student in medieval history, glanced up at the clock on the wall above the whiteboard.

“Call it a day. I’m teaching Antiquities at two.” He rubbed his side. “Damn. I’ll be feeling that tonight.”

“You can handle it. For God’s sake, you’re twice my size.”

“You saying I’m fat?” Far from it. Rob wasn’t as muscular as my buddy Ken Frazier, but fifteen years of Special Forces operations had left him formidable. Rob was big. Ken was huge.

“Yeah, all those tattoos are getting larger.” I spread my hands in a circle. “Too much good living.”

He pointed the stick at me. “Next time I won’t be so gentle.”

Sweat stains pooled on Rob's shirt. He took it off and wiped his face.

Rob likes tattoos. He was covered with them. A tiger with brilliant green eyes stalked the length of his right arm, and ancient Norse runes spelled the names of his son and wife on his left arm. The characters were large, sharp, and angular, starting at his wrist and ascending to his shoulder, continuing around his neck.

His back was most impressive.

From shoulder blade to shoulder blade, neck to lumbar, was a detailed image of the Green Beret's insignia De Oppresso Liber. The dagger that ran vertically upward was perfectly in line with Rob's spine. The two crossed arrows, perfectly centered.

Below the words, to the left of one arrow, were three circular scars. Each one the diameter of a 9mm bullet. The angle of the bullets had missed his vital organs. Another scar formed a long thin valley across his right cheek from a knife that got close.

A series of irregular craters from an IED blast dotted his right side. He still had the shrapnel inside the tissue around his waist. If he liked you, he'd pinch his flesh and show you the outline of a hex nut that was buried in the subcutaneous tissue. The outline of the six sides of the nut became sharper the harder he squeezed.

The metal didn't stop there. Hammered steel loops in his earlobes, sometimes one in his nose. That one made him look like a bull, which was consistent with Rob's disposition. Being around Rob was like being around a temperamental steer. Not uncivilized. Just stand-offish. Maybe it was because of his own abusive childhood, or his military training, or PTSD, but it didn't matter. Our respective damage made us friends.

Rob re-threaded his long graying hair into a tight ponytail, then pulled his shirt back on.

I'd been training with Rob for five years. Jordan had insisted that I get some defensive and offensive weapons training when he deputized me. Rob had been the tactical firearms and martial arts instructor for the Oak Ridge Police Department, so he got the task of inculcating me with his knowledge. I'd been carrying weapons since I was nine years old, but Rob showed me how to use them with expert competence.

His training was brutal. Rob referred to me as College Boy. I didn't argue, and did the exercises and drills he instructed me to do, until I was gasping for breath or retching. We started with firearms, progressed to knives, and now we were using sticks.

Rob didn't teach a formal system, nor was he caught up in the mixed martial arts fad. He'd mastered dozens of various martial arts in his life, but his real world experiences in the military taught him to keep techniques that worked and discard techniques that didn't. The core elements of our training were kali and eskrima, but the overriding theory was overwhelming violence.

His mantra was simple: it's not the martial art that stops the bad guy, it's the impact. Strength was important. It helped that I'd been lifting weights since high school. The same thing was true for firearms: it's not the launcher that gets the bad guy, it's the projectile. The gun is far less important than the bullet.

Rob's specialty was knives. And when the fighting got close, he preferred knives to guns. A knife can damage much more tissue than a bullet can. But with the knife came risk. If you're going into a knife fight, Rob taught, you will get cut. And the person who is more willing to get cut will get close enough to eviscerate the opponent. Hence the scar on Rob's face.

About a year into our training, Rob asked me about college, and I gave him a course catalog from the Department of History at the university. One year later he had his Bachelor of Arts degree. Two years later he completed his Master of Arts degree. Now he was studying for a Ph.D., just like me. His long-term career plan was teaching at the university level. He'd be unmatched among university professors in enforcing class discipline.

"I teach today, too." I mopped sweat off my forehead and picked up the stick.

"What class?"

"Particle dynamics. Newton's laws, engineering mechanics." I tossed him the bamboo stick.

"Better you than me." He caught it and made the sign of the cross against his own.

"Math has got to be the only thing you're afraid of."

"I ever run into it, it's getting two in the chest and one in the head." He inserted the sticks into his duffel bag. "You're still not going to help your friend?" He meant the crash that Judith had called me about. I'd filled him in while we were sparring. He slid the stick into his duffel bag.

"No." I rubbed the bruise on my arm.

"How old was the kid?"

"Don't know."

"You should take the case."

"Rob, I can't. I can't fit it in."

"She's your friend. She needs help." Rob valued friendship. He was used to being part of a team that depended on each other to stay alive.

"If it was possible, I would. You know that."

"Your choice." He shrugged the duffel bag over his shoulder. "Just make sure you can live with turning away a friend."

"Damn it, Rob. I don't want to. I've got two semesters of work to cram into one."

"Did you learn why they shorted you a semester and cut your funding?"

I opened the door. "When I began the program seven years ago I'd applied in the fall. I officially started in the spring, but the administration counted that fall semester. And now they're back charging me for it, in addition to this semester. And Peckem said the funding cut was out of his hands."

"What are you going to do?"

I shrugged. "Teach class. Then hit the weights at Rec sports for an hour. Then keep fighting until they kick me out." I pulled the door shut as we walked out of the room.

~~~

Estabrook Hall was one of the oldest buildings on campus. Felt like it, too. No central air conditioning meant I'd be sweating again by the end of the first class.

I closed my eyes and leaned my head against the doorframe of my office.

This semester made ten years of teaching engineering mechanics.
~~~

I fought the weariness.

Teaching it twice a day, three days a week, kept me sharp in my forensic consulting work. I loved teaching, but not the subject matter. With no benefits or retirement to give me, it was a great deal for the university. Added to my research, and writing, and consulting workload, it was not such a great deal for me.

The bright side was that I'd be done by December, whether I graduated or not.

Twenty-some students were waiting for me to unlock the door of the classroom. Most of them were freshmen, although there would be a few boomerang sophomores coming back for their second try. Or third.

"Is this class going to be hard?" Sweet-looking young girl.

I unlocked the door and held it open.

My feeling: Welcome to the End of Happiness, kiddies.

My words: "Nah, it's a breeze."

They filed into the room mostly silent, then stood fidgeting.

They seemed like good kids. I hoped they were making the correct choice. And if not, I hoped that they had the courage to switch out of engineering into something that would make them happy.

"Find a place to park," I said. "You're choosing a seat, not a marriage partner."

The whiteboards were scrawled with the previous instructor's handwriting. I erased it, then wrote the following:

> Newton's First Law: An object at rest will remain at rest, and an object moving in a straight line with constant velocity will remain in motion, until acted upon by an external force.

"Who can interpret this for me in plain English?" I asked.

No hands. Blank stares.

"Come on. If you've been admitted to this class, you know how to think. Read page thirty-eight of your textbook."

Clean-cut kid with black curly hair spoke up. "If there's an asteroid in space, just sitting there, it'll sit there forever until something hits it and makes it move."

"Good. What if the asteroid were moving at a constant velocity in a straight line?"

No takers. "Okay, the same thing applies to the asteroid if it's moving. The only way an object can speed up, slow down, or change direction is if something else pushes it, pulls it, hits it or otherwise imparts a force to it."

A few heads nodded. "What about a car going around a curve?" someone asked.

"Especially going around a curve," I said. "An object in motion will always want to go straight. To make a car go around a corner, another force has to act on the car."

I picked up a dry-erase marker and drew an overhead picture of a car on the whiteboard. "In our example, it's the force of the car tire on the road. As long as the tire is gripping the road, and the wheel is turned, the car follows the curve. But if the tire loses grip on the road, the car will go straight again."

"It doesn't go sideways?" someone asked.

"No."

"What about centrifugal force?"

"No such thing exists," I said. "Like unicorns and dragons. What you're calling centrifugal force is actually the inertia of the car trying to go straight. Only you think it's sideways because your view is from inside the car."

Couple of confused looks. But it was the truth.

"Let's go back to an object at rest. When your alarm goes off for an early class, do you want to get up?"

"NO." Chorus of voices.

"Do you just want to lay in bed?"

"YES." It echoed through the class.

"So what's the force that makes you get up?"

"Food," one kid said. Everyone laughed.

A girl with short blond hair spoke up. "So if you're working really hard on a project, and someone interrupts you, that would be an external force."

"Excellent metaphor. And you know what I love about metaphors? They're ambiguous, yet strangely illuminating."

~~~

Judith's email message was on the screen. It was an external force I didn't want acting on me.
~~~

Late Wednesday afternoon. The university library was still vacant this early in the semester. The computer lab was empty except for me and the graduate student assistant dozing at the help desk.

Her email had a few more details about the crash. Her nephew had just turned eighteen, and had just graduated from Clinton High School in May. He wasn't a bad kid, she said. They just wanted someone to explain how the crash happened. She'd contacted Dr. Peckem, but he'd never called back.

Reginald Peckem, III, Ph.D., C.I.E., E.I.E.I.O., was one of three professors in the engineering department who specialized in forensic science. He and the other two professors were the reason I'd chosen the University of Tennessee for my graduate work. All of them were on my doctoral committee, but the two others were semi-retired, so Peckem had been assigned as my chairperson and had the final decision on my dissertation research. He also spent most of his time on his own private forensic consulting practice.

Technically, this makes him a competitor to my own business, but his clients were powerhouse defense legal firms based out of Washington, D.C. and Los Angeles. I was a minnow to his Great White, so he didn't feel threatened.

His consulting income dwarfed his university salary, though, which meant that he spent as little time in his university office as possible. He only stayed with the university because it gave him credentials that looked great to prospective clients, which was true for many faculty members in higher education. A person doesn't need to have a Ph.D. or even a college degree to testify as an expert in court, they only need to be recognized by the judge as having specialized knowledge in a particular subject. But just like everything in the human realm, there was a hierarchy to expert witnesses, and a Ph.D. placed an expert at the top level. Being a university faculty member added to the credibility, even if it was largely a position in name only.

I was taking care of his teaching, but he was also one of five deciding votes on my final dissertation exam. This meant I needed his approval of the progress I was making on my own research, which meant I needed to meet with him on a regular basis. Which never happened regularly, because he was never in town.

Judith's next line got my attention: the cop who worked her nephew's crash didn't take any pictures. No measurements, either. He wrote it up as a single car accident and placed the fault on her nephew. Suspected methamphetamine.

But Judith said the family requested an autopsy, and the toxscreen was negative.

A fatality with suspicious circumstances, possible criminal charges. No photographs. That's weird. And way out of line with protocol.

Maybe it was a county cop who didn't know better.

Maybe not.

Her number was under her name.

I reached for my phone. It was next to a three-inch stack of research articles I had to review for the next chapter of my dissertation. I pulled back.

The only email message I needed to compose right now was one to Dr. Peckem. I'd been begging him for weeks for a meeting to review my dissertation. He'd been blowing me off for weeks, too.

It's an old grad school joke: the good part about lack of guidance was that you had a lot of freedom. The bad part about lack of guidance was that you had a lot of freedom.

Problem was, it was entirely possible that I'd get the dissertation completed, only to have him or one of the other five committee members veto it during my dissertation defense at the end of the semester. It could happen. And that would be a very, very bad thing.

The email message was still there.

Judith had been the secretary for the engineering department when I'd been working on my Bachelor of Science and Master of Science degrees. About seven years ago, when I'd tested into the doctorate program, she had taken a better position over in English and Romance Languages.

She'd always been good to me.

Peckem ignored her, but I owed her a reply, even if I couldn't do the work.

> Judith, I'm so sorry to hear about your nephew. I can understand the frustration you must be feeling about his crash, and the way the police

> handled it. I would like to help you with it, but I simply don't have the time. The assistant dean has informed me that this is the last semester

My phone buzzed. Lab assistant was still asleep on the desk. Ken's number was on the screen. I answered.

"Bust anyone famous today?" Every officer has a dream.

Weird silence. "No."

"What's wrong?"

"Dad's back in the hospital."

"University Medical Center?" I saved the draft message and kicked the chair back.

"Yeah."

"I'll be there in ten minutes."

~~~

I dislike hospitals because they lie.

People politely look the other way when death comes. They cover up their discomfort with murmured banal generalities of sympathy and hope. The hospital covers it up with marble entrances and computerized processing systems and a pretense of control. But in spite of the people working there, good people, mostly, it is still a pretense, well-intentioned but useless in the face of inevitable death. It doesn't matter if it's a teenager coughing up blood during his or her last minutes on earth after a horrific car crash, or a stillborn baby, or an old man's body slowing eating itself from within. When your number comes up, no facade of control can stop it. It's up, and that's all there is.

Death is painful, messy, terrifying, and often violent. It's the opposite of that polished hospital façade.

Ken's dad loved Krispy Kreme donuts. I picked up a dozen glazed, hot off the line, on the way over.

I'd met Ken when we were both freshmen in college. Ken was searching for truth through science, and trying to reconcile it with his own unshakable faith in God. He'd chosen engineering over seminary school, but barely. He'd decided that science brought a person closer to God than seminary could.
~~~

Ironically, I had chosen science for an opposite reason: when I'd called God for help, She or He hadn't answered. Science offered a means of staying isolated and cold from emotions and feelings, and I'd willingly jumped on board that train, even though my acumen was in art and not math.

We both had trouble fitting the engineering stereotype. Him, because of his size and creative streak. Me, because of my artistic bent and innate math disability. We both thought engineering was the path to our own salvation, and we pulled each other through the program. When I was drowning in Heat Transfer, he saved me. When he was drowning in Rigid-body Dynamics, I saved him. He'd had a football scholarship early on, but he'd also insisted on doing his own work, which meant the scholarship was gone after the first year. The program was demanding. Triple integrals and dour professors were more easily defeated when you had a good teammate. And Ken was the best.

After graduating with his bachelor of science in mechanical engineering, six months into his graduate program, Ken quit and joined the Knoxville Police Department. They were happy to have him because of his size. When the brass recognized that he had an engineering degree, they fast-tracked him into rank. He hadn't quit graduate school because it was too hard; he just said that his sojourn in school was done, and it was time for him to start doing good work. He'd never been happier than being a cop.

I stayed in school, where it was safe. Graduate school meant more numbers, more isolation, and no danger of feeling emotion. My master of science program gave me a research position at Oak Ridge National Laboratory, but I was back in school as soon as it was over. A doctoral program scared most people. To me, it was a refuge. It kept me frozen so I didn't have to feel anything. As I mentioned, math wasn't my forte, which meant I had to work at it. Hard. Forced mental labor keeps the mind and body cold.

The line of work I'd chosen- or rather, had chosen me- continued the cycle. My clients didn't care about getting to know me. They didn't want to be friends. No dinner invitations, no parties. They want an expert opinion, and they pay for my time to find it. If they don't like it, they hire someone else. I'm not a whore.

And I remain cold.

Artists can see patterns in chaos. Most people can't.

Crashes are like snowflakes. Each one is different. My formal education was in science, but because of my innate ability to recognize patterns in chaotic scenes, that crazy gift that is common to artists of all types, I see the wreckage through different eyes.

Show me art, real art, and there's a flicker of warmth. Give me a blank canvas, and some primary colors of oil paint, and there's a fire.

Even though I'd done my best to kill it, my true love of painting wouldn't die. And in the mysterious way that life works, I found that it gave me an unanticipated edge over other forensic engineers in the reconstruction field.

Car crashes aren't nice and orderly, neat and logical, like engineering science and physics. Crashes are violent, chaotic, bloody, and unpredictable. My passion for shape and color and abstract narrative might have been suppressed, but it bubbled to the surface when I looked at a crash scene or a wrecked car. Deep down, chaos fomented in my soul. And it gave me an unfair advantage.

But that's where it would stay. No feelings, no pain.

Ken was in the lobby. He was easy to spot. Six-seven, three hundred pounds, all muscle. His police buddies called him Copzilla.

He smiled at me, brown eyes lighting up in spite of the reason we were here. "You didn't know what room he was in."

"I'd have found you." I followed him into the elevator. "How bad?"

"Don't know yet. Tests. More tests." Ken shrugged. "Doctors said it was T1 when they resected it. Said he had a chance of recovery. Now they're saying it's TX. And it's spreading."

Ken's dad had liver cancer. Environmental exposure to dangerous metals was the most likely cause, during his work as a machinist at Y-12 making components for nuclear weapons. T1 meant a smaller hepatocellular carcinoma tumor. Changing the 1 to an X meant the tumor on his liver was bigger than they thought. And they didn't know where all of it was.

The elevator doors opened. The odor of bleach and alcohol hit my nose, reminding me of death and pain. The room was at the end of the hall. The yellow paint on the walls was supposed to be cheerful, but it brought back memories of bile and body fluids.

"How's Kim?" I asked.

"She's fine. She's here."

Ken's wife was just inside the door. She took the box of donuts but knew better than to hug me. "Thanks for coming over. I know it's short notice."

She was wearing denim overalls. I pointed to them. "Is that what third-grade teachers are wearing nowadays?"

"It was agriculture day. Had to dress like a farmer."

Ken's father lifted his eyelids, spotted the box in her hands. He shifted his gaze to me. "Son, you make an old man smile."

"Just for you, Mr. Frazier."

Kim put the donuts on the table in front of his bed. Ken opened the box. Tears in his eyes.

Ken's father had been nearly as large as Ken. The cancer had taken away his muscle. He was a living skeleton now. The blanket that covered his bones denied any suggestion of flesh, looking like the final covering on an emaciated corpse. It was pulled up over his neck, tight under his chin, as if he were freezing. He probably was. His beard, turned shock-white during the chemotherapy, fringed the blanket and bordered his ebony skin. My mind stuttered, bringing up an image I'd seen in my art books. It was the painting of John Donne in his death shroud.

"I'll be out of her in a few days. You need to get back to school." His words were spoken with effort.

"Yes, sir. I will. But it's good to see you."

Ken's father smiled. "You too, son."

Ken was cutting up a donut. "Small bites, dad."

I turned to Ken's mom. "Hi, Mrs. Frazier. Don't get up."

She rose anyway. "You didn't have to come over," she said. "Kenny said you were busy writing your dissertation."

"It's okay." I reached out haltingly, placed my hand on her shoulder.

~~~

The hospital cafeteria was crowded. The high-roofed glass atrium amplified the noise.
~~~

"There's a new teacher at my wife's school," he told me. "Really sweet girl. I think you'd like her."

"That's nice of you. But no."

Ken studied me. "My wife is right. You're on the path to spending your entire life alone."

I shook my head. "I'll date when I get around to it."

"You need to see a professional about letting people get close to you." Ken glanced at me. "It helps to talk about it."

"I did. Over at the student health clinic."

Ken arched his eyebrows. "How's it working out?"

"I quit going."

"Why?"

"The guy got too close. Made me uncomfortable."

"Soren, that's his job. That's what psychiatrists do."

I stared at the tabletop. "It's hard for me."

"I know." He pointed at my hands.

I looked down. My hands had curled into fists, fingers white from pressure.

"The nightmares?" Ken asked, not looking at me.

"Under control."

The room was clearing out, the noise abating.

I opened my fingers, massaging blood back into them. "I'm okay. I'll work on the psychiatric stuff later. Right now I've got to finish school."

"Sure." Ken cut into his second chicken breast, then pointed the knife in my direction. "That's why you burned up a day out in Oak Ridge."

"You heard about that?"

"Two former cops killed? Everyone in a uniform heard about that. They also know you're on it, which is good. Maybe the highway patrol will ease up on you now."

"Sure. The earth could rotate backwards, too."

"It did for Hezekiah. He was also having a hard time."

I rolled my eyes. "That passage says the sun moved. And you and I both know the sun didn't move anywhere. It's just tribal mythology."

"You don't believe it?"

"No, I do not believe it." I waved him off.

"It's okay." He smiled. "You might not believe in God, but he believes in you."

"Sure. Great." I sipped my water. "You remember Judith Warner?"

"Who?"

"Judith Warner. Secretary in the engineering department. She left after you graduated."

"Skinny, kind of dirty blonde? She was pretty." Hopeful look. "You interested in her?"

"No, I'm not interested in her. Her nephew was killed in a car crash out in Clinton. Hear anything about that?"

"Thought you only had time for school."

"I'm not taking the case. She called Peckem first, but he never called her back."

"Big surprise. Has he called you back?"

"No."

"He won't, either. Soon as you graduate, you're closer to being his competition."

"*If* I graduate. I have to come up with eighteen grand by November. Besides, Peckem has bigger things to worry about than me. I just need him to get my funding. Somehow."

"How do those attorneys get his attention?" Ken forked some chicken into his mouth.

"They give him ten thousand dollar retainers. Anyway, about this crash."

"Yeah?"

"Judith said the cop who worked it didn't take any photographs or measurements." I omitted the drugs and alcohol. Without proof, it was only an allegation.

"That's odd. Which department worked the wreck?"

"Don't know. Nothing out there about a kid crashing his car in Clinton, though?"

"No. If you see her, tell her she'll be in our prayers. All this pain going around, it's going to be a hard season for crimson roses."

~~~

Wayne gunned the engine of his car and we sped into a gap in traffic. "How's your old Mercedes?"

I glanced over at him. "Fine, I guess. It's just a car."
~~~

He glanced down at his instruments. "This one is my favorite so far. Almost ten thousand on it now." He gunned it again, darting into the far lane. "How about yours?"

"Miles? Too many to count."

"I remember those days, doc. It'll get better."

"Yeah." I stared out the window.

The memory of seeing Ken's dying father hit me. Wayne's father had recently died of liver cancer too, but he'd never been exposed to toxins like Ken's father. They'd both led very different lives, but the deaths were the same.

I substituted my own father lying in the same bed, searching myself for emotion. There was none.

I cleared my throat. "So, for this meeting...do you want me to mention what I found?"

Wayne stroked his chin. "Not right away. Let me talk to them and see if they're willing to negotiate. If they take a hard line, that's where you'll come in."

"Just remember I'm not a doctor yet. When you make introductions."

"You will be, doc."

"It isn't true now. That's what matters. The future is a betrayer."

Wayne shot me a sideways glance. "Don't get too deep on me now, Soren. Eyes on the ball."

He turned the car into the parking lot of the John Deere dealership. We bypassed the loading dock and line of pick-up trucks on the side of the building and pulled in front of the showroom.

An older salesman walked to the front of Wayne's car. "Ya'll here because of that crash?"

"How'd you guess?" Wayne asked.

"Son, none of my customers drive a car like that." The salesman jerked a thumb over his shoulder. "They're waiting on you. His office is in back. Past the showroom and down the hall."

We walked through the showroom, full of gleaming green and yellow equipment.

"Ronald Sims?" Wayne asked, knocking on an open door.

"Mr. Richards. Come on in." The manager crossed the room and took Wayne's hand, then introduced the other person at the table. "This is Clint Bingham, our attorney."

"And this is Soren Graves," Wayne said. I waved but didn't shake any hands.

"Paralegal?" Clint asked.

"Forensic engineer," Wayne answered.

Clint's eyes went wide. "You brought your expert?"

"Is that really necessary?" Ron asked. He glanced at Clint.

"I like to be prepared," Wayne said. "Doctor Professor Graves is just here to answer technical questions if we have them. He was at the scene and inspected the Maxima and the truck and the trailer."

I fought the urge to roll my eyes.

Clint's jaw tightened. "Wayne, we invited you here to see if we could reach an understanding without going through the trouble and expense of a lawsuit. Ron and I would prefer just keeping this between us."

"Does he talk?" Ron asked, looking at me.

"Only when he has something to say. And when he does, it's worth listening." Wayne glanced at me. "Doc, would you mind waiting outside for a few minutes while I listen to these gentlemen? I'll find you when we need you."

I nodded, then exited the office, closing the door.

It was late afternoon, and most of the staff was gone. I walked down the hall, away from the showroom. The door at the end opened to the shop area.

It looked empty, making it preferable to the showroom populated by salespeople. I pushed the door open and walked into it.

It was a large open area, broken into a half-dozen bays that extended to the back of the room. Garage doors lined the left side, one per bay.

The right side of the shop was lined with a long workbench. Machine tools dotted the surface. Parts lay haphazardly in various places. The overhead fluorescents buzzed, occasionally flickering. The smell of oil and dirt and decomposing grass permeated the room.

An enormous riding lawnmower was in the bay nearest to me. The cutting deck was so large that each side was folded upwards to get it in the shop bay, resembling the wings of a giant bat. Gleaming blades reflected the unsteady light, three under each wing, sharp and hungry.

A trailer sat in one of the middle shop bays, similar to the one that hit the Maxima.

Something pulled me toward it. I made my way around other mowers, stepping carefully over air hoses lying on the ground.

An air compressor suddenly roared to life, causing me to jump.

I picked my way around a table piled with dirty parts. The trailer sat there, motionless. It resembled a casket wagon in the sickly yellow buzzing light.

The safety chains were lying on the ground, under the neck. The holes for the attaching bolts were empty. Odd.

I glanced around the shop. There was a personal work area at the back of each bay. Each one had a customized toolbox. This bay had a dirty and dinged chrome toolbox that had seen better days. A calendar from a local adult bookstore was stuck on the side, three years out of date.

The roar of the compressor continued filling the garage, drowning out other noise.

A handheld die grinder with a cutoff wheel was on the table next to a vise. A can of WD-40 sat next to it.

My intuition nudged me towards it. I made my way toward the workbench.

The cutoff wheel on the die grinder was thin. It would leave a small kerf on anything it cut. Almost unnoticeable.

I looked at the vise. A ¾" bolt was clamped into one side.

The old chill came back.

I leaned over the bench, peering at the bolt.

There was a notch in the bolt. Just under the head.

Movement behind me reflected in the grungy chrome of the toolbox.

I dropped and flung myself sideways. The pipe wrench swung through the air, grazing my scalp, eerily silent under the roar of the air compressor.

The man's arm was wound up, ready to backhand the pipe wrench into my head. He mouthed something at me, but the compressor noise drowned it out.

My back hit the workbench.

He was bigger than me.

My right hand snatched up the can of WD-40. I pushed the spout towards him and let it rip as he unwound his backhand at me.

The spray hit his eyes and he jerked back. I ducked the wrench, then hammered the can against the inside of his right bicep as it went past me.

The impact on his right arm, combined with the spray of WD-40, jarred his grip on the pipe wrench, flinging it behind him.

My left hand shot out, slamming my left forearm against his right forearm, holding it back so I could free my right hand.

He blindly pressed forward. His left hand groped outward and latched onto my shirt collar.

I dropped the spray can and pulled my right hand back to my shirt, trapping his left hand on my chest. My thumb covered the metacarpals on the back of his wrist. Then my fingers wrapped over the edge of his hand.

He kept coming. My body yielded to his force, rotating. I stepped toward him as I came up, pushing my body close to his. Into his comfort zone.

His right hand was now curled into a fist, pulling back like a slingshot, away from my left arm. He wavered as he tried to move back and adjust his aim, blinking through red eyes, not expecting me to move closer to him.

My left hand shot over his left bicep. I clamped down like a vise and pulled his left arm towards me. Now he was off-balance. His cocked arm flailed involuntarily.

He was trapped. And I executed the finish.

He tried to punch his right arm around in a haymaker. His fist hit my head, but it was weak, off-balance.

Violent motion. I twisted my right hand and pulled his left arm into my body. My left hand pulled his bicep toward me.

His face went from anger to surprise. His left arm twisted in two different directions. If I held on and followed through, his arm would undergo a spiral fracture. I would let go before that happened.

He turned his body, trying to relieve the torque on his arm.

I stepped to the side, letting his body continue to turn. He grunted as he passed me. A cloud of stale alcohol-breath padded wetly against my cheek. He hit the workbench, bounced off.

The entire sequence took less than three seconds.

He wasn't done yet. He used his momentum to come at me like a defensive lineman, aiming for my waist. Clumsy, and his timing was off.

I swept away his outstretched arm and sidestepped. He tried to catch himself, then hit the concrete.

The air compressor finally stopped. Silence slammed into the space between us.

I backed up, putting about ten feet between us. My right hand dropped to waist level and gripped the butt of the Heckler & Koch USP Compact pistol in my right pocket.

"How about we knock this off?" I asked.

He lay on the concrete, hands outstretched. Didn't move for a minute. I stayed where I was.

"You okay?" I asked again.

This time he groaned. He rolled over, pushed himself onto all fours. He belched. Then he threw up.

I turned my gaze away. That wasn't from my block. It was from a lot of alcohol and a spritz of WD-40.

"What the hell do you care?" he asked. He spit, then pulled out the tail of his John Deere shirt and wiped his eyes and mouth. He tried to stand, but rolled back on his rear. He bent his legs, put his arms on his knees, and hung his head on the backs of his hands.

He was taller than me. And older.

"You hooked up the truck. And rigged it to fail."

He raised his head, squinted at me. "Screw you."

One of the garage doors began to rattle upward. "Soren? You in here?" Wayne's voice.

"Over here," I yelled. I glanced over at the door to the showroom. A long crowbar had been wedged under the door handle.

The setting sun penetrated the dim garage. It hit my back, casting a long shadow in front of me. The light caught him in profile. In his surrendered form I saw my father.

"You killed two people."

"Screw them too." It came out softly, without fire.

I fought the urge to put a bullet into him.

~~~
~~~

There was a package on my doorstep when I arrived back home.

Strange. I wasn't expecting anything. I picked it up and carried it inside. The return address was Los Angeles, California.

My stomach turned.

I opened it. The brown paper fell away, exposing the glossy cover of a book. The title was *The Art of Ferrari: Pininfarina and the Ferrari Berlinetta*. A note was taped to the front cover, where I couldn't miss it:

> Saw this and thought of you. I love you and your sister more than anything else in life. I hope one day you'll forgive me.
>
> Your father,
>
> Gull

I stuffed it in the trash and slammed the lid.

~~~

My backside hurt from sitting in the chair for four hours, typing on the dissertation. The graze on my head had stopped bleeding by the time the police made it to the dealership. My forearm hurt the most, bruised from the altercation, and still hurting from Rob's strike that I hadn't blocked two days earlier. Negative reinforcement, it was called.

There wasn't any doubt about the cause of the trailer crash. Now it was up to Wayne to negotiate the settlement. It would seem obvious that the insurance company for the dealership would pay the policy limits, but it's not that simple.

The drunk bastard wouldn't talk, but the criminal case was solid. Bobby and Larkin would be able to testify with damning evidence. If he hired a good attorney, he might get manslaughter. A not-so-good attorney might get him a lesser homicide charge.

The civil case was another matter. And that's where Wayne would sue the business for negligence.
~~~

The dealership's insurance company would deny liability. The insurance company's defense attorney will fight it because that's his job. For him, it's about billable hours. The longer his law firm drags the lawsuit out, the more hours they bill, and the more money they make.

That defense attorney will get an expert of his own to look at the trailer and the Nissan Maxima. That expert would issue his own report. If he's honest he'll say the latch was up. If not, he might try to say it was down. It didn't matter. The evidence was incontrovertible.

I had plenty of defense attorney clients, but in this case, I was glad to be on the plaintiff side. This case had a clear cause, and the insurance company didn't have much wiggle room to deflect blame. The downside for me was that Wayne wouldn't want to pay my bill until he received the settlement from the insurance company, which could take years.

I shouldn't have to wait to have my bill paid, and I've occasionally sent an interim invoice, but it was the way most plaintiff attorneys preferred to work. They have to pay the costs of the lawsuit out of their own personal pockets, and regardless of how wealthy they are, they can't outspend an insurance company with hundreds of millions of dollars in cash reserves.

The defense attorneys I consulted with, thank God, normally paid their bills when the work was completed. This was because the money to fight the lawsuit was coming from the insurance company, and the insurance company has the advantage of being able to outspend the plaintiff attorneys.

With the evidence at hand in this case, everyone involved already knew that the insurance company would not risk going to trial, and would eventually settle with the families.

Ultimately, Wayne would probably recover the limits of the insurance policy at around three million dollars for the widows and children of the two decedents, structured so they can't spend all the money at once. He'd make himself a nice fee of one-third of the settlement plus expenses, and pay my bill for consulting with him and possibly testifying about the bolt head, the trailer chains, and the unlocked latch.

The defense attorney would make his quarter-million in billable hours, the insurance company would be relieved they didn't get hit with punitive damages and lose more money than they did, and the dealership would stay in business, keep people employed, and continue paying their premiums.

But it would take billable time to get there for everyone involved.

I turned my attention back to the laptop screen.

Judith's e-mail message crept back into my mind.

The cop didn't even take photographs. Something is wrong with her nephew's crash. You know it. You can *feel* it.

Can't. Have to work.

But I still owed Judith an explanation.

I opened my e-mail and pulled up the draft message to Judith.

School was to blame for me not being able to help her, and it made me loathe the university even more. I hadn't known how much work was ahead of me when I applied to the Ph.D. program. Most doctoral students don't. Half never graduate.

I was determined to be in the half that did. I'd pushed myself this far, and I wasn't going to stop now. My dissertation needed to be flawless.

The nightmare of every doctoral candidate is that they don't pass their defense. Seven years of hard work, struggle, starving, and six figures of tuition down the drain.

Some people think that no professor would be cruel enough to flunk a candidate. Truth is, it happens. If a professor finds a fatal flaw in the research, he or she doesn't have a choice. Sooner or later someone else will spot it, too. The committee can't sign off on flawed research. So the mistake gets identified, and the candidate doesn't graduate.

In some cases, the candidate takes matters into their own hands. A guy in a philosophy program was sent back to square one by his committee chairperson. The student must have liked the beginning of Foucault's *Discipline and Punish*, because he killed his chairperson with a claw hammer. And there was one in California where a guy in engineering failed his dissertation defense. He pulled out a 9mm and shot his entire committee.

If I didn't make it, I wouldn't blame Peckem, or the school, or life. It was my responsibility to finish. But without Peckem to check on my work, there was always the chance I'd miss something. As I'd mentioned, science and math weren't my innate talents.

Judith's message was still pungent on the screen.

I picked up the phone. As I did, the screen lit up. The number was unfamiliar.

Could be Ken, at the hospital.

I answered.

"Soren?"

I didn't recognize the voice. "Yes?"

"It's Judith."

My heart dropped.

"It's late, I know. Soren, I just don't know what to do. No one else will talk to us." Pause. "Did you get my email?"

"I did. Judith, I'm sorry."

"It's just been awful." Deep sigh. "Do you remember my sister Cathy? Worked in the dean's office?"

"Yes."

"It was her son. Chris." Her voice caught at his name.

"I'm so sorry." I searched for words. "How did the crash happen?"

"We don't know. He was in Clinton, it was late. The police didn't work it right. Nothing makes sense. Cathy and Steve and Allison are torn up about it. They just want someone to explain how it happened. I tried calling Dr. Peckem, and emailed him too. He never got back to me. I know he's busy. I'm sure you are too. And I know you're doing the same kind of thing, you know, looking at accidents for lawyers, and maybe you could look at the road and the car and tell us what happened..."

This was beyond listening. She wanted a reconstruction.

The calendar on the wall in front of me numbered my days.

"Judith, I can't."

"Please say yes."

"No." It came out harder than I intended.

Her voice went hoarse. "I'm not hanging up. I can't. Please. Everyone's been so awful to us." She was crying now, talking through the tears. "It's tearing up our family. You're the last person I can turn to."

"Judith..."

"I'm not hanging up, Soren. I'm not."

She was clearly hurting. It would take me one day, maybe two, to work the crash.

My head was starting to ache. "How long since it happened?"

"Three weeks."

"And no one has been out there to take photographs? No measurements?"

"The cops never did. Steve did, but he didn't know what to look for." She sniffed. "There's still skidmarks on the road. We tried to ask the police officer who worked the wreck about it. He won't even talk to us, Soren. Can't you at least ask your police friends about it?"

"I already did, Judith. No one knows anything."

"Please. Just come out and look at where it happened. Sulphur Springs Road in Clinton."

Guilt hammered me.

But curiosity did, too.

"Judith..." I rubbed my forehead. "I need to drop off some forms at Student Services tomorrow morning. Can we do it tomorrow after that?"

"You'll do it?" Surprise turned into relief. "Yes. Tomorrow is fine. Great. Oh, Soren, thank you. Thank you so much."

"It's okay." It wasn't, not really. "Where's your office?"

"Third floor of McClung Tower. Room 308."

"Good. See you tomorrow."

"There's one more thing."

"What's that?"

"Steve said it wasn't an accident. He thinks Chris was murdered."

CHAPTER 3

I took a shortcut through the grass to McClung Tower. A murder of crows scattered away from me.

Steve was Chris's father. Lose a son in an unexplained crash, and maybe it would feel like murder.

I hoped I'd be able to help him find peace.

The concrete plaza that surrounded Judith's building was packed with kids. A group of them thronged around the statue of Europa and the Bull. A Methodist evangelical was standing on the edge of the platform.

Get saved, ye sinners. Join my flock. Choose my side.

It was barely ten. I was already sweating. The cold air of the building blew the humidity off my body.

Kids packed the corridor. When I was an undergraduate like them, cellular phones didn't even exist. Now everyone has an iPhone. We used to have huge HP calculators that used reverse entry notation. It made me feel thirty years older than I was.

I punched the elevator button and rode up to the third floor. Room 308 was the main office of the English department. The office door was heavy. I pushed it open quietly.

Judith was at her desk, typing. Her dark brown hair was streaked with dirty blonde. It hung flatly on her head, curling gently as it fell past her shoulders. She was about my height and had always been thin.

She turned as I walked in. Her face registered relief.

"I am so happy to see you," she said. She rose out her chair, came around the desk fast, as if I might suddenly leave. Loose blue jeans and pink t-shirt. That was Judith. She'd never been one for high heels.

"Thank you so much for doing this." She threw her arms around my neck and hugged me. Squeezed hard. "I talked with Cathy and Steve. They can't wait to meet you. Steve was nearly in tears when I told him you'd help us."

I froze as she touched me. "It's okay," I coughed. I forced an arm up, patted her back. Then I pulled away. "But he shouldn't get his hopes up. I might not be able to tell you anything."

"You make it better just by being here," she said. "No one else cares. No one even wants to talk about it."

"You mean the police?"

"The officer who worked it won't return our calls."

"What was his name?"

"Glen Palmer. Know him?"

"No. Is he Knox County?"

"I don't know."

"It would be on the crash report."

"Steve has that," she said. "We can go over there later." Her words trailed off, but I knew what she wanted to say: if you have time.

I nodded. "That's fine."

She smiled, then lowered her head. "It's been so hard."

"Life can be that way."

She stepped back, sized me up. "You're all grown up."

"Are you looking at the wrinkles around my eyes?" I moved over to her desk.

She laughed. "No, not that. I just remember when you were a freshman. Now you're going to be like all those other professors walking around the halls."

"I really don't want to be like those other professors."

"Good. Most of them were awful."

She smiled as she said it. There were more lines around her eyes than I remembered. She had sad eyes, the kind that look constantly weary, waiting for the next piece of bad news to break. She'd been a single mother at eighteen, and a grandmother at thirty-seven. She earned the wages in her family.

"How's your sister?" Judith asked.

"Fine, I guess. I hope. Still in Europe. France, last time I talked to her."

"When was that?"

"Last year."

Judith nodded. "Have you...heard from your dad?"

I closed my eyes.

"I'm sorry- I always say the wrong things."

"No, it's okay. He's still in Los Angeles." I looked away. "Tell me about your nephew."

"Chris. I wish you'd known him. He reminded me of you. So...kind. And honest. He's joining...was going to join the Air Force in the spring. He wanted to study electronics."

She wiped her eyes. The tears had started as soon as she mentioned his name. She snatched her cellphone off her desk, threw it in her purse. Photographs of her family were near her computer.

"Is that him?"

She picked up the photograph. "Yes. That's Chris."

Blue eyes, narrow shoulders. Dark hair combed across his head. He had that look of a teenager trying to be a man but hadn't suffered enough yet.

"That was taken last year." She put it back down. "He would have turned nineteen just after the crash."

"Tell me about it."

"He left his mom and dad's house around eight. Cathy usually called him around eleven, but she didn't that night. Steve went out looking for him around one. They got the call a few hours later."

"What kind of car he was driving?"

"Chris had a 1967 Mustang."

"Classic car."

"Oh, he loved it. He put a new engine in it."

"I'll need to see it, too. Is it secured?"

"Yes. Our friends have a salvage yard in Clinton. The car is locked up, back behind a building. It's gated and fenced and there's dogs."

"Can we go there after the crash site?"

"You can, but I need to get back here after lunchtime. Plus I don't even think I could handle seeing his car. I'll text you the address."

She walked to another doorway, poked her head around the corner. "Lori, I'll be back by one. Thanks for covering for me."

I opened the door for Judith and we walked into the hallway. "Why does Steve think Chris was murdered?"

"Steve adamant that Chris wouldn't have crashed his car. And Chris's sister said he had some trouble at school with other boys. He wouldn't talk about it to us, but it's a small community."

"That's a long way from murder."

Judith shrugged. "I know. Steve was saying all sorts of stuff, like someone cutting Chris's brake lines, or damaging his tires, crazy talk. That's why we need your help."

~~~

Judith led the way to the town of Clinton.

Thursday morning traffic was light. She made a right turn onto Edgewood, which led to Hillcrest, which branched into Sulphur Springs. We drove for a couple of miles, leaving the town behind until the road was an isolated two-lane ribbon of blacktop.

Traffic became sparse. Judith slowed.

The road went straight for about an eighth-mile, then curved slightly left, then straightened out and crossed a small creek. Judith stuck her arm out the window and motioned for a left turn, pulling into the parking lot of a faded old Esso store. Empty, rusting husks of old gas pumps were still standing at attention in the concrete island in front of the run-down store, like obsolete sentinels whose days of service were long past.

It was another Edward Hopper landscape. His painting *Gas* made real in asphalt and concrete. The resemblance was striking.

I parked next to her white Mercury Cougar. We got out. She came over to me, pointing up the road.

"The crash happened up near the curve. Just before the creek," she said. "Chris's car slid off the road and left skidmarks."

"I need to see them," I said. The entire area was flat. A copse of spindly trees bordered the creek. "Any reason why we stopped here?"

She pointed. "Just seemed like the best place to park. The skidmarks are up near the curve. The shoulder tapers off into grass."
~~~

I walked over and stood at the road edge, then turned back to the store. Typical Tennessee charm. Weather-beaten boards and broken glass. "Too bad the store isn't open. Sometimes they have surveillance cameras on the parking lot."

"Carter family used to run it. They went out of business a few months ago. It's happening a lot more nowadays."

We walked further into the road. I scanned the dark grey weathered asphalt, looking for clues. I started near the store's parking lot, reading every square foot.

"Truck," Judith called out. An old Ford F-150 came around the curve and rambled by us, heading north. The driver gave us a wave.

"Not too busy, is it?" Judith asked.

"No, this is great," I said. "Normally I'm dodging traffic trying to get my measurements. Occupational hazard."

I stepped back into the road, following Judith's lead to the curve.

Something bothered me.

I stopped, scanning the road near the old store.

Something nagged at me, an itch in my mind.

Something I'd seen, but wasn't connecting.

Think.

There. About forty feet from the store's parking lot, in the middle of the road. Two faded patches of rubber about four feet long.

My eyes had seen them, but my mind had not discerned them.

Closer up, they were obviously not braking skidmarks.

I'd seen them before. I'd even made marks like them.

They were burn-out marks. They were made by a car spinning the rear tires on the road to heat them up and make them sticky.

I knelt down. Yellowish-white crystals were embedded in the texture of the asphalt. I pulled out my Benchmade knife and dug up some of the crystals. I rubbed the substance between my fingers, then took a whiff.

Sodium hypochlorite. Also known as bleach.

The rubber marks weren't consistent. Two different tire widths, different tread patterns. Two different cars had done a burn-out here. The bleach was used to soften the tires, make them sticky.

But these were not acceleration marks. Any car spending that much time with the tires spinning would lose the race.

I blinked.

Race.

Better grip for launch during a drag race.

"Soren?" Judith looked back me.

"I need my equipment."

I jogged back to my car and opened the trunk.

Every professional has a bag of tricks in which they carry the tools of their work. Mine was a big, black, waterproof, pressure-vented, and tougher-than-nails Pelican case which contained the tools I used.

A Kowa spotting scope for long distance observation.

Digital SLR camera.

Laser rangefinder.

Digital high-definition camcorder.

Infrared thermometer.

Digital inclinometer.

Digital paint thickness meter.

Bluestar blood reagent.

The list went on.

No gun in the case, though. That tool stayed in my pants. The right front pocket, specifically. And another one was hidden in the trunk with four loaded magazines.

Firearms are not toys. They are tools that demand enormous responsibility. Tennessee law allowed concealed carry of a firearm if you took an approved class. As a Tennessee Department of Safety instructor, I was certified to *teach* the class. Most of the course isn't about how to shoot a gun. It's about when to use a gun in self-defense.

I knew the law because I'd taught it many times: deadly force can only be used when a life is in immediate jeopardy. The words were burned in my mind.

Carrying a concealed weapon had a valid place in my occupation. It is a fact that my line of work exposes me to more risk than other people. I'm frequently out in deserted areas and bad parts of town with expensive equipment. Alone. At night. Times like those, I'm not a forensic scientist reconstructing a crash. I'm prey.

Twice in my work I've needed to draw a pistol, and both times I've slid it back in the pocket holster without pulling the trigger. Simply having the firearm had persuaded predators to look elsewhere for less well-armed victims, and bought me enough time to pack up and leave a dangerous area.

But below that veneer, my primary motive for being armed was the sharp and jagged fear of being a victim again.

Firearms are dangerous, loud, dirty, and unpleasant. They are tools that make holes in things. A hole in something is an effective way to drive the life out if it, especially if the hole is placed correctly. I'd counted on this the first time I fired a pistol twenty-six years ago. If evil ran into me again, it wouldn't find a terrified little boy, afraid to resist until the damage was done.

Firearms, or dollars, aren't the root of all evil. The human condition is.

People who have experienced evil are burdened with an understanding about life that transcends race or language. They have knowledge of something that no person should ever have to bear.

They know firsthand what the word *victim* means.

They understand that good doesn't always win.

They know that surviving doesn't equal normal.

Blessed souls who haven't had a run-in with evil tend to be perplexed by the actions of those who have. The behavior of the victims, though, is perfectly understandable to other victims. They know evil exists.

There are people, some of whom are victims, who feel strongly that firearms are part of the problem, not the solution. Their point is valid.

Having a gun and thinking you're protected is like having a guitar and thinking you're a musician. If you don't know how to properly use a firearm, there's a good chance your adversary will strip it out of your hands and kill you with it.

But when you're up against evil, and it's bigger than you, and stronger than you, and there's no other recourse, then it's necessary.

From the open trunk I grabbed a measuring wheel, my clipboard, and my camera. And two yellow reflective vests for safety.

Judith reached me. "What did you find?"

I tossed one of the vests to her and put on the other.

"Chris was racing someone."

Her eyes widened. She followed me back over to the burn-out patch. I measured the marks and noted them on my site diagram, then took some photographs.

"Is this where they started?" she asked.

"No. This is where they did burnouts to soften the tires."

Judith shadowed me as I walked up the road. There would be two more sets of marks. One set in the right lane, and one set in the left.

Fifty feet up. Jackpot.

Black marks in the left lane, facing oncoming northbound traffic. They were shorter and narrower than the first set.

"This was where one of the cars started," I said. "And he was a good driver. He controlled his wheelspin. Didn't sit there wasting time."

I bent down and measured the marks. The tire would have been about eight inches wide. Four center tread blocks. I drew these on the site diagram, took more photos.

I looked on the other side of the double yellow centerline. No other marks. The cars hadn't staged side-by-side.

I zeroed the measuring wheel and walked up the road. Fifty-five feet later I found a similar set of the straight black marks in the right lane.

"This was the starting point of the other car." I laid my measuring tape down. Ten inches wide. And five center tread blocks, different from the other marks.

"Why aren't they in the same place?" Judith asked.

"In drag racing, head starts are measured in car lengths. The kid with the slower car was given a four-length advantage."

Judith looked back at the first set of marks. "Can you tell which ones are from Chris?"

"Not yet." I looked up the road. "Let's go to the place where it happened."

We walked down the road to the curve and the creek.

It was a gentle curve. More of a lazy path to the right. You wouldn't brake for it if you were going at the posted forty-five mph speed limit, or even ten over.

Judith walked ahead of me. She stopped near the single white line on the outside of the curve.

"Here's the first mark we could find," she said.

I walked over. It was about forty-five feet after the curve. This one was clearly a braking skidmark, perfectly straight. Definitely not a yawmark. The tread pattern matched the first launch area.

Chris had been the one further back, without the head start.

He had the faster car.

Chris had braked very quickly, and very briefly, just after coming out of the curve. It had been hard enough to momentarily lock up the outer rear tire. But it didn't make sense. There was no reason to brake after the curve. It was a straight shot to the finish. Throttle wide open, upshift at peak power the rest of the way.

A less experienced reconstructionist would probably say that Chris exceeded the critical velocity of the curve and spun off the road. But I knew that was bogus the moment I saw the skidmarks. Going too fast and spinning off the curve would throw the car to the outside, leaving yawmarks. Chris's car had gone to the inside of the curve, and he left braking skidmarks.

When a car slides off a curve, the tire marks are slightly curved and choppy. They're called yawmarks, not skidmarks.

The marks from Chris's car were arrow straight and solid black, not curved and choppy. And they began just after the curve. Not *in* the curve, when the car's mass is fighting the tires.

The critical velocity of a curve in the road is the maximum speed a car can go around the curve before it slides off. Every curve has a natural critical velocity, based in part on how sharp the curve is.

It went back to Newton's First Law. An object in motion wants to remain in motion until it's acted upon by an external force.

The only thing keeping the car going around the curve is the traction of the tires on the road. The faster you go, the more the inertial force of the car's mass fights the tires and tries to make the car go straight.

At the critical velocity, the force of the car trying to go straight becomes greater than the traction of the tires. The car goes back to traveling in a straight line, tangent to the curve. Simple.

Some people think the car slides sideways off the curve, not tangent to it. It does not. A car begins to roll before it slides, and this rolling is mistaken for going sideways. But it isn't. It's going straight, tangent to the curve it just left.

And no, this isn't from centrifugal force. There is no such thing as centrifugal force. Get over it.

The critical velocity of any curve can be calculated by hand if you just have a few measurements of your car and the curve. I'd be able to calculate the it for this curve back in my office after I'd gotten the required measurements. And I'd be able to calculate Chris's velocity when he lost control, too.

Something else bothered me about the skidmarks. They were made from the rear tires at first. The front tire skidmarks began in the middle of the road, and they were offset from the rear tire marks.

Chris's car had rotated very quickly, so that it was sideways by the time it crossed the double yellow centerline in the middle of the road.

We walked further. Dark black skidmarks cut across the road at an angle. The black skidmarks from all four tires ran off the road just in front of where we parked. The marks were arrow straight, across the dirt field, into a treeline. His car had continued into the treeline sideways. The car had knocked over several of the trees as it went through them.

Judith walked over to me. "He went through the trees and over the creek. His car came to rest upside down on the grass on the other side of the creek."

I kept my face stoic, but that indicated high speed. "Okay. Time to measure more distances."

I reset my measuring wheel, looked for traffic, and measured the path of the car from the road edge back to the curve. I measured the path of the center of the car, not any skidmark in particular. An energy analysis would use the skidmark length, but a kinematic analysis used the rate of slowing of the car's center of mass.

The first number: two hundred feet of sliding and spinning on the road before going into the dirt and grass.

I reset the wheel at the dirt. The tires left black skidmarks on pavement. On hard-packed dirt, though, the tires left furrows. The machine counted a little over a hundred and twenty feet when I reached the treeline.

Damn. Chris's car had slid sideways for over three hundred feet before hitting the treeline. That's enough time to see what you're in for. An eternity, contained in a few seconds. Chris saw death coming.

I'd done plenty of street racing in my younger days. The night was easy to picture.

Rolling up to the launch point.

Shift into first. Bring the revs up.

Hair-trigger adrenaline dump. Left foot on the clutch, right foot on the throttle. The powerful engine rocking the car with each stab of the pedal.

Waiting for the launch.

Then the signal. Hands down, flag drops, girl flashes her breasts, doesn't matter. It's on.

Dump the clutch. Ride the throttle. Not too much or the traction is gone.

Rear tires spinning. Acceleration pressing the seat into your body. The revs rise into a screaming crescendo.

Stab the clutch. Grab second. Speed climbing. Road gets narrower. Tunnel vision. Clutch. Shift. Hard on the gas.

Then something goes wrong.

I stared at the skidmark, playing it out.

Something caused the rear of Chris's Mustang to lose traction.

A theory germinated in my mind. It was like an itch inside my ear that I couldn't scratch.

Massive stab at the brakes. Seatbelt bites into the chest. The car swings around, too far to save it. Sawing at the wheel.

The car is sideways but still traveling too fast.

Total loss of control. Rubber screaming and burning. Going sideways off the road.

And then the trees loom in the night.

Still too fast.

Impact.

A slight breeze whistled around us. Heat shimmered off the pavement.

"Chris ended up over there." Judith had walked up behind me. She pointed through the trees, across the creek.

She coughed. Her face tightened and she turned away, bringing her hands to her eyes, wiping away tears.

I walked over. Probably should've hugged her. But I just stood there.

"I'm fine," she said. "Keep going."

I turned back to the treeline.

The individual trees showed stripped bark and broken wood from the impact of the car sliding into them at high speed. Broken glass and pieces of plastic trim were scattered on the ground.

I picked up some of the glass. It had shattered into thousands of tiny pieces, which meant it had been tempered and non-laminated. I looked back at the skidmarks, visualizing the Mustang coming around the curve. Then braking. Then sliding sideways. Driver's side facing the trees.

This was side-window glass from the driver's door.

The broken glass surrounded one tree. It was bigger than the rest, probably eight inches in diameter, but it was bent and cracked near the trunk. Bark had been stripped away on the side facing the road. I pushed aside the brush and stepped deeper into the treeline to inspect the raw wood. There were bits of glass caught in the splintered wood surface, and a wisp of something moving in the wind, thin and black.

Human hair.

It was always disconcerting to meet pieces of someone who was gone. Especially hair. It was the way it moved. Hair always moved in the wind. Blood and bone didn't.

There were dark stains on the wood, slightly faded. Blood.

I stepped back from the tree.

Across the creek, torn grass and gouged dirt marked the path of Chris's car. The bank of the creek was too steep to climb down, and the creek was too wide to cross. I walked to the road to go over it. A dilapidated white trailer was in the mowed field.

Judith caught up as I walked into the grass. "They said his car was over there, next to the trailer."

"Okay."

It added another hundred feet to the final trip of the Mustang. I walked to the creek's edge, on the other side now, and looked at the ground. Gouges and divots in the dirt showed where Chris's Mustang had landed. It was an abstract narrative reminiscent of Pollock. But to me, the path of the car as it rolled across the ground was obvious.

Judith followed behind me. "His car was upside down when they found it."

Broken pieces of amber and red colored plastic dotted the path of the rolling car. I knelt and picked up a broken Ford emblem. I dropped the emblem and picked up some of the shards.

"What are those from?" she asked.

"Turn signal and brake light housings," I said.

A glint of chrome caught the sun. It was a small figure of a Mustang pony at full gallop, young and vibrant with life. I picked the metal emblem up, wiped it on my pants.

"It's the pony emblem." I handed it to Judith.

She nodded, took it in her hand.

I measured and photographed all of the evidence. The gouges, the furrows, the skidmarks, the trees. Judith stayed with me as I worked. She remained silent until we were walking back to the cars.

"Can you tell anything from the skidmarks?" she asked.

It would be easy to tell her he was going too fast. That it was a tragic error during a stupid adolescent rite of passage. And I'd be done.

Can't do it, though.

"I need to sit down and think about all the data before I form any opinions about how the event happened. I also need to see Chris's car. And the one he was racing." I opened my trunk and put the tools back in the Pelican case.

"He was speeding, though, wasn't he?"

"Chris was flying. But Chris did not slide off the curve because he was going too fast."

Judith's shoulders relaxed. "You're sure?"

"The braking skidmark near the shoulder, on the outside lane, past the curve." I didn't mention my theory. "It's not curved at all. Chris hit his brake hard enough to lock up the rear wheel on his right side, but his car was arrow straight when he did it."

"So he was already around the curve when he hit his brake."

"That's what the evidence shows." I looked back at her. "Do you know anything about Chris's car?"

"Like what?"

"Transmission?"

"It was a five-speed. I rode with him once, after he got it running."

I mentally pulled up the list of possible Mustang engines and power ratings.

"Okay. Do you know if Chris worked on the engine for more power?"

She looked away. "Would it be bad if he did?"

"I'll be able to tell when I start doing the math, Judith."

"You need to ask Steve."

"The evidence shows that Chris had the faster car. The other car was the one with the four-car-length head start, and was on the inside lane," I said. "Chris was in the outside lane." And something made him lose control. The itch came back stronger.

Judith nodded her head. She opened the door of her car and tossed her purse on the seat, then turned back to me.

"Do you...did Chris..." She put her hand over her mouth and looked away.

I waited. I knew what she was going to ask.

How Chris died.

"No," I said. "Not right now. I need to sit down and think about how it happened, and see the cars. Then I might be able to tell you. Maybe."

Judith looked back over the skidmarks. "It just seems so impossible. He was just here. Three weeks ago, he was here and alive."

"I'm sorry."

She sniffed. Inhaled deeply, and straightened her posture. "Okay. I need to get back to work. Can you still look at Chris's car?"

"I'll go there now."

"Can you still come out to Steve and Cathy's house later?"

"Yes." I frowned.

"What's wrong?"

"I have some serious questions for the person Chris was racing."

CHAPTER 4

The junked car bodies appeared before the entrance did, stacked five high behind the fence that ran along the road. The fence ran on for a quarter-mile, and the car bodies did too, a bizarre twentieth-century fortress wall in which the cars were like individual bricks made of rust and faded multiple colors of paint.

I drove through the open gate, nosing my car down a rutted gravel and dirt access road. More bodies of junked cars lined the shoulder on both sides of me. They were skeletons of the dead, warnings to vehicles that could still enter the premises on their own power. This is what will happen to you, the bodies said. This is where it ends.

There was always the danger of picking up a bolt or screw through one of my tires. I steered carefully, trying to avoid metal debris in the wheel ruts.

The business itself was a series of junked-out mobile homes that had been converted into working space. A huge old swaybacked barn behind the largest trailer functioned as the garage. A gutted mobile home just inside the fence held racks of engines and transmissions, spare organs to give dying cars a little more life before their inevitable final journey to a cemetery like this.

I pulled up directly in front of the main office mobile home. The gravel and dirt parking area was streaked with the dark stains of engine oil and brake fluid and power steering fluid and the other blood that circulated through cars to keep them alive. It was in junkyards like this that their lifeblood leaked out into the dirt from their mortally wounded bodies. Those bodies were stacked in rows that went on for acres, becoming emaciated in the hot sun of summer and the cold wind of winter. Over time the bodies would be scavenged for all the usable parts they possessed. Then they were destined to be carried to the large mechanical crusher on the far end of the yard, the great equalizer that reduced the vehicle to a small compact square that would be hauled off to a foundry, melted in fire, and reborn into another object of servitude.

I opened my door. The heat of late summer flooded into my car. The thunder of hammering and the shriek of metal being cut emanated from the barn behind the offices. A pack of dogs barked at me from behind the fenced yard, Cerberus in the flesh. They eyed me as I walked toward the office porch, climbed up the rickety steps, and then turned the dirty, greasy doorknob.

The door opened on squeaking hinges. I stepped inside and shut it. The rattle of loose glass panes in the door echoed painfully in the small confines of the office.

A worn sofa, striped with cloth tape, held a morbidly obese man smoking a bent cigarette. Behind the chipped, scarred, and broken counter was a small, pasty, anorexic man chain smoking his way through a pack of cigarettes. The air was saturated with curling blue smoke and the smell of unwashed human bodies. It was the smell of a thousand salvage yard offices. I would have preferred standing outside but I didn't have the luxury. This was part of my job.

"There ain't no way he's gonna pull it off." The smaller man shook his cigarette at the obese man. "Mark my words. I'm sayin' it now, mark my damned words."

Neither seemed particularly interested in me. There was a faded sign that hung at an angle on the front of the counter that said CASH ONLY and another that read ALL SALES FINAL. In smaller script someone had written in IF IT DON'T WORK IT AIN'T OUR FAULT. Then another store-bought sign said NO RETURN ON ELECTRICAL PARTS. The last one was either redundant or contradictory.

"Halp ya?" the smaller man asked, tossing the butt to the floor and rubbing it out.

"Jeremiah?" I asked.

"Who's askin'?" He grabbed another cigarette from the pack and lit it up.

"I'm here to look at the '67 Mustang."

He looked at me from under his cap, narrowing his eyes as he took a deep drag. "You the scientist from the university?"

I nodded. "Soren Graves."

"Judith said you'd be comin' by." He flicked ash over the counter. "It's out behind the barn." He picked up a handheld two-way radio and mashed the side button. "Mikey, get your ass up here to the front and man the counter while I take this guy to see the Mustang."

"Gimme a minute," Mikey answered through static.

Jeremiah turned to me. "Once he gets here I'll take you to the car. If the dogs don't know you they can get mean."

"Thanks." The smoke made my eyes sting.

He hit the cigarette again, blowing another cloud of noxious smoke in front of him. He leaned over the counter.

"So you do stuff with accidents?"

"Yes."

"Like what?"

"Look at the site, look at the cars, do the math to see how fast they were going before impact."

"No shit."

"Yeah, it's like them CSI folks on that television show," the obese man on the couch said, spelling it out phonetically. "Ain't that right?" He looked over at me.

I nodded. "That's it."

"Shit," Jeremiah said again. "Got them damn airbag computers in them cars nowadays that'll tell you everything you need to know." He scratched his thinning hair. "Hey, you remember when we put that airbag under Earl's chair?"

"Aw, hell," the obese guy said. "You blew that thing just as he was sitting down to eat. Funniest gawdamn thing I ever done seen." He slapped his huge thigh, laughing and squeezing his eyes shut.

"Damn near smashed his balls to grits." Jeremiah chuckled and sucked the last bit of the cigarette. He went through the same motions again. Drop, rub, light, suck. "You ever need to get them computers?" he asked me.

"Many times."

"It's unbelievable how much a lawyer'll give for one of them damn things. Never know if a car I buy at auction has it, but if it does and then there's some kind of lawsuit, man, I can bend 'em over the table, that's for sure."

Those words hit me. My right eye winced. I casually slid my hand in my pocket. The sharp checkering on the grip bit into my fingers.

I'm not insane. Pulling it out never crossed my mind. But it helped steady me.

The obese man spoke up. "You ought to just charge them to look at the damn cars."

"Martin's up in Cumberland Gap does that," Jeremiah said, nodding. "I might. I just might." The phone rang and he picked it up. "Red's," he answered. Then a pause. "Hell, no." He hammered it back on the cradle.

"Yeah, boy, those damn computers'll pay for what I give for the entire damn car at auction." Jeremiah shook his cigarette at me. "It ain't on every one, but I give four hunnerd for a oh-one Chevy Silverado last month that was killed. I mean, there ain't no straight panel on the damn thing. But I figured I could maybe sell the differential and maybe the engine but then I find out the block was cracked after we got it out. Those new damn aluminum engines crack a lot easier than them old iron ones do. But then it turns out that the driver of that truck killed somebody and done put another one in wheelchair for life, and I got five hunnerd bucks for that damn computer. We had to cut the damn truck in half to get it out, but that ain't nothin'." He sucked on his cigarette.

Five hunnerd bucks was too cheap. The attorney probably cleared several million on a case involving a young paraplegic.

The sound of an old engine coughing through unmuffled pipes crept up in volume until it was just outside. Heavy footfalls on the front porch and then the door opened.

"Hey, Jerry," Mikey said.

Jeremiah nodded. "Did ya'll get that rear clip off that Honda yet?"

"Yeah." Mikey glanced at me and then pushed his way through the

half-door that connected the counter to the wall.

Jeremiah nodded. "If that guy calls, you be sure to tell him to come git it. The

deal was no tax if he pays cash."

"Got it."

Jeremiah snatched up his pack of cigarettes and walked around his employee through the same half-door. He motioned for me to follow him and we walked back out into the heat. The sky was patched with high white clouds.

"I need to grab some things out of my car," I said. He watched as I retrieved the black Pelican case from my trunk.

"Nice Benz."

"Previous salvage," I said. "Had to weld in the left rear quarter and floorpan."

"You did the work?"

"Yeah."

Jeremiah looked it over and whistled. "Damn, son. You sure can paint."

"Thanks."

"This here's my yard car," he said. "Ain't near as pretty as yours."

We walked over to a Frankenstein-ish Ford Escort hatchback. Each corner had a different-sized tire so that it sat cock-eyed on level ground. No taillights and no rear bumper, just the blank end of the rear metal body panel staring back at me. The glass was missing from the rear window and the car was covered with a thick layer of dust and dirt. Someone had stuck a huge Cadillac emblem on the hood.

I tossed the Pelican case through the convenient hole where the rear glass used to be and walked to the passenger door. The handle was missing. There was a hole cut in the sheet metal to actuate the door latch. I inserted my fingers into the hole and grabbed the operating rod, jerking it forward.

The door popped open and I dropped onto the dirty red fabric seat, billowing up a cloud of dirt. The inside of the door was bare metal with no door panel. I threaded my fingers into one of the stamped holes and slammed it shut. The noise was harsh, metallic, and empty, echoing in the hollow crevice of the sheetmetal door.

The car had no dashboard or center console. The gravel and dirt lot was visible in a gaping hole between the seats.

Jeremiah popped open the driver's door and fell in the car. More dirt poofed upward. The naked steering column stuck out of the firewall in front of him. A screwdriver poked out of the ignition cylinder.

"Salvador Dali," I said. He could have painted this surreal little car into existence.

"Who?" Jeremiah arched an eye at me, cigarette dangling.

"Nothing. Car reminded me of an artist."

He grabbed the plastic handle and wiggled it sideways. The little four-cylinder engine coughed to life on three cylinders. The missing beat generated a vibration that could shake out tooth fillings.

He grabbed the knob-less shift lever that sprouted from between the seats like a spindly weed and moved it back a notch. Nothing happened, so he wiggled it a bit and the car finally lurched into reverse.

We backed up slowly. Jeremiah used the handbrake to help slow the car.

"Ain't got no brakes," he said. He moved the lever further back, wiggling it again to slip the linkage into drive. It caught with a jolt.

We approached the gate behind the main office but he didn't stop. He pulled up on the handbrake and nosed the gate open with the car.

"Shut the gate!" he yelled out the window. One of the guys in the barn put down a Sawzall and begin to walk toward it. Behind him, a near-new front-hit Honda Accord was freshly sawed in half. The dogs were trotting beside us slowly, unconcerned with leaving the fenced yard.

We came to a crossroad and stopped. An enormous front-end loader drove in front of us and rammed its forks through the side of a Chevrolet Suburban. A cloud of black diesel soot ballooned into the air as he carried the impaled SUV to the large yellow crusher in the back of the yard. The canine escort left us.

"How's business?" I asked.

"Slower after summer," he said. "What's really been a pain in the ass is them Feds from the EPA." We bounced over ruts and risked bending metal. There were no seatbelts and the interior was stripped. My grip on the seat bottom tightened and I held the door to steady myself.

He let off the gas and we coasted to a stop. "Damn Feds are busting people's balls around here, making sure we collect all the oil and fluids and such from the cars now. Used to be a man could do whatever he wanted to on his property. Ain't that way no more."

"Sorry." I pulled on the door handle linkage that was exposed from the inside, got out.

He pointed to an object covered by a dark grey tarp. "That's it."

The tarp lay on the car like a death shroud.

Only gross proportions suggested the plastic was covering something man-made. Dry brown weeds crunched underfoot as I neared it.

Jeremiah helped me pull the tarp back. We dropped it at the rear of the car.

"How long you think it'll take you?"

"Couple hours." I walked back to the Escort and hefted the Pelican case out of the hole in the rear hatch.

He nodded and hoisted himself onto the fender. "Holler if you need any help." He brought the two-way radio up. His words were too soft to hear. I turned back to the Mustang.

It was a 1967 fastback. Beautifully proportioned when intact. This one had been crumpled like tinfoil in a giant hand, then roughly unfolded and slammed back to earth.

Most people see a mass of mangled metal when they look at a wrecked car. I don't. Each bent panel tells a story. If you can mentally separate specific areas of damage from others, the crash will show itself to you. It's shapes and shadows, telling a story. Just like a painting. More Picasso than Van Gogh. His Cubism paintings, in which each shape is a different view from a new angle.

Rollovers like this one, especially at high speeds, tend to demolish a car. As the car rolls, each side of the vehicle gets pounded by the fist of the earth. If it rolls more than once, there are then multiple impacts to each side. This takes the challenge to a higher skill level, because the reconstructionist will need to separate the initial deeper layers of damage from the later, less fundamental ones. Just like psychologists do with people.

The only way to reconstruct a rollover is to work backwards.

This means freeze-framing the vehicle back through its crash sequence to determine which part struck the ground last, and then next to last, and finally back to the time it was still upright.

Only after the rollover damage is identified can the car be examined for evidence of impact with another vehicle. Normally this is made easier by the transfer of paint between the vehicles. In this case both cars were black, which made it near-impossible to identify paint transfer. But there were other ways of identifying contact between cars if you knew what to look for.

The driver's side of the car had hit the treeline. None of the trees had been more than ten inches in diameter, so as the car was deforming, the trees were breaking and bending. The trees had also been the ramp that vaulted the car in the air and across the creek.

The trees had crushed the entire driver's side of the Mustang inward. Looking at the front of the car, head-on, the shape was that of a parallelogram. The massive impact with the treeline crushed the bottom half of the car into the center, so that the roof was sticking out over the ground on the driver's side.

The driver's door told me how Chris had likely suffered the first blow to his head. There was a significant tubular depression, like a trough, in the middle of the door. It was nearly vertical. There was a matching impression in the roof exactly above where the driver's head would have been. The size of the trough-shaped dent matched the diameter of the larger tree I had noticed at the site that had the blood stains on it.

I stuck my measuring tape crossways through the open area where the driver's side window used to be. The tree had penetrated into the passenger compartment twenty-one inches. As the car was stopped by the impact, the driver's head and body would have kept moving into the tree.

It was another final moment described by bent metal.

The passenger's side wasn't as angled as the driver's side was but it was still noticeable. The roof was bent inward in several places. It had hammered into the earth at least once during its roll sequence squarely upside down.

The front fender of the car on the driver's side was pushed inward. At some point during the roll the passenger side fender was squeezed against the engine. The driver's side front wheel was facing forward and up at a broken angle.

I peered inside the driver's area of the car.

'Safety' in mid-sixties cars meant Don't Hit Anything, but seatbelts had been installed in the car by Chris, or someone else. The seatbelt hung limply from the B-pillar. It was pulled out nearly two feet, consistent with being worn by the driver, and there were small dots of blood on the black nylon webbing.

The interior A-pillar that ran along the windshield from the dashboard to the roof was cracked near the top. Dried blood colored the plastic to dark red. Blood and matted hair were on the steering wheel rim. Small blood stains dotted the black vinyl seat. The lining on the ceiling was speckled with more blood and it was torn above the driver's head.

That explained the head injuries.

I focused on the exterior next, carefully going over every panel, mentally unfolding the crumpled metal. The driver's side was easy. Tree bark and tiny wood splinters revealed the tree impacts. Dirt and grass revealed the ground impacts. There were no rubber scuffmarks or flaking paint on that side of the car.

I moved to the front. The hood was barely attached. The left side hinge was the only point of connection to the car, valiantly holding on even after there was no more reason to do so.

The engine was a late model 302 with aftermarket race parts. A higher-voltage ignition coil and bright yellow spark plug wires were further evidence of increased power. The intake manifold was one of those tubular jobs that flowed more air than the stock unit. Equal-length stainless steel headers flowed like thick silver snakes out of the sides of the aluminum cylinder heads. Aftermarket valve covers perched on the heads, larger than the factory originals to accommodate milled steel roller rocker arms.

The passenger side headlamp assembly was still in place. I reached behind it and twisted the ring that secured the headlamp bulb.

The shape of the bulb filament was important.

When a car slows down suddenly during a severe impact, the individual parts and components of the car slow down at a similar rate because they're all connected. In the case of incandescent lightbulbs, the filament inside the glass is subjected to a similar negative acceleration, often colloquially called deceleration. This deceleration produces a force on the filament, similar to the force a body produces on the seatbelt as the car is being crushed and stopped.

If the lightbulb is off, then the filament is just another room-temperature piece of metal, and it's so small and light that it won't bend or deform during the crash as long as it isn't physically crushed. But if the lightbulb is on and the filament is glowing brightly, that tiny piece of tungsten wire is heated to about 4,500 degrees Fahrenheit. That temperature is what it takes to shine the headlight beam several hundred feet into darkness.

For reconstructionists, a nice side effect of this heat is that the tungsten filament becomes ductile, kind of like a piece of cooked spaghetti. If the car hits a tree at 50 mph there's a good chance that the lighted filaments will stretch completely out of shape. In some cases the hot wire will even make contact with the glass bulb housing, and if the glass breaks, air will rush into the evacuated space and the tungsten filament will oxidize immediately. Either way, if the filament from the crashed car is stretched out, the light was on at impact.

I turned the collar of the bulb gently, freeing it from the headlight unit. The high-beam filament was stretched out inside the bulb like a piece of spaghetti that had been thrown against the wall.

The driver's side headlight assembly had detached from the front of the car. The recovery crew had shoveled all of the broken parts and debris into the back of the car. I pulled on some gloves and began sorting through the pieces, searching for that bulb as well.

Most of it was broken plastic. Chrome bumper trim pieces poked out of the pile. It was laborious work. I sifted through all the pieces larger than a quarter. After an hour, I had the driver's side headlight housing pieced together, including the bulb.

Same thing with that filament.

The high beams of the car had been on at impact, and likely during the race. Chris would have been able to see up the road about three hundred feet in front of him.

One piece of debris was incongruous with the rest. The itch inside my ear came back.

It was the center cap of a wheel. This one was made of carbon fiber and marked HRE PERFORMANCE WHEELS. A crack ran through the center. I slid it into my pocket.

HRE was a custom wheel manufacturer, and their products were expensive.

Chris's wheels were stock Ford Mustang GT wheels, about 1992 vintage. There were two center caps missing, but the hole sizes from the missing caps on Chris's wheels were different from the HRE center cap I'd found, and Chris's remaining two center caps were stock Ford pieces.

My back ached from bending over the rear of the Mustang. I stood up, then went back to examining the rest of the exterior of the car.

I resumed studying the sheet metal.

The passenger side damage was more difficult to read than the driver's side. I started at the front, rounding my way from the passenger side headlight to the fender. Roll damage, but no vehicle contact. I moved to the passenger door, kneeling down on the dirt, and scrutinized the panel.

There.

A long scuff mark ran down the horizontal center of the door. It didn't fit with rollover damage. The mark was dull and flat, like a shoe scuff on a tile floor. In the middle of the mark, a shallow dent was barely visible.

I scraped some shavings into a small evidence bag and moved on to the rear quarter panel on the passenger side.

This panel hadn't been directly hit, but it was bent from induced damage on the rest of the car. Lots of damage on this area. But was any of it from another car?

The passenger side rear wheel didn't look right. I stood back and studied the silver paint of the wheel. More circular rubber scuffs became visible. They started on the wheel face and extended onto the rear of the quarter panel. Faint, but enough to scratch off with my fingernail. I rubbed it between my fingers.

Tire rubber.

The scuff marks on the quarter panel were in the valleys of the bent metal, not just the peaks. They had been made before the impact, when the metal of the panel was still flat, before the car rolled over.

It was obvious that the marks were from a rotating tire on another car. Scrapings of the Mustang's paint from around the scuff marks went into a separate evidence bag.

Almost done. I went around to the rear and pulled the taillights out. The filaments of the running lamps were stretched from hot shock, and so were the filaments of the brake lights. Chris had been pushing the brake pedal at impact with the treeline.

Jeremiah leaned patiently against the fender of the yard car. No cigarette. Maybe he was out.

"Finished?" he asked, watching me stand up.

"I need to take some pictures and measure some more things." I opened the Pelican case and grabbed my camera.

"There was something in all those pieces that didn't look right."

"What do you mean?"

"Looked like some kind of wheel cover."

I reached into my pocket and pulled out the HRE wheel center cap. "You mean this?"

He nodded. "Yeah, that was just off the shoulder. Kinda near where he left the roadway." He took the piece from me, scrutinized it. "We tried to pick up the pieces as best we could, even up near the trees."

"Did you find anything else that far up?"

He shook his head. "Nah, this was the only piece up to the treeline. It mean anything to you?"

"I'm not sure yet."

I finished the work, then repacked my Pelican case and tossed it through the broken hatch of the Escort. Jeremiah helped me pull the tarp back over the Mustang. As we got into the little car he glanced over at me.

"How's the family holding up?" he asked.

"Hurting. He was their only son."

Jeremiah plucked a cigarette from his shirt pocket. "Something ain't right about this crash."

"How so?"

"That road is known for drag racing. It's easy to block traffic coming up the other way, and the law never patrols out there."

"You think he was racing someone?"

"Don't you?"

"I'm not certain yet." It wouldn't be right to share information, so I didn't.

Jeremiah eyed me and rolled the cigarette to the other side of his mouth. "Judith said it might be murder."

"Judith said that?" I arched an eyebrow.

"Lot of people are saying that. You believe in the Bible?" Jeremiah made no move to start the car.

"Which part?" I just wanted to get home and wash off the dirt and scent of death.

"Eye for an eye."

"Sometimes."

He lit the cigarette. It sizzled and caught. "So how fast do you think he was going?"

"I don't know yet."

"Damn, son. You either don't know shit or don't want to say shit."

"Sorry." I placed my right hand on my hip, near my pocket. "Look, if this turns into a big lawsuit, an attorney can hit you with a subpoena and suddenly you're in a deposition being asked under oath about what I said to you here."

His eyes went wide. "For real?"

I nodded. "So I just don't want to say something that might not be true. I need to sit down and put all the pieces together before I can see the big picture."

"So it's like a puzzle," he said, the cigarette dangling from the corner of his mouth.

"Pretty much." I closed my eyes. Youth is a fire that so easily extinguishes itself.

Jeremiah tugged the screwdriver sticking out of the column and got three of the four cylinders firing again.

"I hate puzzles," he said. The little car bounded over the dirt, carrying us away from the dead Mustang.

~~~

It was after five p.m. when I texted Judith that I was ready to head to the Cameron's house. Judith texted me their address, said she'd meet me there. Thirty minutes later I found myself following her white Cougar as we both turned off the main road at the same time.

Judith got out of her Mercury and walked over to me. She put her hand on the hood. "This sure is a nice car. I meant to say something earlier."

"Thanks." I patted the roof. "It's older, but it's safe."

"You were always driving nice cars, though. Buying them wrecked and fixing them up."

"Same thing with this one," I said. "Salvage title and all."
~~~

"No one would ever know." She smiled. "That's the way it is with people too, isn't it?"

"What do you mean?"

"At the funeral, Chris didn't look like he'd been hurt at all. No scars, nothing obvious. You can't know how bad a person's been hurt just by looking at them."

"Yeah."

"How did the salvage yard go?"

"Old Testament, not just old school," I said. "Did you tell Jeremiah that you thought Chris was murdered?"

"I just told him what Steve was saying. People talk."

"Why?"

"I don't know." Judith avoided my gaze. "Was it bad?"

"The car?"

"Yes."

"Yeah, it was. Probably good that you didn't see it up close. I took photographs."

We walked up the concrete sidewalk to the house.

The home was late-seventies contemporary. Big windows and stonework on the front. Bluish-gray trim on the sides and back. It sat high on the ridge that ran parallel to the road. I followed Judith up the long, narrow concrete driveway and parked on the pad outside the three-car detached garage.

We walked to the steps at the rear of the house. As we climbed the porch steps the door to the house opened and a tiny yellow Labrador puppy bounded out.

Chris's father, Steve, was standing in the doorway. He was a few inches short of my six feet and heavier than my one hundred and eighty pounds but he wasn't fat. Deeply tanned skin complemented short black hair and a short mustache. His button-up shirt, streaked with dried sweat and dirt, was open to his chest. On one side was a Clinton Utilities Board patch. The other patch said Supervisor. A dirty white ball cap embroidered with the letters CUB was perched on his head. Steve had brown eyes that moved quickly as he sized me up and then recognized Judith.

"Hey, Steve," Judith said, closing the distance towards him.

"Hey, girl." His voice boomed around the wooden porch. He looked back at me, gesturing to follow Judith inside. As I walked toward him he stuck his hand out.

"Steve Cameron." Quick and forceful. Friendly but with a note of impatience.

"Soren Graves." His grip was firm.

He ushered us in and shut the door. Cathy was in the kitchen, near the refrigerator. As Judith and I walked in she moved closer to us and embraced Judith. Then she walked over to me.

"Hi, Soren," she said softly. "Thank you so much for doing this."

"It's okay," I said. "I'm so sorry, Cathy."

I turned to the kitchen area. Steve pulled a chair out from the table for me and then walked around to the other side. He sat down. Cathy and Judith had walked back over to the far side of the kitchen, away from Steve.

"Thanks for coming out and helping us with this." He put his elbows on the table and pushed his cap back high on his head, rubbing his eyes with both hands. "You been out to the scene?"

"Judith took me out there today."

"Could you figure out what happened?" He folded his arms on the table in front of him.

Judith jumped in. "Lord, Steve, he hasn't had a chance to look over the stuff he found today."

"Okay, okay," Steve said. "I didn't meant to be pushy." He pushed back from the table and rose to his feet, pacing to the door and then back to the table.

"It's all right," I said.

"You and Judith go way back?" he asked.

I nodded. "Back to when she was in the engineering department."

He stopped near the table and leaned over the mess of papers, thrusting aside what he didn't want with sharp motions. "Here's something-"

Cathy interrupted him.

"Soren, would you like some tea?" she asked. "I'm sorry, I should have asked you sooner."

"Sure." Judith shot me an apologetic glance. She opened a cabinet and took down some glasses. Cathy opened the refrigerator.

"How is school going for you?" Cathy asked.

"It's rocky." I reached for the glass. "It's been rough in the department lately. The new dean of engineering is getting rid of all the old guard and bringing in new professors. I don't know any of them."

"That new dean was brought in just to axe people and cut costs," she said.

I believed her. It was wise to be nice to the secretaries if you wanted to be warned about the knife headed for your back.

"You're working on your Ph.D., right?" she asked.

I nodded. "Yes, ma'am."

I watched Steve in my peripheral vision. He was pacing again, taking off his cap and then putting it back on.

"Oh, you don't have to call me ma'am," she said. "Are you about done?"

I smiled. "My research is done. Now I'm writing the dissertation." I drank from the glass. The tea was bitter.

Cathy was connecting things. The change in the department faculty meant that I needed to finish up pronto so I wouldn't be caught with a doctoral committee of fired professors. She'd been successful in her job in the dean's office. Her quiet intelligence was disarming.

"And instead of working on it, you were helping us today. Thank you."

"It's okay. I documented the site and I inspected Chris's Mustang. But like Judith said, I haven't really had time to sit down and put the clues together yet."

"There's a bunch of stuff for you here, too." Steve pushed a sheaf of loose papers toward me. Cathy shot him a warning look. He gave it back to her but then he stopped. He moved his chair again and sat down. It was like watching a person with obsessive-compulsive disorder on a caffeine binge.

Judith put her arm around her sister.

"It's okay." I tried to defuse the sudden tension. "What have you got there?"

"For starters, here's the crash report." He thrust it at me like a spring had uncoiled.

My stomach turned. "This is from the Tennessee Highway Patrol."

There are THP troopers who wouldn't mind being called to a fatal single-car crash involving me. It would, in fact, be a cause for knocking off work early, having a keg party, and guarantee an increase in THP trooper church attendance.

Steve saw my reaction. "Bad experience?"

"Previous case. They had a difference of opinion with my professor. But I did some work on the case. Guilt by association."

"Do you know the trooper? Palmer?"

The trooper's name was on the first page. Glen Palmer. "No, I don't."

"You'd think a state trooper would do a good job."

"Most of the time they do an excellent job." It was the truth. They hated me, but that didn't change the fact that they usually did thorough work.

I skipped to the diagram and the narrative on the last page. The officer had only drawn Chris's car and had written it up as a single car accident. I flipped back to see if there were any witnesses listed. None were.

"You think it's normal that he wouldn't have taken pictures or measurements or marked the road?" Steve asked.

"No." Especially in light of the alleged drugs.

The report had a place for illegal substances and intoxication.

> Presence of Alcohol/Drugs – 1 – YES (DRUGS PRESENT). Determination Method – 5 – OBSERVED. Drug Test Type – 1 – BLOOD. Drug Result – 97 – TEST GIVEN, RESULTS UNKNOWN.

Palmer had marked that drugs were found. Whether the driver had them in his body was a question for the medical examiner.

"Judith, you said the toxscreen was negative."

"It was," Steve said, before Judith could answer. He fished through the papers. The medical examiner's report slid my way. The cover page described Chris.

> Christopher Cameron was an 18 year old white male who was a driver in a single vehicle crash on 8/4/2016. According to the ER attending, he was restrained by his seatbelt during a high-

speed rollover event. He was pronounced dead at the scene at 3:17 a.m. on 8/4/2016.

EXTERNAL EXAMINATION:

The body is that of a well-developed adult male who weighs 165 pounds, is 72 inches in height, and appears compatible with the stated age of 18 years. The body is identified by the coroner. Two loose identification tags are between the decedent's feet within the body bag.

The body is clad in a thin polyester jacket, a short-sleeved white cotton T-shirt, blue denim jeans, and white cotton undershorts. One shoe is missing. The shirt and jacket exhibit bloodstains. Pools of thin, bloody fluid are within the body bag.

The body is cool to touch. Rigor is difficult to assess due to multiple closed fractures. Livor is purple and fixed.

The scalp hair is fine, slightly wavy, and black, measuring four inches in length over the crown. The irides are blue. Pupils are bilaterally equal at 0.2 inch. The cornea are transparent. Petechial and confluent hemorrhages involve the left sclera. Excluding trauma, the ears and nose are not unusual. The lips and gums are appropriately pigmented and the teeth are in good repair.

The neck is without masses. Larynx is in the midline. The abdomen is flat and the genitalia are those of a normal adult male. The anus and back are unremarkable.

At autopsy, the arms are over the head. The upper and lower extremities are well-developed and symmetrical. The forefinger and trapezium on the left hand have been severed. The

> fingernails are short and trimmed. The toenails have variably irregular edges. Identifying marks and scars are not apparent.
>
> There is no evidence of emergency resuscitation or medical therapy.
>
> EVIDENCE OF INJURY:
>
> Petechial and confluent hemorrhages involve the left sclera. Two 1.5 inch lacerations in the sagittal plane involve the parietal scalp. The rightmost laceration is also undermined to the right to a depth of 1.3 inches. An oblique, ragged, 1.3 inch laceration involves the lateral right supraorbital ridge, exposing hemorrhagic soft tissue. Two ragged, superficial lacerations measuring up to 0.4 inch each involve the left lateral forehead, above the left eyebrow. One traumatically avulsed tooth is within the oral cavity, and many of the remaining teeth are loose. Multiple hemorrhagic lacerations involve the tongue. Calvarial skull fractures are readily palpated.

The report went on. Mostly arm and hand injuries, including re-mention of the severed finger and thumb. That happens when the arms are flailing during the rollover. Chris's left hand had been out the window when the edge of the roof rolled over it.

Chris's death had been brutal. The tree that broke the driver's window had also impacted his head. After that, his head had struck the interior of the car as it rolled. The injuries matched the blood and tissue transfer in his car.

Something else bothered me. I scanned back over the report.

His arms had rigored over his head. That didn't make sense. It takes about four hours for rigor mortis to set in.

"Judith." I re-read the crash report to be certain.

"Yes?"

"You said Chris's car was upside down."

"It was."

The crash report agreed. "Do you have any idea what time the wreck happened?"

Steve answered this time. "Cathy tried calling him at eleven, but he didn't answer."

The crash report was different. Date Notified – 8/4/2016. Time Notified – 02:23. Time Arrived – 03:05.

My blood ran cold. My grip on the paper tightened until my knuckles turned white.

Whoever Chris had been racing, they'd left him there. Dying. For at least three hours. And then the trooper took forty-two minutes to respond. That's why Chris's arms had rigored above his head.

"What's wrong?" Steve asked.

I picked up the tea. "I'm not sure yet."

The final page held the drug test results.

> Drug Screen, blood serum – NEGATIVE/NO DRUGS DETECTED
>
> Drug Screen, gastric/meconium – NEGATIVE/NO DRUGS DETECTED
>
> Ethanol, blood, urine – NEGATIVE/NO SUBSTANCE DETECTED
>
> Drug Screen, opiates – NEGATIVE/NO OPIATES DETECTED
>
> Drug Screen, cannabinoids – NEGATIVE/NO CANNABINOIDS DETECTED
>
> Drug Screen, amphetamines – NEGATIVE/NO METHAMPHETAMINES DETECTED
>
> Drug Screen, MDMA – NEGATIVE/NO ECSTASY DETECTED

"You understand all that?" Steve asked me.

I nodded. "The blood test would show if any drugs were in his body at the time of the crash. The drugs take longer to metabolize into urine. The urine tests would show if he'd been using drugs prior to the crash." I handed the report back to Steve. "And then they did a series of tests to check for specific drugs. They were looking hard for something."

"My son was clean. He didn't do drugs. He didn't sell drugs. He wasn't around drugs."

"And that's what the tox report shows," I said.

"He went to church more than we did," Cathy said. "He was so pure. He had such a good heart." Her eyes welled as she spoke.

"Okay." This was hard, but I had to ask. "Then how did the drugs get in his car?"

"Someone planted them there." Steve was adamant.

Cathy nodded. So did Judith.

"Have you got the CIRT report?" I asked.

"What?" Steve was blank.

"The CIRT report. There's a very specific protocol for investigating fatal crashes where suspicious circumstances are involved. At minimum the responding officer is supposed to secure the scene, and if he isn't certified and trained to document the scene, he's supposed to call in the CIRT team and they do it."

"What's the Certs team?" Judith asked.

"Not Certs, CIRT, see-eye-are-tee," I said. "Critical Incident Response Team. THP has a special team of troopers that investigate crashes like this. Where drugs are found, or criminal charges might be filed. Trooper Palmer should have called them."

Steve pointed to the crash report on the table. "That's everything," he said, rising from his chair again. Pace. Pace.

This was unbelievable. "Who is this guy?"

"Palmer?" Steve paused. "He lives in Anderson County, and he's the trooper who patrols this area. He arrived at the scene first and found Chris's car."

"Who called 911?"

"No one. County doesn't have a record of a 911 call."

"You checked?"

Steve nodded.

"So who notified Palmer at 2:23am?"

"Good question, ain't it?" He gestured with his tea as he spoke. The brown liquid sloshed against the sides of the glass, threatening to spill over the rim.

"We've tried calling Trooper Palmer numerous times," Judith said. "He's never called us back."

The medical report from the EMTs was on top. I picked it up and thumbed through each page. They had to cut the seatbelt off him. They mentioned the rigor, too.

Steve sighed, keeping his hand on his face. "It's not you. It's just the thought of him, how it happened. It hurts so much."

In one night, after a meaningless race that every American male makes in his adolescence in some way, their son is in a crash, and no one cared enough to even try to help. It was increasingly clear why Steve felt like someone had murdered his son. But there were still too many unanswered questions about the crash.

Steve rotated his chair to face me. And away from Cathy. "What else did you learn today?"

Cathy glared at the back of his head..

I looked at Cathy. She closed her eyes, then nodded.

"A few things," I said. "Chris was traveling very fast when he lost control. And he was racing someone."

"Judith told us," Cathy said. "I don't want to believe it."

"Which lane was he in?" Steve asked.

"Chris was in the outside lane as he went around the curve. He was in that lane when they started, too."

"How did he lose control?" Cathy asked.

Oh, boy. This was delicate.

"There had to be an external force that hit his car."

Steve's brow furrowed. "What's that mean?"

Cathy answered. "It means the other car hit our son's car. Doesn't it, Soren?"

"Yes. But I can't say whether it was intentional. It was probably just a mistake." I recalled Larkin latching onto the comment I'd made about the trailer being intentionally sabotaged, and I didn't want that to happen here. Steve looked ready to kill someone, and all he needed was a reason.

I pulled the HRE carbon fiber wheel center cap from my pocket. "I also found this."

Steve took it. "What is it?"

"It's the center cap of a very expensive HRE alloy wheel."

"Chris didn't have nothing like that on his car."

"I think it came from the car Chris was racing. There was a wheel mark on his right rear wheel and quarter panel. I think this came off the other car's wheel when it hit Chris's car."

"Is there any way to trace it to the other car?" Steve asked.

"Tough call. But it's something to look into."

"What's an HRE wheel look like?"

I pulled up the HRE website on my phone. "There are many different styles. It's a long shot, but do you recognize seeing any of them on a local car?"

He took my phone, scrolled through the different models. "I sure don't. They look like any other aftermarket wheel to me."

"The difference is that these are high quality."

"I'll say." Steve whistled. "$12,000 for a set of wheels? Ain't no one around here has that much money to spend on that."

"Or if there was, we wouldn't know," Cathy said. "You're certain Chris was racing someone?"

"I found the area where they did their burnout to warm their tires, and where they staged for the race. It looked like Chris gave four lengths to the person he was racing against." I paused, watching Steve. "Do you know how much power Chris's Mustang was making?"

"Stock. The at piece of junk had a burned engine when Chris bought it. He found a stock motor from an '88 Mustang and stuck it in there to get it running."

"Damn it, Steve." Cathy took a step forward. "Chris loved that car."

"It was stock," Steve said, ignoring his wife.

"Steve, a 1988 Mustang motor only had 225 horsepower. That's pretty weak. His engine had go-fast parts on top. The evidence at the scene indicates Chris's car had a lot more power than that. Was the bottom end modified for more power too?"

Steve shrugged. He rose from his chair. "Doesn't matter. Some son of a bitch killed Chris. And I want him to answer for it."

Cathy glared at Steve again.

There was more going on here than just the power of the Mustang. There was an issue of power in this kitchen. Steve wanted someone to be responsible for his son's death. He wanted Old Testament retribution. Cathy wanted to grieve in peace.

A storm was forming in the house. The forecast: booming thunder and salt-water rain.

"Anything else?" Steve asked.

"The skidmark past the curve is from braking, not yawing."

"What's that mean?"

"Chris made it around the curve without sliding off it."

Steve sat back down and put his arm on the table. "So why'd he brake?"

"I don't know."

He got up again, moved to the window. "He was a damn fine driver. He knew how to handle a car." He stared out the window as if Chris and his car were in the driveway. "He was good. He could slide his car sideways down the whole length of the road in front of our house. Got videos of him doin' it, just lighting the tires up and sliding 'em all over the road, and putting that car wherever he wanted to make it go."

"You should probably keep those videos private."

"Sure, sure." He took his cap off, ran his fingers through his hair, then put it back on. "So someone hit my son's car and knocked him out of control during a race."

"That's what the evidence indicates."

Steve turned to Cathy. The expression on his face was clear: I told you so.

I kept my voice even and flat. "But again, I can't prove intent. It's a possibility that the other person made a mistake. Racing is dangerous. I can't say anything else about that until I inspect the other car and spend some time analyzing all the data."

Steve came back to the table. "Wouldn't the trooper have had to put the other car in the report if there was contact between them? He would, wouldn't he?"

"Absolutely," I said. "He should have arrested the other person for street racing, if he could find him. Or her. But I can't fault a trooper for not finding evidence of racing on a dark night."

We sat in silence for a moment.

"Have you gone to the Tennessee Bureau of Investigation with this yet?" I asked.

Steve grunted. "We went to the Anderson County District Attorney but all he did was tell us to hire someone to investigate the crash and then write a report on it. Said he'd look at the report and then decide what to do." He looked away in disgust. "But you could tell he didn't want to help."

Tire and engine noise outside.

"Allison's home," Judith said.

I moved my chair back from the table and stood up. The door opened and the girl from the photo on Judith's desk walked in. Older by a few years, but still the same long straight dark hair and her mom's blue eyes and her dad's bronzed skin. She was petite, walking on two-inch heels yet still only coming up to my eyes. Her black blouse disappeared around her shoulders as her hair fell over it. Her tan skirt fell just below the knee. Her wedding ring stopped me from looking closer.

"Hey, darlin'," Steve said.

"Hi, dad," she said. He stood up but Allison walked to her mother. They embraced.

I moved closer to Steve, extending my hand. "I have to go."

"Thanks for coming over." His voice didn't boom loud like before.

"Hi there," Allison said. She walked over to where I stood.

I put out my hand. She ignored it, stepping in and giving me a hug.

I awkwardly returned it, mechanically patting her back. Her hair was soft and

smooth against my cheek.

"So you're Soren," she said. She stepped back, brushed her hair behind her ear.

"That's me. You must be Allison."

She nodded. "Mom and dad have been talking about you ever since Judith said you'd help us."

"Oh, jeez." I wasn't comfortable in the role of savior. "Glad to help. I'm sorry this happened."

Her voice dropped. "It means a lot to us."

"Show him the quilt," Judith said. "He needs to see it."

Cathy nodded. "It's over here."

I followed the women from the kitchen to the great room, stepping down and walking over to the area near the staircase. Steve stayed in the kitchen.

A quilt was folded up on a loveseat. Cathy picked it up and unfolded part of it. She smoothed the fabric, laying parts of it flat.

Photographs of Chris had been transferred onto pieces of cloth. The cloth pictures were woven into the squares on the quilt.

"That's Chris in his third grade Christmas play." Cathy picked up one corner. "And that was him at prom with Kelly."

Allison frowned. "That one shouldn't be in there."

"It's the only one of him in a tuxedo." Cathy looked at Allison.

"Show him the one with Chris and his Mustang at the car show, in front of the other cars," Judith said.

"You made this?" I asked.

"Not just me." Allison said. "Everyone who knew him stitched a piece into the quilt."

The quilt was enormous.

"Here it is." Cathy held up another part of it. Chris was standing in front of his Mustang with a row of cars lined up at an angle in the background.

Allison nodded. "It was at the high school right before graduation. His car was voted best of show." She went to move the quilt. "I think there's one of him working on it, too."

"Wait." Judith put her hand on Allison's wrist, then looked at me. "Can you tell what those other cars are?"

"Couple older Camaros, a few Mustangs." I peered at the photo. "Wait a second. I think those are HRE wheels on that car in the background."

"That newer Mustang?" Judith leaned forward. "I can't hardly tell."

"Maybe. Have you got the original photo? Something with more resolution?"

Allison stepped back. "I think so. Mom, have you got your iPad?"

Cathy glanced back into the kitchen. "Steve, would you bring me my iPad?"

"I'll get it. Stay here with Allison." Judith spun on her heel and darted into the kitchen.

Judith returned and handed the iPad to Allison. Steve followed. "You find something?" he asked.

"I think it's on Chris's Facebook page." Allison typed and swiped. "Here it is."

I reached for the iPad, but Steve grabbed it from Allison. He zoomed in. "You got that center cap?"

I pulled it from my pocket and handed it to him. I moved next to him, studying the photograph.

The car was a new Mustang, 2015 or '16 model. Black, just like Chris's car. The car next to it blocked most of the body, so only the driver's side front wheel was visible, but the wheelwell was filled with a gleaming HRE wheel.

"That's it." I pulled out my phone and searched the HRE website for a match.

Bingo. "It's an S201," I said. "And that's the same carbon fiber center cap." I turned to Allison. "You just found the mystery car."

"Now we need to find the son of a bitch who owns it," Steve said.

"I'll repost it on Facebook and ask who it belonged to," Allison said.

Steve handed her the iPad. Allison logged in.

Something nagged at me.

"Wait." I reached out and stayed Allison's hand. "Ask who all the cars belonged to. Not just that one."

"Why?" Judith asked. They all turned to face me.

"Because whoever owns it will be tipped off that Allison knows something is up. And that means she could be in danger."

CHAPTER 5

The next morning came early. I rubbed my eyes and tried to focus.

I worked on the dissertation for ten hours.

By 6pm I'd reached my limit. My mind was wandering, producing run-on sentences that bordered on gibberish.

I made some tea and a sandwich and went out onto the patio. The sun was on the decline. It was another day down, and another day closer to my deadline.

In the quilt that memorialized Chris, the images and memories of Chris's life were providing warmth and comfort to his family and friends, even after his death.

My life had been filled with darker moments. Not the best quilt material. And my future would be filled with broken bodies and violent deaths and cold equations until it ended.

It wasn't something I looked forward to living.

Allison was working on identifying the Mustang's owner. She and Chris had both gone to Clinton high school, and being a small town, the odds were good that someone would know the car and its owner.

After dinner I dumped everything about Chris's crash on my desk. The photos I'd taken from the site and Chris's Mustang were open on my laptop, and my handwritten notes from the inspections were in front of me. I also had the medical report and the crash report from Steve.

My drawing of the crash site was to scale, and it showed the road where both of the cars started the race. I had also placed all the skidmarks on the diagram as we had found them on the roadway. The final resting place of Chris's Mustang was marked with an upside down Mustang, based on the evidence at the site.

First thing to do was calculate Chris's speed before he lost control. It would have been highest just before his car went sideways. The first law of thermodynamics made it clear that a car sliding sideways and braking on level ground can only lose speed, never gain it. Ergo, the highest speed of Chris's car would be just prior to losing control. In order to calculate that speed, it was necessary to begin at the end, at the point where Chris's car had stopped moving.

I worked backward from his final resting point in the field near the trailer. Looking at the dirt gouges from a bird's-eye on the diagram made it much easier to see how the gouges were created by which parts of Chris's car. His car had hit the treeline almost square-on with the driver's side. After that, his car had undergone a specific sequence of rolling and spinning to the final resting location. I had the most likely motions of his car down in a few minutes of playing with the car on the diagram. It isn't hard. There's limited number of things his car can do, and each time it strikes the ground, there's a gouge in the dirt. I'd be able to confirm it after I'd do some calculations on his speed.

I divided up the distances that his car had traveled from the point he lost control to the final rest based on the terrain. From his skidmarks in the roadway to the edge of the asphalt had been about 200 feet. From the dirt and grass to the treeline was about 120 feet. From the treeline that he went over to his final resting point was about 100 feet, as well. I pulled up research that had been conducted by other engineers regarding how a rolling and tumbling vehicle slows down, then used those numbers to calculate the speed of Chris's car right after the impact with the trees.

The measurements I'd made of the damage to Chris's car came next. Side stiffness coefficients weren't available for this Mustang, but Newton's third law and some coefficients based on other mathematical methods indicated that Chris lost about 30 mph when his car impacted the treeline. This didn't mean Chris was going 30 mph when he hit the trees; it meant that he lost 30 mph during the impact. He could have been going 100 mph when he hit the trees and then 70 mph as his car left the trees. More number crunching would give me the true speed of Chris's car as it impacted the treeline.

Four hours later, I had that number. Chris hit the trees at 80 mph.

This was *after* his car had been sliding sideways on the asphalt, and through the dirt. Simple kinematics could now be used to determine how much speed his car would have lost from sliding sideways through the dirt. The same method worked for sliding sideways on the road.

Two hours later: 105 mph at the loss of control.

It was hard to believe the number. That was a fast damn Mustang if it was true. I reworked the equations again and came out with 103 mph. And I was probably low on the crush energy from the trees.

This was only after about an eighth-mile of acceleration. A stock Corvette wasn't even quite that fast, only hitting about 95 in the same distance on a timed eighth-mile drag strip. The photos of the engine in Chris's Mustang flashed on my screen. Ported heads. Tubular headers. If the bottom end had been bored and stroked, it was possible. I knew why Steve had been evasive. Chris's Mustang had been built to run.

Next up was calculating the critical speed of the curve. One of the inputs to the calculation was the lateral acceleration of the vehicle in question. Chris's Mustang had wide, sticky tires on it and a lowered suspension. Sensitivity analysis for a range of values indicated 130 mph. Chris hadn't been going that fast, so his car stayed on the curve at 105 mph.

This circled back to the impact on Chris's Mustang.

To spin Chris clockwise, the impact had to be on the right rear quarter panel, where I'd found the circular scuffmarks.

The answer was obvious. The driver's side front wheel of the other car was in a perfect position to make the circular scuffmarks on the right rear quarter panel of Chris's car.

The skidmarks showed where Chris's car began to spin. The other car would have been on Chris's right side, back near Chris's rear wheel.

The other driver steers his car into Chris's right rear quarter panel. Chris's car immediately spins clockwise.

Right in front of the other car.

At 100 mph, there was no way in hell the other driver could have gotten on the brakes quick enough to avoid hitting Chris's Mustang.

The quickest drivers in the world require about a half-second to recognize that they need to apply the brakes, and then they take another half-second to actually hit the pedal. That's one second for the best drivers in the world, people who get paid millions of dollars for their knife-edge reflexes in a race car. Average drivers need about three-quarters of a second for each, for a total time of 1.5 seconds.

At that speed, Chris's car rotated sideways in half a second. There was no way another driver could brake that fast. He or she would have hit the side of Chris's car. They *did* hit Chris's car- and that was the shallow dent in the passenger door of Chris's car.

The force of impact would be directly related to how fast and how hard the other driver got on the brakes. It wasn't a big dent.

This scenario also perfectly explained why Chris's car would have gone to the inside of the curve instead of the outside of the curve.

The only problem with my neat little analysis was that there was no way that a stock 2016 Mustang GT could have kept up with Chris's car over that distance and around the curve, even with a four-length head start. Unless the other car had some modifications of its own.

I needed to see the other car.

I rubbed my eyes. My tank was empty, out of gas. The clock in the bottom right of my laptop showed 3 a.m.

Hell. I'd spent way too much time on this. Not just what I'd done tonight, but also for the last two days. I couldn't risk losing my focus. I had to get back on the dissertation.

I staggered to bed and lost myself in sleep.

~~~

It seemed like fifteen minutes passed before my phone rang me awake. The clock on my phone told the truth. It had been five hours.

"Hello?" I croaked.

"Soren, it's Judith. Sorry for calling you so late, but we just found the other Mustang. And it might be gone soon."
~~~

CHAPTER 6

I checked my voicemail on the way to Clinton. One from an attorney, and one from Ken, but he didn't say anything. That was a bad sign. I dialed his number and got his voicemail again. I'd swing by the hospital tonight.

I pulled into the Ford dealership. Judith had beaten me there. She motioned for me to follow her.

Small dealer in a small town. No glitz and polish like the city dealers. The pick-up trucks had the showroom floor space, not the sports cars.

I followed Judith back to the used car lot, near the service bays. We exited our cars. The heat hit me like a brick. The day was warmer than the last few had been, forecasted to reach into the high-nineties by the end of the week.

"Who owned it?" I asked Judith.

She raised her eyebrows. "It's not good."

"Why?"

Judith pursed her lips and looked at the ground.

"Judith, what's the issue? Just tell me."

She glanced up at me. Fear in her eyes. "Soren, promise me you won't stop helping us."

"Of course I won't stop helping you. What's the problem?"

She shook her head. "It explains a lot."

"Judith, have you got a name?" I spread my hands.

She nodded, looked at me, then looked away. "Johnny Harrell."

I furrowed my brow. "Okay. Who's that?"

"You are so innocent." She tried to smile, but couldn't manage it.

"I yam what I yam." I reached out and gave her a playful tap on her shoulder. "C'mon. What's the problem?"

She sighed. "The Harrell family are not good people. Soren, you don't understand, because you're not from here. They're involved in all sorts of bad activities."

I shrugged. "Doesn't matter. I'm here to look at a car. Let's get the facts first."

"Thanks."

"So where is it?"

She looked back at the dealership. "He said it would be out here. I'll go find Stephen."

"Stephen?"

"Salesman I talked to. He's kin."

Small towns had their advantages.

I scanned the area. The used Mustangs were lined up in a row facing the side street. There were at least two black coupes, but I couldn't make out the year.

I grabbed my clipboard and headed that way. The first one was an '11. The next one was a '16, but it was a garden-variety six-cylinder. Definitely not a racer.

A red Mitsubishi WRX drove by. The driver stared at me intently and then motioned to his passenger. Brake lights came on as it passed me. The Mitsubishi stopped just past the dealership, turned around in the road, and then headed back towards me.

The passenger had a grey hooded sweatshirt pulled over his head. Reflective sunglasses wrapped around his face. The car slowed to a stop near the curb.

"You with that white Mercury?" Thick southern drawl. Young man's voice, but the words were slow. He was pointing at Judith's car.

The hairs on my neck stood up. I shifted my weight to my left foot.

He read my body language. "Dude, it's okay. Chris was our friend. You're here for his wreck, right?"

"You say you're friends of Chris?"

"High school friends," the kid said. "We recognized that white Mercury. Chris's aunt, right?"

I ignored his question and asked one of my own. "You just happened to be driving by and recognized the car?"

"You don't believe in coincidences?"

"Not in my line of work."

"Might have had a text saying she was here. It's a small town. Just thought we'd see what was up."

I walked closer to the car. "You know anything about what happened?"

The passenger swiveled his head back to me. "Just sad, is all. Chris got into things he should've just left alone." He smiled. Big white teeth.

"Like what?" A burning smell wafted out of the car. Marijuana. I stepped back.

The passenger saw my expression. "Oh, yeah, sorry. Wake and bake, dude." He reached down and grabbed something on the floor.

I stepped further back. I shifted the clipboard in my left hand and slid my right hand in my pocket. Sharp plastic checkering met my fingers.

Hissing sound. The kid sprayed air freshener in the car, then turned his reflective lenses back to me. "You a private investigator?"

"Forensics."

"Like the TV show? Pretty cool." He tossed the can in the back seat. "So you here for a certain car?"

I nodded. "Sounds more impressive than it is. Has anyone said Chris was racing someone the night he was killed?"

"Kids around here race all the time," he said. "Is that what someone told you?"

"It's what people are saying."

"Not the cops. They said it was a single car accident. Said there was drugs in the car."

"How do you know that?"

"Man, everybody knows that. There's more shit going on around here than Mexico."

The driver snickered.

"It's true, ain't it, Billy?" The passenger elbowed the driver. "We got whores and drugs and guns. Got the best politicians money can buy. Hell, it's home." He looked back at me. "But you still ain't answered me. You're here for a black Mustang, right?"

"You know the car?"

The passenger nodded slowly, the reflective lenses going up-down.

"It belonged to a bad boy, son. Best be careful where you dig. Might end up being your own grave. But you might already know that, being in forensics and all."

It was near ninety degrees. My neck chilled.

He smiled broadly again. "I'm just messing with you. It's a nice car. Black as sin."

I stepped closer again. "You said you were friends of Chris? Got a name?"

"Soren!" Judith shouted across the lot.

The passenger looked up at Judith's shout, then swiveled his head back to me.

"Catch you later, man." He brought his left hand around in front of him, pointed his index finger out the window at me, like the barrel of a gun, and dropped his thumb.

The driver revved the engine and threw the car into a turn. Tires screeched and the rear end swayed. Then they were gone, heading down the street away from the main road that fronted the dealership.

"Soren!" Judith shouted again, this time closer.

I waved my hand in the air, still watching the road where the Mitsubishi had disappeared.

"Who was that?" she asked as we came within earshot.

"No idea," I said. "They said they were Chris's friends."

"What did they want?" She blocked the sun and looked down the road.

"They asked me if I was with you. And they knew I was here to look at a black Mustang."

"Did you get a good look at them?" she asked.

"No, the passenger was wearing a hoodie and sunglasses."

She shrugged, then turned to the man. "Stephen, this is Soren Graves. He's the guy I was telling you about."

We shook hands. "We just took the car in about a week ago," he said. "Is there a lawsuit over this?" His brow was beading with sweat.

"No," Judith said, "it's just to find out what happened to Chris."

"I'd be in a heap of trouble if we got involved in a lawsuit," Stephen said. More sweat beads. He looked at me.

"No lawsuit," I said.

He looked back at Judith. "The car's in the service bay."

We followed him into the office of the service area. This definitely wasn't a place where customers waited. Cigarette smoke hung heavy and blue in the air. Ragged sofa from the Nixon era against one wall. The cinderblock walls were painted decades ago in Ford blue about chest high. The white above that had turned dingy gray. The door to the bathroom was propped open with a plunger. Tattered copies of Field & Stream and Guns & Ammo on the floor next to the toilet.

We stepped through the doorway into the service area. Poor lighting made it look dirtier than it was. The sweet odor of grease and gasoline pressed against my skin. It triggered flashbacks of my own days doing bodywork to get myself through the undergraduate engineering program.

I knew how to handle the tools in here. But the place felt different than other garages I'd worked in. Dark, ominous. Foreboding.

Most of the equipment was old and well-used. Years of dirt and grease and scratches obscured the lifts and the tire changers and the air compressor. Grease lines hung from overhead reels. The concrete floor showed the evidence of stains and spills of automotive lifeblood over decades.

We walked past a Taurus on one lift, raised high off the ground. It was missing a transmission.

The Mustang was on the other side of the Taurus. The car was waist high on the lift. All the wheels had been removed. The empty suspension points drooped like the legs of a cat that had been picked up by its belly.

"Here it is," Stephen said. He shuffled his feet. "What do you need to do to it?"

Judith looked at me. He followed her gaze.

"Nothing destructive," I said. "Just looking for prior damage and fresh paint work, and checking for crash data in the airbag computer."

"Data?" he asked.

"If a car has an airbag, it has an airbag computer controlling it. Some of them can store data if the car is in a crash."

"Like what data?" He wiped his brow.

"How fast the car was going, whether the brakes were on, whether the seatbelts was buckled, what the measured delta-v of the crash was. Lots more."

"Dang."

"It's complicated but it works. You're the new owner of the car and I need your permission to do it. Is it okay if I image the data?"

"As long as nothing gets changed, sure," he said.

"Thanks," I said. "Nothing gets changed."

"Holler at me when ya'll get done," he said to Judith.

He left us standing there. I walked over to the controls for the lift. Vented air from the pneumatic cylinder hissed as the car lowered enough for me to open the door. I went back out to get the Pelican case from my car. The crash data retrieval hardware went on the passenger seat. I reached under the knee bolster for the Diagnostic Link Connector and plugged the cord in. I put my laptop on the driver's seat and turned the vehicle key.

"It doesn't look like the car has any damage," I told Judith as I went through the procedure. "Don't be surprised if nothing comes up. The airbag computer is asleep all the time unless it feels a jolt strong enough to wake it up, and once it wakes up, it has to decide whether or not to deploy the airbag." I initialized the interface between the vehicle's computer and my own, then turned back to her. I was about to say something else when a dialog box popped up.

"Oh, wow," I said.

"What?" Judith asked.

I scanned the data that had come up on the screen. "It's showing that there was an impact. Two impacts."

So-called 'black boxes' in cars these days are regarded with mystery. Truth is, there's nothing mysterious about them. They're not actually black, they're stamped silver steel or gray cast aluminum, and they aren't in the car because of some insidious government attempt to collect data on the drivers. They are the computer that tells the airbag when and how to deploy, and most of the time they aren't 'awake' and powered up until an impact is detected, usually a few hundred millionths of a second after it happens. In most modern vehicles, they can also store data about what the car, and driver, was doing before the crash, and that's the data that everyone is concerned about.

With apologies to Shakespeare, 'to blow or not to blow' is the question that the computer must answer. There is a proprietary algorithm in the computer that looks at different inputs from various sensors and then makes that decision. In most modern cars, the values of those inputs are stored in the airbag computer's memory after the event is over, even if the airbags were not deployed. That's called a non-deployment event, and that's the data I was after in this Mustang.

Deploying the airbag is primarily a function of the negative acceleration that the car, and thus what the person inside the car, experiences during an impact. This negative acceleration, often colloquially called 'deceleration', is how quickly the car slows down in a certain time period. If the negative acceleration is rapid enough, it ends up bending metal and injuring the soft squishy people inside the car.

Here's an example: a driver can use the car's brakes to slow down in a straight line from 20 mph to 5 mph. The overall change in velocity is called the 'delta-v', and in this case the delta-v is 15 mph. If this takes place over ten seconds, like someone coming to a stop sign, it'll be comfortable. No injuries, no lawsuits. No deployed airbag.

Now let's look at the same speed loss happening in a quarter-second, as the car rear-ends another car. Same 15 mph change in velocity, or delta-v, but this time it's very uncomfortable. And the airbag computer wakes up as the bumpers began compressing, watches the sensors, and then decides that yes, this crash needs an airbag deployment, and gives the order to fire the squib.

Here's an example: let's say someone is busy sexting their girlfriend and misses the red light. At the last moment he slams on the brakes and rear ends the car in front of him. The airbag computer wakes up and looks at the inputs. Then it decides to deploy, or not to deploy, the airbag. In a low speed rear-ender, under twelve miles an hour, it probably won't.

The car stops. His body, though, wants to keep going forward. This is where the seatbelt saves his face, if he's wearing it. It pushes back on his chest and hips and keeps him from slamming into the steering wheel and ruining the thousands of dollars of orthodontic work his parents paid for.

If the driver is not belted, the kid will learn firsthand what Newton's Third Law feels like when their face impacts the steering wheel. Good news for the orthodontist. She'll be able to buy another boat for the money she'll charge to reconstruct the kid's teeth.

If the kid is going a little faster, the airbag probably will deploy. The airbag computer doesn't only look at delta-v, or how fast the car was traveling at impact. It primarily looks at 'jerk' to gauge the severity of a crash. This doesn't mean it looks at your boss, or the rude guy at the DMV. Technically, jerk is the rate of change of acceleration with respect to time. If the jerk is increasing rapidly, the computer can predict that the crash is severe enough to warrant blowing the airbag. If not, it won't. Simple.

Going back to delta-v, the same situation occurs going from 45 mph to 30 mph. The delta-v is still 15 mph, but there's a huge difference in the jerk if it takes place over one-tenth of a second versus ten seconds. And this is what the computer needs to measure to determine if the airbag needs to be deployed. Losing 15 mph over ten seconds won't blow the airbag. Losing 15 mph over less than one-tenth of a second probably will. Losing more than 80 mph in less than a second will definitely blow the bags, but it won't help, because the people in the car will be dead from the car crushing up like tinfoil.

I'd investigated many crashes where an attorney thought a blown airbag should have saved the person's life and was considering suing the car manufacturer because it didn't. Then I see the car, and the crash is so severe that the front end of the car is crushed up into the seat. News flash: nothing would have saved the person from dying in a crash like that.

And then there are times when the airbag doesn't blow, but the attorney thinks it should have, and wants to sue the car manufacturer for a defective product. There's many reasons why an airbag won't deploy in a crash: the crash pulse was too low, the impact was at just the right angle to not trigger the accelerometer, or the car has a salvage title from a previous crash and the unscrupulous body shop stuffed rags under a new steering wheel cover and sold the replacement airbag on the black market.

One fatal crash baffled me until I was able to see the medical report. The crash was severe and should have triggered the airbag, but on inspection, the steering wheel looked brand-new. There was a huge amount of blood and tissue on the dashboard and windshield, but neither were broken. The seatbelt had not been worn, either. Why hadn't the airbag deployed?

Turns out, it tried to. Closer inspection revealed that the bottom seam of the steering wheel cover had a tiny slit from the airbag propellant being released. The expanding sodium azide gases didn't unfold the airbag and blow the cover off the steering wheel, but the gases still had to vent somewhere, and the weakest point of escape was the bottom of the steering wheel cover.

So what had prevented the airbag from blowing the cover off the steering wheel and expanding into a big nylon cushion?

The driver.

The medical report listed the driver as a morbidly obese 48-year old male. Cause of death was blunt trauma to the chest. He'd wedged his body in front of the steering wheel so that his arms could still steer the car. During the crash, while his car was slowing down as the front end crushed like an aluminum can, his 450-pound body kept moving forward. His chest and torso impacted the steering wheel hard enough to cause massive internal injuries. The computer commanded the airbag to deploy at the proper time, but because his body was already pressing against the steering wheel with thirty times his body weight from the negative acceleration, which was 13,500 pounds, the airbag couldn't unfold and expand.

In the case of the 2016 Mustang I was currently imaging, the delta-v from the impact was severe enough to jolt the airbag computer awake. But during the millionths of a second of opening its eyes and yawning and stretching, the computer had decided that the crash wasn't severe enough to justify deploying the airbag. Judging by the minimal damage to the Mustang, it was the correct decision to make.

Even without blowing the airbag, as soon as the computer wakes up, it starts recording data until the event is over. That precious data was now being copied into my laptop. The data stays in the computer's RAM until the key is turned 250 times in GM cars or until another event overrides it in the Fords, at which time it erases and resets for the next event. If the airbag does blow, then the data is locked permanently in the memory, and the airbag computer has to be replaced along with the new airbag.

Getting this data made the trip worthwhile. Bottom line was that it showed two separate impacts. The Mustang's airbag computer had two accelerometers, one to the front and one to the side, and in reading the component acceleration spikes I could discern where the impacts had been.

The first impact was a lateral one, hitting on the driver's side of the car. The second impact was longitudinal. Both impacts were sharp enough to jolt the airbag computer awake but short enough that it decided it wasn't a severe crash.

I skimmed over the data.

There was no braking prior to the first side impact.

Different story on the second impact. Hard emergency braking just before the impact on the front. And the indicated speed was 106 mph.

I smiled. My analysis had been less than three percent off.

The rest of the data was related to the occupants.

Seatbelt pretensioners did not fire.

Driver was buckled.

Passenger was buckled.

What?

I double-checked the data. It was correct.

The Occupant Classification System (OCS) showed the front passenger seat was occupied. The OCS consisted of a weight-sensitive gel-filled mat that could report the approximate weight of the front passenger. It was accurate enough to determine if there was an adult, a child, or nothing in the front seat.

It showed an adult had been there during the impact.

"There was someone else in the car."

Blank stare. "You mean during the race?"

"Yes."

She walked over. "Does that say there was?"

"It does right here." I pointed to the data. "There's a weight sensor in the front seat bottom. It's designed to turn the airbag off if it senses a child sitting in the seat. In this case, it sensed an adult, and it kept the airbag on, even though it wasn't deployed."

"So someone was riding with Johnny."

"And they're a witness to whatever happened." I saved the data to my laptop and unhooked everything. "We need to find out who that person was."

"Good luck," Judith said. "If it was one of Johnny's friends, they won't never come forward."

"Maybe. But if you apply enough external force, you'll make someone move."

I put the equipment and my laptop back in the Pelican case and pulled out my digital paint thickness gauge.

"So what are you looking for now?" she asked.

"Damage," I answered. "The computer data tells me there was an impact, but it doesn't tell me exactly where. Now I need to find it."

I placed the digital thickness gauge on the Mustang's decklid.

When a typical production car leaves the factory, it has exactly one layer of primer, one layer of colorcoat, and one layer of clearcoat on the body panels. The combined thickness of all these layers adds up to about four one-thousandths of an inch (with one-thousandth of an inch equaling one mil), or about the thickness of two sheets of regular white paper. The net result is a paper-thin layer of paint is all that stands between your second-largest financial expenditure and the hot sun of summer and the cold rains of winter, both of which want to reduce your precious car to oxides.

Now, if your darling vehicle gets damaged in a crash, and say for example that it needs a new right fender and hood, then those replacement parts will need to be painted to match the rest of the car.

But the painter, being human, will not be able to spray the refinish paint as uniformly thin as the paint that the robots at the factory put on the entire car as it went down the paint line. Which, by the way, is the very least thickness that the manufacturer of the car can squeak by with, because paint is expensive. And if they squeak by with too little, the paint will peel off later. It happens.

The end result is that the paint thickness on cars can be different from panel to panel, and knowing how it got that way can clue you in to where a car has been damaged and repaired. And if you know where it's been damaged, then you know where the impact was, then you continue merrily on your way to finding out exactly how the crash occurred.

The numbers appeared on the LCD display. The decklid paint was thin, about 4.5 mils, and dead-nuts-on to be factory original. I checked the roof. Normal there, too, almost exactly the same as the decklid. I moved on to the left rear quarter panel. Still normal, as was the driver's door.

Things got interesting on the driver side front fender. It showed twice the normal paint thickness. The clearcoat also wasn't uniform, indicating being sprayed by those fallible human hands. The hood showed the same thing.

The hood and driver side front fender had been repainted at some point in the Mustang's life. I popped the hood and checked for VIN tags on the hood and fender. The hood was original, but the fender had not tag. It had been replaced.

The big question now was whether the re-paint I'd found was from the crash that killed Judith's nephew. The condition of the surface of the paint would provide a clue to that.

I looked closer, examining the surface of the clearcoat with my phone camera's magnification. The original paint on the left side of the car showed distinct swirl marks and acid rain damage. There were also tiny white specks dotting the surface, invisible to the naked eye. As I moved to the passenger fender and hood, the swirl marks and acid rain damage and tiny white specks disappeared.

"The left front fender and hood have been repainted." I held the magnifying glass out and motioned for Judith to come over. She took it and bent down.

"See the swirl marks and tiny white specks?" I asked.

"What are they from?"

"The swirl marks are from regular washing and polishing. The white specks are overspray from being parked too close to a building that's being repainted."

"That happened to our cars in the staff parking lot," she said.

I got up and checked the front bumper. My paint gauge showed 9 mils, twice the normal paint thickness.

There were two coats of paint on the front bumper, and the thickness varied all over the place. It was thinnest on the very front center where an impact would have cracked the paint, and they probably sanded that down to the plastic, but they'd just repainted over the original paint on the rest of it.

I checked the surface condition of the paint. It was brand new, same as the fender and hood. I leaned closer and sniffed the paint. The sickly-sweet familiar odor of evaporating solvents wafted into my nose. The paint on the bumper wasn't even fully cured yet. It was still emitting solvents as the polymer chains that made up the paint linked and tightened.

Automotive paint generally takes several months to fully cure. During that time the solvents that are used to carry the paint material slowly evaporate out of the paint itself. The paint feels dry, and it can be safely washed and touched, but don't wax it. Waxing will trap the solvent vapors in the paint, which makes the paint bubble and peel off the car.

"There's no bug guts, either," Judith pointed out. "I hate bug guts. Never can get them off the front of my car."

That was a good observation. "Yeah, you're right." I leaned over and pressed my thumbnail against the painted bumper. It dug into the paint easily. The paint was still soft. It hadn't even set up yet. Whoever repainted it hadn't even used a catalyzed clearcoat.

Judith watched as I did it again in another place. "What does that mean?" she asked.

"It's brand new. It takes a while for paint to cure, and this is still soft."

The hood was still raised, so I pulled the headlight retaining pins up on both sides and took the headlight assemblies out. This exposed areas of the bumper that weren't normally visible. I counted three runs in the clearcoat and dry spray on the edges. This was definitely a repaint, and it was a crappy one at that.

"Can you match the paint form this one to the paint marks you found on Chris's Mustang?"

"That would be great, but probably not." Both black, both Fords, both Mustangs. Being the same color, I wouldn't be able to get clearly separate samples. A gas chromatograph would show combined samples from both paints, but it wouldn't be able to match the sample to the undamaged part of either car. It wasn't strong enough to hold up in a court of law.

Kids think black is cool. For me, as an artist, it reflected a lack of aesthetic. For them, it was all about presenting a stupid facade of toughness and trying to intimidate the guy in the other lane from the other tribe. There was no room for beauty or expression. Just darkness. And as they desire it, so it comes to them.

There was still other damage to look for.

I walked over to the controls for the car lift and elevated the Mustang a few more feet until it was chest high. The compressor kicked on and the steel safety catches clanged loudly against the stops as it gained altitude. I gave the car a push to make sure it was held solid and then walked back to the front of the car, ducking my head to look inside the front wheel wells. The driver's side push rivets that held the wheel liner to the fender were not original Ford fasteners. I popped them out and removed the cover. The mounting brackets that secured the front bumper to the fender were bright red, not black. Part of the fiberglass radiator support was cracked. A chunk had been knocked out on the left side. I walked over to the passenger side front wheel well and did the same thing. Those brackets were intact, and they were the original black color that matched the rest of the Mustang. Interesting.

"There was a side impact to the forward driver's side, probably on the front wheel. The second impact occurred on the very front middle of the bumper."

Judith bent down. I pointed to the red bracket and the broken fiberglass on the driver's side. "The original bracket would have been black, like the other one. This one is off a red Mustang. And the other fasteners aren't original Ford fasteners."

"And I had to replace the driver's side front wheel bearin'," a deep voice said behind us. Judith and I spun around. I knocked my head on the inside of the fender.

"Ouch," I said, rubbing my scalp. The voice belonged to a big bearded guy wearing a Ford service shirt that hadn't been cleaned in years.

"You okay?" he and Judith asked at the same time.

"Yeah." That was embarrassing. "You had to replace the wheel bearing?"

"Yup." He walked over to a pile of grungy parts on the floor. He kicked a starter and a water pump out of the way, then bent down and picked up a wheel bearing. I walked over to him and looked at it closer. He handed it to me.

"Ya'll can see how it's got too much play in the hub," he said.

I pulled the hub in and out and noticed it immediately.

"How did you know it was bad?" I asked.

"The kid who traded it took such a low price, they didn't even have it inspected. After the kid left, they took the car out and heard it roaring when they got above forty."

I offered the bearing back to him but he held up his hand.

"Keep it," he said. "It ain't a warranty part, so it'll just get tossed out."

I looked back at the car. "What's the story with the wheels and tires?"

He wiped his hands on a dirty rag. "The tires were near bald, so we're havin' to put new rubber on it all the way around."

"If the wheel bearing had been damaged, then the wheel should have been damaged, too." I pointed to the driver's side front suspension. "Did this wheel have any damage on it?"

"Nope."

"That doesn't make sense." I spun the wheel bearing in my hands. "Where are the wheels?"

He gestured for me to follow him. We walked over to the far side of the garage.

The answer was obvious.

A set of stock '16 Mustang GT wheels were stacked in a column near the bead-breaking machine.

"He changed the wheels," Judith said.

"Do what?" the tech asked.

"Nothing." I shot her a look, then looked over the wheels carefully. No sign of damage on the rims.

"Tires?" I asked.

"Throwed out," he said. "I gotta get back to work, but if you need something, just holler."

I grabbed Judith and we walked back to my car. "Best to keep things quiet for now."

"I'm sorry. I know."

I retrieved my camera and took photographs of all the things I'd found on the car. I shot close-ups of the paint work, the bumper, the brackets, the wheel bearing, and then took a bunch of general photographs in case I needed to see something later.

I opened the door of the Mustang and pulled the hood release lever. It sprang up an inch. I walked back to the front of the car, bending down to look through the opening before sliding my fingers under the edge and tripping the secondary hood latch. I'd been stung opening the hood on a previous car, literally, when I'd grabbed a handful of wasps on their nest. Once bitten, and all that. Opening car hoods in my business is risky.

No wasps under this hood. I lifted the panel until the gas shocks were fully extended, then pulled out my little Surefire flashlight and leaned over the right front fender. The threaded plugs were on the intake manifold. I stuck some adhesive measuring tape underneath them for scale and then took a dozen shots. I searched for the telltale signs that plumbing lines had been routed to the blocked holes. The stock gasoline lines were routed around the engine and back to the firewall. No signs of more lines.

There was nothing else to suggest that the car had been modified in any way.

"Damn it." I was stymied.

"What?" Judith asked.

"I can't find where he routed the lines."

"What lines?"

I didn't answer.

There, on the bulkhead. I pushed the harness aside and cast the light into the dark space behind the engine.

I walked to the lift controls and raised the car higher. It raised slowly, clacking on the safety catches. I walked partway under the right cowl of the car, just behind the right front wheel.

There were two empty non-Ford brackets that were screwed haphazardly into the base of the cowl. They were sized to hold lines about 3/8" in diameter. I followed the most likely path of the lines that had been held in these brackets, where I would have routed them if I'd done the work. I ended up near the rear axle. There were two more brackets along the way, tucked up inside the reinforcement of the floorpan. Two holes had been drilled into the metal floorpan under the trunk area. I documented and photographed these and then let the car back down.

I walked over to the driver's side and popped the trunk. The decklid jerked upwards and I walked around and pushed it all the way up, then bent down and pulled up some carpeting. Under the insulation and carpet were four holes. Two holes were for the lines leading to the engine and two were for the return lines.

"What is it?" Judith asked.

"Nitrous oxide," I said.

She looked at the empty space. "I don't see no nitrous."

"It's gone now, but those were the brackets for the bottle." I pointed. "The empty brackets I showed you under the car were for the lines that ran to the engine."

She followed me back around to the front of the car. I pointed to the threaded plugs. "That is not an original Ford modification," I said. "Those plugged holes are where the nitrous lines were plumbed into the intake manifold. He would have had a switch somewhere in the car to arm the system and then vent it, but he must have had a quiet purge valve, probably hidden on the firewall so no one could see it."

Nitrous oxide, N_2O, is an artificial way to nearly double the horsepower of a car engine for quick spurts. It's all the rage with the import racer crowds, but the Germans used it in their fighter aircraft in World War II to increase the power output at high altitudes. The nitrogen serves to cool the temperatures of the intake charge so that the oxygen content is denser, and the extra oxygen atoms allow more fuel to be burned. The end result is bunch more power as long as the nitrous lasts.

I pointed to the space where the bottle had been mounted. "The gas is stored in a metal cylinder, probably mounted here. The driver wanted to hide all the lines so Chris wouldn't notice it. That's how he got his head start."

"So he cheated."

"Yeah."

"How did you suspect it?"

"Both cars were going way too fast to be stock. This car had to have it keep up with Chris around the curve. When the damage on the front end was fixed and the wheels were swapped, they must have ripped the nitrous system off it, too."

Something else bothered me. I walked over to the driver's door. The keys were still in the ignition. I reached in and pulled off the parking brake and then slid into the leather seat. My left foot pressed the brake. I shifted the transmission into neutral. The tech had wandered off. I walked over to the lift and hit the lever, raising the Mustang high enough to walk under it.

Judith watched me put a piece of the tape on the driveshaft and then one on the differential so I could judge the rotation of the driveshaft.

"Judith, turn one of the rear wheels one complete revolution, no more and no less." As she turned the wheel I counted the number of times the driveshaft made a complete revolution.

One, two, three, four... "Okay, go slow." The driveshaft barely came around past the tape.

"Did you get it?" she asked, holding the tire.

"Yeah," I said, walking carefully out from under the car. My head still hurt where I'd banged it under the front fender.

"Four-eleven. The stock Mustang should have had a 3.27 ratio.

Someone put a 4.11 gearset in the rear axle. It makes the car accelerate quicker."

"He had all this stuff and still needed a four-car-length head start?"

"Actually, with gears and nitrous and the head start, this car would have beaten Chris to the curve." I was thinking out loud.

"Then why didn't he just win the race?" Judith asked.

I nodded. "Why didn't he?"

The driver could have beaten Chris to the curve. But he held back, behind Chris, so he'd be in a perfect position to nudge Chris's quarter panel.

My jaw dropped. Son of a bitch.

Johnny, or whomever was driving this car, *did* set out to kill Chris. Or at least make him wreck.

"He did it on purpose, didn't he?" Judith had been watching my face. Her words were barely audible.

I looked at her, then at the ground. "Yeah."

~~~

On the way to the Cameron's home my phone buzzed. I tapped the hands-free receiver hanging on my ear.

It was Wayne. "What's ten lawyers on the bottom of the ocean?"

"I give up."

"A good start," he said. "We need a report from you on the trailer case. And you won't believe the latest development."
~~~

"What's that?"

"Remember when we were meeting with Jordan right after the crash, and he mentioned a previous trailer crash in Maryville that killed a lady?"

"Yes."

"Guess where the perp you caught worked before the John Deere dealer."

My eyes widened. "He hitched the trailer in that crash, too?"

"He did. It was a different business, but Larkin put it together."

"Damn. Good for Larkin. Makes your job easier."

"Yours, too. When can you get me that report, doc?"

"Not a doctor yet," I said. "When do you need it?"

"How about next Wednesday?"

"Will do."

I tapped the earbud again. It would take me away from my dissertation but I could bill at least five hours of work for it.

I followed Judith as she turned down the road the Camerons lived on. The last rays of the setting sun were turning the western sky deep red.

There was a small dark blue BMW 3-series parked in front of the garage where I'd parked before. I pulled in next to it, and Judith came to rest on the other side of me.

"Allison's here," she said, motioning to the BMW.

"Okay." I grabbed my laptop and the folder containing the case materials from my car, then climbed the steps of the porch and followed Judith inside. Steve was by the sink but he grabbed a towel and walked quickly over to me, drying his hands on the way.

"Hey, buddy," he said. He seemed more upbeat this time.

I took his hand. "Hello, Steve. Good to see you again."

"Hi, Soren," Cathy said. She walked into the kitchen from the great room. She didn't try to hug me this time. Allison followed behind her.

"Cathy," I said quietly. I looked into Allison's eyes as Cathy walked over to her previous position by the sink. Judith went over and stood by her sister.

"Hey," Allison said. "Thanks again for doing this." Then in a lower voice, "I know it's not easy." She glanced behind me in the direction of her father.

"It's okay."

We turned toward the kitchen and Allison walked over to her mom and Judith. I pulled the same chair out from the table I'd sat in last time. I moved the papers that covered the table to make space for my laptop. I started to pull it out, then left it in the case next to my feet.

Steve pulled the chair opposite mine out from the table but didn't sit down. He stood over my shoulder as I pulled the papers out of the file. His glass of tea tottered near the table edge.

"What'd you find?" he asked. Impatient.

"It'll take a few minutes for me to explain it all." I laid the papers out and scooted back from the table so I could see Cathy as well as Steve.

"There was definitely contact between the two Mustangs," I said. Before I could utter another word, Steve straightened from the table.

"See?" he shouted at Cathy. His arm was straight out, finger pointed at me.

I looked over at Cathy. She had covered her face in her hands. "Damn it, Steve, let him finish." She never looked up.

Awkward silence. I glanced at Allison and Judith and then back to Steve. Steve sat back down.

This was getting difficult.

"What else did you learn?" Steve asked.

I turned back to him. "They were going fast. My calculations put Chris at over 100 mph when he lost control."

I stared at him. He shrugged his shoulders.

"Steve, you and I both know that a stock Mustang would only hit maybe 75 mph in the eighth-mile," I said. "By my calculations, that Mustang was kicking out at least 360 horsepower. That's about 155 horsepower more than stock."

"I don't know," he said. "It is what it is."

I hate that phrase. "If you want me to give you a true idea of how the crash happened, I need honest information."

He nodded, sitting down in the chair. "That's why Johnny had the head start."

I looked at Judith.

"He knows," she said. "About Johnny owning the car before. But not about the stuff you found."

"What stuff?" Steve asked me.

If I told him about the modifications on Johnny's car, it would be like detonating a bomb.

I looked at Judith. She closed her eyes and covered her ears.

It's what I was here for.

"Steve, Johnny's car had gears. And nitrous. It was a cheater system that Chris wouldn't have seen."

Steve's brow furrowed. He knew cars, and he was adding up the horsepower. Then, slowly, his eyes widened.

"*GODDAMMIT!*" His hand lashed out, catching the papers on the table. He slammed the stack against the wall. Papers exploded in the kitchen. The glass of tea shattered. I turned my head as pieces of glass and drops of tea sprayed everywhere.

"STEVE!" Cathy shouted.

"*HE KILLED CHRIS!*" Steve pointed at her. "He murdered our son! I TOLD YOU!"

I'd never heard anyone yell so loud in such a small room. If he went nuts here, I didn't know if I could restrain him.

Steve shifted to me. "Isn't that enough proof for murder?" he yelled.

"Maybe. I don't know." I spread my hands.

"Well, you're the damn expert! Is it?"

"Probably not."

Steve was incredulous. "Why not?"

"It's criminal court. Has to be beyond the shadow of a doubt. His defense attorney will argue Johnny's a bad driver." I dropped my hands. "If it was even him driving. There's a thousand ways for him to weasel out of it."

It was the truth. It also might have caused Steve to swing at me. But better me than Cathy.

Steve's eyes glistened. Tears streamed down his face.

"I get so mad," he choked. "I'm so goddamn angry."

He wanted to say more, holding his hands out and his palms upward, trying to make more words come but not being able. His son was gone forever. His shoulders dropped and he sat down heavily in the chair. He held his hand over his face. He was trembling.

"Damn it." He took a deep, shaky breath.

"I'm sorry, Steve."

The papers were a mess on the kitchen floor. Dark drops of tea stained the pages like dried blood.

Judith was in front of Allison. Cathy had turned her back to us. She stared out the window over the sink.

I fought the urge to clean up the mess.

"Where do we stand now if it goes to trial?" Steve finally asked.

"You mean if they arrested Johnny?" I asked.

Steve nodded.

"I still can't prove it was intentional."

"What about the passenger?" Judith asked.

"Passenger?" Steve looked at her, then me.

I nodded. "The data showed there was a belted passenger in the Mustang at the time of the event."

Steve stared at the floor. "We need to find out who it was. He could prove it, couldn't he?"

"Or she," I said.

"Steve, think about it. You think one of Johnny's friends would testify against him?"

"I'll make the son of a bitch testify," Steve said. His hands curled into fists.

"Have you guys called Wayne?" I asked.

"No, not yet," Cathy said.

"Have either of you been through a criminal trial before?"

"No." They said it in unison.

"They're ugly," I said. "If Johnny's dad gets a decent attorney, you can expect that he will make Chris look as bad as he can, and make Johnny look as good as he can. They'll use every lawyer trick they can get away with to prevent Johnny from going to jail."

"But he killed-" Steve began.

"Damn it, Steve!" Cathy shouted, cutting him off.

I looked at her. She had been pushed past her point of patience. Steve sat still but he curled his fingers into fists on the tabletop.

"I do not want my son's name dragged through the mud." Her tone was solid granite. Final ruling.

"But-" Steve tried again. He turned his gaze to Allison, looking for solidarity. She avoided his eyes.

Cathy interrupted the silent interplay. "Don't push me, Steve." Clear warning.

Judith glanced at Steve, then at me, sadness in her eyes.

Steve turned to me. “What would happen in a trial?” He deliberately ignored Cathy. “Wouldn’t Johnny go to jail if the jury found him guilty?”

“Depends on what he was convicted of. Manslaughter without prior convictions, maybe a year in jail.”

Steve looked at me in disbelief. “He kills my boy, and he gets a year in jail.”

“I’m not certain. You have to ask an attorney. But I’ve been in this business a while, and I can tell you that jurors need to perceive a big imbalance of justice to produce a guilty verdict. Chris was illegally racing on a public road, and nothing can prove the contact was intentional.”

“Bottom line it for me.”

I ran my hand through my hair, looked a the tabletop. “The only thing it would do is disparage his memory and put you and Cathy through a lot of stress.”

“I know,” Cathy said quietly. “I know.” She sniffed and looked up at me. “It isn’t worth it. He’s gone and there isn’t anything that’ll bring him back.”

Steve glanced from Cathy to Allison to me. He was losing support for his argument.

“Well, I’m not giving up,” he said. “Like I said before,” he said, addressing Cathy, “if this does go to court, he’ll get the right judge, and he’ll get a stiff sentence. You know that. You have to know that.”

I recalled Steve’s comment during my last visit, about Johnny being found guilty if he went to trial. I still didn’t understand what Steve meant.

Cathy clarified it. “Steve, we don’t even know that he would. Chris and Kelly broke up before the crash. Kelly didn’t want anything to do with him.”

Allison spoke. “I wouldn’t count on Kelly’s help.”

“Hell, that don’t matter!” Steve pounded on the table. Pieces of glass jumped. “Chris and Kelly was together since he was a junior. Chris spent Christmas before last with them. Ain’t no way she’d let her dad not do justice.”

Allison shook her head.

“What about contacting a lawyer?”

“We don’t know any.”

I knew plenty of them. I wrote down Wayne’s name and number.

"Call this guy." I slid the paper to Steve, but Judith stepped over and took it before it got to him. I turned to her and Cathy. "Tell him you know me, and then explain the case to him as concisely as you can. Don't get long-winded, just let him know what I've found, what you think happened, and then tell him you'd like to pursue a civil case against Johnny."

Steve looked back to me. "Civil case? I want that boy in jail for what he done to Chris."

"He deserves that," I said. "But I've seen my fair share of cases tried by juries, and criminal court standards are higher than those in civil court. You'd have to prove manslaughter, at minimum, to get Johnny put away. Depending on the evidence I find, that's going to be very difficult to do."

"Why?"

"Steve, even if I can prove there was contact, I can't prove intent."

"What about the passenger?" Judith asked.

"Passenger?" Steve asked.

I'd forgotten about that. "The download showed that a passenger was riding in Johnny's Mustang." I nodded. "Whoever it was could potentially testify to Johnny's intent."

"Someone else was in Johnny's car?" Steve was still shocked.

"I don't know how to identify him, though." I emptied the tea. "Can you ask the kids?"

"Or her," Judith said. "It could be a girl."

"Damn straight I'll ask the kids." Steve stood up again. "So if we get the witness, and he- or she- is willing to testify, then we have a shot at convicting Johnny for killing Chris?"

I sighed. "Steve, it's tenuous. A long shot at best."

"That don't mean we can't try," Steve said. "Ain't no harm in trying. But I'll tell you this, he'll get convicted if it goes to trial. With or without a witness. If that little bastard goes to court, that judge is going to put him away." He was working himself up now, pacing faster. "If he goes to trial, we got more than God on our side." He shot me a sideways glance. "Better believe it."

"Guys?" I interceded. "What's going on?"

"Chris's girlfriend," Steve said to me. "Ex-girlfriend, I mean. Her dad is an Anderson County judge. And I bet he'd get the case if it came to it."

"Are you certain he's in criminal court?" I asked.

"Yeah, yeah," Steve nodded. "I see him at the courthouse when I'm working over there."

"Even so, there's no way that could happen," I said. "It's a clear case of conflict of interest. He'd have to recuse himself."

"Son, this is Anderson County," Steve said quietly. "We do things different around here."

There's no way. No way. The attorneys wouldn't let that happen. Steve is disconnected. And when it doesn't work out the way he thinks it should, he's going to be in bad shape. I'd seen other families struggle through similar tragedies, and if they didn't immediately pull together, they usually fell apart. Maybe months or years later, but it was a slow decay. I didn't want this to happen to Chris's family but it was beyond my control.

I looked at Cathy. Her expression softened as Judith put her arm around her sister. Her feelings toward Steve were palpable. Allison moved in closer to her mother, still not looking at her father.

"Could you learn anything about how he died?" Allison asked, breaking the uneasy silence.

This wasn't the best time to broach the subject, but I did have information on that, if they could stand to hear it.

I looked at Cathy and Steve. "Are you ready to hear it?"

"No. No, not now," Steve said, shaking his head. "I appreciate that you looked into it."

Cathy turned away. "I can't." She moved her hand from her face to her throat. "If Allison does, then just go on up to her room and you all can talk about it there. I'd prefer it stayed in this house."

I nodded.

"Come on," Allison said. She walked past me into the living room and toward the stairs at the far end. Judith whispered something to Cathy and then followed Allison, glancing at me as she passed by. I picked up my laptop and walked after her, following the two women to Allison's bedroom on the second floor.

Allison closed the door behind us. The room was feminine and soft, pastels and pink everywhere. Trophies from cheerleading competitions on a shelf. Photos of Allison and her friends and some of her and Chris. Plush pillows and stuffed animals decorated the bed. Allison tossed them aside.

I placed my laptop on the lower corner of the bed and opened it, then pulled up the images of Chris's car and the treeline. I showed them the tree that matched up to the door. I didn't mention the blood or hair that I'd found. I showed them the burnished areas of the headliner and pointed out how the impacts on his head most likely occurred.

"So..." Allison tried to ask, but her voice clipped. Her eyes filled with tears as she struggled for the words. "So...when do you think he was unconscious?"

"First impact," I said. "The one with the tree. I think he was out at that point, and he didn't feel anything after that." I eased the words into the air, trying to blunt the sharp edge that knifed into her heart. The wound would never stop hurting.

Judith grabbed a handful of tissues from a box on Allison's nightstand and pushed them to her, then took a few for herself. Allison didn't break down like I thought she would.

"Okay," she said. Tears flowed from her eyes and she wiped them away with the clumsy bundle of tissues but as soon as she did so, more came. She didn't sob, and she didn't shake. She just sat there, absorbing the information. "Okay," she said again, this time from a distant place. A few more tears, then she nodded to herself.

Judith was watching her intently. I powered my laptop down and closed it. We stood for a moment of silence, each alone with our thoughts.

"Mom and dad can't handle that right now," Allison said, her voice congested. "Maybe later."

I nodded, picking up my laptop and moving to the door. Judith sat down next to Allison and they hugged each other.

"You need a report?" The words hung in the air.

"Yes," Judith said. "It doesn't have to be real long."

"I'll take care of it," I assured her. "When do you need it?"

"We're supposed to call the District Attorney whenever we get it. Don't feel you have to hurry. I know you've already sacrificed a lot."

"Thanks again," Allison said, turning her head from Judith's shoulder.

"You're welcome." I shifted my laptop to my other hand. "I'll call you when it's done."

She and Allison nodded. I let myself out.

I moved down the steps slowly. The kitchen was empty. The mess was cleaned up. I opened the kitchen door. As I stepped onto the porch, the little yellow puppy bounded across the yard and barreled up the stairs. He stopped short and retreated a step.

"He thinks you're Chris," Steve said. He was over by the cars. "But when he gets up close to you he knows you're not."

"Sorry, little guy," I said. The puppy took a tentative step toward me. I bent slightly and extended my hand. The puppy rushed it. I scratched and rubbed his head and neck while he teethed on my fingers.

I stood and walked down the steps, the puppy bounding around me, begging me to play, to be the person that he knew and loved, to be the person that played with him and slipped him treats and let him in the house at night.

To be the person that he knew was gone but didn't know why.

I shrugged the strap of my laptop case higher on my shoulder as I approached Steve. I extended my hand. Steve met it with a grasp that tried to push something into my own. Clumped-up bills rubbed against my palm.

"No," I said, pushing it back into his hand. "Steve, I can't."

"Why?" he asked, bewildered.

"I appreciate it," I said quickly. "I really do. But I can't." I looked up at the sky. "God as witness, I won't take a dime from you on this case."

"Hell, son, you can't work for free." He pushed the money against my chest.

"I'll be okay," I said. "Instead of you giving me something, let me give you something."

"You mean advice?" he asked.

"No one listens to advice."

"Then what?"

"You have a wonderful family. A great wife, a smart, beautiful daughter, and a beautiful home." I gestured towards the house. "Cathy needs you. Allison needs you. Keep going down the road you're on and you'll lose them."

Steve shifted his gaze down to the concrete driveway. He nodded his head in short, sharp strokes. "I know. I know." He looked back up at me. “It’s so hard. When I think about what happened it just makes me go crazy.”

“Wish I could make it easier.”

“You can’t,” he said, exhaling the words. “No one can.” He offered me the money again.

“No.” I moved past him and toward my car. “I’ll have the report done for you soon. Judith has my email address and phone number. Don’t hesitate to call if you think of something else you want to talk about.”

He nodded. “Sure.”

I piled my gear in the trunk and got in my car. I backed up slowly, turned the wheel, and guided my car down the long driveway. Steve receded in the mirror, not moving as the puppy jumped around his legs.

CHAPTER 7

Dark night, no moon. The narrow back roads unwound to the main highway. As I neared the city I merged onto I-275 towards downtown, then connected to Alcoa Highway and headed to the University Medical Center. To my left, in the sleeping darkness, the lights of the city huddled together. I took the bridge over the river, passing by the University campus.

I tried to reach Ken several times but kept getting his voicemail. Turning off his phone wasn't a good sign. When did he call me about his dad? Had it been last week? I mentally ticked off the days, shocked that five had gone by since we'd talked. It was Friday. Today was Friday. Another week gone, and eleven remained between me and my deadline.

The hospital parking garage was nearly empty. My footsteps echoed off the concrete.

I knew this place well. I'd spent a solid year here doing research on wound ballistics for my master of science thesis at the medical library right next to the main hospital building. I ducked in a side entrance and took a shortcut to the main hospital wing. It was a maze of mismatched hallways and dull yellow corridors. I hurried through the halls, taking two separate elevators to reach the floor where Ken's dad was.

The odds of being stopped by an over-protective nurse grew higher as I neared the room. I strode past the nurse's station with a doctor's arrogance. I could feel eyes on my back as I rounded the corner and stopped at the door of Ken's father's room.

The door was open. And the room was empty.

Damn. Must have been moved somewhere else.

I turned quickly, almost crashing into a wall of Snoopy cartoons on light purple scrubs. The nurse wasn't amused.

"Watch it," she growled. "You're not supposed to be up here."

I was caught. No sense in lying. "I'm looking for the patient who was here. Ken Frazier. Senior. I'm family."

Her lips narrowed. She sized me up. "Back to the floor desk. Now."

Walk this way, I thought, wishing Mel Brooks was here and that it was just one big comedy. But I knew it was a tragedy.

Everything is, in the end.

She picked up a phone and made a call, then told me to wait a few minutes. I tried calling Ken again. No luck.

A few minutes later, a short and stocky woman was following the nurse's outstretched hand in my direction. She marched over to me.

"You're not black," she stated.

"Maybe I'm light-skinned," I replied.

She drilled my blue eyes with her own.

"Look," I said, "he's my best friend's father, and he's like a father to me, too."

Her eyes softened. "I'm sorry," she said.

"You're sorry you can't let me see him?"

"No."

I knew.

"He passed away three days ago." She'd squared her shoulders when she had approached me. Now she dropped them as my face registered the news.

"Okay." My voice was choked.

Regret slammed into me. Ken's dad has said he'd be out of there in a few days. He'd known the ending then.

I turned away and pushed past her, walking back down the corridor, retracing the steps to my car.

It was going on nine p.m. I headed towards Ken's house. Kim's car was there. His squad car wasn't. I kept rolling, redirecting to his parent's house on the western outskirts of Knox county.

I neared the subdivision and turned in, moving slowly to the familiar driveway. His KPD cruiser was in the driveway along with several other cars I didn't recognize. Lights were on in the house. I inched up the driveway, placing my car where it wouldn't be blocking anyone in.

The front door was closed but there were voices in the kitchen. I pressed the latch on the screen door, pulling it open, then rapped my knuckles lightly on the hard wood.

From inside, there was an exchange of words, a scraping chair, and footsteps to the door. The deadbolt was thrown and the knob turned and I found myself looking at Ken. His massive frame blocked out most of the light of the hallway behind him.

"Hey," he said.

"Sorry." It was lame and it wasn't enough.

"It's okay."

He held the door open. I stepped up into the entry hall, blinking as my eyes adjusted to the light and the moist heat of the house. The smell of food made me queasy. I moved further in and he closed the door.

"I had to turn off my phone," he said.

"Did it go hard?" Like everything else.

"Yeah," Ken said. His eyes welled up. "Funeral was yesterday," he said. "I called you but it just kept ringing. Didn't even go to voicemail. I just figured you were swamped."

Yesterday. "Yeah, I was."

He nodded. "It's okay. I don't even remember it. Everything has been a blur."

"Sorry for not being there," I said.

He looked over at me. "Don't beat yourself up about it. Look, all our family is here now, and they were there, too. He wasn't coherent after the first couple hours." He rubbed his hand over his closely-cropped scalp. "It's tough now. But it's going to be really hard when everybody leaves and then the silence comes in. That's when I'll be calling you."

Wisdom.

"And you have to focus on finishing up, and you can't let anything get in the way of that. My dad understood. He was trying to go back to college when he got drafted for Vietnam. He wouldn't have wanted you to put him before school. So don't let it eat you up, alright?" He clapped me on the shoulder.

I swayed from the impact. "How's Kim?"

"She's fine. She's at home. I don't want her to be worn out from staying here all night." He motioned to the door. "Let's go out to the barn. I need to walk."

We pushed past the screen door.

"How's your mom?"

"Sleeping. It was a rough day for her. The settlement papers came."

"Today? Jesus."

He shook his head. "I know."

"So it's over now?"

He nodded. "Thirty thousand."

Ken walked to the corner of the barn, reached down, and retrieved the key from under the sideboard.

"Their timing is awful," I said.

"Wouldn't expect anything less," Ken said to me as he walked back to the doorway. He reached for the door, then pulled his hand back. "Damn."

A large brown spider hung in the doorway, barely visible in the moonlight. The web stretched across the entrance.

"There's a stick somewhere around here," he said. "Don't..."

"No big deal." I reached out. My fingers pushed through the web. It darted toward my hand, eager to kill and feed. My fingers curled around it slowly. It struggled, tiny claws scratching my skin.

I squeezed hard. The struggling faded. I wiped my hand on the doorframe.

"Jeez, Soren, what if it bit you?" Ken's ebony skin looked a shade paler.

"There's worse things to be scared of." I cleared the rest of the web from the doorway.

He pushed the old wooden door open.

Two '65 Oldsmobile 442 coupes sat on the concrete floor. Rough shape, not running. They were his Dad's last reminder to the glory of his youth.

The fluorescent lights flickered, gained strength. I went to the sink against the wall, washed off the mess.

"He gave you that one." Ken pointed at the blue one.

"What?"

"Before he died. He said to give you the blue one. The black one is mine."

I dried my hands. "Ken, they'll always be your dad's."

"I know. But I can't afford them both."

He could. He was just trying to make me feel better about taking it. "It'll be fun to restore them," I said.

"How's the dissertation?" Ken asked. A mouse scurried out from behind a stack of old tires and made a break for a gap in the wall planks.

"Going." I picked at the paint. "Hey, you know anything about a family named Harrell?"

Ken scratched his chin. "Name's familiar."

"Evidently they're involved in criminal activity. Mostly up in Clinton and in the rural areas."

Ken nodded. "Yeah, peripherally. What about them?"

"Their son is the kid that Judith's nephew was racing against."

"Really?"

"Yeah. Looks like the guy steered into her nephew's right rear quarter panel. Caused her nephew to spin-out and crash."

Ken nodded. "PIT maneuver. Pursuit Intervention Technique. The Germans invented it back in the sixties. Police departments teach it as a way to stop a high-risk pursuit."

"That's what I'm thinking, too. How does your department teach it?"

Ken walked over to the right rear of the other Olds, pointed at it. "I want this guy to stop. So I come up on his passenger side quarter-panel with the nose of my cruiser. Then I just jerk my wheel to the left. Not hard. Just enough to make his rear tires break free. Once that happens, he's sideways."

"That's exactly where I found the tire marks on Chris's Mustang. Right rear quarter panel." I frowned. "But where would Johnny learn something like that?"

"Anywhere. Maybe a cop used it on him."

"Any idea what the yaw rate usually is?"

"Depends on speed, but usually about a hundred-fifty degrees per second."

"Chris's car spun about ninety degrees."

Ken did the math. "So the other kid got on his brakes in less than a second?"

"More like half a second."

"Kid's got quick reflexes."

"He was prepared for it. He knew what was going to happen."

Ken nodded. "So if it's a PIT, then he did it intentionally?"

"Looks like it. Turns out he had gears and nitrous. With that head start, he should have been able to pull Chris's Mustang. He held back and sandbagged him. The cars definitely show contact, but I can't prove it was intentional."

"So what can you prove?"

I shrugged. "Nothing that'll convict the kid, unless a witness comes forward. But I think I was able to help the family come to terms with how he died, and how the crash happened. You would not believe how the investigating officer completely mishandled the reconstruction."

Ken was impassive. Back in high school and college he'd had his share of uncomfortable encounters with law enforcement, even though he'd never even remotely associated with any kind of criminal activity. He was a Rotary Club Award recipient, for God's sake. But I'd driven around with him during our college days enough to have witnessed firsthand him being pulled over for DWB, or Driving While Black.

"Who worked the crash?" he asked.

"Some guy named Palmer. THP," I answered.

"They didn't call in the CIRT team?"

"No."

He shook his head. "Something isn't right." He shifted his weight against the car, rocking it gently on its suspension. "Want me to look into it?"

"Maybe later." Ken had enough to worry about right now.

He drummed his fingers on the sheet metal. "Okay."

I weighed whether to tell him about the Mitsubishi. "I did get threatened."

"By who?" He turned to look at me.

"I think it was the kid her nephew was racing against. Harrell's son Johnny."

"How'd he know you?"

"Judith and I were at the Ford dealer, looking at his Mustang. He sold it to the dealer to dump it. Someone at the dealership told him we were there."

"Did he get up in your face?"

"No." I scratched my neck. "I don't think he was serious. Besides, he's only nineteen."

"Old enough to pull a trigger."

"He won't have the chance to see me again. I'm nearly done with the case. I have to write a report, and that's it. He won't even know who I am. It's not my job to get involved on a personal level."

"Don't underestimate evil," Ken said.

~~~

I stayed until midnight, then drove home. I pulled into the garage and made it to bed a little after one.

My nights had gotten later from working on the case. I was losing the cadence of rising early and working all day on the dissertation. In the morning I forced my body in front of the computer, trying to get back into the academic mindset.

And the nightmares weren't diminishing.

My body wanted to do anything but type. I wanted to crawl back to bed and sleep for eleven weeks. Black coffee helped, but my mind kept springing back to Chris's death.

Two hours of getting nowhere. I closed the document and began working on the report for Steve and Cathy. I hadn't been doing quality work on the dissertation, and I couldn't stop thinking about Chris's crash.

The report took the rest of the day to complete. It was five pages long and summarized all that I had gleaned from my inspections of the cars and the site. My final opinions were supported by the calculations I'd run and how they contradicted the crash report. It wouldn't do anything to increase my standing with THP, but that was a lost cause anyway.
~~~

CHAPTER 8

Monday morning. Judith answered on the second ring.

"Got your report done," I said. "How do you want me to get it to you?"

"Are you coming into town anytime soon?" she asked.

"Wednesday would work best for me." That way I could deliver Wayne's report, too. I'd write his this afternoon. "Is that soon enough?"

"That's fine. Steve finally got hold of the DA and let him know we got a reconstructionist who's looked at everything and wrote up a report. Steve said his eyes got real big, like he didn't ever expect to hear from us again," she laughed. "Oh, I love it."

"Just remember that the evidence doesn't prove intent, it only proves there was contact." People see what they want to see, not what's actually on the page.

"It's enough to show that the crash report is wrong, and Steve said that it'll prove that Johnny was racing Chris and that they could at least charge him with reckless driving. And then because he left the scene and came back in a different car, Steve is pretty sure that they can charge him with leaving Chris there."

"Judith, we can't even prove Johnny was driving. This is a big bunch of heartache for the Camerons."

"I know. Maybe you can tell him again on Wednesday. Come out to Steve and Cathy's place around five pm or so. That way Allison will be there too."

"Knock it off, Judith."

"What? You'll have to explain the report to them. You have all those numbers and technical terms in there. Me and Steve are going to have to explain it to the DA. We'd be like a monkey with a shotgun if we went in there without knowing how to read your report."

"Okay." It was reluctant. I didn't want to get inside that storm again.

"Thanks, Soren. You are a sweetheart."

I shook my head and ended the call.

~~~

Wednesday came. I made the drive into Knoxville on autopilot. My mind chipped away at Chris's crash. I went back over the report for Steve and Cathy while sitting in the waiting room of Brannon's law office.

"Whatcha reading?" Wayne asked as he came down the hallway.

"My report on the drag racing case."

"You already know the ending."

"Maybe." I followed him into his office. "Here it is." I handed him the report.

"I really appreciate this," he said. He slid it out and flipped through the pages. He nodded a few times. "Looks good." He dropped it on his desk. "I'll need to know what your bill is for the settlement negotiations. Ballpark?"

"Four thousand," I said. "Not just ballpark." I extended my invoice to him.

He glanced at me, surprised. "You need it that badly?"

"Yeah. Wayne, I do." I looked down. "Normally I don't mind waiting until it settles, but I'm really getting tight on money."

"School?" he asked.

"Yes."

Wayne's expression softened. He wrote something on the invoice and handed it back to me. "Give it to Karen on the way out. She'll give you a check."

"Thanks." I took the invoice back.

"You earned it," he said.

"One more thing," I said, turning to leave. "This drag racing case. The victim's girlfriend's father is a criminal court judge in Anderson County. The victim's father thinks he'll preside at the trial. I'm not a lawyer, but that can't happen, can it?"
~~~

"No way." He sat on the corner of his desk. "You know his name?"

"No," I said. "Only that he has a daughter named Kelly."

"Find out the name. I'll discuss it with Miss Cynthia we'll see if there's anything we can offer," he said. "And it's okay for them to call me." He shook his head. "Heartbreaking case."

"Yeah, and the family isn't pulling together," I said.

He grimaced. He knew the ending, too.

~~~

The day was heating up. The sun illuminated a bright blue late July sky devoid of any clouds. I had dressed nice for my meeting with Wayne and I loosened my collar and took off my jacket as I left the office building.

The check from Wayne's office was drawn on the same bank I used. There was a branch two blocks away.

I handed the teller the check.

"All in the savings?" she asked.

"No. Fifteen hundred goes to an account in London."

"You have the IBAN number?"

I wrote the number down and slid it under the glass, hoping my sister was still passing open windows.

~~~

I wheeled my car into the Cameron's driveway. Judith's car was in front of the garage, but no BMW. Twinge of relief.

I grabbed the envelope off the passenger seat and walked to the porch. Before I could knock on the door, Judith opened it. Her face was downcast.

"What's wrong?" I asked, not moving.

"Oh, God." She sighed. "Come on in." She stood back and pulled the door wider. The odor of exhaled coffee-breath flooded out from the kitchen. I was glad Steve didn't smoke like his brother.

"Hey, Steve," I said.

"Hey, buddy." He said it without his usual fire. He was sitting at the table with a cup of coffee in front of him. Judith's cup was near the chair that I had occupied during my earlier visit.

"Sit down." She pulled out another chair from the table. "Coffee?"

"Sure, thanks," I said. I looked back at Judith. "What's going on?"

Judith looked at Steve, and he nodded to her. "It's okay," he said. "He's damn near family now anyway."

She took a breath. "Allison and Travis had a fight," she said.

That didn't sound bad. She had said things were rough between them.

"Travis hit her," she continued. "In the face. Hard."

"What?" Anger flushed my own face.

"She's okay," she said. "Bruised and black and blue, but okay."

Steve was staring into space. His hands were wrapped around the mug, squeezing it tight.

"Good lord," I said. "I'm so sorry."

Judith nodded. "Cathy's at the hospital with her right now. Allison didn't want to go but Cathy made her. The police came and got him. They're holding him overnight." Her voice trailed off as she looked at Steve.

Steve looked like he wanted to straighten this out himself.

"They'd only been married a year," Judith said. "There's been trouble ever since Allison decided to go back to school. And then when Chris was killed, things just went from bad to worse."

Steve stayed silent. It was uncharacteristic of him. I would have been more comfortable if he'd been rampaging around the kitchen like he'd done before.

"Did she say anything else about it?" I asked.

"No," Judith said. "We haven't heard anything more."

Judith could see that I was searching for something to say.

"It's okay," she said. "It's just life. We'll make it."

"Here's the report." I placed the envelope gently on the table. Steve glanced at me, then moved to pick it up. He pulled out the report and thumbed through the pages, narrowing his eyes at several points.

I sat down in the chair. Judith asked if I took milk and I told her no, just sugar. She asked how much, but I told her just to bring the bowl. This might take a while.

We finished up before dark. The sun was sliding behind the western ridges of the Tennessee valley as I walked across the driveway to my car. My mind drifted to Allison. Steve might yet kill the guy. He was unbalanced by his son's death. Anyone could feel the tension and rage that churned inside him. The assault on his daughter pushed him closer to the edge he was already near.

I opened the door and fell into the wide, comfortable seat of my Mercedes, grateful the day was almost over.

A folded piece of paper was stuck under the wiper blade.

I glanced around my car, then at the house and garage. Nothing unusual.

I opened the door and got back out, walking around to the front fender so I could see the note more clearly. It had the ragged edges of being torn from a spiral notebook, then folded in half. The thin blue lines that crossed the page horizontally were too far apart to be college-ruled, resembling more the ones used in middle-school. I glanced around again, then reached out and picked it up. I retreated back into my car and shut and locked the doors. I opened the page and read the handwritten script, marked in pencil:

> We need to talk. Old store, Sulphur Springs Road, tonight

Girl's handwriting, full of swoops and bubbled letters. I wondered why the mysterious stranger hadn't just knocked on the door and told me this in person.

I was tired.

Curiosity burned inside me. Might be the person who was riding in Johnny's car.

I dug out my cellphone.

"Ken, call me back ASAP."

I hung up and put the earbud on. Three minutes later my phone rang.

"You okay?" Ken's voice.

"Found an anonymous note on my windshield. Someone wants to meet with me about this drag racing case. Any advice?"

Pause. "Friendly or hostile?"

I hadn't considered that. "Friendly, I guess. It could even be the passenger from the other car."

"Where's the meet?" Ken asked.

I told him about the old store.

"Be careful," he said. "Come at 'em from a different direction."

"Like from above? You want me to stick my arms through the sunroof and flap like a bird?"

"You want advice or not?"

"Sorry." I pressed the earbud closer to my cheek.

"Come down the road the opposite way they're expecting you. You got that spotting scope in your case?"

"You really think this is necessary?"

"Pull off the road and scope them out before you get close. If there's more than one car, they're hostile."

"How do you know that, Kreskin?"

"Fights are never fair. They're about overwhelming firepower."

"You're paranoid."

"You're calling *me* paranoid?"

"Point made. Okay. Do you have time to back me up?"

"I can head that way on patrol. Thirty minutes or so. Dinner's on you afterwards."

"Wait, wait," I said. "Don't pull in. I don't want to spook them. If they see you, they'll probably get nervous."

"What's scary about a big angry black man with a gun?"

I laughed. "Not you, the uniform."

"I'll hang back. If you get in trouble, give me a sign." He hung up.

I wound down the miles of multiple curves that linked the Cameron's house to the main highway, then made the turn toward downtown Clinton instead of heading home. The sky had turned a blood shade of red as the last of the sun's rays hit the atmosphere at an extreme angle, causing Rayleigh scattering.

I steered my car past the middle school and the police station, then began the back roads, making my way to the road where Chris had lost his life.

The turn for Sulphur Springs Road came up.

Okay, Ken. I bypassed the final turn onto Sulphur Springs, heading straight instead, then pulled onto the shoulder. The map on my smartphone screen gave me a bird's-eye view of the entire area. Four miles and a maze of back roads later, I was headed towards the old store from the north.

Hazy twilight. I turned on my headlights.

When the screen showed me closing within a half-mile of the store I killed the lights and pulled off the road again. No traffic. I opened the trunk and reached for the Pelican case. The 60-power Kowa spotting scope was nestled in foam next to my camera and other tools. I attached the compact tripod, put it on the decklid, and increased it to maximum zoom.

It was almost a straight shot to the old store. There were a few scraggly pine trees lining the road, but the lack of foliage revealed a single car, black eight-series Audi sedan, sitting in the middle of the parking lot. The lights on the corners of the building were already on and illuminated the driver and passenger sitting in the car. Dull orange pinprick of light glowed from a cigarette. Easy targets for a sniper.

The driver flicked his cigarette out the window, then exited the car. Definitely male. He walked around the corner of the building and stood against the wall, legs apart, partially in shadow of a carport. He turned his head to the right and mouthed words. I followed his lead.

Damn. There was a car tucked in the carport, just behind him to his right. It wouldn't have been visible to a car driving up to the store from the south.

I didn't see anyone else walking around the building, or in the grass field on the other side of the road. The question now was whether to drive down there or just let Ken handle it when he showed up.

Neither of the cars was a red Mitsubishi.

I wasn't taking unnecessary chances, though. I slipped the HK from my trouser pocket and pulled the slide back just enough to press-check the round that sat in the chamber. The slide returned to battery. I ejected the magazine, pushing down on the top round. It sprang back up against my thumb. Good. I slapped the spine of the magazine against the base of my palm to seat the rounds, then ran the magazine back in the gun in one fluid motion. The mag clicked in place. The gun returned to the pocket holster.

A firearm is a weapon of last resort. My escrima training with Rob was a way of using a baton to settle disputes before a gun entered negotiations. It's not easy to conceal a three-foot-long bamboo stick, so I kept an ASP collapsible baton locked in the glovebox for those times when the heavy artillery isn't available. I slid the ASP inside my waistband, behind my right kidney.

I weighed the odds. It was unlikely that my life would be in jeopardy if I just pulled in to talk. They had to be the same kids Judith chased away from the Camerons, the ones who'd been talking to Steve. I wanted to talk to them, too.

The spotting scope went back in the case. I hit the ignition and put the high beams on, accelerating smoothly back onto the road. I pulled in so that my brights lit up the car parked on the side of the building. Pontiac GTO, dark red, two kids inside. I paused long enough to let them know they'd been made, then swung into the parking lot and wheeled the car around in a circle. This positioned my sedan between me and both of the parked cars, and the nose of my car pointed to the road for a clean exit.

My circle had put me too close to the car parked in the open. I shifted into reverse and backed up, turning the wheel and then pulling my car forward again. My pulse was up and I hit the brakes hard, jerking the car to a stop. Still need more room. I repeated the motions, thoroughly embarrassed by the time I'd positioned my car correctly.

I shut the car off but left the key in the ignition. I opened the door slowly, taking my time in getting out. The pistol stayed in my right front pocket. Simply pulling it out slightly could get me charged with assault with a deadly weapon. I scanned the kids in the cars, glancing away briefly to check the surroundings for other participants. No one else was around.

The passenger door of the Audi opened. The distance was maybe sixty feet. The passenger got out and began moving toward my car. The driver who had pissed against the building earlier walked back over to his car.

Sound of door latches to my right. The kids in the parked car by the side of the building started to get out, but I didn't want the odds tipped that far against me at this distance. Hell, at any distance. I wasn't in denial about how quickly I could get my ass kicked.

"Stay in the car!" I shouted at the car in shadows. I yanked the Surefire flashlight from my rear trouser pocket and lit the car up. They were about fifty feet away but they blinked and turned aside under the intense little beam of light. They stayed where they were. I kept my body behind the B-pillar of my car, ready to hop back in and leave if things got rough.

I turned back to the two kids near the Audi. The passenger had advanced halfway to me. Heavy but not huge. The driver leaned on the fender. He spoke first.

"That was one hell of a parking job. I got motion sickness just from watchin' ya." Familiar voice.

The passenger belted out a deep laugh. He started toward me again.

"Hold up, buddy." I pointed at the guy halfway to my car. The kid paused, looking at the Audi driver.

The driver nodded. "Keep going, Billy." Then he hopped up on the hood of the Audi. He flashed a big smile at me.

The passenger, Billy, resumed his shuffle towards me. He had a dark blue sweatshirt on, loose around the waist, and the loose, saggy, torn denim jeans that were all the rage with the miscreant set these days. A ball cap turned one-eighty on the kid's head topped off the slacker ensemble.

Billy closed within twenty feet of my car. Hairs rose on the back of my neck. Bad feeling.

I held up my hand. "Far enough, or I'm gone," I shouted.

This time the kid stopped

I stayed by the driver's door of my car, keeping the GTO in the shadows in my peripheral vision as best I could. Hanging around past dark would be bad. I'd lose them if they got out.

An old Clash song played in my head. *Should I stay or should I go now?*

I made the trip. Let's hear what they have to say.

I closed the door of my car and walked up to my fender, but kept my car between me and them.

The guy sitting on the hood of the Audi stuck his hands in his pockets. My fingertips glided to the edge of my own pocket.

His hands pulled out a cigarette and lighter. I relaxed slightly. At this distance and light level it would be a tough shot to make with a handgun.

Billy cracked his knuckles. "Anything else you want me to do?"

"Yeah," I said. "Tell me what happened that night."

He shuffled his feet and looked back at the guy on the hood of the car. The guy on the hood held up a thumb. I glanced at the car in the shadows. The silhouettes of the two occupants were still inside.

I started calculating times. Billy was the first threat. He could reach me in about two seconds, coming around the front of my car. He could try to hop over the hood, but judging by his size and weight, that didn't seem likely. And he'd dent the hell out of the hood if he tried. I moved closer to the front of my car to help discourage him from choosing that path. The guy on the hood of the car behind him would take about five seconds to get to me.

I glanced again at the kids in the GTO. They'd need about two seconds to get out and then four or five seconds to get to me, so they'd be on me a little later than the Audi driver. They'd also step into the light from the building lamp that was becoming brighter by the minute. The light cast on the Audi guys was good, but it also killed the contrast of the Pontiac in the shadows.

I could draw my baton and strike with it inside two seconds. My pistol could be out and engaging three targets in about five seconds, which cut it too close for comfort if I really did have to shoot. Under Tennessee law I could justifiably use a firearm to defend myself against multiple attackers but I absolutely did not want it to go that far. Just because these kids were immature idiots, they didn't deserve being shot. The baton was preferable. The nuclear option for last resort was not.

Billy spoke. "Well, they was lined up back there." He pointed behind me. "And Chris's Mustang was way the hell ahead of Johnny's when he got to the curve."

He rotated to point at the curve just south of the store. "We was all watchin' his brake lights and we could see clear as day that Chris's Mustang was goin' round the curve when he lost control. It wasn't nobody's fault but his own for takin' that curve too fast." He looked back at the guy on the Audi hood half the time he was speaking.

I followed his outstretched arm to the curve. "And you're obviously an unbiased third-party witness."

"Yeah."

"That's great. Thanks. You saved me a bunch of work. Guess I'll be going now." I didn't move.

Billy looked back at the kid on the Audi.

I cleared my throat. "One more thing. Did Johnny drive over and hit Chris's car after it was already upside down in the field? 'Cause that would make him a true, bona-fide asshole, if he did." My words gave Johnny the benefit of doubt. I glanced at the Pontiac, then back to Billy.

His face soured. "You got some fancy way of provin' Johnny hit him?" He took a step toward me. My body shivered as adrenaline shot into my system. I held up my hand again, hoping he couldn't see it trembling slightly in the parking lot lights.

Billy looked back at the guy on the hood of the car. So did I. The kid tossed the last part of cigarette away.

"What part of the story didn't you understand?" he said in my direction. The voice clicked. Red Mitsubishi.

The kid on the hood was Johnny Harrell.

He tossed his hands up, pointing to the road. "I was there, and your boy was way down there when he lost it. That's God's honest truth and you'd better believe it. I come out here in the cold and dark to make your job easier and you give me the third degree. Pretty ungrateful if you ask me." He slid off the Audi's hood, then leaned against the fender and reached behind his back.

My body went rigid. "Hands," I said. I stepped back and shoved my right hand into my trouser pocket.

He paused for a moment. Studied me. "It's Skoal, dude. Lighten up." He smiled, then pulled the flat can from his jeans.

I tensed.

He tapped the can against the palm of his other hand.

Billy chuckled. It was the laugh of a kid who tortures animals to death.

Johnny toyed with the can. "Chris's friends are sayin' that Steve is bragging pretty loud these days. Saying you're gonna prove that I done killed Chris." He stopped tapping the can and shifted his eyes to me. "And I was talkin' to one of 'em, and I said, 'is that right?'"

Johnny opened the can and pinched a wad of tobacco. "And this friend of Chris says 'that's right'. Steve said that you got computers and paint evidence and all sorts of shit to prove I ran Chris off the road."

I glanced back at the Pontiac GTO. It was almost too dark to see the occupants. I looked back at the guy between us, then at Johnny.

"But that's same as gossip, and you know how bad that can be." Jimmy brought the wad to his mouth, then paused. "So I figure I'll ask the man himself." He gestured to me, then stuck the wad in his lip. Big smile again.

"Oh, yeah." The adrenaline made it hard to keep my voice steady. "The computer in your car said you did it. Steered right into Chris's quarter panel. No doubt. Why don't you just go turn yourself in to the law?"

Jimmy spit on the broken asphalt. "Oh, damn, boy," he said. "Whoo-ee. That's a good one." He hefted the can, tapping on the lid with his finger. "I own the fucking law around here," he said, gesturing around the parking lot. "It ain't like back in the city and on campus, where you're *safe.*" He shook his head. "Son, you best just tell them what we told you and go back to town and forget about all this out here. You don't want it. Just go back to your college and books and get your knob polished by some sorority girl. It's better than gettin' hurt."

The kid between us chuckled again. He looked at me from under his brow, squaring his shoulders and bending his knees, like a wrestler. Heavy on top, probably weak on the bottom.

I shifted my hand to my waist, near the ASP. Another glance at the GTO in the shadows.

Okay, Ken, now would be a great time for you to save my ass. I glanced back up the road. No police car.

"Aw, fuck it," Johnny said. "He ain't listening. Hurt him anyway, Billy."

Billy charged.

Billy the Wrestler kicked up gravel in his haste to get to me. Car doors opened to my right, near the building, but my attention was dominated by Billy as he came around the front of my car, lumbering but not running. I slid my hand inside my waistband. He rounded the corner of my car and put his hand on the hood to get around it faster. I brought my left hand up to my chest, indexing it so it wouldn't get in the way, and I drew the ASP baton with my right, jerking it violently upward so that it opened toward the sky.

Rob's words: aim for the middle of the extremity.

Billy was almost on me. I stepped closer to him and brought the ASP around, aiming for the elbow of his arm as his hand was planted on the hood of my car. Fear made me swing hard, putting more force into the blow than necessary. The end of the baton made a whooshing sound as it cut through the air. The weighted metal knob impacted Billy's elbow and there was a loud crack. His elbow bent the wrong way into his body and he stumbled forward in my direction. I sidestepped as he fell into me.

Rob's words: where the head goes, the body follows.

I caught his head with my left hand and redirected his momentum, propelling him into the asphalt with all the force I could muster. He hit the ground face first, hard.

Seconds were ticking away. Movement on my right.

I dropped the baton where I stood, jamming my right hand into my right front pocket. The HK came out in a blur. I swiveled and stuck my right foot behind me, backing up the way Rob had taught me, dragging my left foot, repeating the motion so that I wouldn't trip over something behind me as I frantically tried to put distance between myself and the two kids rushing at me from the shadows. I bent my knees, dropping my body behind my car so that Johnny wouldn't have a clear shot at me if he tried. I lined up on the two kids just as they broke into the pool of light that bathed the parking lot.

My left hand met the gun in my right hand as I brought it up to my chest and then pushed it toward the threat. My arms locked out in an isosceles stance.

The little green tritium dot in the front sight came into view, glowing brightly in the darkness. My finger slid onto the trigger, taking up slack and beginning to apply the seven pounds of force needed to trip the LEM trigger and send a 230-grain .45 caliber hollow-point screaming out of the stubby barrel. The green dot lined up on the kid nearest me. Both of them stopped short. Something black in left kid's hand.

Training took over. Shoot or be shot.

Small video camera. Too late.

Muscle memory from a thousand quick-draws during shooting competitions overrode my voluntary will to stop. I moved the sights off the chest of the left kid just as the trigger broke. My gun barked. Dim light, flamethrower muzzle flash.

Instant hollow thudding sound of the bullet striking a pile of loose wood next to the kid's car.

The muzzle blast shocked everyone into silence and stillness.

I kept the gun straight out, bringing it back onto the pair of kids in front of me, and then jerked around to line it up on Johnny. I rested the sights on him long enough to see that he had dropped the can of Skoal. I swiveled back to the kids on my right.

"HANDS!" I shouted. "Up! Open!" I alternated between the three young men, then remembered Billy on the ground in front of me. I began watching him, too. He looked out of it but I wasn't taking any chances.

Almost instantly, the lights and siren of a white KPD cruiser roared toward us from the road. It swung into the parking lot and screeched to a halt in front of my car.

Johnny darted to the Audi's door, opened it halfway.

Ken got out with his Glock drawn. He immediately drew a bead on the kid with the camera.

"It was him!" Johnny yelled, pointing at me.

I swiveled my pistol to the kids on my right. Ken shifted his aim to Johnny.

"Away from the door!" Ken moved around his car and ran towards Johnny. "On the ground. Spread eagle."

Johnny put his hands up and stepped toward Ken. "He pulled the gun on us, you idiot."

Ken reached Johnny, and with his gun in his right hand pulled back to his waist, reached out with his free left hand and put Johnny on the ground. Hard.

"Hey, you fuc-" was all he got out before Ken pushed his face into the gravel of the parking lot. Then Ken zipped a set of plasti-cuffs on him.

"Keep still," he ordered. He went through Johnny's pockets. Didn't find anything. He glanced in my direction, shook his head. "Did he throw anything in the car?"

"I don't know." I kept my eyes and my gun on the other two kids.

Another couple of pats. Once Ken was satisfied that Johnny was unarmed, he stood and walked to the car. Johnny had locked it, but he peered in the window.

"There's a revolver on the passenger floorboard," Ken shouted to me. "Stainless Smith & Wesson. Looks like a three-fifty-seven." He drew his Glock again. "Soren, stay on them." His voice was low.

He walked back over to Johnny. "That yours?"

"Hell, no," Johnny said. "I hate guns. Too damn dangerous. It belongs to Jason." Johnny raised his head and shouted to one of the kids I was covering. "Jason, ain't that your gun?"

"Knock it off," Ken said.

"It's mine," Jason said. He kept his head down.

Ken picked up Johnny- literally- and walked over to the two kids I was covering.

"What the hell is the camera for?" Ken asked them.

The kids didn't answer. Ken looked at me.

I shook my head no.

He shrugged, dropped Johnny a few feet away from them, and zipped their hands together behind their backs. "Got any weapons on you? Anything sharp in your pockets? Knives? Needles?"

"Yeah," the camera kid said.

"Yeah, what?" Ken demanded. His Glock came out again.

"Pistol under my shirt." He jutted his chin towards his waist. "And a knife around back."

Ken's face went hard. "Do not make any sudden moves." He kept the Glock tucked into his waist and moved his free hand where the kid had indicated. He carefully pulled out what appeared to be a Beretta 9mm, then stepped back. He glanced at me.

"Stay on them."

I nodded, kept the front sight alternating between the kids.

"So you needed two pistols?" Ken asked.

The kid didn't answer. It was obvious that Johnny had dropped the revolver in the Audi. And I hadn't even caught it.

Ken dropped the magazine out of the gun and racked the slide back. A glint of metal flashed in the light of the parking lot lamps, then ticked onto the gravel.

My stomach flipped. The kid had a round in the chamber, ready to shoot.

Ken retrieved the knife from the kid's back pocket. Long Bowie.

The other kid had a another pistol on him, too. Couldn't tell what it was. And a folding knife in his right front pocket.

If I'd seen any of those weapons in their hands, I wouldn't have moved the sights. If I'd seen Johnny pull that revolver, I would have shot him.

An old memory triggered a rise of bile in my throat.

"You okay?" Ken tossed the guns on the ground in a pile.

I stared at the guns.

"Soren?"

Maybe they did want to kill me. I shouldn't have moved the sights.

"Hey, Soren." Ken was watching me closely. "Soren. You're safe now. It's okay."

If they tried once, they'll try again. I'm not safe.

They'll always be a threat to me.

My grip on the HK tightened.

"*Soren!*" Ken yelled.

His voice pulled me back. I stopped, then realized I'd taken several steps toward Johnny.

"You okay?" Ken was peering at me in the darkness, one hand still on the shoulder of the camera kid.

"He ain't okay. He's gonna fucking kill me." Johnny glared at me.

"Zip it," Ken growled at Johnny. He looked back at me.

I blinked my eyes. "Yeah. I'm good. I'm good."

Ken gave me a long look, but he didn't say anything else.

"Why'd you wait so long?" I tried to defuse the sudden tension.

Ken shook his head. "Me? I thought the gunshot was the signal."

"Guess it was."

"I knew you could handle it," Ken said. "And I wanted to wait until they did something stupid. Now they're mine." He glanced my way. "As long as you press charges. You are, right?"

"Yes." My breathing was still rapid and shallow. I fought to steady it.

There was a moan from the pavement near my car. Ken jerked toward it, running around the back of my car and proceeding over to Billy. I stepped around and covered him with my HK, occasionally turning to watch the other kids, too.

"Okay now," I heard Ken say. "Easy." Ken frisked Billy while he was on the ground, gently rolling him over and being careful of his shattered elbow. Ken lifted Billy to his feet easily and held him by the shoulder as Billy cradled his left arm. His jaw was cocked at an awkward angle. Ken led him around to the other three kids and sat Billy down on the asphalt.

"What in the hell is going on here?" he asked.

"What's it look like, Barney?" Johnny asked Ken. "We was having a talk, and your boy here pulled a gun on us." He nodded at me.

"That's not what I saw." Ken used his alpha-male voice. "I saw four against one, then one go down, and then this guy-" he jerked his thumb at me, "pull a firearm in accordance with Tennessee Code Annotated 39-11-611 and defend himself from serious injury or death as a result of the assault of three young, violent, armed men." He stabbed each one with his gaze as he spoke. "And that's the way this is going to be written up when I process all of you down at the City-County Building."

Johnny glanced up at him. "Figures. All you cops are lying sacks of shit." Johnny spit on the ground. "And I hope you got more than one bullet, Barney. Your boy here done used up his. We ain't gonna be in for long."

Ken looked down at Johnny. "Are you threatening me?"

Johnny grinned. "Oh, no, Mr. Barney."

More sirens split the night, far off.

"Don't worry," Ken said to me. "It's Knox County Police, not THP." He looked at the kids, then at the flashing lights growing larger as they approached us from the south. He tapped me on the shoulder and gestured to step back several feet.

"They didn't have any weapons out when they rushed you, did they?" His voice was hushed.

"No."

Ken pointed at Johnny. "Did you see that kid toss his gun in the car?"

"If I had seen a gun, I'd have shot him." I shook my head. "And that's Johnny Harrell."

Ken's eyes went wide. "The drag racing kid?"

I nodded, keeping my eyes on them.

"The armed kids will be in serious trouble. But Johnny will be out on probation in a couple weeks. Or sooner."

I shook my head. “Can’t lie. No deadly weapons out. Just assault, four against one.”

“I’m not saying to cross over to the dark side by lying. Just making sure.”

I nodded. “I’m okay to draw my gun against multiple attackers, right? That’s what the law says.”

“Yeah, you’re safe.” He motioned to my gun. “You can put that away now, too. And don’t forget to pick up your baton.”

~~~

Judith called me on Monday.

“We met with the District Attorney and the THP guys on Friday,” she said.

“And?” I asked.

“They didn’t like your report.”

“Not unexpected.” I picked up my earbud and turned it on, slipping it over my right ear. As the call transferred to the earpiece I put the phone down and turned back to my computer screen. “Who’s the DA?”

“His name is Dwayne Matthews. Know him?”

“No. Did he seem like a decent guy?”

“I guess so. I think he used to be a Marine.”

“What else?”

“Well, me and Cathy and Steve walked in there and the DA was behind his desk, and it was only supposed to be the THP captain but Palmer was there, too. We sat down and the DA said the same thing he said before, about how this was a terrible tragedy but that it didn’t look like there was anything that could be done. Then Steve turns to the THP captain, completely ignoring Palmer, and asks why the CIRT team didn’t work the wreck, like you said they should’ve.

“The captain says that ‘They don’t call the CIRT team for single fatality crashes’. So Steve pulls out five newspaper articles that showed single fatalities and single-vehicle crashes where the CIRT team did investigate them. The captain gets all red in the face, and then he turns to Palmer and says ‘why didn’t you call in the CIRT team?’”

Judith laughed as she spoke the words.

I smiled, too. “What did he say to that?”
~~~

"Palmer said there weren't any suspicious factors involved and that it was clear that Chris had just lost control going too fast around the curve. That's when Steve pulled out your report and tells the captain and the DA how you found that straight skidmark after Chris was past the curve. Then he tells them about the damage you found on Chris's car that matched up to the damage on Johnny's car, and how the computer in Johnny's car recorded two impacts, and then how the crash happened.

"Palmer gets all upset and starts yelling. He said you couldn't tell there were two cars on the road that night. Steve shows him the photos you took of those burnout marks and then how you matched up the marks on Chris's right rear quarter panel to Johnny's left front wheel.

"Then out of the blue Palmer just starts ranting about how you were helping Dr. Peckem try to get that girl off who killed those Nashville cops and that you were lying then and you're lying now. The THP captain told Palmer to shut up, and then he reads your report real careful, and we're all sitting there and everyone's quiet and Palmer is sweating and looking like he's 'bout to have a heart attack.

"After a few minutes the captain hands the report to the DA and he reads it, too. It was horrible to sit through that silence. But we sure enjoyed watching Palmer squirm. Then the DA puts the report on his desk and he says there's enough evidence to charge Johnny with reckless driving and a manslaughter charge."

I nodded. The words I'd been writing glowed on my laptop screen. "That's what I thought. If he's convicted it might be a year in jail."

"Well, Steve was all over him about that, because he wanted Johnny to be charged with murder. We were all happy when he said the thing about arresting Johnny, and it took a few minutes for us to understand what the DA was saying, that it wasn't for homicide, you know, and once we did, Steve jumped up real fast and knocked his chair over and made a big scene about Johnny killing his son and only getting slapped on the wrist.

"Palmer and the THP captain both got up and told him to calm down, and then we were all afraid Steve was going to do something dumb, you know, but then he just kind of got all quiet and said 'so that's how it is' and the DA nodded. Then the DA said unless there was someone to prove that Johnny intentionally hit Chris, there wasn't a way to charge Johnny with anything more serious, and the THP captain told him that manslaughter was a serious charge and that they could probably make that work and like you said it would be a year in jail for Johnny. And through all this, Palmer was sweating so bad that the DA asked him if he was feeling okay. That was funny. I guess he thought he was gonna be in trouble or something."

It wasn't what it should be. But it was something. "What happens next?"

"Well, we asked him that, and they said there'd be some court stuff and then the trial."

"Did they say anything about a pre-trial hearing?"

"That's it," she said. "Something about a hearing and then the trial. The judge granted Johnny's bail on the assault charge against you, but he has to report to the hearing or else they'll arrest him again."

I rubbed my eyes. "It worked out, I guess. As much as it could have."

"We never would have gotten this far if it hadn't been for you finding the damage. At least he's going to be arrested now. After all that he was saying and doing and then trying to kill you. We feel horrible about that."

"They weren't there to kill me, Judith." I tried to ease her guilt, even though I felt otherwise. "They just wanted to scare me and rough me up. Johnny will probably just get probation for the assault. It'll be the manslaughter charge that'll lock him up for a while. Not long enough, not what he deserves, but it's better than nothing. And hopefully give the Camerons some closure."

"What happened to those other boys that were with him?"

"The guy who rushed me broke his jaw when he hit the asphalt, and between that and the broken elbow, I think he's had enough. He might try to sue me, but Wayne said he'd help me out if he did, and Ken witnessed the whole thing. It's on their video camera, too. It's pretty damning for them."

"For YouTube."

"YouTube? They were going to post it online?"

"Pretty sure. That's what Chris and all his friends were doing. Using those adventure cameras and posting videos."

"Oh. I don't think they'll post it now."

"I'm still sorry," she said.

"Yeah, well, no harm. But I'm staying away from Anderson County for a while."

"Wish I could, but I live there." Her voice went quiet. "Can I ask you something?"

"Sure."

"What was Palmer talking about with the girl that killed the two Nashville cops?"

"Long story," I told her. "She did kill two state troopers. It was a high-profile case, and Peckem took it because he knew it would get his name in the news. And it did- and mine, too, because I did the reconstruction on the crash."

"Yeah, it sounded more like Dr. Peckem than you, and I figured there was more to it."

"There is," I said. "But THP doesn't care much for me because of it."

"The THP captain seemed like a good guy."

"They are good guys," I said. "It's like anything else. It only takes a few bad ones to stand out. We have our share of those in science, too."

"And in the English department," she agreed. "That's the way things are, I guess."

"I guess."

Judith cleared her throat. "Allison wants to buy you dinner for your help with the case."

"How is she?"

"She's okay. The swelling is down and so is Steve's anger. Nothing broken, but it looks like hell. She doesn't want to do it until she looks better."

"Tell her I'm sure she's still gorgeous."

"I will. She'll like that." Judith paused. "She's also filed for an annulment."

"That's hard to go through."

"It's for the best."

"Did the DA say anything about me testifying at the hearing?" I steered the subject to safer waters.

"No. Do you think you will?"

"It's up to him," I said. "It's not a problem if I have to. I do it all the time."

Judith was quiet for a moment. "It's over, then."

"A hearing and a trial, unless they cut a deal. It's over."

But it didn't feel over.

CHAPTER 9

The next week crawled by. August fell. September rolled in. No break in the sticky heat.

The dissertation was growing every day. My phone was quiet. Attorneys get occupied with their kids going back to school. It would pick back up in October and November as they tried to settle their cases before Christmas.

Allison called me on September first.

~~~

"You need to be free on September fourteenth," Allison said.

"For what?" I asked.

"The hearing for Johnny's manslaughter charge."

"Wow. That's fast to get on the docket."

"I guess my dad was right about Kelly."

I tried to remember the name. "Kelly is the girl Chris was dating? And her dad is the judge?"

"Yes." She paused. "Soren, do you think they'll make me testify?"

"It's possible."

"Can you help me prepare for it? Not now, but maybe over dinner?"

I squirmed in my chair. "Allison, I'm not sure..."

"Just this once."

"Allison, you don't need to buy me dinner."

"I do. You've been too good to us. It would mean a lot to me."

"Allison-"
~~~

"Not taking no. We need to prepare for the hearing, too, like you said in your email. Come on. Don't make me beg."

"I don't want anyone to beg."

"Then say yes. Come on. Then I'll feel better. Please."

I sighed. "All right. I can do it Saturday. But it's easier if we meet at the restaurant."

"Actually, I need you to pick me up. My BMW is in the shop. And besides, I want to see what your Mercedes is like."

"It's like a big boat. You don't drive it so much as you skipper it." I sighed, then opened my phone's calendar. "Okay. What's the address?"

"I'm living at my parent's place now. I'm leaving Travis."

"Oh, wow. I'm sorry."

"I'm not."

I searched for words. "No, I was talking about your Beemer."

That made her laugh. "Good one. But a Beemer refers to a BMW motorcycle. A Bimmer refers to the car."

"No kidding?" It was news to me.

"Seriously. You sure you're a real engineer?"

"You got me. I'm really an artist."

She laughed again. "Then we're in trouble. You need to testify at the hearing, and I'm pretty certain the judge won't let an artist testify against Johnny."

~~~

Early Saturday evening I made my way to the Cameron's house. Hot, humid air and an azure sky with stratospheric clouds rolled above me, reflected on the glossy clearcoat of my car's hood. Steve's truck was in the driveway. Cathy's minivan was off to the side.

As I got out of my car the house door opened. Steve walked out onto the porch. I threw him a wave and he nodded, trotting down the steps and covering the distance to me quickly.

"Hey, buddy," he said, extending his hand.

"Hey, Steve." I felt like a complete heel for coming over to pick up his daughter, even if it was strictly about the case. "You doing okay?"
~~~

"Oh, gosh, yes." He was more upbeat than I'd ever seen him before. "Trial's set and things are rolling. Man, you know, it's all about faith. Just have to have faith."

"Sure." I tried to sound sincere.

"Allison's been trying to get you back out here. She couldn't wait to buy you dinner for helping us." He smiled. "Hell, I wish you'd let me pay you."

"Steve, I'm not...I mean, nothing's going to happen there."

"You saying you don't like my daughter?"

"No. I mean, not like that." I blushed.

Steve laughed. "I'm just messing with you." He clapped my shoulder. "Come here for a minute," he said, putting his hand on my shoulder. "Come on over here."

I walked with him over to the detached three-car garage. He pulled out a key and unlocked the door at the end. The knob turned. He pushed against the door with his shoulder, bumping it a few times until it swung inward. The magnetic weather-stripping around the perimeter of the doorframe peeled off the door loudly, like ripping cloth.

The air had the musty, damp smell that permeated every garage in the Tennessee valley. Steve stepped through and I followed him. He hit some switches on the wall and the space lit up under rows of fluorescent lights.

In front of us was a late-model black Chevrolet S-10 pick-up truck, missing its bed. On the other side of that I could make out the roofline and hoodline of a white late-eighties Corvette.

"This was Chris's," Steve said, pointing to the S-10. He walked around to the front. I followed him.

Spots of body glaze dotted the doors of the cab. It was ready to be sanded smooth and make the metal surface flat again, filling in the dings and insults that the truck had accumulated as it made its journey from the assembly plant in Canada through various owners and eventually finding a home in this garage.

"This thing came through Jerry's yard," Steve began. "They bought it at auction 'cause no one else even bid on it. No bed and the motor was all burned up. Chris always did like Fords but he asked Jerry how much he wanted for it. Jerry just gave it to him. Said it was his early Christmas present."

I walked around to the front. The hood was gone. In place of the little four-cylinder was a small-block Chevy LS1 V-8.

"Chris got the engine out of a Camaro that had been killed in the rear. I think he gave five hundred bucks for it. He was planning on making a fast little truck that'd cream everyone else at the drags. His Mustang was fast but by God this thing'd leave it behind if he ever finished it." He turned away. "I never did care for Fords but he liked 'em enough. Sometimes I think he liked them just to spite me."

I nodded at the truth of the last sentence, but not in sympathy with Steve's dislike of Fords. People were funny that way, loyal to a certain brand of car. It wasn't enough to be American. They had to pick a team to be on, a group to side with. It was a manifestation of the tribal nature again. Ally or enemy. Friend or foe. Pick a color, pick a side. It wasn't enough to simply be part of the human race together.

"Anyway, these engines got a ton of damn anti-theft electronics on them, and this thing drove Chris nuts trying to get it all straightened out. He worked on it for months. Months," he said, repeating the word to himself. "But he never gave up. Working out here all night sometimes. Finally he figured it out. Damn if he didn't figure it out."

"That's impressive."

Steve faced me. "He was unbelievable, I'm telling you." He wiped his eyes. "He was gonna go places. He was smart and he was gonna do things that would leave you amazed."

"I believe it, Steve." I stood as witness more than anything else. Steve needed a bearer to hear his words so that they meant something, so that the words would carry weight and have substance and truth. Without a witness, the words were just ephemeral sounds lost to the unfeeling concrete block walls that surrounded us, entombed in the garage just like this little truck. I stood and listened and nodded, wishing there was more I could do to make his pain go away.

"You know, you're right about how it happened," he said.

I turned and looked at him. He was staring at the engine in the truck.

"What do you mean?" I asked.

"Johnny killed Chris," he said, still looking at the engine. "Ain't no doubt. You figured it all out, and it all makes sense."

"Steve, I can't prove intent."

"Aw, I know you got to remain objective and all, but I read you loud and clear. Whoever was in that car with Johnny can say it, and I'll find him eventually."

"How?"

"Hell, he had to be a friend of Johnny's, and that means he was from around here. Chris had friends too, and I'm for damn sure that they know he the kid was. I've already set things in motion to find out who he was."

I wasn't certain I wanted to know, but I asked anyway. "How are you doing that?"

"Eh, we've had some kids stop by, and I made some agreements. Best leave it at that." Steve stepped closer to the truck. "Judith thinks it's bad that they come around."

"Steve, it would be great if we could find that witness, but what makes you think he'll tell the truth?"

"Because Johnny crossed the line on this one," he said. "All them kids live around here, and they go to the same schools, they go to the same parties. Fightin' is okay. But killin' ain't. That's why Johnny tried to make it look like an accident. But you found the truth, and I explained that to some of them. People need someone to side with, I guess, and some of 'em run with Johnny and his crew and some ran with Chris, but we all know we're part of the same damn redneck family."

As he said his son's name, he reached his hand out, toward the engine. "People got to have something to hate or fight against, maybe, but it's all a bunch of shit because we're all from this same little town."

Steve's hand hovered near the engine. Then he pulled his hand back, never touching it. "You need to be careful, too," he said. Soft words.

"About what?" I asked.

Steve glanced at me. "Johnny. He's cut from the same cloth as his daddy. And he's not going to like you testifying against him." He reached his hand out again, this time toward the radiator support, then pulled it back. Thick dust had settled on the metal.

The door creaked on its hinges. Steve and I turned to see Allison standing in the doorway. Wide sunglasses covered her eyes, and she had on a light breezy blouse over a short blue skirt.

"You guys okay?" she asked quietly.

"Oh yeah," Steve answered quickly. He looked at me and nodded sharply, as if we had shared a moment that was separate from life and not to be spoken of again. I didn't mind. It joined the solemnity of the other deaths I'd witnessed.

We turned and walked back around the truck. Our shoes made soft scuffing sounds on the concrete. We crossed the threshold of the doorway. Broken spiderwebs floated in the doorframe, broken aside when Steve had opened the door.

We stepped out into the open air and fading sunlight and Steve pulled the door shut, then locked it again. He turned to face us.

Allison walked over and stood next to me. "Ready to go?"

Shame washed over me. I stepped forward to Steve, extended my hand. "Thanks, Steve."

He took it. "Ya'll have a good time," he said. Then he stepped around us and walked back up the porch and through the door of the house.

~~~

Traffic was light as we drove toward the restaurant. The sun had almost set and the stifling heat of the day had reduced to a simmer. I kept steering the conversation toward Chris and the crash. She kept steering it back to me.

"So with testifying, you just need to tell the truth," I said, refolding my napkin for the umpteenth time and placing it on the table between us like a barrier. "But don't let the other attorney rush you into an answer."

"Why would they rush me?" Allison asked.

"Ninety percent of communication is non-verbal. They want to get you into a cadence of talking and not thinking. They're hoping that you'll say something they'll be able to turn against you, or Chris."

"But if I'm telling the truth, why would it matter?"

"As the witness, you're sworn to tell the truth, but the attorneys aren't. They'll be looking for anything to twist into an advantage for their side."

"I don't see how you do this work." Allison looked down at the table and shook her head. "Judith said you had a sister."

"Yes."

"Are you close to her?"
~~~

"More than anyone else." I picked at the dessert. "It's complicated. She does her own thing."

"Is she in Knoxville?" Allison asked.

"She's not in any one place. Always on the move. Last I heard from her she was in London."

"London. Wow. I've always wanted to go to Europe." Allison smiled. "Judith said your father is in Los Angeles. And that he had a funny name."

I nodded. "He is, and he does. He's the laid back type who never met a beach or a boat he didn't like. He goes by Gull, like the bird. It fits him well."

"Do you ever see him?"

"We don't talk much." Or at all.

Allison looked sad. "She also told me about your mother. Soren, I'm so sorry."

My right eye winced. "Thanks."

She sensed my change in mood and decided not to press further. We sat in silence for a minute.

"So you and Chris were close?" I asked, using the edge of my spoon to delicately slice off a small corner of the tiramisu.

"Very close," she said. "I was ahead of him in school by two years, but we were always looking out for each other." She scooped some of the filling from the side. "It's like there's an enormous hole inside me now. Like I lost part of myself."

"How so?"

"Sometimes I'll catch myself talking to him, you know? I'll do something stupid, and I'll hear Chris's voice laughing at me."

"I'm sorry, Allison. I can't imagine losing my sister."

We ate in silence for a moment.

"Dad keeps saying that Johnny is going to prison," she asked. "Think that'll happen?"

"I don't know." I studied her face. She'd tried to cover the bruise Travis had given her with make-up, but the more I looked at her the more obvious it became. Rage flickered inside me. I fought it back.

"You okay?" she asked. "Something just happened with your eyes. They got hard or something."

"Just tired from working on my dissertation." I shifted topics. "It's hard to say about Johnny, especially at his age.

Maybe a year in prison, like I told Judith, especially if he hasn't been in trouble with the law before."

She shot me a quizzical glance. "Don't you know anything about him?"

"Not really," I answered. "Other than he likes big shiny revolvers."

She looked down. "Johnny's bad," she said simply. "And his dad is worse."

"Bad like how?"

"He's no stranger to violence."

"Yeah, I ran into that. Is there more?"

She nodded. "He pushed meth when we were in high school. Never got busted. If there was something bad going on, Johnny was involved. There was a kid that got crossed up with Johnny over some drugs and he ended up dead."

I almost choked on my tiramisu. "What? Are you serious?"

She nodded. "Eddie Jarnagin. He was doing the same thing Johnny was doing, pushing pot and meth. Johnny didn't like the competition. So he killed him."

"Tell me it wasn't a car crash."

"No. Johnny hung him from one of the goalposts."

It sounded like a sick joke. "Hung him from a goalpost at your school?"

"It was awful. Everyone says there's a curse on the field now, because our football team never had a winning season after that."

"If everyone knew he did it, why didn't they arrest him?" I asked.

She nodded. "No hard evidence connecting Johnny to it. The police wrote it up as suicide, but Eddie didn't do any of the things we were taught to look for in our social problems class. He wasn't depressed or anything." She brushed her hair down so it covered more of the bruised side of her face.

"Did they even investigate it?"

"Not anything thorough. It never went beyond the local police. Eddie wasn't exactly a nice guy, either. And his family was poor. There was never any proof, just rumors. You know how people talk, especially kids in high school."

"Yeah." I scooped up another piece of the dessert. "So what about Johnny's dad?"

She cut into the desert too, coming closer to my own spoon. As the cake diminished, so did the distance between our hands. Pretty soon we'd be fighting over the last portion like precious real estate.

"He taught Johnny everything he knows. Johnny's dad makes the stuff. But it's not like his dad cooks it. He's got plenty of people working for him and they've got places all over the county. His dad is into everything. You know that place called the Emerald Club?"

"Judith told me about it."

"That's his, and he runs a few more. Some of the girls I went to school with fell in with Johnny and drugs and then they ended up working at those places. And I don't mean dancing."

"Prostitution?"

She nodded. "And then there's the chop shops. Johnny and his crew were always driving different cars and it was an open secret that they could score any parts someone wanted. They just ran the stuff out of his dad's places."

"How is it that they're still in business?"

"That's a great question." We both reached for the tiramisu at the same time. She smiled and knocked my spoon away with her own and dug in.

"Have you talked to these kids that Steve knows? Chris's friends?" I asked.

"Only at the funeral."

"Has anyone said anything about who was riding with Johnny that night?"

She shook her head, but then put her own spoon down and extended her arm across the table. "Give me your hand," she said.

"What?"

"Give me your hand," she repeated.

"Uh, no offense, but I'm kind of sensitive about people touching me-"

Allison reached out and clasped my left in her own. Her hand was small and soft and her fingers were delicate. There was a pale band where she had removed her wedding ring. I shifted my glance from her hand to her eyes.

"It's okay for you to be here with me," she said softly. "Without discussing what brought us together."

Uh-oh. "Okay."

"Really," she insisted.

"Sorry." My mind scrambled for words. "It's just that I feel bad about it."

"It's okay. Don't." She squeezed my hand. "My dad said you were a good guy."

Warning bells rang in my mind.

~~~

The distant marimba ringtone of my phone woke me the next morning. The digital clock next to my bed showed ten a.m. My hand clawed on the nightstand. No phone. That's right, in the office. Next to my computer, still humming from where I'd left my dissertation five hours ago.

I rolled out and tried to get to the damn thing but slammed my left foot on the doorframe of my bedroom. I went down hard, breaking my fall with an outstretched hand. I got up and limped to the desk on the last ring.

"This is Soren," I croaked.

"Soren?" my doctoral committee chairperson asked.

"Dr. Peckem," I said, clearing my throat.

"You okay?" he asked.

My foot throbbed with each one of my heartbeats. I'd stayed until eleven with Allison, then hammered on my laptop after getting home. I coughed.

"Yes, sir. Just worked too late last night." I sat in my chair and rubbed my toes.

He'd been in my position before. But he played nice.

"How's it coming along?" he asked.

"Good," I said. "Good. Great. Cranking it out."

Awkward pause. "You've been persistent about meeting with me."

"Yes, sir."

"I emailed you yesterday and told you I could meet you in my office. Here on campus. About now."

Hell.

"Sir, I didn't check my email yesterday. I've been working hard to get the draft complete." My mind raced with excuses but it didn't matter. I stifled the urge to keep talking.

"You're still planning on meeting the deadline, aren't you?"

"Yes, sir."
~~~

"Great." He muffled the phone for a minute. "Do you still need to see me?"

"I do. I need...I'd be grateful for your advice on my work."

"I have a few minutes this Friday. Same time."

"Yes, sir."

"That would be ten a.m."

"Yes. I'll be there. Thank you, sir."

"Don't work late Thursday night."

"I won't," I said.

The line clicked.

~~~

I worked without sleep for the remainder of the week.

Allison called me Thursday.

"Hey, I might have some information for you."

"Like what?"

"Stefan's high school yearbook. I was thinking whoever was riding in Johnny's car might be in there."

"Wow," I said. "That's brilliant. Have you gone through it yet? Any names?"

"Not yet. I wanted to go through it with you. You've already had a run-in with some of them, and I can show you who they associated with."

"Okay. When do you want to meet?"

"I'll be downtown tomorrow." She paused a beat too long. "I'll just stay there for dinner if you're free. Calhoun's by the river."

~~~

"That's one of them." I tapped the photograph. "He had the camera."

"Matt Barnard," she said. "Yeah, I remember him. Kids called him Barnyard." She rotated the book back to herself.

"Ken checked him out after he arrested them. The kid was already detained by the Knoxville police the night Chris was killed. Busted for motorcycle street racing."

"And the other two weren't talking?" she asked.

"The one wasn't. The kid with the broken jaw couldn't."

"That was Billy." She made a face. "He's a pig. You did a good thing there."

She looked at the list we'd made. There were still seventeen kids that could have been in the Mustang with Johnny. Too many to check out before the hearing. But I knew Allison would try.

"Got time for a walk?" Allison asked.

I looked around. I'd picked up the tab, although Allison had fought me for the check. I had to get back to the dissertation. But a walk sounded great.

"Sure," I said.

The evening was comfortably warm. Allison and I left the restaurant, headed to the waterfront, strolling the riverwalk.

"How's school?" she asked quietly. She walked closer to me. I kept my arms by my sides.

"I had a meeting with my committee chair this morning about my dissertation."

"How did it go?"

"Hard. He said it still needs a lot of work. He implied that I might not make the deadline."

She arched an eyebrow. "Do you think you will?"

"Yeah," I said dismissively. "Well, maybe."

"Maybe?"

I shrugged. "I'm doing my best."

We both walked to the railing.

She looked out over the river. "I'm so sorry for pulling you into this."

"No, no. Don't say that. It beats sitting in an office writing for twelve hours a day."

The river was lazy, lapping at the bank below us. It pushed against the shoreline softly but relentlessly. The firmament was unyielding, containing the massive hydraulic pressure of the water, channeling it further south. Cradling it but never merging with it.

"I can't believe he's gone," Allison said.

She leaned her head into the hollow of my neck. Slow night breeze pushed her long hair over my back. She was so small. She smelled wonderful.

The soft sound of the water played to our ears, keeping time with the dancing reflections of the bridge lights on the surface. It was van Gogh's *Starry Night Over the Rhone* alive in front of us. My heart softened as the beautiful canvas billowed into my mind.

Van Gogh had seen water like this. It had moved him, creating powerful currents deep inside his soul. We stood there for several minutes.

"Hold me," she said. She pushed against me. Tentatively, I put my arm around her. She came against me harder.

Guilt. You shouldn't be here. With her.

Her left hand moved across my back, down to my waist.

She turned her head to me. Her eyes were closed.

Something sparked inside me. Something I'd tried to beat to death but wouldn't die.

Desire.

"Just...a little comfort. Please," she whispered. "No one else understands loss like you do."

My lips brushed gently against her, then lower to her neck. My left hand found her waist and we turned slightly towards each other.

She exhaled hard against my cheek, blowing away the last vestige of the awkward formality that had existed between us. She pulled me closer and our lips met, delicately, first contact like a butterfly's wings, and then harder as she crushed against me.

She had lost much. She wanted this, needed this. She moved her lips over mine in a desperate passionate dance. The tip of her tongue brushed against mine, caressed along my upper lip. I did the same to her, tasting her, taking her in, as much as I could, inhaling her essence as our lips came together again. She pushed against me harder and her movements became more intense. I fought to keep us upright, leaning on the metal railing in front of us for balance.

With my left hand I caressed her shoulder and neck, bringing it up and cupping the back of her head, slipping my fingers through her hair. I lightly touched her ear with my fingertips and then my thumb, intoxicated with her. She smiled with her eyes closed and moved her hand to the small of my back and then lower still. She pulled my body against hers, pulled me hard, surprising me with her strength.

I pressed into her, helpless. Desire overwhelmed my reservation. Her gravity had trapped me. I couldn't pull my body away. Her hand moved on my back in a slow circle, pulling me into her. She gasped each time I pushed my weight towards her, her sighs blowing across the side of my cheek. We turned further until her back was to the railing. Her hand slid from my shoulder to my waist. She slid her fingers between my abdomen and my pants, hooking her fingers around my belt and using that as leverage to pull me closer still.

Her fingers caressed my torso through the fabric of my shirt and I immediately and involuntarily responded. I blushed, heat rising into my cheeks, and she giggled lightly between the embrace of our lips. Her lips pulled away to smile. It made me want her more. I moved my hands to her back, opening my hands and fingers so that my thumbs rode around her sides and pushed lightly under her arms. I inhaled deeply, pulling her breath into my lungs, crashing into her body. Her breasts stretched against the silky sheen of her blouse, warm as they pushed against me.

The sound of approaching people brought us back to reality. We pulled apart. The atmosphere of intimacy faded. Two older couples passed and then we were alone again.

"Wow," she said.

"Wow," I echoed.

"That was nice," she said.

My smile faded into an expression that finally betrayed my guilt.

"What's wrong?" she asked.

"Oh, God." I shook my head. "We can't do this."

Her brow furrowed. "Why?"

Because it leads to sex, which then distills a poisonous maelstrom of shame and guilt inside me. And I'll be pulled into it and drown in it every time I think of you. It will fill my lungs and suffocate me, just like it has with the few other women I've been with. Just like it does when the nightmares come. And I'll never want to see you again.

"Conflict of interest. It could cost us the case," I said.

She moved away from me, shrugging off my hand. "That hurts."

"It's not you. It's just...we can't, Allison."

She was looking at the river now. "Okay."

"Allison."

"No. You're right." She turned to me again. "We shouldn't. I shouldn't."

I let my body hit the railing. “Sorry.”

Silence. Anything I said would make it hurt more.

“Can we be friends?” she finally said.

“Sure. I just don’t think it’s right to go further than that.”

She swallowed hard, nodded. “Okay.”

“So we’re cool?” I asked.

“We’re cool.” She inched away from me.

Silence. Without grace.

I rested my elbows on the rail, dropped my head in my hands.

“You need sleep. You can barely stand up.”

“I’m fine.”

She looked at me with skeptical eyes.

“C’mon, I’ll walk you to your car.” I stepped back and held out my hand. She pushed herself off the railing.

~~~

Monday.

Blood dripped onto the old wooden floor.

“Damn it.” The skin on my knuckle was hanging by a flap.

“Need to stop?” Rob asked. The bamboo stick rotated in his hand.

“No.” I squared against him again.

The heat in the room wouldn’t leave. We’d opened all the windows we could. Some had been glued shut by decades of paint. Sweat ran off my arm and into the red wound on my knuckle, stinging.

Rob advanced. His stick jabbed at my stomach, angle five. I parried, my stick flashing in front of me, knocking his sideways as I twisted my body. Clacking sticks. My motion stayed fluid, the stick in my hand rotating upwards, a strong, short arc that whipped the end toward Rob’s head. Angle two.

Should’ve been a decent head shot, but Rob’s stick materialized in front of mine. It deflected my blow, not stopping it and wasting energy, but keeping my stick moving, the arc opening up and heading to the floor.

The bamboo sticks separated. Mine was pointed to the floor, which left my upper body exposed. His was jerked back to his shoulder, wound up, ready to uncoil into my face.
~~~

Shit. I swiveled my body just fast enough to catch the blow on my shoulder. The impact stung my arm down through my hand. I held onto the stick, barely.

"Stay fluid. One motion."

"Easy for you to say." I grunted more than said it, rotating my body to diminish the shock. My left hand followed his right hand around. I whipped the bamboo upward, angle seven, jabbing it toward Rob's face.

It should have connected. But his face wasn't there.

"That would've hurt." He stepped back and dropped his arms. "Break."

I dropped my guard and brought my knuckle to my mouth. I sucked the blood off it and spit out one of the open windows.

"Got time for lunch?" Rob asked.

"Sure." I dropped my telephone back in my pocket. Then it chimed with an incoming call. Allison.

"Hey," I answered.

"Soren, I know you're going to think I'm crazy, or think I'm nutty girl, but...it's probably nothing, but I didn't know who else to call." Allison sounded rattled.

"What's wrong?"

"I'm at work, and I just got a text that someone is watching me."

"At the bank?"

"Yes."

"Okay. Don't leave the building. I'll call Ken, and I'm going to head out there now. I've got a few hours before I teach."

We hung up. I looked at Rob.

"Let's go." Rob walked to the door.

"What about your Antiquities class? Can't skip if you're the instructor."

"We'll be back in time. This is more important."

~~~

The bank was a main branch, busy with post-lunch errand runners. We circled the parking lot once, taking our time, waiting for cars to pull out, waving people to walk in front of us.

Rob spotted them first. "That's them."

"Where?"
~~~

He didn't point. "Silver Crown Victoria in the corner space. Two guys in suits. Don't look over."

He was the expert at this, not me. "What now?"

"Keep going. Park in the back."

I wheeled the Mercedes around the building. "They looked like cops."

"I hate cops." Rob cracked his knuckles.

We exited the car, looking like gym rats. "Rob, we don't even know if they're here for Allison. And I don't know who sent the text message."

Rob nodded. "You're right. Call her. Get her to come out the front entrance and walk around the building."

I called her. She didn't argue.

"Give her a minute. She's with a customer."

Rob walked along the side of the building until he could see the car.

My phone rang.

"Okay, I'm going through the front door now," Allison said. Through the phone came the sound of doors opening, then wind. Car noises.

"They're pointing," Rob said. "Is she out?"

"Yes."

"What?" Allison asked.

"I was talking to Rob. Sorry." I looked up. Rob was slouched against the wall.

"They're moving," he said.

"Don't look, but there's a car pulling out of the far corner space."

"Someone *was* watching me?" She was walking faster now. "Are you around the corner?"

"Yes, but don't stop near us. Keep walking to your car." Her BMW was in the back lot, near the fence. Away from curious eyes.

Allison came around the building, a flash of beauty in a business suit, heels clicking on the concrete. She glanced at Rob, almost stumbled. Running into a real-life Viking would make a person do that. She brushed past him and kept moving.

The silver snout of a Crown Vic rounded the corner. I kept the phone to my ear. Rob let his eyes linger on Allison as she walked by him. The two guys in the Crown Vic glanced at Rob but didn't stop. The car trolled behind Allison.

She was passing me now. I moved aside to let her by. We kept our phones to our ears, not looking at each other. "Keep walking. Get to your car. Unlock it, get in, start it up. But don't leave."

"What are you going to do?"

"Make new friends."

The Crown Vic passed us. Heavy tint on the side windows. Government license plate, black letters on a white background. I jotted the number down on my phone, not wanting to risk a photograph. Rob waited a beat, turned my way and walked past me, then I followed him.

Allison cut through a row of cars. The Crown Vic turned to maneuver around the row, then rounded the end and came toward Allison. Slow. Hunting.

Allison spoke. "This is starting to scare me."

"You're doing great. Dodge in front of their car and get to yours."

Allison darted in front of the Crown Vic. It braked. She kept the phone to her ear, leaning her head on her shoulder while she fumbled for her keys.

"Get in and lock the doors." I wanted her out of harm's way. Rob's demeanor had changed. His body was tense. Electricity in the air. Hairs on my neck started to stand on end. Something was going to happen.

"Rob, if they're cops, don't do anything violent."

He didn't acknowledge me. Not even a wave or a harsh word to shut up.

He flexed. He was a little shorter than Ken, and maybe a size 50 compared to Ken's 56. Still big, and fully educated with the knowledge of how to inflict a horrendous amount of damage to a human body. His triceps bulged under the T-shirt. His trapezius muscles stretched the fabric neck. He looked like a wrestler, flexing and stretching before stepping on the mat. He swiveled his head from side to side, scanning for threats. I glimpsed his face. He was *grinning*. His skin was shining with an exuberant joy.

The Crown Vic stopped behind Allison's car, blocking it in.

Allison had the key fob in her hand.

The passenger got out. Big, bald. Thick chest under the suit. Wraparound sunglasses.

"Soren," she said. She fumbled with the door handle, almost dropping her phone.

"Get in the car," I said. Rob and I broke into a run.

Allison opened the door. Heat from the interior of her car shimmered into the air.

The guy moved toward Allison. Something in his hand. Billfold.

Rob and I were entering the row of cars, approaching from behind the Crown Vic. The driver of the car was watching his partner.

Allison held the phone away from her ear and turned to the guy. "Can I help you?"

"Miss Cameron?" The words were gruff, muffled. More words, a name, too faint to understand.

It didn't matter. Rob and I were rounding the Crown Vic.

Rob closed the distance to Allison fast. I pocketed my phone and ran after him.

A car door opened. The driver of the Crown Vic got out, one foot on the sill. One hand near his jacket. I reached Allison, but kept my hands away from my pocket.

"Is there a problem here?" Rob asked. He stepped within inches of the bald guy standing in front of Allison. Intimidating. No fear of authority.

I circled around Allison. She put her phone in her purse. My hand on her arm, in front of her, pushing her back towards the open door of her car. The driver swiveled toward me, then back to Rob.

Blinding bright sun.

"Official police business." The bald guy squared against Rob. He was bigger than Rob, taller and wider. "Get lost." He thrust his wallet in Rob's chest. Black ink tattoo on his wrist, winding onto the back of his hand.

Rob glanced at the badge and ID card.

He exploded.

The movement was almost too fast to see. Rob's left hand snaked out, grabbed the guy's wrist, and bent it towards his chest.

It was the same move he'd taught me that I used on the tech at the John Deere dealership. Only Rob didn't let go of this guy. The modern day Viking stepped close into the guy, arms moving in a tight circle. Something popped, then cracked.

Bald guy screamed.

Rob just broke a cop's arm. Oh, God.

The driver of the Crown Vic reached into his jacket. Gun.

I moved completely in front of Allison, shielding her with my body, pushing her into the BMW. "Get in!"

I tried to follow her. My t-shirt caught on the door. It ripped. My head slammed into the edge of the roof as my body followed hers. Her shoulder bounced off the steering wheel, then hit the horn. Loud honk. She balled up in the passenger seat. I twisted around in the driver's seat. My temple throbbed.

No shots.

I pulled my head up to look.

The driver of the Crown Vic had his gun out. Finger on the trigger, aimed at Rob.

Rob had the bald guy in front of him. One of Rob's hands on his neck, the other twisting the guy's broken arm behind his back. Bald guy was sweating, mucus blowing out of his nose. His sunglasses were cockeyed on his forehead.

"Who are you guys?" Rob shouted.

The Crown Vic driver didn't answer. Something was wrong. Maybe these guys weren't cops.

Allison's face said it all. Terror. I moved my hand to my right front pocket and pulled my HK. I used it to lever myself up and draw a bead on the Crown Vic driver. The front of my gun sliced the pie around the B-pillar of Amanda's BMW.

"Let him go," the Crown Vic driver said. He saw the snout of my gun and dropped his body down behind the rear passenger door, below the roof of his car, making my shot difficult. He swiveled the gun to me.

I pressed the slack out of the trigger. Tracked him with my front sight. I could barely see his forehead, but he couldn't get a bead on me, either.

Might have to shoot through the door glass. But the heavy tint made an exact shot impossible. If I missed, my bullet would fly out toward the bank and the busy road. Can't risk it.

"Nah, I'm not done playing with him." Rob twisted the guy's arm. He screamed again. "The real cops should be here soon. Let's wait for them."

The Crown Vic driver cursed, glanced around quickly. Pointed the gun at Rob, then me again, then Rob.

"You got a gun on you, sweetie?" Rob pushed on the guy's arm.

The bald guy rammed his head back against Rob's face.

Rob cursed and staggered back. He lost his grip. Bald guy jerked out of Rob's grasp. He ran for the open door of the Crown Vic. Rob fell back, moving past me behind the open door of the BMW.

Hair trigger. Tracking front sight. If the driver stood and pointed his gun, I'd ventilate him.

The Crown Vic driver didn't stand up. He dropped farther out of sight, falling into the driver's seat. He reached out and yanked the collar of the bald guy, pulling him into the passenger seat. Screeching wheelspin from the Crown Vic, rear end swaying as it shot away from us, passenger door flopping open then slamming shut as the car rounded the row of cars and roared into the street.

Stunned silence.

"You okay?" I asked Allison.

"I think so. My shoulder hurts."

Rob stepped around the door. Blood dripped out of his nose. He wiped at it with his shirt.

"How'd you know they weren't real cops?" I asked.

"Badge was for a security guard, not a cop. No comm equipment in the car, either."

I reached in and helped Allison out of her car. "We got you now. You're safe." I patted her on the shoulder.

She turned to me. "He wanted me to get in the car with him. Said it was about the hearing." She arched her head back. "You're bleeding."

I reached up to my forehead. My fingers came away with blood.

"You'll live," Rob said to me. He closed one nostril and blew through his nose, spraying red on the black asphalt.

~~~

"The plate was registered to a Chattanooga municipal van. Reported stolen a week ago." Ken slammed his phone shut. "Damn it."

"What about the number that sent the message to Allison's phone?"
~~~

"Burner phone. No contract. Best we can do is find out where it was sold."

"How long will that take?" I asked. My head was throbbing from hitting the BMW's roof.

Ken shot me his get-serious look. "Probably won't happen. I'll request it, but it's low priority. Not likely to lead anywhere, either."

Ken had put a BOLO out for the Crown Vic as soon as I'd called him. Allison had gone home with a police escort. I'd dropped Rob off at the Humanities building just in time for his class. I hadn't seen him so happy in years. Adrenaline junkie of the highest order.

"I'm worried about Allison." We were standing in Estabrook Hall. I had to teach my class upstairs in ten minutes.

"The KPD cruiser will stay at her parent's home for a few hours. They're real cops, and she'll be okay." Ken watched the students filing into the building. "I'm pissed about it, too. Impersonation is a felony. Anything else you remember about them?"

"The tattoos on the bald guy's wrist, cheap suits. That's it."

"Never saw them around town?"

"No." I ran my hand through my hair. "Do you think they would have hurt her?"

"Wouldn't make sense to bring the heat of murder down just to avoid a manslaughter charge on Johnny. Probably trying to intimidate you from testifying at the hearing."

"That's speculation."

"True." Ken hooked a thumb in his belt. "But."

"But what?"

Ken looked from the ground back to me. "Now they'll probably try something else."

"That's fine with me." The words shot out of my mouth.

Ken studied me. "You're not okay, are you?"

I ignored the question. The answer was obvious. "I want to kill them, Ken." My hands suddenly ached. I looked down. My hands were balled up into tight fists. I stretched them out, rubbed my palms on my stomach.

"I don't need to hear that," Ken said. He grasped me on the shoulder. "Just stay cool. Teach your class. And focus on giving it back to them when you testify at the hearing on Thursday."

There wasn't time to clean up before teaching. I walked into the room in my gym shorts and ripped t-shirt. The gash on my temple had swelled up. My knuckle was still weeping. My head still throbbed.

"What happened to you?" one of my kids asked.

"Graduate school," I said.

Some murmurs. "Looks like you got in a fight," a girl said.

"No."

"Who was that cop outside?" another kid asked. "He was huge."

"Did you get arrested?" someone else asked.

"No, I did not get arrested. Long story." I erased the board, then wrote the following:

> Newton's Second Law: An object acted upon by an unbalanced Force will accelerate in the same direction of that Force and at a magnitude proportional to the Force divided by the object's mass.

"Someone sum it up for me. Plain English." I put the marker down.

Minute of silence. "Think about the asteroid in space," I prodded.

"Is the asteroid sitting still?" Kid at the back table.

"Doesn't need to be. It could be moving at a constant velocity. But for simplicity, let's say it is just sitting still," I said. "The point is that some force gets applied to the asteroid. Let's say someone strapped a rocket motor to it. Or it gets pushed by debris from an exploding star. Either way, some force gets applied to the rock."

"So as long as the force keeps pushing, it starts moving faster," another student said.

"Exactly. It starts gaining speed. And what do we call that?"

"Acceleration." Young girl in the front.

"Excellent. Newton's Second Law tells us that we can calculate that acceleration if we know two things: the force being applied, and the mass of the object on which the force is applied. And if we know the direction the force is applied, then we also know which way the asteroid will go."

I stepped back to the board and picked up the marker.

$$\mathbf{F} = m\mathbf{a}$$

"That's what the equation looks like. Force is equal to mass times acceleration, where the force and the acceleration are also vector quantities with specific directions of travel. But Ol' Newton never wrote it that way. Jacob Herrmann did, years after Newton published his Principia."

Okay, that lost them. Blank stares abounded.

"Give me an example of how this applies to people." I waited.

Another girl spoke. "If you wanted to make a person get a job done faster, you have to keep applying more force."

"Good. Anyone else?"

One of the guys raised his hand. "The force could be like pressure. The closer you get to a deadline, the harder you have to work to get the job done."

The kid was prophetic, because at that time, a certain THP officer was being put under some serious pressure to get a certain job done before a certain deadline.

And it involved me.

~~~

"How's the trailer case going?" I was on Wayne's speakerphone.

"Good. The prosecutor agreed to drop the charges against the kid," Wayne said.

"And the insurance company?"

"We made the demand." Rustling papers. "But it'll be a few more weeks before they respond. Turns out that the guy you found, the one who hooked up the trailer, is the supervisor's brother-in-law."

"The supervisor had to know about the drinking problem."

"Looks that way. He was written up previously. More than once. We'll need to schedule your deposition soon."
~~~

"Delay it as long as you can. I'm stressed enough right now. Listen, do you remember that case I told you about where the kids were drag racing?"

"I sure do."

"I just learned that the defense lawyer for the kid is a guy named Tom Gaines. Know him?"

Wayne whistled. "He's supposed to be good. Word is that he gets hundred-thousand dollar retainers."

Just like Wayne's dad used to, before he died. "Okay, but could he really get Johnny off the hook here?"

"I don't know," Wayne said. "I do mostly civil work, not criminal. He's sharp. Don't underestimate him. Are you going to testify?"

"It looks like it," I said. "Manslaughter charge is the big one. The others are leaving the scene of a fatal crash and reckless driving."

Muted voices. Wayne spoke to someone else in his office, then came back to me. "Did you learn who the judge is yet?"

Damn. "No, I forgot to ask," I said. "The hearing is the day after tomorrow, so it's a moot point now."

~~~

I showered and changed back into my business casual clothes at the Rec Sports building. My only thought was getting home, making dinner, and hitting the dissertation again. The interstate turned into a two-lane rural highway as I navigated the familiar roads back to my rented house near the lake in the backwoods of northeast Knoxville. The setting sun cast a long shadow of my car on the road in front of me.

Traffic was light this far from the city. A solitary diesel pick-up truck passed me, angry and loud, blowing soot and smoke over my car. I reached forward and hit the recirculation button on the climate control. Ahead in the distance was the black and tan of a THP Crown Victoria sitting on the shoulder. The placement was odd because he was visible for nearly a half-mile. I took the opportunity to pass him going well under the 55 mph limit.

I glanced in the mirror. His headlights came on and he pulled out smartly. He'd locked onto the diesel pick-up truck. The diesel in front of me slowed.
~~~

I smiled. Served the jerk right.

The Crown Vic surged larger in the mirror. Instead of passing my car, he slipped in behind me.

Damn it. It couldn't have been for speed. More likely he recognized my car.

His blue roof lights came on a few minutes later. I prepared myself for the hassle that was certain to follow.

The woods were dense in this area, but there was a gravel pull-off into an old logging road just ahead. I hit my blinker and braked to a stop, angling my car so it was well off the shoulder and close to the treeline, trying to keep him out of traffic, giving him as much room as I could to make it safer for him to harass me. I shut the car off and hit the hazard lights. I powered the window down and kept both hands on the wheel where he could see them, doing what I could to make this go easy.

Gravel crunched under duty boots. I ticked through the list of troopers it might be. He reached my window. Small dark stains pooled under his armpits. I looked up but didn't recognize him. Thinning hair, matted with sweat. He'd left his rigid-brimmed hat in his car.

It was odd that he'd doffed his hat. THP policy required the troops to keep the hats on to look more formal. And intimidating. Evidently we'd progressed beyond that in our relationship.

"Mr. Graves?" he asked. "You can shut your hazard lights off if you don't mind."

"Sure." I turned the key on the dash off.

"I hate to bother you, but this was the only way I could make contact with you. Can't nobody know I talked to you. You're working on that crash that killed Chris Cameron, right?"

I leaned forward to try to make eye contact with him. He hadn't been out his car for three minutes and the dark patches of sweat under his arms had grown larger. His eyes were narrow, recessed gray orbs above pudgy cheeks that hung downward and fell into the fat around his neck.

"I am. I didn't catch your name, Trooper." I let the sentence hang, waiting for him to fill it.

"I'd feel better if we just left it that way." He glanced up the road and then back again. "Listen, you know the trooper who worked that boy's crash? Glen Palmer?"

I turned my head to look at him. "Never met him, just seen his work. And I wasn't impressed."

"Well, neither am I. He let that boy die in that car."

That got my attention. "How do you know that?"

"Son, that man is trouble. We've all been suspecting it, but you've got to understand that there's a wall of silence when you're part of the brotherhood."

He meant being a cop. I nodded. "And you're willing to tell me? Why?"

"Because you had the guts to go against us before. And if you got the guts to do that, then maybe you can figure a way to solve this thing and get Palmer in the process."

He looked back towards the road. "Look, I ain't gonna stand here all day. There's a cut in those trees up there. Pull up there. If word gets out that I talked to you, I'll be in a world of hurt."

"Where do you want me to go?"

"Just pull forward a little more, into the trees. I'll pull my car next to yours."

I shrugged and did as he asked. His Crown Vic pulled behind my car. We were no longer visible from the road.

He got out and rounded the car, again from the back. This time he had his clipboard in front of him. I pulled the handle and opened the door. As I got out of the door he shuffled closer to me.

He held the clipboard out. "I know it's getting dark, but take a look at this."

I reached for the clipboard. Too late I saw the canister cupped in his left hand.

The pepper spray, or mace, or whatever the hell it was, caught me full in the face. I staggered backwards, trying to breathe and not being able to. My eyes were burning. I was blind.

His baton slammed into my stomach. I dropped to my knees, gagging, then threw up.

One of his hands grabbed my right arm and pinned it behind my back. A boot cracked into my back and pushed me flat. A rough hand dug into my right front pocket, pulling out my HK.

My left arm flailed and I twisted under the boot. That earned me a blow to my right kidney. Bile stung my nose as my face dug into the gravel. I was still gagging and choking.

Handcuffs ratcheted across my wrists, pulling my arms behind my back. Then the muzzle of the trooper's Glock pressed cold and hard against my right ear.

"Get up."

I didn't move.

The muzzle moved to the inside of my elbow.

"Get up, you son of a bitch, or I'll pull the trigger and take your arm off."

His free hand pulled up on the inside of my right tricep. He wasn't strong enough to pull me up by himself. He grunted as I pushed my knee forward and stood. My body was shaking.

"Walk." He pushed the Glock's muzzle into my kidney. The pain nearly doubled me over. My vision was reduced to a narrow slit of dim light. He pushed and I shuffled. The gravel turned into dead leaves. We walked a minute or two. The leather soles of my shoes lost traction. I fell, nearly taking him down with me.

"Fine, then." He kicked me again, this time in the stomach. I doubled over again, heaving.

Silence.

My breathing was ragged. So was his.

Crunching sound of a plastic bottle being squeezed. A boot shoved my shoulder, rolling me face up.

Water poured down on my eyes and mouth. I gagged again, trying to breathe, swallowed some, then coughed and spit as it went down the bronchial passage.

My vision began to clear. Which was what he wanted.

The Wilson County fiasco was coming to a head. These guys truly hate me.

He dropped the empty plastic bottle on my face. "You really ain't that smart, are you?"

I took a short breath, coughed again. "No." The word wheezed out of my throat.

I shook my head to clear the water from my eyes, then squinted to make out my surroundings. We'd gone maybe a hundred yards into the woods. Green leaves were silhouetted against the yellow-red of the early evening sky.

"You had some bad things happen to you when you was a kid, didn't you?"

I lifted my head off the ground, straining my neck to look at him.

He poked me with his boot. "Asked you a question, boy."

I stiffened. "How...?"

"Out in California, wasn't it?"

I didn't answer.

"California. Land of left-wing hippy faggots. Should've stayed there." He surveyed the surrounding woods, then dropped to his bulk down, closer to my face.

"How? You asked me how? How I know?" He chuckled. "You remember a little girl named Misty Carver?"

This confirmed it. The Wilson County case.

"You and that professor of yours pissed off every law enforcement officer in the country on that case. Cracking a sealed juvenile record in another state wasn't nothing." He scratched the stubble on his fleshy cheek. "You got some suffering to do." He smiled. "Suffering like you had before at that day care. Only in this case, I ain't sleeping later, and you ain't gonna kill me with my own gun. Even if they was a bad man and a bad woman."

My skin went white. Edvard Munch. The Scream.

"Shame how your daddy's drinking problem got worse after that. Bet your father won't never forgive himself for causing that crash that killed her. I bet he's even still drinkin' and driving, isn't he?" He laughed. "Ain't it funny how one bad thing just ripples out and destroys an entire family? You and me, we see it every day in our work. All it takes is one bad thing, like breaking the leg of a table. And then the whole family falls down."

He paused, glancing around the woods. "But don't worry, boy. You'll be with your momma directly."

Tears rolled down my cheek at the mention of her. I closed my eyes.

He poked me again, this time with his hand. "Goddamn it, boy. I'm talking to you. You *will* look at me when I talk to you."

I struggled to open my eyes, then glared at him.

"Now tell me you're sorry." He pointed his pudgy finger at me.

I closed my eyes again.

"Stupid scientist. What's it going to take to teach you some southern manners?" He reached back to his pocket and pulled out the spray canister again.

"Sorry. I'm sorry."

He paused, canister in his hand. It was a commercial pepper spray, the kind sold in retail stores, not the more potent mix that state troopers were issued.

The other mix could be traced back to the highway patrol.

He was going to kill me.

"I asked you a question, boy. You remember Misty Carver?" He kept the canister out.

"Yes."

"Yes what?"

I coughed. "Yes, sir."

"Good boy. And you remember who she killed, don't you?"

"Yes, sir."

He threw the can of pepper spray at me and pulled his Glock out of the holster. He kneeled on my chest and jammed the gun hard against my knee.

"The hell you say. You say their names, you lying prick. You can't, I'm pulling this trigger right now. Then I'm moving to your elbows."

He pushed the gun harder against my kneecap.

"Gerald Connor and Les Mundy," I said.

His face went slack. The Glock eased off my knee.

"I agreed with you guys." It was the truth. "Peckem testified, but I didn't agree with him. I knew it was murder. I knew it was deliberate. That's why they didn't put me on the stand."

His face fell. "You're lying."

"It's the truth. You all judged me guilty because of my professor. Not one of you stopped to think about why they didn't ask me to testify." I coughed hard. "I'll never forget their names."

Or the names of the other people who haunted me, whose remains I had to sift through in the vehicles in which they died.

Death walked with me in my job. Things had gone wrong early in my life. I'd been living in fear since then. It was comforting to think that it would be over.

But the thought of being violated again was worse than death.

He stood up, keeping his eyes on me. Backed away two steps. The Glock was limp in his right hand. He rubbed his forehead with his left hand.

My HK was stuffed in his waistband, nearly hidden by the stomach fat that drooped over it. He holstered the Glock, then pulled out a small bag of powder. He dipped something in it, held it up to his nostril, and snorted.

Something was on the ground between us. It hadn't been a baton that he'd hit me with, it was a broken broomstick handle. A bolt of fear shot through my heart.

"Don't matter," he said. He pinched his nose and inhaled, then tucked the bag back in his pocket and pulled out the handcuff keys. "This is business. Now stand up."

I struggled to my feet.

"Turn around," he said. "Walk toward that poplar tree."

I did so. It was mid-growth, about a foot in diameter.

He bent, picked up the broomstick, and tossed it near my feet.

Suffering. Like before.

A key scraped in the cuffs. The metal slid off my left wrist. He put his hand on my back, but I turned around, my back to the tree.

"Don't turn around, goddamn it." The trooper drew his Glock again and rammed it against my chest, pushing my back against the tree. He pressed the gun hard against my sternum with his right hand and pocketed the keys with his left.

He pressed hard enough to leave a bruise.

Hard enough to push the slide of the gun back a little.

His left hand reached out to grab my shoulder and spin me around.

My trembling stopped.

Rob's words: No one can react faster than you can act.

I was ready to go, anyway.

The move was quick and violent, just the way Rob had taught me.

I pushed my sternum into the muzzle of the Glock, hard. The muzzle moved rearward, keeping the slide out of battery just as he reacted to my movement. His eyes opened wide and he pulled the trigger.

The gun did not fire.

My left hand clamped down on the rear of the gun, curling my fingers around the top of the slide to keep it out of battery. I twisted away from the muzzle, bringing my right palm upwards, slamming it against the right side of the Glock, locking his hand on it and rotating the muzzle away from me as he tried to jerk his hand back and pull the trigger again. The empty handcuff attached to my right wrist slapped against his face. He jerked his head back involuntarily, teetering backwards, off balance. My right hand curled around the barrel and slide of the gun, using it as a lever, wrenching it toward him.

He grunted like a pig. His left hand clawed at mine, but I was stronger.

My left hand let the slide forward into battery. My right hand pushed the muzzle under his chin just as I jammed my fingers into the trigger guard, pressing his own finger back.

The shot was deafening.

His right eye bulged out of the orbit, like a soft-boiled egg cracked through with tiny red lines from burst blood vessels. Blood leaked behind it. The back of his skull and the sweaty, thin, matted hair over it flapped upward briefly from the exit of the hollow-point bullet.

Blood and brain matter spattered behind him, falling on the leaves like a gentle rain. Red mist hung behind his head like a halo before dissipating like fog in bright sunshine.

Overloaded knees buckled. His body collapsed and crumpled to the ground. Dead hands pulled the Glock from my grasp. It thumped onto the body armor covering his rotund chest under his tan shirt.

I stood frozen. My hearing was muffled, as if my ears were stuffed with cotton. It was gradually subsiding and being replaced with a high-pitched ringing as the cilia in my inner ear recovered from the pressure wave of the gunshot.

Seconds crawled by.

I was glad he was dead.

Think.

I checked my hands. No blood.

My shirt was a mess, but not with any of his blood.

There would be gunshot residue on my hands. And possibly on my shirt.

The ground was hard, not moist. My shoes were leather-soled. They left no tracks in the dirt or ground cover.

Think.

I checked my pockets. Everything was there.

The black plastic grip of my HK poked out of his waistband. I knelt, pulled it out carefully, and instinctively did a press-check of the round in the chamber.

Think, damn it.

I pulled out the tail of my shirt and wiped down the Glock's slide and Palmer's fingernails.

There had been no car noise up to the shot.

I picked up the broken broomstick handle and the can of pepper spray, cursing Palmer's body on the ground. I resisted the urge to empty the magazine of my gun into him. And empty the remainder of the bullets in his gun into him.

Hard to explain that as a suicide.

Sudden emotion overcame me. My body wracked with each sob, more tears pouring down my face. My chest tightened as if a steel band were being cinched around it.

I cried for several seconds.

Rage still burned inside me. I wanted to tear his body apart.

Breathe. Slowly. Keep thinking.

His handcuffs were still locked on my right hand, saturated with my sweat and skin cells and some blood. They had to disappear.

The handcuff keys were in his pocket. I couldn't risk leaving my DNA on his body to dig them out. But how can missing handcuffs be explained?

I caught a glimpse of chrome in the handcuff case of his belt. Simple: he hadn't used his duty handcuffs, either.

My breathing was steadying. I snapped the open bracelet of the cuffs just above the one that was still tightly locked around my wrist. They hurt, but I could still use my fingers and thumb. And I wasn't bleeding. I pulled my shirtsleeves down, stretching the fabric over the metal cuffs, then smoothed out my shirt and tucked it back in my pants. It was dirty and wet. I'd need to change before being seen by anyone.

I backtracked through the woods, straining to hear any activity.

Nothing.

I reached the treeline. Our cars were dark, silhouetted in the rapidly fading twilight.

Latex gloves were in the Pelican case in the trunk of my car. I drew a pair on.

The clipboard lay face up next to my car. It was still readable in the remaining light but I drew my flashlight and cupped the beam. Entries for three vehicle license plates were listed on the sheet from prior stops. Mine was not written down.

His THP cruiser was behind me, blocking me in. It was unlocked. He hadn't planned on being gone long.

The interior light stayed off as I opened the door of his cruiser. His hat filled the front window, hanging by the brim on the camera underneath the rear-view mirror. He'd placed it there to prevent the camera from recording footage of my car when he stopped me.

My fingers brushed against the steering column, meeting the jangle of keys. I ran each key through shaky fingers, searching for a handcuff key. No luck.

I started the Crown Vic and moved it back far enough to free my own car, then drove it further into the treeline.

His voice recorder was on the passenger seat. So were his badge and nametag, upside down. I reached in and flipped it over.

The letters were black lines engraved in shiny gold.

PALMER.

CHAPTER 10

I placed the clipboard on the seat, over his badge and nametag. Nothing else looked out of place. I hit the button to open the trunk, then got back out and opened the rear door, looking for any clue that could link this car to me.

The radio crackled. I jumped. They'd be looking for him soon.

I closed the door, went to the trunk. The sound of an approaching car caused me to run for the far side of the Crown Victoria. Even though the Crown Vic and my Mercedes were obscured from the road, I waited for it to pass, then went back to the trunk.

It opened easily. The trunk light came on, dimly illuminating the contents of the trunk: road flares, measuring wheel, tire iron, and a plastic box full of forms and papers. I reached for the corner of the trunk carpet and pulled it up, shining my little flashlight on the spare tire underneath. A compact jack and another lug wrench framed the tire. Nothing else of interest.

I dropped the trunk carpet. A canvas bag with the Tennessee Highway Patrol emblem on it was tucked in the corner of the trunk, barely visible. I reached for it. A tag was sewn on the side: PALMER - TROOP 6.

Intuition from years of inspecting wrecked cars and trucks urged me towards it. The top part was packed with empty ammunition boxes for .40 caliber pistol rounds. I dug deeper. My hands met a plastic grocery bag.

My heart was racing. Every tiny noise emanating from the night made me glance back over my shoulder. Part of me was terrified of seeing Palmer, eye bulging from his orbit and scalp flapping with each limping step, slowly creeping toward me from the maw of the black woods where I left his body.

I fought the panic away. The bastard was dead. And the world was a better place for it.

I unwrapped the plastic bag.

A bundle of stacked bills came out first. Ben Franklin's face smirked up at me in the shadows of the trunk.

Next came a tightly wrapped plastic bag of what appeared to be crystal methamphetamine. Then a smaller clear bag of fine powder, probably cocaine.

Taped to the underside of the large bag of crystal methamphetamine was a note. I held it near the trunk light to read it.

> Plant the coke. Use the broomstick. Make him suffer. Don't screw it up like J&L did. Get this right and you'll have Brit and Jen tonight.

Handwritten, hard to read. Different handwriting from the one that had been left on my car.

A marimba ringtone split the night. I jerked back, startled, expecting to see Palmer looming over me.

My phone was ringing. I reached down, turned the switch to silent. Nothing else of interest was in the trunk. I'd only been there for a few minutes, but it felt like an hour. I had to get moving.

I stared at the stack of money.

It could solve a lot of my problems.

The money was dirty. I didn't know how much it totaled. Twenty thousand? Fifty thousand? I'd never asked my bank teller for a couple inches of hundreds.

Enough to finish paying for school, for certain.

It's dirty. But Jesus, I needed it.

I peeled the note off the bag of methamphetamine and stuck it on the bills, then put the stack of money inside my shirt. I put the drugs back in the grocery bag, then put the grocery bag back in the canvas bag, under the empty ammo boxes. I started to put the canvas bag back where I'd found it, then had a second thought.

I moved to the passenger door, opened it, and placed the canvas bag on the front passenger seat. I dumped the ammo boxes on the floor and pulled the plastic bag of drugs back out, leaving it in plain view. Then I pulled the key out of the ignition, dropped it on the driver's floor mat, and locked the car doors manually.

I transferred the money, the pepper spray, and the broken broomstick into my backpack in the trunk of my car. I climbed back in my car and pulled across the gravel carefully, avoiding mud and dirt that would leave imprints of my tires. The road was empty, and I turned onto it heading back to the city.

I would not be heading home.

If they'd come after me, they might go after Allison again. I dialed her number.

"How are-?" My voice was loud and shaky. My throat was raw. I coughed and took a breath. "Sorry, Allison. How are you holding up?" I asked her.

"Still nervous," she said. "I can't believe what happened today. You okay? You sound strained."

"I guess I'm still a little nervous, too," I said, although I was thinking of a different event. "The police are still there, right?"

"They are. I took them some biscuits and coffee a few minutes ago."

"That's good, that's good." I wasn't certain where to go with this, and I was silent for a moment, which Allison took as me working up some courage.

"I haven't eaten yet," she prodded. "You?"

"No," I said.

"Think you have time for dinner?"

Perfect. "Of course I do. Pick you up in an hour."

The hum of the V-8 beneath the hood of the Mercedes helped steady my nerves. My hands were welded to the leather rim of the steering wheel. When I wasn't looking straight ahead, I was looking in the rearview mirror, expecting to see flashing blue lights gaining on my car.

I dialed Ken's number. He answered on the last ring. "This is Ken."

"Hey, I need a favor." I checked the mirror again.

"Sure. Everything okay?"

"Yeah, yeah. I just had a minor car thing, and I'm filthy, and I'm on way to meet Chris's sister Allison for a late dinner. Can I stop by your mom's house and use the barn to clean up?"

"Why don't you just come on over here?" Meaning his house.

"I would, but I'm closer to your mom's place."

Pause. "You in trouble?"

Damn it. Ken and I were like brothers, and he knew every inflection of my voice. I tried to control it better.

"No, not at all. Just a little out of breath and a lot of dirty."

"You got your backpack? Need me to bring you anything?" He was referring to a backpack I keep in the trunk with a few day's worth of clean clothes. I'd learned to keep one in there the first time I'd been called away to work a heavy-truck crash that had turned into a three-day job.

"No, just call your mom and let her know I'll be out there."

"You sure everything is all right?"

"I'm fine. Just still a little shaken from what happened today."

"If someone has a gun to your head, say the word *tomorrow*."

"Ken, I'm fine. There's no gun at my head." A shiver went down my spine at how prescient my best friend was. "I just need to clean up, that's all."

Long pause. "Okay. I just got a weird feeling."

"Like the time you ate that undercooked burger from the university cafeteria?"

Ken finally laughed. "Don't remind me of that. Call me back if you need anything else."

~~~

The barn behind his mom's place was perfect.

I pulled up as close as I could to the doorway, then used my flashlight to illuminate the key under the sideboard. Once inside, I clicked on the main lights and dropped my backpack on the workbench.

Ken had to have a set of handcuff keys around here. And if he didn't, I'd find another way to get these damn bracelets off.

I went through the drawers of the workbench. Nothing in them but basic hand tools. Next were the small plastic bins of parts and other little fasteners. No keys there, either.

Time was becoming an issue, too. I didn't want to linger longer than necessary. If I ever became a suspect in Palmer's
~~~

death, I'd need to account for every minute of the night. And those minutes were adding up by the...minute.

There was a grinder on the end of the workbench. Redemption, in the form of a bench grinder.

I'd need to be careful, but it should work. The metal would get super hot by the friction of the grinding wheel, so I grabbed a bottle of water from the mini-fridge in the corner and doused a shop cloth. I snugged it between my wrist and the handcuff, then poured more cold water over the handcuffs and the skin of my wrist. I flipped the switch. The stone wheel of the grinder began spinning.

I grabbed the face shield from the peg on the backboard and snugged it on my head. Slowly, I advanced my wrist toward the grinder, bracing the back of the cuffs with my free hand.

The sound was loud as hell. A blast of sparks erupted from the wheel, showering all over my body and the face shield. Each spark was a tiny bit of steel that had been chipped away by the stone of the grinding wheel, and the friction of the grinding superheated the steel until the edges were smoking. Most of the sparks died out as they bounced off me, but a few dug in and stung my skin.

The grinding was also creating a lot of heat in the cuffs, too. I pulled away and poured the rest of the water in the bottle on my skin. The liquid sizzled and steamed on the cuffs.

This was going to hurt. I was only halfway through the thickness of the metal. I'd have some serious burns to explain later.

I approached the grinder again. My teeth were gritted.

In my peripheral vision, the door of the barn opened.

Shit. I jerked my arm away and tore off the face shield. It bounced on the workbench. My sopping wet right hand reached for the HK as I darted towards the rear quarter-panel of the nearest Oldsmobile 442.

It could be Ken's mom, wondering if I was okay. But if someone had followed me, and they were here to finish the job, this time I'd be shooting first.

I trained the front sight of the HK on the barn door. The bench grinder kept whirring.

I trained the front sight on the doorway. My finger slid inside the trigger guard, taking up the slack of the trigger.

The muzzle of a Glock appeared around the edge of the doorway, identical to the one Palmer had used. My stomach turned. It couldn't be. It couldn't be. He's dead. They're all dead. They can't come back.

And then Ken's head became visible as he slowly sliced the pie around the doorframe, increasing his viewing angle into the room.

"Soren?" he called out.

"Here. I'm over here." I took my finger off the HK and lowered it slightly.

Ken poked his head a little further into the barn, the Glock still locked out in front of him, tracking for targets. His eyes met mine.

"It's just me, Ken. I'm okay."

He studied me. "Like hell you're okay. You didn't get that messed up from changing a tire."

I dropped the HK down to waist level, slid it back in my pocket, and tried to keep my right arm slightly behind me. "You can't be a part of this. Trust me. Just turn around and leave. I'll be okay."

His eyes focused on my right arm. "What happened to your wrist?"

"Ken. Listen to me. You don't want to know. You can't know."

Ken holstered his Glock. "You made me a part of this when you came here. I might as well be all in. Is it that bad?"

"Worse."

"Let's hear it."

"A Tennessee Highway Patrolman tried to kill me tonight. He maced me, then handcuffed me, then was going to sodomize me with a broken broomstick before murdering me." I paused to let it sink in.

Ken's jaw dropped.

"How...?"

"He pulled me over in that wooded area off Asheville Highway. Just after the state park." I stepped out from behind the Oldsmobile.

"He cuffed you?" Ken asked.

I held out my right arm.

"Both on one wrist?" He stepped forward to inspect the handcuffs.

"No. He unlocked the left one and told me to put my arms around a tree."

Ken looked back up at me. "And you're standing here, which means you got away. And you didn't have a chance to unlock the other cuff. Which means that he still has the keys. And he's probably looking for you to finish the job."

"He's dead."

Ken's jaw dropped again. He backed up a step. "You killed a cop?"

"Not exactly." I rubbed my face with my left hand. "He shot himself with his own gun. His hand, his finger on the trigger."

"You convinced him to commit suicide?"

I shrugged. "Something like that. Ken, he was dirty. I found a pound of crystal meth and bag of cocaine in the trunk of his car."

"It was probably confiscated." Ken rubbed his scalp. "Soren, I'll stand behind you, but you're going to need to talk to an attorney."

I went to my backpack and pulled the stack of cash from it, along with the broomstick and pepper spray. I put them on the workbench. "Read the note on it."

Ken looked at me as if I'd pulled a rabbit out of a hat. He walked over to the bench, shut the grinder off. He looked at the broomstick and pepper spray, then picked up the stack and read the note.

"Who's J and L?" he asked me.

"I don't know."

Ken put the stack on the workbench. "Did you count it?"

"I haven't had the luxury yet." I held up my right arm.

Ken walked back over to me. He studied the cuffs, then pulled out his own keys. "I thought you said he was a trooper."

"He was."

"These cuffs are made by Thompson. THP uses Smith & Wesson."

"I told you, he was planning on killing me. He didn't use his issue spray, either."

Ken tossed the handcuffs on the bench next to the money. "What was his name?"

"Palmer." I rubbed my wrist with the wet cloth. "The same guy who worked Chris Cameron's crash."

"That's not a coincidence. And this isn't about the Wilson County incident."

I nodded. "You wanted to know. And now that you do, you can't unlearn it. What happens now?"

Ken exhaled loudly. "Someone will find Palmer. There'll be an autopsy."

"That'll show he had drugs in his system. He snorted something to work up the nerve to kill me."

Ken turned to face me. "Are you positive that nothing links you to his death? Tire tracks? Prints on his gun?"

I shook my head. "I wore gloves when I checked out his car, and we were parked on gravel. Palmer hung his hat on his camera and didn't record pulling me over."

"There's one more thing," Ken said. He pointed at the money.

"I know." I looked at the ground. "You don't think I should keep it, do you?"

"Doesn't matter what I think. It's what you can live with."

"He was going to plant it on my body anyway. So he was going to give it to me, in a way."

Ken didn't smile. "Soren, that much cash wasn't to frame you. He was carrying it for someone. Probably to be laundered. Palmer was probably the only guy Harrell has enough dirt on to prevent shrinkage."

"Shrinkage?"

"Think of it as frictional losses. Like thermodynamics. Whenever a sum of money gets handled by criminals, a little bit of it is lost. The more criminal hands touch it, the more that gets lost."

We stared at the stack.

"You want it?" I asked.

Ken shook his head. "Hell, no. And put it away. It's making me nervous."

I returned the money to my backpack.

Ken turned to leave. "You really have a date with Allison now?"

"Yes. And I need to get cleaned up." I started unbuttoning my shirt.

Ken opened the door and stepped out, then poked his head back through the doorway. "One more thing."

I smiled. "You'd help me hide the body?"

"No. But take Allison to the Summit Street Diner. That's where all the cops go, and it'll help your credibility if..." Ken's words trailed off.

I nodded. "If I become a suspect."

~~~

We followed the hostess to a booth near the window. Ken wasn't kidding about the cops. I'd counted more uniforms than civilians as we walked.

Allison studied me. "You're trembling. And you're white as a ghost."

I jerked my hands back, massaging them. "Just stress. School."

She cocked an eye at me, but let it go.

We ordered. Allison slid the menus out of the way. "What's this Wilson County incident? Is it why THP hates you?"

"Among other things. But yes, it's why they hate me."

"Can you talk about it?"

I looked out the window and rubbed my chin, thinking about Palmer.

"About a year ago, a twenty-three year old girl was released from a Kentucky state prison. Busted for crack possession. She'd been in and out of Elkinridge as a minor."

Allison nodded. "Over near Memphis. Bad place."

I cocked an eyebrow. "You've been there?"

"Of course not." She rolled her eyes. "But a girl from my high school was sent there."

I flexed my fingers, trying to stop the trembling. "The first thing she does when she gets back to Knoxville is score some drugs. She went on a crack binge with some old friends. One of the kids had driven his dad's Mercedes there. This girl needs a car, so she trades him some cocaine and a couple of sexual favors for the Mercedes."

"A Mercedes like yours?"

"Smaller than mine. Hers was an E-class."

"Don't tell me you got yours the same way she did," she smiled.

That made me smile. Being here, with her, was helping me.

"Not quite. I had to un-wad the rear end and weld mine back together. Her way was lot less work, though."
~~~

"Anyway. So she gets the car..."

"And she picks up her girlfriend. Then they head down to Lonsdale to score some more crack."

The waitress came over. We ordered.

I resumed the story. "They're sitting in the car getting high when a KPD cruiser pulls up behind them. He tells them to exit their vehicle, and the girl panics. She's been out of prison less than two days. She puts the car in reverse, floors it, and crashes into the front of his car. Then she tears out of there. He tries to chase her, but she got lucky and pierced his radiator, so he drops out of the pursuit."

"She got away?"

"No. It gets worse." I pushed the menus out of the way. "You sure you want to hear this?"

"I can handle it. I want to know why they're so mad at you."

"She can't outrun a police radio, so eventually a few other cops spot her. She gets on I-40 heading west, towards Nashville. Then THP gets in the mix. She floors it and outruns them."

"What? How?"

"Her car was faster. Her Mercedes could top out around one-sixty. The cops had underpowered and overweight Crown Vics loaded with gear. And they had to contend with the mayhem she was causing ahead of them. She caused a few wrecks along the way."

"How far did she make it?"

"All the way to Nashville."

Allison's jaw dropped. "Nashville? They couldn't stop her for a hundred and eighty miles?"

"They tried. THP would radio ahead for troopers to lay down a spike strip, but the guys with the strip had to wait for traffic to clear before they put it on the road. They don't want an innocent driver to run over it and lose control. Normally there would be a car ahead of the suspect, but she was going too fast. They couldn't get a car on the road between her and other traffic."

"For three hours they couldn't do it?"

I shook my head. "It wasn't three hours. She made it to Wilson County in about an hour."

"My God. She was flying."

"You bet. Those Mercedes are designed for autobahns. Long distance running at high speeds."

"How'd they finally stop her?"

"Ten miles outside of Nashville, a couple of officers had a chance at stopping her. They were far enough ahead, but they only had one spike strip. You know what I mean by a spike strip?" I asked her.

She nodded. "Blow the tires."

"Exactly, but it isn't like the movies. The strip is big and heavy and sharp. Not easy to deploy. It comes in a plastic case, folded up, and it has to be carried out into the highway and pulled open like an accordion by two officers. They can't just run out there, either. They have to time it just right. They have to avoid getting hit by regular highway traffic, and get the strip out there just before the suspect comes into view.

"How wide is the strip?" Allison asked.

"It covers one lane."

"But the interstate is five lanes wide out there. Plus shoulders."

"Yeah. They have to wait until the last second to see which lane she's in. Turns out she was in the fast lane. They had to run across one shoulder and four travel lanes while she's racing towards them."

The waitress interrupted me with two chocolate milkshakes.

I unwrapped the straw in mine. "The thing is, this girl had been stopped by a spike strip before. Her previous jail stint was for running from police in a stolen car in Kentucky."

"Seriously?'"

I nodded. "Anyway, it later came out in court that she was quoted as saying that she knew what they were doing and they wouldn't stop her that way again. Now, as you approach the area where the officers were laying out the strip, the sight distance, or the total line of sight distance from you to them, is nearly seventeen hundred feet."

Allison held up a hand. "Doesn't help me."

"Almost six football fields long."

"Okay," she said. "So she could see them a long way off."

"Yes. So, even though the Mercedes flew down the interstate at one hundred and sixty mph, or two hundred and thirty-five feet every second, she had nearly seven seconds to see them and what they were doing and then decide what to do about it. That's when she slowed down a little and decided to aim for the cops."

Allison covered her mouth. "Oh, no. They couldn't get out of the way before she got to them?"

"They did get out of the roadway. That's the point of the murder charge. She hit them when they were in the shoulder area. She had four open travel lanes to bypass the spike strip, and she aimed at them and the squad car on the shoulder. They were both running. One of them made it to the shoulder area between the slow lane and the merge lane, and the other was on the shoulder trying to make it back to their car."

"How did she kill them?"

"She struck the first one with the left front of the car so hard that his body crushed the front fender into the left front tire. He died immediately. The impact severed his body in two pieces. His upper torso and his legs were thrown forward three hundred feet."

Allison paled.

"You sure you want to hear this?" I asked.

"Keep going." Quiet voice.

"In less time than a normal person could react, she then struck the other officer with the right front of the car. The impact was severe enough to send his body through the air for nearly two hundred feet. He landed on the grassy bank on the side of the interstate. His shirt and pants were ripped off his body. Then she continued on and rammed the Mercedes into the cruiser so hard that the car was bent into a U-shape when viewed from above."

"Did the girls die?"

I shook my head. "No justice that day. As the pursuing police cruisers got on the scene, and their windshield mounted video cameras were recording the event, you could see the doors of the Mercedes swing open. Then the girls rolled out of the car. They both had sense enough to buckle up before the impact. They walked away with minor injuries."

"They put their seatbelts on?"

"Yeah," I said. "I was at the trial, and I heard the accounts firsthand from the girl and the officers. The girlfriend testified that the when the driver saw the spike strips, she told her girlfriend to buckle up because this was going to hurt."

"Oh, God."

"I saw the same video. The officer that came up on them had his gun out and a perfect sight picture. Hard not to pull the trigger, but he didn't."

Allison was silent. I glanced over. Her eyes were wide open.

Our food arrived. There was a moment of silence before I reached for my burger.

"So how did all this involve you?" She reached for the ketchup.

"Well, in a court of law this girl was entitled to a defense. Being indigent, this defense had to be provided by the state. And in this defense, a crash reconstructionist will be required."

"Okay."

"The extent of the analysis is pretty much what I explained before about how much time she had to see the officers and then decide what to do. And the fact that she slowed down from one-sixty to around ninety, and that she nailed both officers, tells me that she was aiming for them. She had time to perceive the situation, react to the situation, decide on a course of action, and execute that course of action."

"Seven seconds is enough for that?" she asked.

"Absolutely. The average person requires about one-point-five to two seconds to perceive and then react to a developing situation. It's like sitting at a red light. If you're not watching the light like a hawk, then it'll be about a second and a half for you to see the light change and then react to it by taking your foot off the brake and press the accelerator."

"Seven seconds is long enough for what you say she did, though?"

She was serious, so I stopped. "Look into my eyes. I'm going to count to seven. Don't blink or move, just keep looking in my eyes."

She put her burger down and our eyes met.

"Okay, go."

I counted slowly in thousands. By the time I reached seven, it felt like an eternity had passed.

"That's seven," I whispered.

"That did seem like a long time," she said.

I tilted my head at her.

"No, really, I can see that now." Her expression grew more serious. "So what next?"

"So, the state counsel needs a reconstructionist for her. I couldn't fathom who would argue that she had no time to decide where to steer her car. And in the open lanes she had available to her, it is awful coincidental that she chose to steer all the way over into the shoulder that was occupied by men trying to run away from her. And this is pretty much what the state-appointed defense counsel found as they called every reconstructionist in the state of Tennessee to work on her defense."

"Until they called Peckem."

"Exactly," I said, nodding. "I still remember the telephone conversation when he called me about possibly taking the case."

"So he talked to you about it? What did you tell him?"

"I told him he was nuts. He believed she was entitled to a fair defense, and still does. And I agree with him on that. I've worked cases where the law was unfairly trying to put someone under the jail. But that's where the agreement ends. The truth is that it was a high-profile case, and it gave him a chance to get his name in the news. His opinion was that she didn't have enough time to react, and steering towards the officers wasn't intentional."

We dug into our burgers. "Did Chris ever take you out in his car and drive fast?" I asked.

"When he first got it he took me for a drive, and he picked me up in it a few times, but not like what you're talking about."

"This girl made it through traffic from Knoxville to Nashville at twice the speed limit without running into anyone, and that's a good indication she was watching the road. And anyone who's driven near those speeds on a wide-open, flat highway will tell you that your knuckles are white because you are actively *looking* for objects in the distance at that speed. And the more sight distance you have, the more time you have to react, and she could see them a long way off."

"I can see why they don't like Dr. Peckem." She held her burger over her plate as ketchup dripped from the back. "But why do they hate you?"

This is tough. "Grad students are like indentured servants. Major professors exert enormous leverage over their student's work. They can make life miserable for a student in a heartbeat. Peckem knew I was going to Nashville every couple weeks to do research at Eskind Medical Library at Vanderbilt, so he asked me to stop by the crash site and take a measurement of a lane line right before the trial began. I didn't want to upset him, and I thought I could do it quick enough that I wouldn't arouse suspicion from officers in the area. Before I was able to get back in the car, though, a Wilson County deputy stopped and did everything short of arrest me. Then my name came up in the courtroom at trial."

"Oh, God."

"Yeah, the prosecuting DA tried to use me being out there as an example that Peckem hadn't done his own work on the case. But my own opinion on the matter didn't count because no one ever heard it. I was branded as the bad guy along with Peckem, and ever since then THP has had us in their crosshairs."

"And then my family calls you up and almost gets you killed by someone else."

I stiffened. "You mean Johnny?"

Allison tilted her head. "Of course I mean Johnny." She studied me closer. "Soren, has anything else happened? Your eyes are awful red. And you've got some scratches near your ear."

"No." If she only knew about tonight. "Allison, I'm still breathing."

She didn't laugh. "I feel so bad about this."

"That's what Judith said. Look, don't beat yourself up over this." I searched for levity. "I can honestly say that this is the most exciting case I've ever worked on."

"We almost got you killed." She wouldn't look at me.

My body didn't want to move. I forced it. I dropped my burger and slid out of the booth. She glanced up at me as I sat down and slid next to her. I closed the distance and our bodies met. The heat of her body pushed through my clothes.

She looked over at me. Tears filled her eyes.

"Hey," I said. I forced my arm to move. My right hand went around her and pulled her close. She turned to me and slid her arms around me, burying her head against my neck. Her tears cascaded down my neck and onto my chest. My eyes welled up, too.

I fought back the urge to leave. I whispered softly to her, searching for the right words to ease her pain. This was about

Chris and not me but I didn't say anything about that. I waved the waitress off and held her for a long time.

CHAPTER 11

Early Thursday morning.

"You don't look so good," Dwayne Matthews said.

We were sitting in his office in the Anderson County courthouse building. An American flag was in one corner and a United States Marine Corps flag was in the other, next to Matthew's honorable discharge certificate.

Matthews was in his sixties, a few inches shorter than me, and heavier. Wavy grey hair made him resemble Burgess Meredith. Greyish-blue eyes matched his hair.

The laceration on my temple was noticeable, but it was the dark spots under my eyes that betrayed my condition.

"Busy couple of days," I said. Three hour's sleep, too. "I'm okay. Hoo-ah. Let's get this over with." I sipped my coffee.

He knew I was stretched thin. But he nodded.

"Okay." Matthews picked up the report I'd written about Chris's crash. "They agreed to a bench hearing."

"Why would they do that?" I arched an eyebrow.

"Prejudice," Matthews said. "There's no way we can find a jury here that wouldn't know of Johnny's background, and they think they'll get a better shot if there's only a judge to hear the case."

"Who's the judge?" I asked.

"Ron Bailey," he said. "He has a daughter named Kelly. Know her?"

Steve was right. Somehow Kelly's father had gotten the slot.

"Not personally." I shifted in my chair, suddenly uncomfortable. "Are you sure he's the correct judge for the trial?"

Matthews ignored my question. "Steve tells me you've testified before?"

"Several times. State and Federal."

"Criminal trials?"

"Nearly all civil."

He pursed his lips. "Things can get downright vicious in the criminal venue."

"Tell me about it."

He smiled. "Yeah, I guess you know that."

"Do you think they'll have an expert of their own?"

Matthews shook his head. "They haven't declared one, but they could always spring one on us. It would be highly unusual. They'll have one for the trial, but probably not for the hearing."

"Less to worry about for me," I nodded.

"Me, too." He nodded, then frowned. "When I filed the charges, I had planned on calling Palmer as a witness to testify to what he saw that night, and about how Johnny was the person who called it in. Now, with what's happened, I only have the evidence you've uncovered in your report."

I arched an eyebrow. "What happened?"

Matthews narrowed his eyes. "Palmer killed himself yesterday."

"Are you serious?" This was taking effort.

Matthews nodded. "Bag of undocumented meth and coke in his car, too. It's been all over the local news. You haven't heard?"

"No. You think he was dirty?"

"Looks that way." Matthews grimaced.

"What about using the crash report in his place?"

"It's still not admissible in his absence. Can't use that either."

I tried to express the right amount of curiosity. "It sounds like there's more to the story there."

Matthews nodded gruffly.

"What about the paramedics that responded to the call?" I asked.

"They can only be fact witnesses. They can testify that Chris had rigored upside down, and that he'd been there a while. But you're going to need to explain how Johnny's car knocked Chris's car off the road, and that he left the scene of a crash. And you'll need to do your best to show that Johnny had a faster car, which gives us intent to make Chris wreck."

My hands began trembling again. I held them in my lap, out of sight.

Matthews grimaced. “It’s always best to have an officer on the stand,” he said. “We can get past the hearing, but when it comes to a jury trial, I may have to re-think the strategy.” He flipped through my report. “I think there’s enough evidence to make the manslaughter charge stick. But it’ll be on your shoulders to convince the judge.”

~~~

The politically correct term for the Anderson County courthouse was ‘historic’. Century-old hardwood floors blended into mid-sixties linoleum at the building seams where more space had been added on. There were metal detectors at the front doors, and a guard with a wand blessing everyone who made it through the metal detector frame.

“Why the redundancy?” I asked Matthews.

“It’s an old building. Lots of outages lately. It’s getting upgraded, though.”

We walked down the hall. There was another metal detector frame outside the courtroom doors as well.

“Back in a minute,” Matthews said. “Wait here.”

I took a seat on a hallway bench near the men’s room. Sleep begged me to close my eyes.

An older man in a charcoal suit rounded the corner. Gray hair slicked back in a ducktail. Penetrating eyes swept over me. He walked further into the hall. Polished black cowboy boots clicked on the floor as he approached me.

“Hell of a nice day outside. Shame to waste it in here, going through these motions.” His voice had a dirty roughness, as if he took his whisky poured over gravel instead of ice.

“It is nice outside. But it’s going to be another hot one.” As an expert witness, it was not a good idea for me to talk to people in the building, but I tried not to be rude.

“Not as hot as in there.” He jerked a thumb toward the courtroom doors.

“I’m a friend of the Camerons. Steve and I grew up on the same road.” He took a seat on my left, on the bench, closer than comfortable. “Pretty much family.”
~~~

"Okay." I slid closer to the end of the bench, opening up some distance between us.

"Damn shame to have to be here," he repeated. "You the scientist from the university that worked this horrible crash?"

"I don't mean to be rude, but I can't discuss the case." I crossed my left ankle onto my right knee to buffer the space.

He nodded. "I understand. But I know who you are. I guess this is a workday for you, then, ain't it?"

I looked over at him. His features looked vaguely familiar. Sharp nose, hard jawline.

He scratched the stubble on his chin. "Not for me. I'm losing money just to be here. Can't miss it, though."

"Evidently no one else can, either. Half the county is in the courtroom already."

He laughed. "That'll give a person stagefright, now, won't it? Or maybe you're used to it, what with all the testifying you do, this being your work and all. How much you make in this racket?"

"Not as much as you think." Sweat beaded on my palms. I wiped them on my pants, hoping they wouldn't begin trembling again.

"Hell, I'm a businessman too. You could tell me. Say about fifteen thousand an hour?"

"Maybe in yen, not dollars. Not even close."

"How would you like to? Say fifty grand for the day, then you and me and everyone else can just get out of here and go home." The tone was jocular. He nudged me on my arm.

I jerked my head around. "What are you talking about?"

He smiled and lowered his voice. "You already took the money. I'm offering you a way to keep it. Trust me, you don't want to turn me down."

I glanced at him. His voice was still light but his eyes were dead flat. Chills went down my spine. The voice, the mannerisms. Familiar somehow.

This was Johnny's father.

My throat tightened.

"Son, I'm not the hillbilly hick you think I am. I've got a measure of intelligence and sophistication, and I'm a reasonable man."

I moved further down the bench, away from him, wishing Matthews would get back here fast. “Why are you telling me this?”

“Because this doesn’t have to be done the hard way. I’m a powerful person in these parts right now. In another few years, though, I’ll be a very powerful person in this state. I’d rather head this problem off now and save us both a lot of trouble.”

My stomach flipped. I couldn’t face him.

He leaned toward me. “Look, we both know how this works. You say what you’re paid to say. Ain’t nothing wrong with that, it’s the way life works. I’m just saying I understand that, and I’m a higher bidder.” He straightened up as a woman walked by.

“It’s not the way I work.”

“We’ll see. I been impressed with your work so far.” He cracked a smile. “How’d you do it, anyway?”

“Do what?”

“Son, you are piss-poor liar. How’d you get him to off himself?”

I shook my head. “I don’t know what you’re talking about.”

“Cut the shit. Hell, it makes me respect you. But I ain’t gonna hesitate to drop a hint to the DA about you if you won’t play ball.”

“And if I do play ball?” I asked.

“There’s more money where that came from,” he said, “in addition to not being implicated in a state trooper’s murder.”

“You said it was suicide.”

“Things can change.”

An old emotion was beginning to rise in me, replacing the fear. Anger.

I fought to control it. “I heard there were drugs found, not money.”

“That’s because *you* took the money.”

I shrugged. “Wouldn’t it be more fair to say that this money you lost was simply compensation for a severe beating and attempted murder?”

The man smirked. “That’s an interesting point of view. I told you I’m a reasonable man, so I could see it that way. But the money had a job to do. As long as the end result is the same, I don’t care who it goes to.”

I shook my head again. "I just don't think I've got the personal flaws to do this particular job."

"Oh, I think you do," he said. "And I think you're just holding out for more. Make me a counter offer. You got balls, son. It's hard not to like you."

"That's kind of you to say." I stood up. "But you aren't going to like this.

My testimony isn't purchased. It's based on the evidence I uncover in the case."

"Bullshit," he said.

"Then get your own expert. There's whores in every profession."

He grinned. "You got it backwards, son. Every profession is some kind of whoring. Some people are just better at making it seem real than others."

I turned around and began walking away.

"I gave you a chance," he said. "Don't forget that."

~~~

"All rise for the Honorable Ronald Bailey."

We all stood. My hand rested on the back of the wooden pew-bench to steady myself. Johnny was in a navy blue suit at the defense table on the right. His longish blonde hair had been slicked back against his head. Tom Gaines, his attorney, stood next to him. Taller, and with graying hair that matched his five-thousand-dollar suit. Next to Gaines was his paralegal, a tall, slender blonde in a designer skirt that rode halfway up her thighs.

Matthews was at the table on the right. An old, worn briefcase was open in front of him. Next to him was his legal assistant, a kid with thick glasses who couldn't have been more than twenty-five, wearing a brown double-breasted J.C. Penny special. It was obvious where the money was.

Johnny's dad was behind the defense table, directly behind his son. He was alone in the pew.

Allison was up front near Cathy and Steve in the benches behind the DA's table. The benches behind them were packed with the Cameron's family and friends. I had to turn my head to glimpse them. The benches on Johnny's side of the courtroom were nearly empty except for his father.
~~~

In spite of the trials I'd testified in before, this was my first hearing. There was no jury to appeal to. It would only be the judge to hear the arguments of the two attorneys and the testimony of the witnesses. Then it was in his hands to decide if the charges brought against Johnny were solid enough to warrant a full trial.

The judge came into the courtroom quietly. Tall and thin with a full beard and wire-rimmed glasses. He went up the steps to his chair loudly. He pulled his chair out with a flourish. The long wide sleeves of his black robe fluttered and he sat down without looking at us.

"All present in the matter of Tennessee versus Johnathan Earl Harrell?" he asked, reading from a folder on his desk.

"Yes, sir," each attorney answered.

The judge nodded curtly, then addressed the entire room. "At this time we are going to be taking up the preliminary hearing in the State of Tennessee versus Johnathan Earl Harrell, if I understand correctly. Are we invoking the rule on this, councilor?"

"No, sir. Witnesses can remain."

"Very well, then. Call your first witness."

"The People call Soren Graves."

My pulse raced faster. It always did. The adrenaline dump and caffeine helped chase away the fog of pain and lack of sleep.

Giving courtroom testimony was an intense exchange of words and intellectual strategy. It was my job to report the truth, the facts, and show how physical events happened. The attorney on my side was supposed to ask me the right questions to allow me to do this. That's called the direct examination and it's always smooth.

The opposing attorney, though, gets to do everything he can to ruin me, ruin my reputation, and try to discredit me so that the jury and judge won't believe the testimony I've just given. This is called the cross-examination. It's always an intense mental chess game where I have to think three steps ahead of the opposing attorney to keep myself out of his traps. He or she gets wide latitude in asking nearly any question they want, and they can ask it in the most aggressive and intimidating way they can, in order to throw the expert off-balance. Their goal is to destroy the expert on the stand.

Making matters worse is that the expert, in this case me, is *not* allowed to freely talk about the case. I can't ramble on about the details and all of the information I have. I can only talk about things that were disclosed in my deposition (in a civil trial, not criminal) or that the judge approved before the hearing with the two attorneys. The opposing attorney knows this and so will avoid areas that he or she knows would hurt their side, and they can focus on the points that only hurt me. If they slip and open the door by mentioning something that damages their side, I can run with it, if I recognize it. That's where an expert's skill comes in.

The cross-examination is like being in a fight where I have one hand tied behind my back and I'm not allowed to do anything but jab, while the opposing attorney is allowed to jab, punch, grab my hair, and kick me in the crotch as much as he or she wants.

I stood up from the hard wooden bench. All eyes swiveled toward me. Johnny and his father watched me as I walked past. Their gaze was cold, unemotional. I walked down the center aisle and opened the small wooden gate and stepped into the open court area. I glanced up to acknowledge the judge but he didn't look at me.

Johnny's father kept his gaze on me. He was expecting a favorable performance. But he'd be disappointed.

"If you would raise your right hand, sir," the bailiff said. He administered the oath and I took my seat in the witness box. Matthews got up from the table and walked towards me.

"Mr. Graves, would you tell us your name, please, for the record, and what your occupation is."

"My name is Soren Isaac Graves, and I reconstruct motor vehicle crashes."

"And what qualifications do you possess that enable you to do such work?"

"My formal education consists of a bachelor of science and a master of science in engineering and I will be graduating with my doctorate in engineering in December."

"And what is the research focus of your doctorate?" Matthews asked, studying the floor.

"I conducted thirty-one crash tests at varying speeds between two vehicles and then quantified the damage that was created by the impacts."

"So your degree is specifically concerned with car crashes?"

"Yes."

"And what about your master of science degree?"

"I worked at Oak Ridge National Laboratory to develop and evaluate new bullets for the United States Special Operations Command. My work was to design prototype bullets and shoot them into cadavers to see how they perform. The work grew out of the need to develop bullets that could be used in sensitive areas like nuclear control rooms and around nuclear weapons that would not damage equipment but would still penetrate soft body armor and incapacitate an adversary."

Johnny and his dad both looked up.

"And how does that relate to what you do now?"

"Bullets hitting tissue and cars hitting each other are both impacts, and the same physical equations apply to each analysis. They both involve the same principles of energy and momentum of engineering mechanics, which I also taught for many years at the University while working on my master of science and doctoral degrees."

"Okay. And are you still teaching those subjects?"

"I am."

I glanced at the judge. He was leaning back in his chair, watching me.

"And do you have any practical experience in dealing with car crashes?"

"Yes, sir. My first involvement began in high school when I worked in a body shop, painting and repairing wrecked cars, and that's how I paid for my undergraduate education. Because of my experience with cars my college professors hired me to assist them with their own crash investigations. Eventually I began taking cases on my own and I have been reconstructing crashes for the last decade as a private consultant."

"And do you hold any certifications?"

"I passed the eight-hour written exam to be accredited by the Accreditation Commission for Traffic Accident Reconstruction, and I am also a Ford and General Motors-certified automotive painter."

"Anything else?"

"I'm a state-certified firearms instructor, but that's not usually relevant to car crashes." I glanced at Chris's family, and

Judith and Allison smiled. Cathy sat close to Allison. Steve was a few feet down the bench, separated from the girls. He kept his eyes fixed on the back of Johnny's head. His hands rested on the short wooden divider that separated them from the open court area. His fingers were tapping so fast on the top surface that it looked like they were shaking.

"And have you been recognized as an expert in the area of vehicle crash reconstruction by prior courts?"

"Yes, sir. I've testified nine times in state court and three times in Federal court, and I've been through approximately fifty depositions."

"Okay," Matthews said. He paused, then walked back to the table and flipped through some notes. He turned back to the judge.

"Your Honor, we respectfully request that the court recognize Mr. Graves as an expert in the field of crash reconstruction."

"I think I'd like to hold off on that. Proceed with your direct," Bailey said.

What?

Matthews' expression mirrored my own. Those words had no basis to be uttered. The legal definition of an expert is someone who has specialized knowledge about a subject area. More so than an average person. That was me in spades. This was my job. To not be recognized by the court was literally a career-ending event. It only takes one to set a precedent, and then under the Daubert ruling, it was over for the expert in other courtrooms.

Matthews cleared his throat. "Your Honor, I don't mean to be argumentative, but Mr. Graves has clearly met the legal standard of being an expert in his field, and has been recognized as such numerous times before."

Bailey shot Matthews a glance that could have shattered stone. "Mr. Matthews, this is my courtroom, and I will be the judge of testimony here. I didn't say that I would not recognize Mr. Graves, I said I would wait until I've heard more of his testimony."

"Your Honor, that is highly unusual..."

"Mr. Matthews, I suggest you continue your direct."

Matthews blinked his eyes several times. He turned back to me.

"Mr. Graves, were you asked to reconstruct a particular crash last month involving the death of a young man named Chris Cameron?"

"Yes, sir." I leaned forward and adjusted the small microphone.

"And what did you do in your investigation?"

"I inspected and documented the site, the vehicle of the decedent, and then used engineering mechanics to reconstruct the kinematics of the event."

"And what did you learn in the course of your investigation?"

I cleared my throat. The opposing attorney was watching me intently. "I found evidence that the decedent was involved in a race against another vehicle at the time of the crash."

I swiveled to face the judge. "Your Honor, may I leave the stand and present my drawings for the Court?"

He seemed uncertain for a moment. "You may," he finally nodded.

I stepped down and retrieved my laptop, setting it and the small projector on an empty table so that the image was projected on the right wall of the courtroom. I brought up an overhead view of the roadway and the evidence of the tire marks where the cars had staged and then traveled around the curve.

"I was able to determine that the vehicles staged a burn-out here." I aimed a laser pointer at the area I was referring to. "They proceeded to accelerate down the road towards this curve. Shortly after exiting the curve, Mr. Cameron's car left the roadway and slid, rotated and rolled over before coming to rest in this field."

Mathews nodded. "And you performed a scientific analysis of Mr. Cameron's crash?"

"Yes. Mr. Cameron's vehicle did not leave the roadway as a result of traveling too fast around the curve of the road."

"And what evidence suggests that?" Matthews continued.

"Two things. The straight braking mark of Mr. Cameron's car after the curve, here," I said, moving the red dot to the skid marks I'd found, "and the fact that Mr. Cameron's car went off to the right side of the road, on the inside of the curve."

"Did you determine what exactly did cause Mr. Cameron's vehicle leave the roadway?"

"Yes. There were two impacts to Mr. Cameron's vehicle. One was a circular mark on his right rear quarter-panel that matches another car's wheel, and the other was an impact on the passenger door on the right side of his car."

"Was that also from a wheel?"

"No. That mark appeared to have been made by a flexible surface, like a front bumper."

He paused again, looking through his notes. He bent down and conferred with his assistant, then returned to questioning me.

"So you believe that there was another vehicle in close proximity to Chris's car at the time he lost control?"

"Yes."

"And were you able to identify the other vehicle?"

I glanced at the judge. "Yes. That vehicle was a 2016 Ford Mustang and was found at the Ford dealership in Clinton."

"Objection," Gaines suddenly said.

"Overruled," the judge said.

Steve slapped the top of the wooden divider. The sound caused the judge to look over at him with a frown.

"How were you able to determine that 2016 Mustang was in fact the vehicle that was racing Mr. Cameron?" Matthews asked.

"Upon inspection of the 2016 Mustang, I found evidence that the vehicle had experienced two impacts that matched up to the impacts found on the decedent's vehicle."

I glanced at Johnny, but he looked positively relaxed. He'd pushed his chair back and had rocked it against the wooden divider, and one boot was on the edge of the table. I wondered why the judge didn't say anything about it.

I moved my gaze to his father, who was in the same position, only with his boot heel on the edge of the divider a few feet down from his son. His eyes were still locked on me.

Matthews addressed me again. "And what did you learn from inspecting this vehicle?"

"That the front bumper had recently been repaired and repainted, some damage to the left front fender had been fixed, and the left front wheel bearing had been replaced by the mechanic who was readying it for sale."

"Anything else?"

"Yes." I pulled up the data I'd downloaded from the Mustang's computer showing the two impact spikes. "The computer of the 2016 Mustang showed two separate brief but sharp impacts. The first one," I said, gesturing with the laser, "is on the left front of the car, and the second one occurred about one second later, directly on the front of the car."

"And what did this allow you to determine?"

I pulled up a diagram of the two vehicles as they would have been positioned at the first impact. "The first impact matches the circular marks on the right rear of the victim's car, and the second impact matches the marks on the passenger door of the victim's car."

He nodded. "So you believe that the second vehicle you found was, beyond any doubt, the vehicle that the deceased was racing against that night."

"Yes, sir."

"Okay. And did you also learn who had sold that vehicle to the dealership?"

"Yes, sir."

"Who was that?"

This time Gaines rose to his feet. "Objection, your Honor. The witness is basing this on hearsay."

The judge looked at Matthews. "Do you have any evidence regarding who owned the vehicle prior?"

"Yes, sir." Matthews walked over to the table and picked up some documents.

"Your honor, we request that a copy of a sales receipt and a certified document from the Tennessee Department of Motor Vehicles be entered into evidence as People's first exhibit."

"Granted," the judge said. He nodded for us to proceed.

"At the time of the crash, that vehicle had been owned by Johnathan Harrell. Mr. Harrell sold it to the dealer shortly after the crash occurred. The documents introduced reflect that."

"Okay. So Johnathan Harrell owned the vehicle, and he was listed as a witness to the crash that night. He was also listed as being the person who first called the police, is that correct?"

"Yes."

"What is your final opinion on how the crash happened?" Matthews asked, looking at the judge and not me.

"My final opinion is that the 2017 Mustang and the 1967 Mustang were racing against each other that night, and that both vehicles reached the curve in the road at the almost the same time.

"Mr. Cameron's 1967 Mustang was in the lead, and it was also in the left lane of the road. As the cars made it around the corner, Mr. Harrell steered into Mr. Cameron's lane. The left front wheel of Mr. Harrell's 2017 Mustang struck the right rear quarter-panel of the 1967 Mustang. This impact caused the decedent's car to rotate in front of the Mr. Harrell's car, who could not react quickly enough to prevent his car from hitting the right door of Mr. Cameron's vehicle."

"And do you believe that this act was intentional on the Mr. Harrell's part?"

This was tricky. "My opinion is that the contact was intentional."

"And what leads you to believe that?"

"Several things," I said. "Mr. Harrell's car had a head start of nearly sixty feet. Also, his car was equipped with certain modifications that would have made his car clearly faster than Mr. Cameron's Mustang."

"What else?"

"The marks on the rear quarter-panel of Mr. Cameron's Mustang are consistent with a certain maneuver used by police officers to end a pursuit. The police car is steered into the rear quarter-panel of the pursued vehicle. This causes the rear end of the vehicle to swing around and lose control."

"Is this something that is formally taught in police driving schools?"

"Yes. It's called a Pursuit Intervention Technique." I looked at the judge. He was focused on some papers on his desk.

"Okay," Matthews said. "How fast were the vehicles going at the time of impact?"

"Approximately one hundred and three miles per hour," I said.

"And which vehicle was in the lead at the time of the first impact?"

"The 1967 Mustang was in front of the 2017 Mustang when the first impact occurred."

"Is there any way this crash could have been avoided?"

"Certainly. Both vehicles could have proceeded around the curve without incident if Mr. Harrell had stayed in his lane of travel."

"Thank you, Mr. Graves. No further questions."

The judge nodded, then shifted his eyes to Gaines. "Your witness."

"Thank you, your Honor," Gaines said, rising. He studied me for a moment from behind the table and then stepped around it, slowly approaching me.

"We've all been in hearings and trials before, Mr. Graves, and I think you'll agree in the spirit of cooperation and fairness that just giving me a 'yes' or 'no' answer will be best for everyone involved. Can we agree on that?"

This was an old trick to prevent the witness from explaining an answer. Matthews was watching me to see how I fared against this opening round.

"No, sir, I don't think that's fair. I have no idea what you intend to ask me, and I don't want to mislead the Court with an incorrect answer to a complex question."

"Well, now, I'm an honest man. Aren't you?"

"Sir, I am honest, and I request that I be allowed to explain in a narrative if the question requires it."

Gaines continued without acknowledgement. "Mr. Graves, you certainly have an interesting curriculum vitae. Guns and cars and accidents. Almost sounds more like playtime than a formal education."

"Is that a question, Councilor?"

"No, but here's one. You aren't yet a doctor, correct?"

"Yes, that's correct."

"Then how can you call yourself an expert?"

"Sir?" This was a completely off-base question. Most reconstructionists are not Ph.D.'s, they're former law enforcement officers or engineers.

"Answer the question, please." Gaines' tone was rough.

"As I told Mr. Matthews, not yet. But I will be grad-"

"Not yet. So you, in fact, aren't a doctor, but you want us," he gestured to the judge, "to believe you're an expert."

"Sir, I am done with my research-" but he cut me off again.

"I didn't ask you a question, *Mr.* Graves."

This was unbelievable. My head swiveled back to Bailey, who again avoided looking at me. I looked at Matthews, who wore a pained expression.

"Who are you looking for, Mr. Graves? I don't believe they can help you now, unlike earlier, when Mr. Matthews was undoubtedly coaching you what to say to the court."

"Objection, your Honor," Matthews interjected.

"Overruled," the judge said. Now he turned to me. "Mr. Graves, did you meet with Mr. Matthews prior to this hearing?"

This was bizarre. "My testimony is not coached."

"Just answer the question, sir," Gaines said.

"Of course we met prior to trial. I reconstructed the crash. He's the DA who filed the charges." I fought to stay cool. This wasn't how hearings usually went. The natural question to follow was 'what did you discuss in the meeting?' I hoped Matthews would note it for re-direct.

"Okay, Mr. Graves, let's move on. Your entire opinion in this case assumes that my client was actually driving the 2017 Mustang, doesn't it?" Gaines stepped back to the table and picked up a legal pad.

"Sir, my opinion is that the 2017 Mustang owned by your client was the causal factor in the subject crash."

"But how can you say he was driving?"

"Sir, it was Mr. Harrell that knew the crash had occurred, and he was the one who called to report the crash."

Gaines made a show of looking around the courtroom. "Well, how does that prove he was driving?"

"Again, the evidence shows it was his vehicle. It is true that I can't definitively say that he was the driver."

Uncomfortable silence. Someone in the benches coughed.

"Alright, Mr. Graves, let's talk a little about the so-called evidence you presented today." Gaines reached into his suit jacket and pulled out a pair of glasses, slowly unfolding the arms and slipping them on his face. "One of your conclusions was that the radial scuff marks on the right rear quarter of the 1967 Mustang were caused by the rotating left front wheel and tire of the 2017 Mustang. Is that correct?"

"That is one piece of evidence among many others." This was better. Less personal attack, more science.

"Would you please tell the court the diameter of the scuff marks?"

"Absolutely." I flashed through the photographs until one with a measuring tape against the scuff marks came up. "You can see in this photograph that the diameter is approximately twenty-five inches."

"And you're certain of that?"

"That is what the measurement shows."

"Okay." He nodded. "And what is the diameter of the left front wheel and tire assembly that was on the car when you inspected it?"

"Sir, there are photos that show the larger wheels on the car prior to the crash. The wheels and tires I saw were not on the vehicle at the time of the impact. I found the center cap to the larger wheels and tires in debris collected from the roadway at the scene of the crash."

"Mr. Graves, I don't care if he did own another set of bigger wheels. That's not what I asked you, sir. I specifically asked you for the diameter of the wheels and tires that were on the 2017 Mustang when you conducted your inspection."

"The wheels and tires that were on the car when I inspected it were stock Ford Mustang, about twenty-one inches in diameter. The wheels on the car during the crash were a set of very rare and expensive HRE forged aluminum wheels."

"So the diameter was not twenty-five inches?"

"No, sir."

Gaines took off his glasses, rubbed his nose. "And yet, Mr. Graves, you not only opine that my client was driving, but that he intentionally contacted Mr. Cameron's Mustang." He put the glasses back on. "What grudge do you have against my client, sir?"

"No grudge at all." I knew where he was going.

"No grudge. Even though you had a physical altercation with my client, you say you bear no grudge."

"Your client attacked *me*."

"Precisely, Mr. Graves." Gaines looked at the judge, then back at me. "Mr. Graves, your weak and self-promoted reconstruction skills might work in a civil court, but this is a criminal venue, and we require higher burdens of proof than hearsay." He stepped closer, closing the distance between the defense table and the witness stand.

Matthews snapped up. “Objection, your Honor. Mr. Gaines is commenting.”

Bailey looked at Gaines. “Sustained. Stick to asking questions, Mr. Gaines.”

“Certainly, your Honor.” Gaines turned back to me. “How much are you charging for your opinion today, Mr. Graves?”

My shoulders went forward. “I have never charged for an opinion, Councilor.”

Gaines looked surprised. “You work for free?”

“Sir, I charge for my time, not my opinion. My time is billed at two hundred dollars per hour, which is probably a fifth of your hourly rate.”

“And how much is your bill in this case so far?”

“I’m providing my services gratis in this case.”

Gaines arched his eyebrows. Bailey looked at me in surprise. “You’re not charging for your time in this case?” Gaines asked.

“No sir. The family can’t afford it, and I’m doing it pro bono.”

Gaines looked at the judge. “Your Honor, I think it’s clear that Mr. Graves has a vested interest in the outcome of this case. He’s not charging for his time, and as such he has personal connections for his client’s family.”

My hands slapped the witness bar. “Your Honor, my investigation in this case has followed all of the same rules of ethics and integrity I use in every case.”

“Strike that from the record,” the judge snapped. “Mr. Graves, you will not speak unless addressing a question by counsel. Anything else and you’ll be held in contempt. Am I clear?”

My skin flushed crimson and my heart was hammering against my chest. “Yes, sir.”

Allison and Judith were wide-eyed. Cathy had her head against Judith and Steve had his head on the railing in front of him.

Gaines turned to the judge. Then he went in for the kill. “Your Honor, we respectfully request that Mr. Graves’s testimony not be recognized by the court in this matter. There are clear ethical concerns with respect to his involvement in the case, and furthermore, even the assertion of his supposed expertise in the matter is in doubt.”

No. No way. He can't grant this. This is completely unreasonable. I searched Bailey's face. This is my life. This is my career. Please don't end it. Don't end me.

The judge was impassive. Silence hung in the courtroom.

Bailey finally cleared his throat. "I agree with you, councilor."

His words struck me harder than any physical blow.

"The court hereby disregards the testimony of the witness and furthermore rescinds the assertion of the witness as an expert." He glanced to me. "Get off the stand."

My mind was too numb to move. The judge went back to flipping through some papers on his desk. I rose slowly, still not comprehending the entire event that had just unfolded.

Johnny's father was smiling at me.

I fought the urge to vomit.

Matthews looked at me helplessly as I walked by him.

Allison caught my eye. I was too humiliated to hold her gaze. I'd let her down. Let her family down. Let her brother down. The desire to run the rest of the way to the back of the courtroom assailed me. I fought it down and kept my steps even. I muscled the heavy door open and stepped through into the indifferent banality of the hallway outside. There was a bench at the end of the hall and I made a beeline for it, letting gravity pull me onto it.

A few minutes later the courtroom door opened and Allison peeked around. She closed the door quietly and slowly walked towards me.

"So what does this mean?" she asked, when she got within a few feet.

"It's bad," I said. I couldn't look at her.

"If I ask how bad, would you tell me?"

"You'll find out."

She stood in front of me in silence. Her hand touched my shoulder.

I stiffened. She pulled back.

Ten minutes later the doors to the courtroom were both opened and people started filing out. The last thing I wanted was to face anyone who had just witnessed that debacle. I stood up quickly, looking around for an exit.

Allison read my mind. "This way," she said.

We walked quickly towards the stairs at the end of the hall. I hit the push bar on the door hard enough to make it ring out in the stairwell. Allison followed me down the steps, her short heels echoing off the hard concrete around us. As we hit the bottom floor she dashed in front of me. She stopped me cold.

"I know you did your best," she said.

I stopped. "I did. Jesus, I did." The words gushed out. I glanced back up the stairway.

"No one is coming for you," she said.

My focus went from her face to the door behind her.

She put her hand out, hovering it in front of my chest. "You look like a trapped animal."

I just wanted her to move. "I'm sorry, Allison. I don't understand what just happened in that courtroom. But I need to get out of here."

"That makes two of us."

We stood there in the hall. Me fidgeting, her searching. "How is this going to affect you?" she asked.

It would have ramifications on my life. I couldn't lie to her. "Not good."

"What do you mean?" she said, arching her eyebrows.

"I'll never be able to testify again. My career is over."

CHAPTER 12

My cellphone buzzed as I walked Allison to her car. It was Matthews.

"The judge granted the motion," he said. "The charges were dismissed against Johnny."

I expected it, but the words still cut me. "And it's my fault."

Matthews sighed. "Look, we've both been through this before. What happened in that courtroom was absolutely bizarre."

"Doesn't change the outcome," I said. "And now I'm junk as an expert witness."

Allison touched my arm. "You're not junk," she whispered.

I turned to her. Her dark hair caught the last of the sun's rays as the breeze caught it. Waterhouse, no doubt, the way the light moved and caught her skin. His *Windflowers* piece. The curve of her jaw as it swept to her chin, the arch of her cheekbone. Oh, God, I could paint that. Her perfume drifted to me. I could paint it into life. I could capture her essence in delicate oils on a stretched pure-white canvas. As surely as John William Waterhouse had caught that beautiful woman in the meadow.

Matthews' voice seemed far away. I realized I'd dropped the cellphone away from my ear. "What?" I asked him.

"I said that it's not a justice system, it's a legal system. He'll screw up and get caught again, and next time we'll get him."

"What do you mean, get caught again? He's still in for the assault charge against me."

Matthews coughed. "Uh, actually, the judge let him off on probation for that."

"*What?*" I almost screamed the word.

"I still don't know the details. But Johnny's free. The other kids are, too."

A thousand curses went through my mind. "Something's wrong with this."

"Look, he'll screw up again, and we'll get him solid next time."

"Sure." My heart wasn't in the answer, though. I ended the call. At this moment I just cared about Allison's safety. I'd assess the wreckage of my career later.

Her BMW was in the corner lot. As we neared it she paused. "I need to eat dinner. And so do you."

"I don't have an appetite," I said.

"Then let's just get drunk."

"I don't drink," I said.

"Then just keep me company."

"Sure."

"Your German car or mine?" she asked.

"Yours," I said. "I don't know that I can drive." My hands were trembling again.

She unlocked the car and opened her door. I started to open the passenger door, then paused. "What about your mom and dad? Should you be with them right now?" I asked.

"No." She didn't hesitate. "Mom will be okay with Judith."

I dropped into the taut leather seat. "Stop by my car. I need to get something from it." Without the HK, I felt naked.

~~~

"It's not what you think," she said.

Dinner was over. The lake was a black void, reflecting the lights of the pier in shallow ripples.

"What's not what I think?" I turned the glass up, drained the rest of the bourbon down my throat.

"Our family." She sipped her wine. "I thought you didn't drink."

"Oh. I don't. Haven't. This is the first time in like...seven years. I think." I struggled to remember the last time. "I'm hoping it gives me some ideas on how to tell my clients I can't work for them anymore, and that all the cases they have with me are going to be compromised. And how I'm going to handle being sued by all of them."
~~~

I motioned to the waitress, pointed at my glass. Again.

"Your family," I prodded. "Tell me."

Allison stared at the rivulets of red that ran down the inside of her wine glass.

"My father and Chris never got along." She said it matter-of-fact. "Just a few weeks before the crash he blew up at Chris and told him to get a real job and move out, that he was tired of supporting him. But it went further than that. Dad was critical of Chris, always putting him down and trying to make him feel like he wasn't a man. Some kind of male competition thing. Chris could never do anything right in his eyes."

I struggled to focus through the alcohol. "You wouldn't know it by the way he's acting."

She rolled her eyes. "He's consumed by guilt. He treated Chris badly, and now my brother is gone, and dad can't stand it."

"What about your mom?"

"She loved Chris. He was her favorite."

I winced. "Ouch."

Allison shrugged. "It's okay. She loved us both, but he was the baby. Dad always spoiled me and treated Chris hard, so I was okay. But Chris wasn't. He couldn't do anything to get dad's approval. If he got a motorcycle, then dad had to make sure that Chris knew he would never ride it better than dad. When Chris got a car, dad made sure Chris knew that it was crap compared to what Steve had when he was Chris's age. It was torture to watch."

"How did Chris handle it?"

"The only way he could, I guess. Kept trying to make dad proud, and kept loving him."

"He did?" My fifth glass arrived. The waitress gave Allison a concerned look.

"Oh, yeah," she said, smiling. "He always said he loved dad and that he knew dad loved him. He was very forgiving."

Steve's vengeance began to make sense. "So Steve hates himself for treating Chris badly?"

"Yes."

"Is that why Chris was out racing that night? To prove himself to your father?"

"No. I think it was about Kelly."

I put the glass on the table, barely. "What?"

Allison nodded. "Mom and dad don't know it, but Kelly broke Chris's heart. He begged me not to tell them, because he knew dad would just add to the humiliation. It would be one more thing Chris screwed up that dad could torture him about."

I waited. "There's more, isn't there?"

"Just before the hearing, when I was still talking to Chris's friends about who might have been in Johnny's car, I learned that Kelly dumped Chris for Johnny." Allison drank the rest of her wine. "I knew you were stressed enough already, and I didn't think it would make a difference if you knew." She put her glass on the table.

"So Johnny humiliates Chris, and Chris challenged Johnny to the race to try to regain some respect." That made a lot of sense.

"He never said it to me, but I think that's exactly what happened." She closed her eyes. They welled up but she didn't cry.

"You said Johnny plays for keeps."

She nodded. "To Chris, it was a drag race. To Johnny, it was a threat."

I carefully reached for the glass, took a sip. It went down too easy. The flavor was long over. It was solely about the anesthetic effect now. "Do you think Bailey would have thrown this hearing just because his daughter is dating Johnny?"

Allison shrugged. "I don't know. It's the only reason I can see, but it seems weak."

"Very weak. And stupid. And Bailey isn't stupid." I tried to puzzle it out, but the bourbon made it hard to think. I changed the subject. "What's going on with your mom and dad?" It came out too bluntly. "Sorry," I said.

"It's okay." She set her own glass back down. "You really don't drink much, do you?"

"No. Not at all." I picked up the glass of bourbon and ginger ale again. "My dad drank Jack Daniels. I never drink Jack Daniels. Never, ever, ever."

"But you're drinking bourbon," she said.

"Not the same. I'm not like him." My words were rounded off, not sharp. "Back to your family."

"Family relationships are like triangles, and Chris kept mom and dad stable. I moved out as soon as I could, and Chris would have been leaving soon anyway. They're on the brink of divorce now, only dad doesn't know it. Mom has been moving things over to Judith's for few weeks, ever since dad made the decision to go after Johnny. She's talked to me about getting an apartment."

I didn't say anything. There isn't anything to fix the way things are. They just are, and all you can do is bear witness.

The server brought the check. Allison reached for it but I grabbed it first, stuck the bills in, and handed it back to her. I tried to fold my napkin, failed, and tossed it in a lump it on the table. "Ready to go back?"

"Not if you're driving."

"I'm most emphatrically- emphatally- I'm definitely not driving," I said.

"So where are you going to stay tonight?" she asked.

"Oh, man." Ken and Rob both had families. They couldn't see me like this. "I didn't think about that too well."

"I can drive you home."

I waved her off. "No way. It's like a half-hour drive."

"Let's go," she said.

I didn't argue anymore.

~~~

Allison guided the BMW off the main highway and onto the back roads. We threaded our way through the hills until the lake came into view around a bend.

She gasped. "That's beautiful."

The moon was up and full. Gravel crunched under the tires as we drove deep into the woods. At the end of the road the small house was perched on a bluff above the lake. The car transitioned to the concrete apron and we got out.

"You own this?"

My head was still light, floating gently on the bourbon. "No. Just rented. It's a drive from the city but it's quiet and cheap."

"Need help?" she asked.

"No." I opened the door, fell out of the car.

"You okay?" Allison asked.

"All good," I replied. My hands grabbed the door, pulling myself up.
~~~

I wobbled my way up the loose pavers that led to the door. She followed me into my laundry room.

"Holy crap," she said. "You must like art."

Every wall had something on it. A Botticelli print of *The Birth of Venus* above the washer.

"Because the clothes are reborn clean when they're done," I said, pointing to it.

Above the dryer, *Umbrellas at Blue Point* by Glackens. "That's because people are drying off on the beach," I said.

The kitchen was next. Manet's *A Bar at the Folies Bergere* was wedged between the cabinets and the refrigerator.

"She looks sad," Allison said, pointing to the lady behind the bar.

"It's because she knows the ending." I flicked on the lights.

The living room held a Del Cossa, and Van Gogh's Starry *Night Over the Rhone*, a couple of Degas works, Sargent's *Madame X*. And more. Many more.

"They're all reproductions," I apologized.

"They're beautiful," she said. She surveyed the room. "Where are yours?"

"I don't have any," I said.

She glanced at me, skeptical. Then the outdoor patio caught her eye. She dropped her purse on the coffee table and made a line for the patio door.

I floated after her, into the night. The wide expanse of the lake stretched out before us.

"The wonderful thing about alcohol," I said, "is that it makes your fear surrender to carelessness."

It sounded brilliant, probably wasn't.

"What are you so scared of?"

The alcohol made it hard to remember, now. "Them."

"Who's them?"

I didn't hear her. "I'm always afraid they'll come back."

She walked over to me. "Your eyes."

I reached up, wiped them. "I'm so sorry, Allison."

"It's okay."

"I'm so sorry for all the shit you've been through."

She put her hand on my arm.

"I don't want to see anyone hurt," I said. "I hate seeing people hurt. If I could take it all away, I would. All the stains from everyone."

"I know." She moved closer to me. Her lips closed on mine. "It's okay now. It's done."

No. This shouldn't happen. My stains will bleed onto her.

"Make me forget. Please," she said.

My body responded with pent-up desire. I moved to her, pushing her against the low stone wall that bordered the concrete patio. The weight of our lives had crushed us into each other. Now our bodies met with the same force. The longing and desire that had been held back by the walls that brought us together crumbled in an instant. My hand circled her waist and I brought my head down. She pushed against me with an aggressive force, recoiling from the restraints that we had both respected until this moment. Now it didn't matter. We had tried and failed to obtain justice. We had tried and failed to find reckoning in her brother's death. She was standing in the wreckage of a shattered family and I was standing in the wreckage of my career. The final wall of formality between us was collapsing. No more faith existed to keep it standing.

Her lips met mine again. She pulled away after a moment.

"Now," she said. "Hard."

Her hands reached to my shirt. Her fingers were shaking as she grabbed the first button. She found the edge and pushed it through the slit in the cloth. She moved to the next one, then the third. That button caught. She swore. She pulled harder and the threads broke.

Desire overcame reservation. I surrendered.

I moved my hands to her waist, sliding my fingers up under her arms and peeling away her outer jacket. Her white blouse hung on her shoulders with thin straps. I laced my fingers under them and pulled up. She dropped her right shoulder, then her left, but didn't stop wrestling with my shirt with her free hand. As her blouse fell to her waist she reached my beltline. Her hands pulled up and my shirt came with it and the last buttons were undone.

September evening air cooled my skin. I dropped my hands to her hips and slid my fingers inside the waistband of her skirt. The soft smoothness of the satin against her skin was tempered by the lace that bordered the edges. Her hands were attacking my belt, brusquely pulling the end. Anxious fingers clawed at the metal catch. I slid her skirt down over her hips and down her thighs and over her stockings. It fell softly to the floor. My slacks followed as she found the zipper and roughly pulled them down.

She pressed her body against mine, feeling me through the silk of my boxers. Her hands frantically dug inside the waistband, scratching my skin, pulling the fabric down and letting it drop to the floor. Then her hands found me. I shivered. I pushed against the satin that remained between us and then moved it to the side.

"Hard," she said again.

She was light and I picked her up. We exhaled in unison as our bodies came tightly together. I pushed deep inside her and she tightened her fingers on my shoulders. Her thighs closed tightly around my hips. Her heels dug into the back of my legs. I looked at her in the light of the moon. Her eyes were closed. She moved her body against me, trying to push me back with each blow. I pressed her harder against the rough stone, keeping my hands under her. Her hair flew around us as we moved against each other with violence. Like *The Lady of Shalott*, by Hunt. Her hair. Soft. Alive.

"Everything...is...hard."

I stopped listening. Everything in me was held captive by this moment of rough intimacy. Nothing mattered except possessing her, hurting her, defeating her. Every thrust of her body was met by the force of my own. Everything in our lives lost its meaning except for this moment.

Her eyes closed. Her lips separated enough to let a soft moan escape. Her head arched back and the force of her blows intensified. She brought her eyes back to mine. They hardened, then her head arched again. Her legs and body squeezed against me tighter and I pulled her to me harder still, trying to harness her, control her.

She was somewhere else now. The movements of her slender body in the moonlight were attempts to throw off the weight of death, of divorce, of losing stability in life. I ground against her hard, abandoning any pretense of gentility. It wasn't about love or intimacy or modest restraint. It was about primal pleasure, the desire to satisfy the inner beast at the expense of everything that surrounded us. The selfishness in our pleasure made us drive against each other like two competing countries, neither willing to cease the assault. Our only impulse was driving deeper into each other, trying to capture the essence of the other, outlasting the other to claim their spirit in triumph, in our ecstasy.

"Damn it." Her body trembled.

And as she trembled, her thrusts weakened. Something broke inside me. The pyrrhic victory was mine as she consumed me in the fall. There was no more fight left in either of us.

~~~

Running.

Sweat streamed off me. But the fog was cold.

Footsteps behind me. Measured, loud, haunting. Deep in pitch.

I ran harder, but the footsteps grew louder, closer.

My arms pumped but the fog was too thick. It surrounded my arms, made it hard to move. Hard to breathe.

Something reached out, brushed the back of my neck. Fingers on my shirt, lifting it up.

I turned, flowing through a studied and practiced movement that should have brought my right arm down with violent force against the thing touching my back. But the fog was a thief, stealing my speed, slowing my strike to a feeble touch. My arm bumped lightly on the extended limb grasping the back of my shirt. The arm wasn't attached to anything but the fog.

It lifted off my shirt, leaving me bare. Then the hand grabbed my arm. Another hand shot out of the fog, grabbed my bicep. I knew what was next. And I was too weak to break the grasp. Helpless.

My arm cracked like thunder.

~~~

I cracked an eye. And found myself looking straight into hers. And an apple.

"What was that?" she asked. She took another bite. The apple crunched loudly.

Gray dawn filled the bedroom window. I glanced over the edge of the bed. My pants were there. The butt of the HK peeked out from the pocket.

One overwhelming thought consumed my mind. It drove out the last vestige of the nightmare, blinding it into ephemeral oblivion. The thought: Don't hurt her.

Be calm. Don't say anything. Choke it back if it comes.

I raised my eyebrows. "Unbelievable."

"Not last night. What you were doing just now."

"Which was?"

"Thrashing around. Mumbling."

I tried to move, but my arms had rolled the bed sheet tight against my body, like a straightjacket. I rolled my body off my arm, shrugged out of the fabric, and sat up next to her. "Just dreams, I guess. I don't remember too much of it." Change the subject. "I see you found my pantry."

She offered me the apple. I took it, bit into the firm skin. Sweetness followed.

"The French always have an apple on the nightstand," she said. "So when the lovers wake, they don't kill each other with morning breath."

"That would be a bad way to say thanks," I said. "Mal élevé."

"Est-ce que tu parles francais?"

"Un petit peu," I said, holding my thumb and finger up to indicate just a little.

"Quel dommage," she said.

We chewed our apple bites in silence.

"What now?" She turned and moved closer to me. She brought the apple up, took another bite.

The urge to run assailed me. I fought it down. Eventually it would grow too strong to resist. Just not right now. "I don't know."

"You've got that trapped animal look again."

"No, no," I said. "This is what I look like with a hangover."

She laughed. "You're not even close to that." She studied me. "No, there's something else there, I think. Do you regret last night?"

"What? No," I said.

"Are you a butterfly?" she asked.

The question was so far out of left field that it made me laugh. "A butterfly?"

"It's from a song I like. The girl who wrote it says she only sleeps with butterflies because they always flutter away afterward."

"I don't-"

"It's okay," she interrupted. "Look, I needed last night. Even if you didn't."

I searched for words. "It's not that I didn't want it." Jesus, this territory wasn't just uncharted, it wasn't even in the same universe as any conversation I'd ever had with a girl. I took a deep breath. The answer was the truth.

"Okay, look," I said. "I've got some issues. It's hard for me to get close to people. Really hard. And when I become...intimate...with a girl, it brings up a lot of bad memories. After a while I become completely dysfunctional. I'll grow increasingly distant until I won't even want to see you. And it'll tear your heart out."

Her eyes were wide. "So are you freaking out right now?"

"Not right now. It takes some time."

"Oh." She leaned back against the headboard. "Well, thanks for the warning."

"I don't want to hurt you. I'm being honest. I tried to fix myself. Didn't work."

"Even if we aren't an item? I mean, it's not like we're married. I don't want to get married again. At least not for a long time. Years." She handed me the apple again.

I held it up. "This is appallingly symbolic, you know."

Now she smiled. "Ha. It is. You already ate of it, though." She brushed her hair out of her eyes. It flowed like an obsidian river across her shoulders.

She wanted me to explain more, to reveal more of the damage inside me, but she was afraid to press. Finally she shrugged. "Look, we've been though a lot. Maybe you've been through more than me." She glanced sideways, looking for a reaction. "Let's just take it day by day. No pressure."

"Day by day," I repeated. Same thing the psychiatrist at the university clinic had said. Maybe it would work.

She nodded, took the apple again. "So are you going to run away now?"

"Truthfully," I said, "running away might not be a bad idea."

"What about your doctorate? School?" She propped herself up on her elbow. Her eyes studied me. "Your bus-" and then she stopped in mid-sentence. "Sorry."

My business. I closed my eyes. "Doesn't seem to matter so much anymore."

"Yeah." It was unconvinced.

"God, I don't know," I finally said. "Someone told me life is hard."

Her cheeks turned crimson and she buried her face in the pillow. That made me smile.

"Leave it all," I said. "I've got a master of science degree. And I've come into a little bit of money. Enough to get established somewhere new. Maybe take a leap out west. I liked Seattle when I was out there last year."

"It rains a lot." Her voice was muffled as she talked into the pillow.

"It only rained one day when I was there."

"And how long was that?"

"Two days." I smiled. "Seriously, I don't know. I just don't want to face the world right now. I don't want to go back to reality."

"Me either."

We lay there, each in our own thoughts.

"You have to finish school," she said.

"It's not a necessary condition for sustaining life."

She shook her head. "No. If you finish up you'll be okay. You can recover."

"I don't know if I want to."

"Why?"

My stomach growled. I rubbed my eyes. "For starters, I hate math. Never liked it. My mind isn't wired for it. And then there's the death and the pain. Every case that comes my way means someone's permanently injured or dead, usually in a horrible manner. At first it wasn't bad, I didn't mind the tragedy, because I was familiar with it myself. But after a while it starts eating away at you, like a slow cancer. And what happened yesterday, for example. I hate testifying. Hate it. I do my job, and find the truth, but then the other attorney lies and does every unethical thing you can think of to attack me personally. They do the same thing in depositions. It's never about the truth, it's about winning the case. Like Matthews told me, it's not a justice system, it's a legal system. And I'm tired of it."

Her eyes fixed on mine. "So why do it?"

"Forensic engineering sucks the life out of me."

"That doesn't make sense."

"For me it does. It's sterile. No color, no joy. That's why I do it. To stay cold. If I'm frozen, then there's no pain. Another reason is the money's good. Money buys security."

"But not happiness."

"No."

"What pain?" she asked quietly.

"It doesn't matter," I said. "Life is hard for everyone." I stopped there. She didn't need to hear about an instance of sexual abuse whose damaging effects destroyed an entire family.

She studied me. She started to say something, thought better of it, and remained silent.

"I'm sorry, Allison. You didn't need to hear that."

"It's okay." She kept studying me. "You've never told another girl that, have you?"

I closed my eyes. "No."

~~~

Afterward, she drove me back to my car. As we idled in the parking lot of the courthouse, she turned to me.

"It'll be okay," she said.

"Sure," I lied.

Then she was gone, and it was time to pick up the pieces.

~~~

My first stop was to see Cathy Cameron. Chris's mother. She worked in an old building on campus called South College, on the hill next to Ayres Hall where students are tortured by the math department. The commuter garage across Cumberland was nearly full and I had to cruise to find a space. Rain started as I stepped onto the foot bridge that crossed over the boulevard to the main campus. I snapped the umbrella open and took measured steps. By the time I made it to her building the rain was tapering off.

The smell of the aged building greeted me like an old nemesis. The odors were all the same in campus buildings. I had paid a ton of money to inhale that for fourteen years.

Cathy's door was cracked halfway open. I knocked lightly anyway.

"Come in." Her voice was formal.

"Hi, Cathy." I stepped inside and shut the door.

"Soren," she said. I braced myself for punishment, for a harsh tone and harsher words, but it didn't come. She rose from behind her desk. "It's not your fault."

Relief flooded over me. "I thought you'd be angry."

"No, that's Steve," she said. Then, quickly, "but not at you, either. He knows you did a good job. What happened in there wasn't right. Steve's got the judge on his list right below Johnny's daddy now."

I tried to smile but it came out awkward. "Look, I just wanted to apologize. I don't know why it happened like that. But I wanted to tell you that I'm going to try to find out."

She stepped past me and pulled a chair out from the corner. "Sit down."

My eyes fixed on my shoes as I took the chair. The glossy leather of my captoes glistened with rainwater. Cathy walked back behind her desk.

"I knew Chris was not going to be with us this Christmas," she said.

I arched an eyebrow.

"It's true. The first feeling I had was at Easter of this year. We had just gotten home from church, and Judith and I were in the kitchen, and something just hit me. I almost dropped then and there. And I knew one of us wouldn't be there for Christmas. I didn't realize it would be Chris until a bit later. But I knew."

The rain began falling again. The drops crashed hard against her window.

"I could have saved him from that race." She said it plainly, as a statement of fact.

I winced. "Don't put that burden on yourself, Cathy. There's no way you could have done that."

"No, there is." Cathy folded her hands in her lap. "I go to bed around nine, but when Chris stays out late, I'd always wake up at eleven and call him and go get him if I had to. I did that ever since he started driving. There was never a time that I didn't wake up and call him."

She was looking out her window now. "Except for that night. I didn't wake up. The phone rang about two a.m. and that's what got me. And even before I answered it, I knew it was about Chris."

Raindrops lashed the window.

"When Chris graduated last year, I wanted to do something nice for him. I had a small life insurance policy that I cashed in. Wasn't much, but it was enough to buy him a motorcycle he'd been talking about for a while. Steve was against it. He said Chris should use it to move out and get into college or get an apprenticeship, but Chris told me that he just wanted to take some time and play with his cars and computers. He told me that he was thinking about joining the Air Force.

"He just looked at me one day and said, 'Mom, you'd be proud of me if I went into the military, wouldn't you?' and I told him I was already proud of him no matter what he did. And then he asked me, 'Do you think dad would finally be proud of me?'"

She cleared her throat. "He ended up crashing that bike. Gave me such a scare that I swore he couldn't have another motorcycle as long as he lived in the house. He took the insurance money for the bike and was going to use it to get his car painted and finish that little truck, but then one of Chris's friends had his car repossessed. This friend had dropped out of school to get a job to support his pregnant girlfriend, so Chris gave him the money to get a car so the guy could keep his job. Chris always said it was a loan, but he knew he'd never see it again. That's the kind of person my son is."

She used the present tense but I didn't correct her. The rain pelted the window harder now. Thick rain clouds were turning the late morning dark. Through the glass I could see students dashing from buildings, trying to avoid the torrent from the sky as classes changed.

"I wish I could have known him." When I first said those words to Judith, many weeks ago, they had been flippant. Now, after all that had happened, they were sincere.

"Oh, you all would have gotten along great." Her phone rang but she ignored it.

"There was another time, right before his graduation, when some kids were outside the school kicking something around. They were part of that violent crowd that dresses in dark clothes and listens to that horrible music, you know, the Manson guy that's always trying to shock people and such. Chris walked over to them and saw that it was a Bible that they were kicking around in the dirt."

"Oh."

"Chris got so mad that he shoved a couple of them aside and picked it up and slapped it against the biggest kid's chest and told him he needed to read it, not kick it. No one else had the guts to do that. And instead of fighting Chris, they actually said they were sorry. Can you believe that?"

"That's a brave thing to do."

Cathy nodded. "That's what everyone was saying. Chris never lived that down."

"What did Steve think about that?"

"He said that Chris should have fought them, even if he knew he would've gotten beat."

"I think Chris did the right thing."

"So do I."

"How is Steve doing?" The chair was making me numb. I shifted my position.

She shook her head. "He can't deal with it. He's just having so much trouble coming to terms with it. We've never discussed it. He can't. He gets so angry."

"Sorry."

"It's not just now," she said. "Even before, if he was upset at me or Chris for something, he'd not be there for Thanksgiving dinner or Christmas. He'd just get mad and storm out and wouldn't be able to calm down for a long time."

"That's awful. He's lucky to have you and his children." The rain was still pounding the world outside the window.

"He's got a temper. It's just life, I guess."

"It's hard," I said.

"It is." She looked up at me. "There is something I need to tell you. Steve has been calling everyone he can about what's happened, and he got hold of Pete Stryker from Channel 2. You know him?"

"Sure," I said. "Why?"

"He's agreed to do a story on the crash and how THP didn't really do their job in this instance. Steve contacted him a few weeks ago, but after that trooper shot himself, Pete called back for the story."

Figures. Blood draws cameras like poop draws flies. "How does this involve me?"

"He wants to interview you and learn how the crash happened." She gave me a sad smile. "Would you be willing to meet with him?"

Crap. I didn't like the spotlight. "Generally it's best to keep a low profile in this business. If this ever goes to civil trial, even without me, you can bet that the attorney will get his hands on the footage and try to twist whatever I say totally out of context. And I'd have to be very careful to not accuse Johnny of anything."

"Sure," Cathy said. She studied her desk. "This might be the only way to ever get the truth out, though. It might not be in court, but it will make a difference to the people who matter."

Her words had wisdom. It was her call. I still wasn't entirely convinced to do it, but I also wasn't entirely convinced it was a bad idea. I pulled out one of my cards and laid it on her desk.

"There's my contact information," I said. "Have him call me to set up a time."

She picked it up. "Thanks."

Thunder rolled across the building, rattling the window panes.

~~~

I needed legal advice. Wayne wasn't in, but Cynthia Carter rescued me.

"Hey, stranger." Cynthia's voice had the soothing quality of slow jazz.

"How's things?" I asked.

"Busy as always. Wayne's got me running hard this week. You okay?" She must have known about the hearing.

"Getting by," I said. "Kind of rough lately."

"Sorry, darling." Pause. "Is there anything I can do to help you out?" Her voice flowed into my ear like aural honey. I smiled.
~~~

"Maybe. Can you check for some legal connection between Ron Bailey and James Harrell? You know, like courtroom proceedings or hearings, that kind of thing?"

"You mean the Anderson County Judge?"

"Yes."

"Who's the other person?" she asked. It sounded like she was writing it down.

"James Harrell. I don't know anything about him, other than he's the alleged boss of all that's bad in Anderson County. And the surrounding areas, too."

"Okay."

"Cynthia, I really appreciate this. Sorry to add to your load. You can send me a bill for the time if you want."

"Oh, darling, you're so sweet. I don't think you could afford me if I charged you. But for you it's completely free. All you have to do is ask." Sultry tones the color of twilight carried the words.

"You do know how to make a man lose concentration," I said.

"It's one of my many gifts, darling. But don't feel too indebted. This is a perfect task for our young intern."

"Don't ride him too hard."

"He should be so lucky. I'll call you if anything should pop up. With your request, I mean."

"Thanks, Cynthia."

"You owe me, darling."

~~~

"You have to finish," Ken said.

"Why?" I chucked another tortilla chip at the birds in the corner of the patio.

"I'd have to arrest you."

I played along. "What charge, copper?"

"Embezzlement."

"I'm innocent."

"Who says you're innocent?" He folded his comic-book-hero arms across his massive chest. "You're only thinking about yourself. You're not thinking about all the people who've helped you get this far."
~~~

"I'm thinking about myself because I'm the one who's in my situation." I stopped. "What kind of circular mind game are you pulling on me?"

"You're wrong." He cocked his head as he looked at me. "As I recall, you have five professors who are expecting you to finish. And there's also the entire Engineering Fundamentals program that gave you a teaching position to help you pay for school, even if you're actually teaching Peckem's class for him. You need to remember when they gave you that position, someone else didn't get it. You're obligated to finish just for that. But then there's also the twelve hundred students that you taught during that time that looked up to you and respected you as a leader. And I'm not even mentioning all the folks that have helped you get where you are today. If you walk away now you're betraying all of them." He swiveled his head to the street. "You ain't innocent, brother. And it isn't only you."

"Most people don't even finish their Ph.D.," I said.

"Since when are you most people?"

The birds were edging closer. I tossed another chip their way. "I don't know."

Ken raised his wrap-around sunglasses and rubbed his eyes. "You will finish."

My eyes closed. This wasn't support. This was boot camp. "I've already lost a bunch of time."

"So don't sleep."

"That's all I want to do."

"Scarcity comes to the man who slumbers."

"Scarcity is already coming. I should at least get some sleep out of the deal."

He chuckled. "Remember working on that hybrid electric car? Senior year? Under Dr. Snider?"

"Good lord." We'd worked our butts off on it. We took it to Detroit to compete against twenty other schools, and failed miserably. "What about it?"

"To get it done, we worked all week. Saw the sun rise and set six times in a row. You and I were the only ones standing at the end."

"Lot of good it did us."

"We got it done. Some teams didn't even make it to the competition." He leaned back. "You can do it again."

"No more all-nighters. I'm done." I crumpled a tortilla chip in my hand, then threw it at the birds. The last three chips went in my mouth. "Whah iff I join tha forth?"

"It's rude to talk with your mouth full. And no, I don't think you'd be happy on the force. You don't like taking orders."

That was true. He knew me well.

My phone chimed. Cynthia's number was on the screen. I tried to swallow the mouthful of chips too fast and the lump got stuck in my throat. I coughed but it got worse. Searing pain made my eyes water. I pounded my hand on my chest. Didn't work. I lunged for the plastic cup of water just as Ken reached out his large hand and pulled it to him.

My face screamed at him in panic. I gestured frantically for the cup. Ken sat there like a damn statue.

"Ahhrrgg," was all I could manage.

"You agree to finish, I save your life. And you get the water."

"Ffaack yaa," I gurgled.

He shrugged.

Light started to fade.

I nodded my head.

"Deal?" he said, leaning forward a little.

I nodded harder. My eyes were closing.

He stood up, leisurely walked behind me, and pulled his hands around my thorax hard. The mess of partially masticated chips flew onto the concrete. The birds hopped over to it.

"Nasty," he said.

I pushed my chair back and coughed out the rest of the detritus. "Jesus." Air surged in and out of my lungs. He kept his hand on my shoulder, squeezing gently.

"Exactly," he said. "Everything happens for a reason."

"Bullshit." I coughed again. "Things happen because they happen. And because people can be really damn stupid." My phone chimed with a voicemail. I didn't bother to listen to it. "That was harsh, man."

"That," he said, "was providence." Ken walked back to his chair and pushed the water towards me. "In some parts of the world I'd own you for saving your life."

"I thought providence was supposed to be a good thing." I pulled the phone from the case on my belt and dialed Wayne's office. "I need to call Cynthia back. Give me a minute. This isn't over."

"Sure it is. Take your time, though. I need to call my mom and tell her I own a white guy now." He chuckled.

I rolled my eyes.

"Cynthia, it's Soren."

"That was quick."

"I could say the same. Any good news?"

"Maybe. It's kind of convoluted but I think it's what you're looking for. Turns out that James Harrell and Ron Bailey have crossed paths before. Every time Harrell or one of his goons came before Bailey in a courtroom, the charges got dropped and he walked out a free man. The most serious case happened three years ago. Harrell was arrested by the local PD for running an illegal gambling ring out of one of his strip clubs. The cops raided the club, but they didn't find any gambling machines."

"Go figure."

"Anyway, they rounded up all the girls that were working there and ran them through the system just to harass Harrell. Turns out one of the girls was sixteen."

"Big surprise. How does it fit in with Bailey letting Johnny off?" I glanced at Ken. He really was calling his mom.

"Don't know. But when James Harrell came up for trial, guess the judge at the criminal hearing to allow evidence."

"Ron Bailey."

"You're so smart, darling. The brief my intern wrote says that the case was dismissed for unlawful search and seizure."

"There might have been a credible basis for that ruling."

"You're also naïve. It's very sexy, really."

My skin flushed. "That I am. Naïve, I mean." My throat was still raw from the chips. "So there might be some connection between Bailey and James Harrell that allowed Harrell to exert some leverage to get his son off at the motion hearing."

"It looks that way."

I sipped the glass of water. "Have you got some names?"

"The attorney who prosecuted the case is Greta Wilson. You might be able to learn more from her. She's in private practice now here in town."

"Anyone else?"

"Not right now."

"Okay," I jotted the name down. "If I can't get anywhere with her I'll be calling you back."

"That implies you'll be able to get somewhere with me. I love that unspoken confidence."

"Thanks for doing this, Cynthia. I truly appreciate it."

"Anything for justice, darling. Bye."

Ken was laughing into his own phone. "So then his lips started turning blue..."

"I have to go," I said. "But this isn't over."

He pulled the phone away from his ear. "You'll finish," he said.

I opened the web browser on my phone and looked up the number for Greta Wilson, Esquire. "Keep the shiny side up," I said, pushing my chair back and walking past him.

~~~

Greta's office was on the corner of Market street and Church street in the middle of downtown. The office had character. Renovation had brought new woodwork but the old brick was still exposed on the interior walls.

"I don't have much time," she said as she walked into the reception area. "I've got a motion in limine against the other side's experts at three." She flashed azure eyes at me. "As an expert witness, I'm sure you've been on the receiving end of one of those."

"Been there. Thanks for taking the time to meet with me."

She gestured. "This way."

We stepped in her office and she shut the door behind me. "So, James Harrell, huh?"

"Yes."

"I heard about Palmer. Shocking." Her tone was flat, indicating otherwise.

"You don't sound shocked. Did you know him?"

"He was the coordinator between THP and the sheriff's office that conducted the raid you asked me about."

"So you had your suspicions?"

"Not at the time. After last week, it all kind of fit."

"What about the ruling that Bailey made at the hearing?"

She shrugged. "It was disappointing, but it was within the law. We didn't find the gambling machines, and the warrant
~~~

wasn't executed with intent to find two underage girls working at his club. His manager took the heat on that."

"Two girls? I thought there was just one."

The look on her face told me she'd given something away. She was professional, though, and kept her eyes focused on her desk. There was an internal battle being waged. I prayed it would come out in my favor.

"You know what professional courtesy is, right?" She leaned forward in her high-backed chair.

"It's a euphemism for looking the other way," I said.

She fidgeted with a pen on her desk. "You didn't hear this from me."

"Hear what?"

"As you pointed out, there was another underage girl there that night." She paused for effect.

"I'm not the sharpest knife in the box," I said.

"Bailey has a daughter who just turned nineteen."

My eyes widened. "His daughter was there? Kelly?"

Now her eyes widened. "You know her?"

"She was Chris's girlfriend." I shook my head. "Damn."

"Oh, boy," she said. She dropped the pen and sat back in her chair. "Look, I don't want to get the blame for connecting the dots on this. I'm in private practice now, and there's always the chance I'll wind up with him on the bench. And he wouldn't like me very much if he knew I spilled the beans about his daughter."

I waved my hand. "This is all confidential. But why is Bailey worried about his daughter's behavior coming out? He didn't do anything wrong."

"Actually, he did. "

"How?"

"Both girls were caught with cocaine. More than enough for an intent to distribute charge. They also had forged licenses that showed they were eighteen. But I saw Palmer single out one of the girls at the club, so evidently, Palmer recognized Kelly before they made it to the station. Palmer called Bailey, and he told Palmer to bring his daughter home and disappear the drugs."

"You were there?"

She nodded. "Supervising the legal aspects of the operation. The cops were pissed that they'd come up empty, so they arrested all the girls on prostitution charges. I knew it wouldn't hold up, but it shut Harrell's club down for the night."

"You knew what Bailey and Palmer had done with Kelly that night?" I asked.

"No. Not then. But I realized we were missing a girl when we got to the station. Palmer was adamant that I'd miscounted. Then I remembered Palmer singling out the girl, and she looked familiar, and I realized it was Kelly Bailey a few weeks later."

"What happened to the other girl? No one realized she was underage?"

Greta shook her head. "You need to realize that half of the girls we arrested were pleading they were underage or just innocent waitresses. No one knew the other girl was underage until she was processed and printed. But then Bailey made sure he presided at her hearing. He sent her to Elkinridge Detention Center, over near Memphis."

"Elkinridge is a tough place."

"You know about it?"

"It's the same place that Misty Carver was released from before she killed those troopers."

Greta nodded. "Look how well that worked out."

Sad. "Why Elkinridge?"

"He wanted her as far away from Kelly as possible. He blamed her for Kelly's wild streak."

"Do you remember her name?" I asked.

Greta started to speak, thought twice, and shook her head. "No."

"Because she was juvenile? Sealed record?" I searched her face for a clue to why she wouldn't mention the last detail.

She nodded. "Can't disclose that. The walls might have ears." She gestured around her office.

I smiled at the joke. "Okay, okay. I won't press. But you didn't say anything about what Bailey did? Or Palmer?"

She sighed, looked toward her window. "No proof. It was all circumstantial. And it would have been career suicide if had raised any questions."

Evil flourishes when good people do nothing to stop it.

"How dirty do you think Bailey is?" I asked.

"Well, it's not like there's a sliding scale." She focused on me. "We all push the boundaries sometime. Then we hope we're forgiven for it."

Evil also flourishes when people don't want to see it.

"I don't know how bad he is," Greta finally said. "But his main problem is political. He's got bigger aspirations than simply being an Anderson County judge. He's eyeing a Senate seat. Bailey can't afford to have his daughter's story come out."

"Palmer's gone now. So why wouldn't Bailey throw the book at Harrell?"

"Seems like he would, doesn't it?" She had that unsurprised tone in her voice again. "Political campaigning requires a lot of money. Harrell has the money, and Bailey has the ambition and ability. Maybe Harrell has some influence over Bailey. Look, when I was the DA, it was like pushing a rope to get a conviction in Anderson County. Every time we had a tip for a raid, we came up empty. And when we did manage to collar someone, Bailey let the guy off easy."

"Palmer was the leak. And it sounds like Bailey is dirty, too. Especially after what he did to me at the hearing."

"Bad experience?"

My lips tightened. "That bastard cost me my career. Why isn't anyone doing anything about it?"

"Sorry." She was sincere. "The wheels of justice grind slow."

"If they're still moving. Sometimes I wonder."

"They nabbed a lot of corrupt officials with the Tennessee Waltz sting," Greta said.

I chuckled. "Looks like they missed a few, doesn't it?"

We both stood up. She walked me to her office door.

"Thanks again for your time on this," I said.

She winced. "We never talked about this, okay?"

"Sure."

My shoes echoed on the hard wooden floor as I walked to the front door.

Bailey's daughter was a bigger part of this than any of us suspected. The question now was how to use the information to help the Camerons find peace. And maybe justice.

The heat wave had broken after the rain had moved through. Autumn was harder in the air now, and my spirit was more upbeat. My heart was warm in spite of losing my career. In truth, I was happy at being forced out of the expert witness business. No more depositions with rabidly aggressive lawyers. No more cross-examinations in trials.

I'd find something else to do. Maybe work part time and teach at a community college. Somewhere no one knew me. It could work.

The thought of running away was still making me smile when a couple of stiff guys in black suits approached me on the sidewalk. I'd seen them coming, but assumed they were Mormons.

"Mr. Graves?" A badge flashed in front of me. "We're from the FBI, and we need to talk."

CHAPTER 13

"Your place or mine?" I asked.

Neither of them smiled. "Our field office is in the Federal building around the corner," one of them said. He had a thin mustache. His partner gestured for me to walk with them. He went for the clean-shaven look.

"I don't suppose I have a choice." I looked around for a bystander to grab as a witness.

"Of course you do. This isn't the movies. But then we'd have to get a warrant and it would end up getting messy, legally speaking."

"And it's just more work for us," the clean guy said.

"Work makes my partner irritable," mustache guy said.

Clean guy shrugged.

"Can I see your ID again?" I asked. I reached for my phone but mustache guy cleared his throat.

"Please don't touch your phone."

My demeanor stayed relaxed but internal alarm bells went off. Allison. The bank.

Rob's words: no one can react faster than you can act.

At this close distance it would be brutally quick and violent. Clean guy goes first. Punch to the throat, step in and pull, two in the chest of mustache guy, then swing around and put two in clean guy.

My guts tightened up.

I raised my left hand to scratch my ear so it would be closer to clean guy's throat and slid my right towards my pocket.

They stepped back.

"Goddamn it, we're Federal agents," mustache guy said. He slid his own hand towards his jacket.

We both froze, hands near our steel.

"You really want to go down this road?" I asked. I had once been ranked third in the Southeast in drawing and firing a shot into the ten-ring. I also knew who the first and second ranked shooters were. And it wasn't these guys.

Mustache guy relaxed first. "You do it, and the last thing you'll see is a needle in your arm."

"How about names?" Maybe they were legitimate.

"Jesus Christ," clean guy said. He inched his hand away from his jacket.

"Okay. And you?" My eyes shifted to mustache guy.

"Paul."

"Okay, Jesus and Paul, the last time I dealt with two guys in cheap black suits, they tried to abduct a friend of mine."

"If we wanted to hurt you, you'd be dead already. You never saw us coming."

"Actually, I did, but I thought you guys were Mormons. So why can't I invite my lawyer to our little meeting?"

"Because you've stumbled into a rather sensitive operation." The voice came from behind me. I straight-armed Paul. He stumbled into Jesus. I whirled to face the threat but didn't pull the gun. Older man, gray suit.

The two agents righted each other. Paul took a step towards me, retribution in his eyes, then stopped as the older guy held up his right hand.

"I said to keep it quiet," the older man growled at them. He jerked his thumb over his shoulder. Paul and Jesus kept their eyes on me and retreated to a safer distance.

"We can talk here," he said. "You'd have to surrender your pocket buddy if we went to my office anyway." He extended his hand. "William Kidd."

"Can I call you Billy?"

"I get that all the time. Call me William, please."

I shook his hand. "What's with the Christians?"

He ignored the question. "We could arrest you for assaulting a Federal agent with that stunt you just pulled."

"I'd be grateful if you didn't."

"Then please cooperate."

"How?"

"Shut up and listen." Hard words, spoken through a false smile. "You said you were familiar with the FBI sting operation that concluded a few years ago? Tennessee Waltz?"

Chills ran up my spine. I hadn't said that to Jesus and Paul. I narrowed my eyes and nodded.

William nodded back. "We have another underway. This one deals with judicial corruption."

"I see." These guys weren't following me. They were watching Greta Wilson.

He nodded. "You understand that things are of a sensitive nature, then. Can we agree on that?"

"Yes." I shifted my weight.

"And I think we can also agree that your last courtroom escapade had a rather deleterious effect on your career?"

God, these guys were everywhere. "Yup."

"Okay, I think this is working," William said. He stared out at the street, rocking back on his heels. "You might be provided with the opportunity to rectify the situation in the future, albeit not in this particular case. All you have to do is not interfere with what we're doing. Does that sound amenable to you?"

"Absolutely," I said. Jesus and Paul were hanging back, pretending to talk to each other. "But I still have a job to do." Judith. Cathy. Allison. And that little son of a bitch who ran her brother off the road.

"Understood," William said. "But if your job interferes with ours, and I don't get my bad guys, then you don't recover your career, and I don't get my promotion. And if I don't move up, then my agents don't get their promotion, either. And then you have a bunch of people in the Federal Bureau of Investigation who are extremely upset with you. Does that sound like someplace you really want to be?"

"Is that a threat?" I asked.

"Not at all," William said. "An example of a threat would be that I would charge you with conspiracy against the United States government and make you disappear for a while. Or that you've been accused of aiding and abetting foreign nationals who have clear links to terrorism."

My blood chilled. "That's not true. None of that is true."

"Doesn't matter. You'd still be tied up for years trying to clear your name while a dozen U.S. prosecutors try to use your case to advance their careers. But it rarely comes to that." He shrugged, then scratched his chin. "People usually begin to cooperate much earlier than that, when the financial pressure increases. How's your tax situation?"

"I'm clean," I snapped.

"No one's clean, Mr. Graves." William smiled again. "But even if you were, the financial toll of an aggressive IRS audit is expensive and time-consuming. And it's just the beginning."

A lady with peppermint-striped glasses and a Greyhound came speedwalking down the sidewalk. We stepped back to let her pass.

William smiled at her. As if she were clairvoyant, she eyed him suspiciously.

"I'll ask you again, Mr. Graves. Do you want us to be upset with you?"

His words angered me. But I didn't see a way out. "No."

William studied me. Our eyes probed each other. He pursed his lips.

"Good," he said. "We have an understanding."

I nodded. "Tell Jesus I'm sorry for pushing him away."

"He'll get over it." William extended his hand again. "We're not the bad guys, Mr. Graves. Just let us do our jobs."

I forced my hand to meet his. He turned to leave.

"One more thing," I asked. "Did you know about Palmer?"

He stopped, fixing his gaze on the ground. "It's always women that get them. They might say it's drugs, or money, but it's always the women." Sadness tinged his voice.

I puzzled over his words. Billy the Kidd collected Jesus and Paul to resume their covert crusade.

~~~

Driving home. I reflected on Billy the Kidd's words about recovering my career.

Instead of bringing comfort and hope, they brought consternation.

I wasn't certain I wanted my career back, even if I could have it.

The loss of my career was having a strange and euphoric effect on me. The weather was cooling down, the sky was bright blue, and I suddenly ached for a new car. The Mercedes was large, heavy, and safe, but the imposing mass of the car that had made me feel protected and isolated now felt cumbersome and leviathan. With my career over, I felt the desire for protection slipping away. The physical barriers that I
~~~

was in the process of constructing around me were formidable, yet unfinished, and without the income from my consulting job, they'd never be complete.

The loss was also liberating. It was nearly the worst thing that could happen to me, to lose the career that I'd invested nearly half of my life in building, not to mention the debt I'd incurred in building it. Yes, I had lost it, but I was still breathing. I still had my health, and my life, and I could still eat and drink and sleep and watch the sun set. All of the effort I'd put into building my ramparts and fortifications had been washed away in one event, like a fisherman losing his boat and all of his nets and tools in a violent storm and then finding himself alive and washed up on a rocky coastline.

Losing everything had nullified the fear of losing everything. I smiled at the lesson.

And the other side effect was feeling my compulsive desire for physical safety begin to release its steel claws from my heart. And with that came the desire for a small, fast car. Something fun, and unusual, and unique. And affordable.

My mind played through the options, grateful for the distraction.

If I made it through this semester and this case, I'd find a way to buy one.

My right hand tapped the Bluetooth headset. "Allison."

The phone took over and dialed her number.

"Hey," she said.

"You okay?"

"Great. How about you?" Her voice probed cautiously.

"Oh, fine," I said. "We're cool, right?"

"Cool. We are cool. Iceberg cool. Polar bear cool-"

I interrupted her before she made another arctic reference. "I learned some interesting things about the case today."

"You have my complete attention."

"Turns out that Johnny's dad and Judge Bailey had met before. Three years ago one of Harrell's strip clubs was raided by the local police. They didn't find any gambling equipment so they rounded up all the working girls to harass him. One of them was Bailey's daughter. And she had a significant amount of cocaine on her. Enough for a felony conviction, if she'd been an adult."

Now Allison interrupted me. "No, that wasn't Bailey's daughter. That was a different girl. I remember hearing something about that after I graduated."

"Yeah, but Kelly was there with her, and she had a bunch of cocaine, too. Two underage girls were there."

Allison took a minute to process it. "Well, it doesn't surprise me. Kelly was a wild one. Did her dad get her out of it?"

"That's what Greta said."

"Who's Greta?"

"The attorney who prosecuted James Harrell. She was there that night and knew Kelly was Bailey's daughter. Did you know this other girl?"

"I remember her, but not her name. Started with a J... she ran with Johnny's crowd. Hard life story. Mom died young, dad was abusive. She dropped out of school about a year after I graduated."

"Another victim of abuse," I said quietly.

"So what are you thinking?" she asked.

"One possibility is that Bailey threw the hearing for Johnny because Johnny's dad threatened to expose the flap with his daughter. Ruin his senate bid."

"And hurt your career in the process."

"That too."

"What's the other possibility?"

"Bailey is being investigated by the FBI. He's got to be in deeper than just covering up a scandalized daughter."

"Like what?"

"For starters, he asked a THP trooper to get rid of the cocaine that his daughter had. Then Kelly went home, and the other girl went to Elkinridge."

Allison laughed quietly. "Yeah, that might be a little negative. And illegal."

"You knew Kelly Bailey, right?"

"Only through Chris, and not very well. She was two years behind me in school."

"Do you know where she is now?"

"Last I heard, her dad sent her to Europe on some kind of Baptist college exchange program. Do you need to talk to her?"

"Even if I could, do you think she'd be cooperative?"

"No way." Allison said it bluntly. "She broke my brother's heart. She left Chris for Johnny." No room for debate. "But hang on a sec."

I waited, listening to things being tossed on the floor. Then she was back.

"Okay," she said. "Here's the yearbook. And the winner is..." She paused again. "Jennifer Cox. Wow. God, she looks so young in this photograph."

"Think she's still around?" I asked.

"I'll find her for you." Allison was resolute.

~~~

"You can't do it," Allison said. "You can't go to the club. We'll find another way to talk to her."

We stood side by side against the breakroom counter. It was the first time I'd returned to see her at her bank since the attempted abduction.

"It was your idea." I took the cup from Allison's hands.

"They'll kill you if they recognize you."

"You're certain she's at The Emerald Club?" The coffee was bitter. I glanced around for sugar.

"Yes. No. I don't know."

"Won't hurt if I pop in and take a look around."

"It might."

"Jealous of a lap dance?" I elbowed her gently.

She grabbed my arm and held fast. Just as quickly, as if she sensed she'd made a mistake, she let go. "Soren, this is serious."

"I'll be in and out within an hour. Just long enough to make contact. I promise."

~~~

My tires crunched on the gravel of the Emerald Club's parking lot. Bright neon slit the night on the building façade. There was a space near the road out of sight of the club's entrance and I backed my car in so it would be easier to leave if things went sour.

I hung back until a group of other guys walked to the building. I fell in behind them, closing the gap as we climbed the wooden stairs to the main entrance. My body language mirrored theirs. Clumsy movements, nervous laughter.

"Ten," the steroidal bouncer said. His juiced buddy hung back, arms crossed. It was hard to see his fingers for the tattoos stitched on his arms. Something familiar about him.

The Crown Vic driver. The one who tried to abduct Allison.

My head stayed down. My heartbeat accelerated. I handed over two fives and followed the group inside.

Loud. Smoke. Overwhelming pressure waves from the bass of the music pushed on my chest.

I glanced behind. The bouncer didn't follow me. He was focused on the next group of men coming up the steps.

The guys in front of me provided cover as I took in the room. The place was dark but the décor looked like someone had sprayed dark red velour over every exposed surface. In the center of the room was the stage, an elongated 'T' ringed with tiny bright lights. Dark brass poles connected the stage floor to the ceiling at each end. Individual tables ringed the stage. Deep high-backed booths buttressed the walls. The main bar was against the right wall. It was packed with fully-dressed men and near-naked girls. The girls were doing their best to separate the men from their money like they'd been separated from their clothes.

A few girls had already identified the prey in front of me and were making beelines for them. I ducked to the left, keeping my head down and threading my way over the thin carpet to a dark booth. Within a minute of my body hitting the tainted cloth there was a girl at the table. She bent her leg and slid her knee onto the space next to me, leaning in closer.

"Hi, baby. Been here before?"

She had innocent brown eyes but a soulless voice that betrayed the sin she'd seen. Impossibly long brown hair swept over her shoulders and down her back, cascading over her arm as she leaned in.

"First time," I said. Nervous smile. I looked past her, trying to find the girl who matched the yearbook photo Allison had shown me.

More scrutiny. She leaned forward and pulled on my collar, then ran her hands down my chest, pushing aside the suit jacket. I stiffened.

"There's a first time for everything." She said it slowly and worked me with her eyes. "My name's Britney. Lap dance is twenty. If you want to go back in the club rooms it's fifty."

I nodded. "I think I need to relax first."

"Oh, honey, I'll make sure you're totally relaxed." She ran her fingers around the inside of my belt.

I fought the impulse to grab her wrist and break it into two pieces. *Get your goddamn hand out of there.* Sweat broke out on my forehead.

"I was thinking more along the lines of a drink," I said. This was going to be hard. *It's just an act. It's all an act.* My body flushed, ready to vomit. I reached into my pocket, popped a stick of spearmint gum in my mouth.

She pulled her hand back. "Will you buy me one, too?"

The mint helped steady me. She was trying to keep my attention but I looked past her, fixing on the girls on the floor and on the stage. They all wore heavy make-up, as if it shielded them from the hazards of their job like a welder's visor. A glimpse of straight blond hair behind the stage caught my eye. I followed it around. The facial structure matched the photo.

Britney got the message. "You see something else you like, sugar?"

"Oh, I don't know." I said it awkwardly. Blond girl was trolling the tables.

"Come on, now. Maybe we can all party together."

"Yeah, sure." If she didn't get the message, this was going to be a long night. Blond girl was cruising the booths now.

"You like blondes, baby?"

"Gosh, I don't know. Yeah." Blond girl sauntered past us without looking at me. Occupied customer. I made a show of turning to watch her pass.

Britney called after her. "Nicki!"

Damn. Wrong one.

The girl stopped and turned. Britney motioned and she walked towards us, slowing on the approach.

"Hey, baby," Nicki said. Britney moved over. Nicki slid onto the seat next to me, pushing hard against my thigh. I slid over to make room. Two girls would not be cheap. The way things were going I'd have a dozen over here by the time I found Jennifer.

Nicki's face was more visible in the dim light now. Her eyes were the same as the photo Allison had shown me. Wait a minute. Had to be her. I hoped it was. Coming back here again would be too hard.

"Hi," I said. My eyes lingered on her nearly exposed chest. "Wow."

"You like what you see?" She traced a long slender finger over the delicate curve of her breast. My face flushed hot. Britney burst into laughter.

I stammered out a reply but kept my eyes on Nicki. Britney understood. She slid out of the booth and whispered to Nicki that I was clean, then disappeared among the tables.

"I really need a drink, baby. Can you help me?" Her fingers tickled my thigh.

"Sure. Uh, how do I..."

The server came out of nowhere. "Shots?" she offered.

"No thanks," I said. "Crown and ginger for me and something for my friend."

Nicki reached for one of the tall thin shot glasses on the server's tray. She knocked the amber liquid back in one motion.

"I guess that'll be it," I said. The server took off for the bar.

"Thanks, baby. This is thirsty work." She ran her tongue over her lips and giggled.

"Yeah." I resumed the ping-pong game of looking at her chest and eyes.

"Twenty for a lap dance, fifty for the club rooms." She was watching me while scanning the rest of the club for more prey simultaneously.

The server dropped my crown on the table. Nicki reached up and grabbed another shot.

"Eight for the two shots, eight for the crown," she said.

I dropped another twenty on her tray. She turned without a word.

Sweet soda hit my tongue, tinged with the familiar subversive medicinal bourbon. We sat through another song.

"So how about that club room now?" Impatience in her voice this time.

"Sure."

She slid out of the booth, pulling me with her. I grabbed my drink and kept my head down, but my eyes scanned for

Johnny or anyone who might recognize me. We brushed through a heavy dark curtain that looked like part of the wall and entered a black-light hallway. She checked a couple of doors and then opened one. She pushed me in and then followed behind.

There wasn't anything obvious in the room that could have hidden a camera or microphone, but they had to have some way of keeping an eye on the girls. Discretion was in order.

"Sit down, baby."

She gestured to an abused low-backed loveseat. I pulled out my wallet instead, counting out ten hundreds. She was in the process of going back out in the hallway but stopped when she saw the cash.

"What do have in mind, baby?"

"More than what fifty would get me."

She took her hand off the doorknob and moved closer to me, reaching for the cash. I pulled it back to my chest.

She gave me her most seductive look. "Three-fifty for half an hour, six for a whole. Six buys you half-and-half."

"Half and half?"

"Suck and fuck." She whispered it but the crudeness hit me hard.

"I was just hoping to talk."

It was the first time I'd seen anything other than a dead expression on her face. "Talk?" Unbelieving and uncertain. Nervous.

"Relax. I'm not the law." I peeled off a hundred and pressed it in her hand. "Do you know Kelly Bailey?"

She raised an eyebrow. I sat down. She stood there. Internal battle in her mind. "Is the rest of that mine?" She pointed at the cash in my hand.

"Yes. All you have to do is talk to me. If you don't know something, then just say 'I don't know'. And I'll make it six if it takes a half-hour."

Nystagmus took over her eyes. Me. The door. Me. The door. If she went out, then I'd have to follow and get the hell out of here in a hurry.

"Please," I said. "I'm a friend of Allison Cameron. You're Jennifer, right? I'm just trying to piece things together for them."

"About Chris," she said. She blinked back to me. "Oh, Christ."

I held up another hundred. She groaned. She rubbed her hand over her face. "Oh, man. Oh, man." She stepped closer to me. I gave her the bill.

"Okay, look, I need to do something right now, okay?" She fidgeted with her small purse.

"If you leave the room, I'm gone." I waved the hundreds at her.

She shrugged. "Fine." She went over to a small table in the corner. "You'll just have to watch, then."

She pulled a small make-up compact and vial from her purse. She opened them both and spilled a small mound of white powder on the compact mirror. She cut it with a razor and rolled up the hundred I'd just given her.

My stomach turned. My eyes stayed on the far wall as she snorted up the drug. Oh, yeah, what a glamorous life. The pathogen count on the average bill is off the charts, worse than the dirtiest public toilet you've ever seen. The room was probably crawling with nightmare germs. Nausea rose up in me for the second time.

"You party?" she asked, sniffing back mucus.

"No."

"Don't know what you're missing." More upbeat now.

Sure. An overload of dopamine and glutamine into the cerebral cortex that eventually prevents the body from making its own. Then nothing can make you smile except the drug. Nothing but the drug activates the pleasure center of the brain. Not seeing your newborn child smile for the first time, not seeing your lover on a bright sunny day. The drug becomes the idol of worship that replaces everything good in your life. It's not a ride up, it's a descent into hell.

"Goddammit," she said.

"What?"

"The look on your face. You're a real buzzkill."

"That's what my sister says."

She sniffed again. "I bet I'd like your sister."

I nodded. "You have something in common with her."

She smiled. "Yeah? What's that?"

"You've both seen your share of pain." I watched her face as I said it.

Tears formed in her eyes involuntarily. "Screw you," she said. She got up and walked to the door.

I waved the hundreds. She stopped.

"I wasn't trying to hurt you. I'm sorry. For whatever it is you've been through."

"You don't understand. Guys never do." She wiped her eyes.

"I do," I said. The pain radiated off of her. I peeled off another hundred and extended it to her.

She looked at me, then walked over and took the bill. "Did they get to you, too?" she asked quietly.

"Yes."

"How old were you?"

"Eight years old. It went on for almost a year."

She searched my eyes. "Family?"

"Neighbors. My parents both worked late, and they left me and my sister with them after school. They ran a day care out of their house." I had to turn away. "I can't..."

"It's okay," she said. "I'm sorry."

I nodded, tears filling my own eyes.

She sat down on the loveseat. "Look, I'll try to help you out, but what makes you think I know anything important?"

I sat down at the other end. "Do you remember when this place was raided by the cops? About four years ago?"

"When I was sent to Elkinridge." She nodded. "Yeah, I remember that. Don't want to, but I do."

"Kelly Bailey was here with you, wasn't she?"

"She was. Jesus, that girl could party." Jennifer's mouth twisted into a wry smile.

"What exactly happened that night?"

She shrugged. "Cops came in, went in the back rooms, then came back out pissed and rounded us up. Kelly and I got caught up with them. We weren't really working so much as just hanging out. Well, Kelly wasn't really working. I was. She was crazy. Had a wild streak you wouldn't believe. If it could be done, then she did it. She always had money from her dad, but I didn't."

"What happened after the cops got you?"

"One of them recognized Kelly. She got a ride home with a cop, and I got herded in with the other girls. They didn't believe I was underage until they ran my fingerprints." She opened her purse again. "I need to smoke. Smoke or coke."

"Smoke. It's okay."

She lit the cigarette. "I went through all the legal stuff, but I didn't testify against the boss at trial."

"The boss?"

"Harrell. Johnny's dad. Kelly's dad was the judge. Man, that was crazy. The whole thing was just weird. Bailey told me before I got on the stand that I needed to stay silent, otherwise I'd be sent to jail for a long time."

"When did he do this?"

"At the detention center that night. He scared the shit out of me. He said that the government would take me away and lock me up for a long time if I said anything about working in the club. Said it was for my own good. He told me if I said anything about Kelly they'd lock her up, too, and that we couldn't ever be friends again. So when I went on the stand, he kept looking at me, and I clammed up. Then the bastard sent me to juvie anyway. But it wasn't bad. I had someone looking out for me. When I got back here, Kelly never got into any of the clubs again. She was running with Johnny and his crowd but they never let her in."

"They didn't send you to Elkinridge?"

She nodded her head. Ashes fell onto the carpet. "They did. But like I said, I had someone looking out for me. I knew I needed someone to watch my back."

"Kelly's dad?"

She laughed. "Hell, no. The same cop who took Kelly home that night." The tip of the cigarette glowed bright orange as she took a drag.

"What do you mean?"

"He kind of singled me out. Came to visit me at Elkinridge a lot. I could tell he was interested in me. Men are so easy to see through. He wanted to fuck me in a bad way." She glanced at me. "Look, if you ever get locked up somewhere, you've got to have someone on the outside to help you out. Send you money and smokes. None of my family is worth a damn. And having a cop is better than anyone else, because whenever I got threatened by another inmate, he'd tell the guards, and they'd set the other girl straight."

"That's the way life works," I said.

She nodded. "Anyway, there was a girl here at the club who got stopped for speeding by a cop, and she offered to fuck him if he'd let her off with a warning. He did it, but she pulled a Monica on him and got his jizz on her clothes, and then later she accused him of rape and got him fired. Nearly got him thrown in jail." She chuckled.

"Is that what you did with the cop who took you home?"

"Something like that." She blew a cloud of smoke toward the ceiling. "He wanted it, and I let it happen. Made him feel safe, then got him wound up, so horny he was about to pop like a zit. Then I fucked him in his police car." She smiled. "He was mine from then on. From there, he just got in deeper and deeper."

"How could he get in more trouble than that?" I asked her.

"You ever been high?" she asked me.

"No."

"And you've never had sex while you're high, then." She grinned. "Baby, it's the best feeling in the world. That's how I got him to try it."

"Is that how you got hooked?"

"I'm not hooked."

"Sorry."

She was silent for a minute. "Fuck, maybe I am. He sure got hooked. Then Johnny's dad found out about him, and then it was over for the guy. But I got all the blow I could use out of the deal."

I already knew who it was, but I needed to hear it from her to confirm it. "His name?"

She lowered her gaze to the dirty carpet. "He's dead now, so it don't matter. His name was Glen Palmer."

The doorknob wiggled.

"Busy," Jennifer yelled. Then she looked at me. "I should come over there in case someone comes in," she said.

"Sure." I slid over and put my arm on the side of the loveseat. She rubbed the cigarette out and threw it in the corner of the room. She was a different person now. No longer the shrewd business prostitute, more of a broken little girl. The heavy make-up looked clownish. Her posture slumped. The lingerie lost its effect with her vulnerability.

"So you know about Johnny? About his dad, what they do?" She brushed her hair back.

"Some of it. Only what Allison told me."

"She always seemed nice. And her brother was so sweet on Kelly. She probably screwed half of Johnny's friends while they were dating, and he never believed it."

"Love is blind, I guess."

She nodded. Her fingers tapped my chest. I peeled off another hundred.

She folded it into her bra. "You're the guy who was supposed to prove Johnny killed Chris when they were racing."

"Yeah, I am. It didn't turn out that way, though."

"You can't win against them. They own everything around here."

"Seems that way." I shifted my body. "Did Johnny say anything about the race that night?"

She tapped my chest again. I placed another hundred in her hand.

"This was the first place he came after it happened. He pulled the car in the garage out back and did something with the wheels. We all heard about what happened and went to see if he was okay and he just told us all to shut up and that we didn't see anything."

The thing about the wheels got me. "He was changing the wheels?"

"Yeah."

"Out back? Of here?"

She gestured with her hand. "That's what I said. They run a chop shop in the building behind this one."

"You think they're still there?"

She shrugged. "Gosh, I don't know."

Wheels. Paint damage. If the wheels had a shred of paint that came from Chris's Mustang, then that would put the cars together. Finding them here would connect them to Johnny.

Her hand brushed against mine. She leaned in close to me. "You sure there's nothing else you need while you're here?"

I straightened up and put some distance between us. "Yes. I need to see those wheels."

"From Johnny's car?" Her eyes widened.

"Quietly," I said. "If you can help me without getting yourself into trouble."

I didn't want to call Ken or Matthews without first seeing the wheels myself. If the cops swarmed all over this place Johnny or his dad would add things up and Jennifer would come after the equal sign. My plan was just to sneak out the back and check the other building out, verify the wheels were there, and then call the cavalry tomorrow.

"Can I have the rest of those?" She pointed at the bills in my hand.

I handed them to her.

We got up. She inched open the door and checked the hallway. "All clear," she whispered. We walked down the dim corridor toward the main room.

"Are you going to be safe?" I asked.

She looked at me the same way other people do when I ask a naïve question. "You understand what I do, don't you?"

"Right. Sorry."

"The building is fenced from the outside, but if you sneak through the back of the club you'll come out in the alley between the buildings. The tricks go out that way all the time. After that it's up to you."

"Tricks?" I asked.

"Customers," she said.

I nodded. We came to the heavy black curtain. Jennifer pulled it aside.

And there was Billy.

CHAPTER 14

We stared at each other like idiots. He couldn't shout a warning because of his broken jaw. He grunted like a wild pig and tried to turn back into the club. My right arm shot out and caught him in the gut. I stepped close into him and swung my left arm around his neck and pulled him into the hallway. The curtain fell back across the opening.

My punch landed solid but he was big. He reared up and brought his right arm around in a wild haymaker. I pushed myself against his body and it was his bicep that connected to my head. I brought my right hand up hard against his jaw, smashing the wires that had set it in place for the first fracture. Bad breath and saliva speckled my face. The cast on his left arm cracked me on the back of the head and I saw stars. I rammed the heel of my open hand against his injured jaw twice more, feeling it crack again on the third blow. Then he went limp and I had the strain of two-hundred and fifty pounds pulling me to the floor.

I twisted my body so he was on my back. I limped and dragged him into the room Jennifer and I had just left. The cord from a lamp bound him like a trussed hog. The awkward angle of his jaw told me he wouldn't be shouting for help. As I was pulling the door shut behind me Jennifer grabbed me and pushed me against the wall. Her mouth met mine. Her lips and tongue danced around my own, heavy with the taste of cigarette smoke. I nearly gagged.

"What the fuck was that about?" The voice was heavy male and came from one of the other doorways in the hall. "Is that you, Nicki? You okay?"

Jennifer pulled her face away from mine. "Fuck off, Jake. Customer."

In my peripheral vision I saw a big bald guy covered with tats. Black cast on his right arm. Rob had broken that arm. He stared at us for a moment, then closed the door.

"Did Billy see you?" I asked. My gaze stayed on the door Jake had closed. If he recognized me, that door would be opening any second.

"I don't think so. No. Too dark in here." She wiped her lipstick off my face with her hand.

"You should go. Get out of here. They'll figure out I was with you."

She gave me another pitying look. "Whatever happens, happens. I have to make my living."

"It's not a living, it's a dying."

She shrugged. She checked the door to make sure it was locked. We walked to the end of the hall.

She peeked out the curtain this time, then moved it aside. I followed her through it. She walked for the tables, and I walked for the back door.

My head stayed down as I followed some other guys on their way to the bathroom. The exit was just past the bathroom doors. No alarms on this one. I pushed the door open and was greeted by chilled night air. I slipped out, easing the door closed, then walked quickly over to a dark pool of shadows on the corner of the other building. A minute went by, then two. Nothing else moved in the alley.

I inched my way along the wall and around the corner. This part of the building was more exposed, opening into a large lot surrounded by the perimeter fence. Bright overhead sodium vapor lights illuminated the lot and building front. I walked quickly to a recessed doorway. Two roll-up garage doors braced the other side of the door and lined up with the fence gates across the lot. Soft yellow light emanated from the wire-reinforced glass in the door. I could barely see through the dirty glass. It looked empty.

I tried the door anyway. The metal doorknob turned and clicked. It was open.

I glanced around me one last time and then turned the knob the entire way. I pulled back on the handle while pushing the door open with my body to keep the door in tension as it swung open. Faint strains of hard rock reached my ears. Panic swelled inside me. The sound was coming from a battered stereo on the floor next to the paint mixing area. An open pack of cigarettes and a paint-stained lighter were next to the stereo, but there wasn't a hint of tobacco smoke in the air. I moved quickly through the doorway, then locked the door as it latched. The shop was empty. No one was home.

It was a typical body shop, but the cars were exceptional. A spanking new Z06 Corvette was missing all its glass on one end. Two Mustangs flanked it, one missing front sheetmetal and the other missing an engine. A bright red Dodge Viper looked intact. A mid-sixties Corvette convertible was in the air on a lift. Two late-model BMW 6-series convertibles were in the process of being clipped. The damaged back half of one had been sawed completely off and an undamaged rear half was being welded on from the donor car next to it. The donor car wasn't damaged in the front, though. Probably stolen. They were cutting up a perfectly good $80,000 car to fix one that had been junked as salvage.

Then I saw it. My breath caught in my throat.

Next to the donor BMW was a gorgeous dark grey Ferrari F12.

A paint booth took up one corner of the building. Drums of reducer and paint solvent were stacked underneath and around the main electrical box next to the paint booth. These guys definitely weren't OSHA compliant. There was also way too much solvent just to be used for painting. Clean burning fuel for cooking methamphetamine was more likely.

There were three stacks of tires near the car lifts. They were too far away for me to make out the tread design or the wheel faces. As I reached the halfway point between the tires and the cars, my emotions took over. I veered over to the Ferrari.

The car was art in its truest sense. The curves of the hood and the rear flanks evoked emotion and lean power. Heavy tint colored the glass black. It was beautiful, a rolling sculpture that rebelled against the banality of convention and compromise. The shape of the body made it seem indecipherably foreign, sensuously alien. The surrounding cars looked banal in comparison. Pininfarina was the Italian design house that created the shape for this Ferrari. The founder, Battista Farina, had built his company on the philosophy that the lines of a car should be like those of a beautiful woman, so that even as she ages one can still see the beauty of her youth. This car was the essence of those words.

My fingers caressed the latch. A little upward pressure told me the door was unlocked. A little more pressure and the latch tripped and the door popped open. The interior light immediately illuminated and the car chimed loudly. Resisting the urge to slam the door shut, I yanked it open further and leaned in, fumbling with the key that had been left in the ignition. The chiming stopped. I raised my head, listening. Still nothing. My right hand went to the seat bottom to push my body out and pressed on a bunch of metal tags in a plastic bag. I looked closer. They were US VIN tags, faked, but accurate right down to the rivets that were supposedly unattainable outside the factory.

The speedometer was marked in kilometers per hour, which meant it was a European car that had been imported into the States. Normally this is an expensive proposition, but the VIN tags indicated that they weren't concerned with meeting Federal emissions regulations, and it was probably stolen. That would also mean the car wasn't easily marketable, so it must be someone's personal vehicle. Probably Johnny's father.

Wow. That meant he had great taste. And the rivets and VIN tags indicated these guys were sophisticated.

I inhaled the scent of the leather one more time before righting myself and closing the door softly. I knew everything about the car, including the price. Even on the used market, this thing cost twice as much as I owed in student loans. Maybe in another life. It sure as hell wasn't likely to happen in this one.

With that spell broken, I shifted back to the reason I was in this damn place: finding Johnny's wheels and tires. On my way to the stack of tires I passed the paint mixing area again. A Tyvek paint suit and respirator hung on a hook next to the racks of BASF paint cans. I paused for a moment, remembering my own days of working in a body shop, mixing paint and reducer, and spraying clearcoat so fine that it flowed out like a glossy curved mirror of liquid. There was something intensely satisfying in that labor of art and craftsmanship, I suddenly realized, that was absent in the forensic work.

A noise outside the building brought me back to reality. I froze. My sense of hearing magnified until I heard the buzz of the electricity flowing through the lights above. Nothing followed it.

The tread pattern on the first set of tires indicated that they were for light trucks. The second set looked more promising. The silver spokes were definitely from a performance car. Closer inspection revealed they were off a Corvette Z06. Strike two.

The third set were from a Dodge SRT-10 Viper. Strike three. I turned to head back out when I discerned a covered column of tires in the shadows of the corner. I pulled out my flashlight and cupped it in my hand, damping the bright beam so I could make my way to them. I doused the light and pulled the cover up and off, then lit them up again.

An HRE S102 alloy wheel stared back up at me. The light reflected off the polished finish. The rim on it was pristine, though, and the center cap was in place. I hefted it off the stack and put it on the floor. The next one had its cap and wasn't damaged either.

The third one showed scrapes and gouges on the rim. The wheel face was scuffed. Tiny flecks of black paint were embedded in the scratches of the aluminum. No center cap.

Gotcha, Johnny.

Voices outside. Shouting. I killed the light and lifted the other two wheels back on the stack. My adrenaline spiked. I threw the cover back on the tires but it snagged on the rubber treads. Precious seconds were lost as I frantically yanked on the canvas.

Hiding was out of the question. With my car out front it was only a matter of time until enough people left the parking lot to expose it. Every second that elapsed was one more closer to me being trapped with a bunch of thugs outside who would love to make me disappear. Making matters worse, I was the one trespassing, and under Tennessee law, they had every right to shoot first and never get around to asking questions.

I dashed back to the paint racks and grabbed the respirator and the paint suit. I paused, then grabbed the cigarette lighter as well. Through the glass in the door I could see flashlights heading this way. It was only a matter of seconds before they were in the building and I was a perforated engineer. I stuffed my feet in the legs of the suit and shrugged it on. Then I grabbed a rag from the bench and a can of slow reducer from the shelf, balling the rag in my hand and dumping reducer over it.

The Ferrari.

As I raced to the F12, I grabbed a crowbar on a table. Then I pulled out my Benchmade knife, flicked it open with a wrist snap, and sliced off a ten-foot section of half-inch rope from a coil in the corner. Almost ready.

I dropped the solvent-laden rag on the floor in front of the drums of paint solvent, then lit it on fire. The solvent erupted with a whoosh. I tossed some more rags on it to keep it burning and spread the flames.

Back to the driver's door of the Ferrari. I yanked it open and sat on the doorsill. I pulled both paddle shifters behind the wheel back to engage neutral, stepped on the brake, my hand turned the key, and the 6.3 liter 730-horsepower V-12 roared to life. I engaged first gear, pulled the car forward, and aimed it at the garage door. Then I engaged reverse and backed it up as far as I could. The more distance it had to accelerate, the faster it would be going when it slammed through the door. And I wanted it going *fast*.

"Sorry, baby," I whispered. I caressed the steering wheel, the curve of the dashboard. They didn't make many of these. Now there would be one less.

It had to be the Ferrari. For starters, I knew it had keys in it. More importantly, though, it had a special kind of transmission that suited my plan perfectly. Called the F1, this transmission used paddles instead of a traditional shifter, and it had an automatic mode as well. It had been designed for the rich customers who could afford these cars brand-new but didn't like the traditional gated manual shifter. To launch the car, all they had to do was rev it up and then pull back on the right paddle behind the steering wheel. The car would be at 60 mph in less than three seconds. All the driver had to do was point the car in the right direction and let off the brake pedal and pull the right paddle once.

To accomplish that, I looped the rope from the right spoke of the steering wheel to the passenger door handle. I yanked it hard, stretching the rope taut. The black leather on the steering wheel tore off the stitching. I looped it again, stretching it until it was like a steel cable. I reached over and pushed the button to put the car's transmission into automatic mode.

I snugged the crowbar against the accelerator pedal and then powered the seat forward. As it moved up, the pedal went down, and the muted burbling engine revved into a roar and then a scream. The tachometer was registering six thousand RPM. I hoped it would be enough.

My hand clawed inside the paint suit for my HK. I twisted my body on the doorsill, careful to keep the brake pedal pressed. The front sight lined up on the drums of solvent. I squeezed the trigger quickly, letting it return forward only far enough to reset the action to prevent slapping the trigger. Three quick double taps sent six .45 rounds into the bottoms of the nearest drums. The percussive booms echoed off the galvanized walls.

My right foot came off the brake. I reached over the steering wheel, pulled the right-hand paddle. The odor of burning friction plates drifted up as the clutch face engaged the flywheel. Then it grabbed and the tires screeched. I fell off the doorsill as the car jerked forward. The clutch engaged fully and it shot away from me like a rocket, gathering speed impossibly fast, seeming to defy physical laws as it raced to the garage door across the shop area. The engine screamed, wailing, pulling harder every second.

It hit the door like an Italian cruise missile.

The bottom of the garage door broke away from its tracks and flapped upwards, breaking the windshield and slamming down on the roof of the Ferrari as it streaked through. I had just enough time to cover my head before the solvent from the drums reached the flames.

Screw you, James Harrell.

The blast was enormous. The heat of the shockwave pummeled my body. The Tyvek suit and the respirator protected me from the brunt of the explosion.

I slung the respirator around my neck and ran towards the door.

"He's in the car!" I shouted it as loud as I could, then raised the HK and fired after the Ferrari. One round struck the rear taillight panel. Another whacked into the bumper. The car continued towards the fence gates, screaming, as if a demon were at the wheel.

Half a dozen guys were still trying to make sense of the situation. No further encouragement was needed. They aimed for the Ferrari as it was breaking through the fence. Volleys of pistol rounds hammered into the beautiful flanks as it broke the gate and screamed into the night.

"Get him! Don't just fucking stand there!" I shouted. They responded brilliantly, taking off after the vanishing car. I followed behind just long enough to get outside the fence and then ducked to the right. The Ferrari had crossed the gravel lot and zoomed over the main road. Harrell's men were running after it like armed marathon runners.

Time was running out. I stripped out of the suit and tossed the respirator in the weeds. I hit the magazine release of the HK and performed a tactical reload. I pocketed the HK and the nearly-empty magazine and rounded the front of the club. Patrons were beginning to congregate outside. I slipped next to the fringe and then crossed into the parking lot. A flash of blond hair in the entranceway might have been Jennifer. I hoped she'd be okay.

My car was within sight. Trembling hands dug in my pocket for my keys. My mind was processing what I'd done as my car slipped in between two other cars and headed out of the parking lot. On the main road I fumbled with my phone.

"Yeah?" Ken's voice.

"Hey, I got some great news." Two fire trucks screamed past me, headed for the club.

"It couldn't wait until tomorrow?"

"I found the wheels and tires from Johnny's Mustang. They're in the chop-shop behind the Emerald Club."

"Great, great. I'm happy for you. Now, I actually have a real job that requires me to get up early."

"The place is on fire. Physically burning. And they might know I found the wheels, so they'll probably try to move them. Oh, and there's a million bucks worth of stolen cars there, too. You don't have to come out, but if you don't mind, it sure would be great if you called some of your cop buddies who'll be here and let them know what to look for. Someone is going to want to take credit for this bust."

"You're shitting me." Ken was awake now.

"Nope." I veered to the shoulder to avoid a careening ambulance. "Come on, Ken. Just make the call."

"Yeah, yeah, okay." He was moving around. "Let me hang up so I can do it. Did you have anything to do with this?"

"I didn't shoot anyone, and if you find some shell casings, they won't yield any prints. My cop buddy told me to wipe them clean before they went in the magazine."

Ken groaned and hung up.

I'd debated telling him about Jennifer but figured she might be in more danger if the cops singled her out. I prayed I made the right call as I dialed Allison's number.

"How did it go?" she asked.

"Fine. Things got a little hot at the end."

"Are you okay?"

"Yeah, I'm fine. Little shaky, but okay." I checked my mirror out of habit.

"Did you find Jennifer?"

"I did. We talked. She was the one who corrupted Palmer. Harrell found out and blackmailed him."

"Oh, wow," Allison said. "Did she know anything about what happened between Harrell and Bailey?"

"Bailey scared Jennifer into not testifying against Harrell at the hearing, in return for Harrell keeping his daughter out his clubs. It completes the picture that we knew parts of. And it would be even worse for him if it got out."

"It's going to get out now." Firmness in her voice.

My promise to the Feds came back to me. "Yeah, but let's think carefully about how to handle that." The chance for redeeming my career was precarious.

Allison went quiet. "Think carefully about what? He's dirty. All it takes are some well-placed media stories and his political career is over. The upcoming interview my mom arranged with Pete Stryker is perfect for that. You're going to do that, aren't you?"

"I'll do the interview. But the rest of it isn't that simple."

She paused, sensing the truth. "It is, unless there's something more that you're not telling me." She waited for me to confess.

Damn it. "Allison, you can't repeat this. Not to anyone, especially your dad."

"Okay."

"Seriously."

"Look, if you don't want to tell me, then fine. Don't."

I prayed it wasn't a mistake to tell her. "The FBI is investigating Bailey. They're building a case, but if Bailey gets wise to them, he'll cover his tracks. It'll make it harder for the Feds to convict him. He might even be able to beat the charges."

Allison hesitated. "How do you know this? Did Ken tell you?"

"No. They had Greta under surveillance. When I met with her, they heard our conversation, and they realized I could jeopardize their investigation. They caught me as I left her office."

"And you didn't tell me," Allison said.

"I couldn't. It was better that you didn't know. Still is." I knew she was hurt.

"My brother was killed, Soren."

"I know. I'm sorry." This was making me uncomfortable. "Look, it's not all bad news. I also found the wheels and tires from Johnny's Mustang."

Noticeable pause. "How'd you do that?"

"They were in the building behind the Emerald Club. It's okay, I think the cops will have them by midnight. If Bailey goes down, then Johnny might be in court again, and they'll certainly be useful then."

"You think he'll be in court again?"

"Yes. But we can't say anything about Bailey until that time."

She didn't press me on the answer, but she didn't like it. "Where are you now?"

"Just leaving the club." I glanced at the clock. "I should be back at my place by one." Fatigue suddenly nailed me. My body was crashing as the last swirls of adrenaline dissipated from my blood.

"Okay." Uneasy silence. "I just..." her voice hung in the air.

"Something else?" She still couldn't let Bailey go. Or maybe she was sorry for what she said to me.

"No. Just be careful."

~~~

When left to our own devices we all determine the extent of our own punishment, and I was no exception. The chance to
~~~

get another shot at convicting Johnny had me motivated me to get on with my life. Running away wouldn't buy me anything. I had started down this road and I needed to see it through. Ken was right. As usual.

And that meant heading to the Bursar's Office at the University.

"Next," the lady at the window called out.

I advanced. "Can I pay my tuition in cash?" I asked her.

"Certainly!" she said. "We take all forms of payment. Cash, check, credit cards, you name it."

"Even livestock?" I asked.

She smiled. "You got me there. No livestock."

I began counting out the bills. "It's a large payment," I told her.

~~~

I worked on the dissertation the rest of the day. Short break to the weight room. Lunch was quick, cup of coffee to fight the nods, and back at it. I sent a brief email message to Peckem and the other committee members to update him on my progress. I fought the urge to surf the net and closed the browser when I was done. Then my phone interrupted my flow.

"This is Soren."

"Pete Stryker, Channel Two News. Steve Cameron gave me your number. Do you have a minute to talk?"

"Absolutely." I hit the floppy disk icon on the toolbar and watched my computer labor to save the dissertation. I wondered how many incoming freshman even knew what a floppy disk was.

"Steve tells me that you've found evidence that implicates the other person who was racing his son that night."

"It's complicated."

"I'm willing to listen."

The next fifteen minutes were spent bringing this guy up to speed on how the crash happened based on the evidence that I'd found on each car and the markings on the roadway. I made certain to keep the information as unbiased as possible.

"So this person, Johnny, intentionally killed Chris?" Pete asked at the end of my spiel.
~~~

"I'm certain of it. But I can't prove it. Like I said, the evidence just shows definitive contact between the two Mustangs. It doesn't indicate who swerved into who first."

"And then at the hearing, which you believe was a biased event, you weren't recognized as an expert, and the result was that the bad guy walked free."

I winced. "I'd really like to leave the hearing and the judge out of this. I don't need the heat from them." Or from the Feds who were after Bailey.

"Sure, sure." More writing. "So would you be willing to come down to the studio and do a short presentation of how you think the crash occurred? You know, with one of those airbag computers you mentioned?"

"Be glad to."

"And do you have any kind of computer animation that we can put on the air to show how it happened?"

The exhibits I'd used at the hearing were perfect for that. "No problem. When do you want to do it?"

"Tomorrow afternoon, about two?"

"I'll be there."

~~~

Ken met me for lunch before the television gig with Pete Stryker. He made a show of looking me over. "Your eyebrows are a little singed."

"Real funny." The server came over and we ordered.

"So how did it go?" I asked.

He whistled. "Unbelievable. Except for the BMW hit in the rear all the cars were hot. And not from the fire."

"How far did it spread?"

"Not far. The building was all steel, and the other cars were far enough from the drums that they only had minor damage. The Viper got it worst."

"Too bad." Moment of silence.

"So who got credit for the bust?"

"We did." Ken meant KPD. "A couple of our guys made it out there before any other departments. It was tense for a few minutes. They were armed to the teeth and ready to kill."

"Did you secure the wheels and tires from Johnny's Mustang?"
~~~

"I took care of that personally." He crushed a lemon wedge into his water. "They're at the station, tagged and bagged with the other evidence. TBI is coming back down to catalogue the cars."

"So what about James Harrell? Can you arrest him on this?"

"The DA is wrestling with that. The place is owned by a shell corporation and he needs to trace it back to Harrell for an arrest to stick."

I crushed a lemon into my own water and followed it with a few packs of sweetener. "The Ferrari?"

Ken looked pained. "Completely burned up. Couple of bullets penetrated the fuel tank, leaked onto the exhaust. Sad."

"It is." The Ferrari was an inanimate object, but Ken and I both felt a twinge of pain about it being destroyed. It was akin to watching a beautiful sculpture be demolished.

We sipped our lemon water in silent bereavement.

"You really pissed them off," Ken said.

I spread my hands. "They would have killed me. I didn't see another way out. I was an armed trespasser on their property."

"Your choice to carry a damn gun."

"Rather have it and not need it than need it and not have it." The food arrived and we cleared space for it.

"If you get to it in time."

"I always do." I sipped the water. "Did you round up the girls in the club?"

"Yeah, the usual." He tried to bite the dough, then dropped it on the plate. Hot calzone.

"Remember any blondes?"

He pursed his lips. "Got a name?"

"Stage name Nicki. Real name Jennifer Cox."

He shook his head. "Doesn't sound familiar."

~~~

After lunch I drove downtown to the Channel Two studio. It was off Broadway in a rough part of town. The sad, falling roof and upper story of the Fifth Avenue hotel was buttressed by the legion of homeless that sat on the sidewalk with their backs against the white block wall. The methadone clinic and homeless shelter stood proudly next to it and St. James Episcopal was a little further down on the same side.
~~~

The studio was housed in an old converted manor. Huge blocks of gray stone made up the exterior walls. I parked in back and was buzzed in the side door.

The college-intern receptionist took my name. “He’ll be with you shortly.”

I took a seat and waited, working on my dissertation on my laptop for a half-hour before the guy came out.

“Sorry for the wait. Crazy day.” He extended his hand and we shook.

“No problem.” I closed the laptop and put it back in the padded case. I followed him downstairs into the bowels of the building. The studio was in the basement. I opened my laptop back up and pulled up the crash event from Johnny’s Mustang. I had a dissected airbag computer with me to show him how it triggered to start recording when it sensed an impact.

“What I’d like to do is essentially go over the same thing you told me on the telephone,” Pete said. He straightened his tie and looked at the camera while he spoke to me.

“Okay.” A young girl was busy fitting a microphone to my belt. Then she reached for my lower shirt buttons. I reflexively grabbed her hands.

“It needs to go up inside your shirt,” she said. I took it from her and threaded it up to my collar and clipped it on the edge of the fabric. She did a mic test and nodded at the camera guy.

“Turn the ringer off on your phone,” she said quietly.

“Can you move your computer around?” the guy behind the camera asked. He was panning with the camera, trying to get a shot of the screen and myself and Pete. I moved it until he gave me a thumbs-up.

“Rolling,” the guy said.

Pete squared with the camera. “This is Pete Stryker with Two for You. Thanks for tuning in. Some of you may know about the strange and tragic suicide of a Tennessee State Trooper a few weeks ago. What you probably don’t know is how it is intricately connected to a crash that occurred earlier this year between two young boys who were drag racing in the outskirts of Clinton. One of the boys was killed in the race. And here in the studio next to me is the man who links both of those events together.”

The camera zoomed out and captured me in the frame. “Soren Graves, welcome to Channel Two for You.”

"Thanks, Pete. Glad to be here."

"Now, you were asked by the family of the deceased to reconstruct this crash, correct?"

"Yes, I was, a short time after it happened."

"And you learned some interesting things in the subsequent investigation, didn't you?"

"Yes. The crash report only lists the deceased's vehicle. It was ruled as a single car accident."

"But you found evidence to the contrary, didn't you?"

"I did. I located the other vehicle that the deceased was allegedly racing against, and a thorough inspection of both vehicles revealed that there had been contact between them that likely sent the victim's car out of control, resulting in his death."

"What kind of evidence did you find?"

"The airbag computer, or 'black box' of the other car showed two sharp but brief impacts. The first occurred to the left side of the vehicle, and the second occurred to the front of the vehicle. The one to the side corresponds with an impact to the right rear of the deceased's vehicle, and the one on the front corresponds to damage found on the right door of the deceased's vehicle." I turned the laptop so the camera could zoom in on the crash data on the screen.

"And was there any sign of damage to the other vehicle that corroborated this black box evidence?"

"There was. The left front wheel bearing of the other vehicle had been replaced immediately after the crash event, and the bumper had been repainted very recently after the event."

Pete made a show of looking into the camera. "And the shocking connection between the crash and the dead trooper when we come back."

He turned to me. "You're doing great."

The same young girl brought us two cups of water. I gulped mine down. The minutes flowed by.

"Welcome back to Two for You," Pete announced. "We're here with Soren Graves discussing the recent suicide of a Tennessee State Trooper and his connection to a mysterious crash that occurred earlier this year in Anderson County." He swiveled to me. "We had just finished talking about the evidence you found that the two cars had made contact with each other. What significance is that?"

"Well, the crash report showed that it was a single car accident, which clearly wasn't the case."

"And who wrote this report?" All he lacked was a drum roll.

"That would be Glen Palmer, the trooper who tragically took his own life."

"And is it obvious that the omission of the second car was intentional?" Pete made a grim face for the television camera.

"Without a doubt."

"Shocking," Pete said, looking into the camera. "And what is more shocking is the subsequent investigation by TBI into Palmer's personal life. Although we certainly don't know the all of the details of that investigation, it does appear that he may have been involved in illegal activities linked to the father of the young man who was driving the other car that ran the deceased's vehicle off the road, resulting in his death. Isn't that correct?"

My face must have blanched. This was off-script. He knew I didn't want to talk about this part of it. He was after the shock value.

"Ah, my investigation is relegated to the physical evidence between the vehicles involved in the crash," I said.

He pressed me. "Certainly. But it is true that Palmer had methamphetamine in his system and illegal drugs in his police car?"

The urge to pull a Bill O'Reilly and walk off the set overwhelmed me. "I don't know that I can comment on that. It's part of an ongoing criminal investigation." I kept a poker face. Pete backed off.

"There's certainly more here than meets the eye, though, isn't there?"

I nodded. "Yes."

That seemed to satisfy him. "Okay. Let's move to the crash itself. Were you able to determine how the deceased's vehicle left the road?"

"Yes. After the first impact to the right rear by the left front of the 2017 Mustang, the 1967 Mustang driven by the victim rotated out of control. It happened to rotate directly in front of the 2011 Mustang, which resulted in the sharp but brief impact on the front of that vehicle. After that, the 1967 Mustang slid sideways off the asphalt road surface, through the dirt shoulder, through a short section of grass, then impacted a line of trees bordering a creek."

"When do you think the killing blow occurred?"

I grimaced at his words. "There is evidence that indicates the fatal injury occurred at impact with the tree line."

"Can you tell us a little about how that happened?"

No, I wanted to say. I can't, and your bloodthirsty viewers will have to turn off their tubes unsatisfied and your ratings will just have to suffer for it. Then I thought of Cathy and Steve and Allison. They wanted the truth disclosed.

"The first major blow came from an eight-inch diameter tree that impacted the driver's door almost exactly where the driver's head would have been. This blow broke the driver's side window and intruded a significant distance into the passenger compartment, bending the rocker panel and the roof severely in toward the center of the car. The car then rotated up and over the tree line, coming down hard on the other side of the creek on its roof. This impact also likely caused major blunt force trauma to the top of driver's head. This was reflected by damage to the vehicle's headliner. After landing on its roof the car rolled several times, and further blunt force trauma that caused the subdural hematoma in all four quadrants of the driver's head would have occurred during that sequence."

Pete had placed his hand over his mouth as if in shock over my words. "That's horrible," he said quietly. He seemed to be genuinely affected by the description of the injury, even though I'd told him the same thing yesterday over the telephone.

"It is."

"And the police still deny the involvement of another vehicle?

"Not after my investigation. They rewrote the crash report to include the other Mustang."

"I see. Now, didn't this go to trial?"

The camera rotated back to me. "Not to trial. There was a preliminary hearing to see if the evidence warranted the charges brought against the other driver."

"And what was the result?"

This was dangerous ground. "The hearing essentially dismissed the case against the other driver."

"Did you feel it was a fair hearing?" Pete leaned in closer.

"No."

His eyes were begging for more detail. "Could you say any more about that?"

"No, not at this time."

C'mon, his face said.

No way, mine replied.

"This is certainly a crash that devastated a family." He recovered quickly. "And the entire story is yet to be heard. Viewers, if you have any comments or insights regarding this event, please call into the studio by the number on your screen and let us know. The lines are open." He paused a few seconds. "For Two for You, this is Pete Stryker reporting."

The camera guy gave him a thumbs-up. Pete immediately stripped off his mic. I did the same, pulling it down through my shirt and unclipping the receiver from my belt.

"Sorry, Pete. I just couldn't say anything more about the hearing." I placed the mic and receiver on the studio desk.

"There's something else. It goes further." He squinted his eyes. "I know a good story. There's more to this than you told me."

"I don't know. Maybe." I dug out my card and handed it to him. "If anyone calls that seems credible, would you send them my way?"

"I want exclusive rights to follow-up when the whole thing does break."

"That's fine. Great. When will this air?"

"Tomorrow afternoon. It'll lead the five-thirty segment."

He took the card. I gathered my items and left the studio.

~~~

I tapped my earbud and called Ken.

"Frazier." Gruff answer.

"Hey, it's me. You think I could see those wheels today?"

"Yeah, sure. Where are you now?"

"On Broadway, heading into town."

"They're at our storage facility off Cedar Bluff." His radio squawked. "I can meet you there in half an hour."
~~~

They had decent security. The parking lot was open but I had to be buzzed into the building. Ken was waiting for me.

"Sign in."

No metal detectors to pass through. It was a warehouse, not a jail. We pushed our way through heavy doors into the cavernous storage area.

"Where are the cars?"

"From the club?"

"Yeah."

"Outside." He gestured to the right.

We walked along the narrow aisles until we came to the same stack with the same cover I'd seen at the shop behind the club. Ken wrote something on the evidence card and then cut the plastic tie holding them together.

"They are nice," he said.

"Yeah. Do I need gloves?"

"Did you handle them at the club?"

"I did."

"Then you should probably skip the gloves here, too."

I lifted the top one off. The one underneath had the damage. They must have stacked them in opposite order when they were brought in. I pulled out my Surefire and lit up the rim. The gouges on the rim were still there. So were the flakes of black paint.

Ken slapped a plastic evidence bag against my arm. I used the tip of my folding knife to scrape off the paint flakes and drop them carefully in the bag.

"If the paint matches, doesn't it only prove that the wheels made the contact? How can we extend it to Johnny's car?"

"There's photographs of Johnny's car with these wheels on it prior to the crash," I said. "The wheels are rare and expensive, and the Ford dealer he got them from can be subpoenaed to produce the order sheet."

"If he didn't steal them."

"Doubtful. There aren't hardly enough around to steal. But it's a safe bet he bought them with dirty money."

Ken gave me a sideways glance. "You don't have much room to talk about dirty money."

"I spent it on my education. Think of it as a scholarship."

"All of it?"

I peeled off the tape and closed the bag. "Some of it."

Ken signed and dated the wire tag. "Who's going to do the spectroscopic analysis?" he asked.

"Eric is working out at ORNL. Y-12. He's got access to the equipment."

"Eric? How's he doing?" We'd all been in the undergraduate engineering program together.

"Fine, I guess. He transferred back here from the Savannah River nuke plant a couple of years ago. Two-year old daughter now."

"I remember when he got married." Ken helped me restack the top tire, then ran another plastic strap through the wheel spokes. The cover went on smoothly this time. It would when there's no one trying to kill you.

"So what happens now?" Ken asked me.

"It's, uh, complicated." My hands were black. "You got a sink around here?"

Ken led the way. "Complicated how?"

"If Matthews re-files charges, then Johnny gets arrested again." We washed the carbon off our hands. "The problem is that I can't testify."

"Okay." Ken knew there was more.

"If something were to happen to the first judge, say an indictment on corruption charges, then the previous hearing is invalidated."

Ken stopped scrubbing. "You're shitting me." He understood immediately.

"It has to stay quiet." I dried my hands. "Anyway, the short answer is that Johnny will be arrested again, and there'll be another hearing, but I can only testify after a new judge is needed."

Ken whistled. "Man, this got all crazy."

"Tell me about it. In the meantime, Allison and I just have to stay alive."

~~~

"High Temp Materials Lab, this is Eric."

"Hey, buddy, it's Soren."

"Hey! Been a while." I heard him close a door and start walking.
~~~

"I know. It took me a while to locate the exact color you asked for."

"Hang on a sec." More doors opening and closing. Footsteps. I waited.

"Okay," he said finally. "Whatcha got?"

"Those paint samples you asked me about. The lime green for the kitchen, the shade Kristen wanted."

"Oh, the paint samples. Right. How about dropping them off tonight? You in town?"

"I am, and I will. You still in the same place?"

"Roger that."

"What did you say the budget was for just painting the kitchen?"

"Ah, I think it's around a grand."

My surprise almost broke the cover. "Asshole...doubles his price since June? Last time the guy only charged you five hundred."

"Well, that guy moved up in the world, and good luck finding someone else, you know? A lot of the bigger renovation firms want seven thousand. Can you believe that?"

That was true. Private labs charged absurd amounts of money for this kind of testing. "Gosh, I guess he's still getting a good deal, then."

"Yeah, and the cost just gets passed on when we sell the house."

"Usually. But what if there's not a buyer?"

Silence. "Personally?"

"Yes." C'mon, Eric. Just because I'm in private practice doesn't mean I'm rich.

"Jeez. The guy might do it for five one more time. But he'd have to know it was for a good cause."

"It is a good cause. Hopefully not lost."

"Hopefully, sure." Sound of a car going by. "So, then, how about you? Still at the same old address?"

"I sure am. We should get together sometime, catch up."

"We should. Just leave the samples on the porch, and toss the paperwork in the mail slot."

"Will do."

"Work's calling. Take it easy."

"Bye." I hung up and negotiated the afternoon traffic to my bank. Ten minutes to closing I was walking back to my car with the cash.

In a stroke of stupidity I'd left the paint samples from Chris's '67 Mustang in my glovebox instead of locking them in my fireproof gun safe. My mistake saved me a seventy-mile roundtrip back home. Those samples along with the samples from Johnny's wheel and the five crisp hundreds were sealed in an envelope. I wrote the word 'Match?' on the outside with a black marker.

Eric would know the job. We'd done it before. The cute talk was so the Department of Energy security personnel who monitored all incoming and outgoing calls wouldn't catch on to the private practice Eric performed on the side with the taxpayer-funded multi-million dollar scientific equipment used for making nuclear weapons that littered the buildings out there.

Twenty minutes later I was at a typical middle-income four bedroom, two-and-a-half bath Knox box with attached two car garage in a nice little middle-income neighborhood just off the parkway to Oak Ridge. Kristen was home but I dropped the envelope in the slot without bothering her. Whether or not the paint samples were statistically identical would be in my post office box next week.

My car knew the way home, but I steered it to the Camerons instead. Halfway there I pulled off the road and put my head on the steering wheel.

There were too many forces pulling me in too many different directions. Chris's family. Pete Striker. My career. I still didn't know how to handle the Feds. My dissertation deadline was looming over my head like a falling anvil. It couldn't get worse.

My phone chimed.

"Hello, this is Soren."

"Is this the son of a bitch who burned up my cars?"

CHAPTER 15

"Who is this?"

"James Harrell. We saw each other in the courthouse not too long ago. Saw you get your ass kicked. I gave you a chance to avoid it and come out way ahead and instead you got hit hard. You looking for another beating?"

"No, sir." Acid rose into my mouth.

"Sure as hell gonna get one. You went over the line, son. I've put more pricks like you in the ground than I can remember."

"You intend to kill me?"

"Damn straight I do. But I'll give you a chance to live. I'm a businessman." The voice was the same rough tone, whisky on gravel. I recognized it now.

My throat was dry. "How?"

"Insurance don't cover stolen cars. So you will. Counting the fifty grand that I let slide for the hearing, I figure you're into me for about five hundred thousand. Now, you get me that much, and we're even. You get me less, and I make the balance on you. Get me three hundred thousand and I'll take your arms. Two hundred, and it's your arms and legs. Sound fair?"

"Not to me. Those cars weren't yours to begin with."

"Listen. If a person can take something, then it's theirs. You understand? That's how the world works, son. It don't matter if you're a politician in Washington or a po-dunk farmer in Arkansas. Those cars were mine, son. That Ferrari was supposed to be a replacement for my other one. Jesus Christ, you don't know how hard it was to find one in that color, you son of a bitch. My son don't even get to touch that one, and I love him more than anything else in my life."

Harrell paused and took a breath. "That *had* to be the car you picked to set on fire. I should waste you just for that damn stunt. Now you damn well better make things right with me. You ain't hard to find. Hell, the damn teevee studio gave me your number without me having to say three words. Now, I sure as hell hope you got a trust fund. You owe me five hundred thousand."

Great. James Harrell, crime boss of East Tennessee, watches the five o'clock news. I wondered if he liked Oprah, too. Might be something we had in common, besides being smitten with V-12 Ferrari automobiles. And being pissed off at each other.

"You're nuts." I reached the end of my patience. "I already owe the government a hundred and fifty thousand in student loans. Get in line."

"You don't pay, then I'll take it out on your girlfriend, too."

"Girlfriend?" Then I realized he meant Allison. My vision flashed red. "You'll stay the hell away from her."

He laughed. "That got you. Next time my guys won't botch the job. And I'll kill her before I kill you. Maybe tie her up and put her on railroad tracks like in those old cartoons. Yeah, that'd be fun. Johnny would like that. 'Course, that's after he's done with her. And Jake and Leroy have their fun, too. Five hundred grand."

"What are you, deaf? It isn't going to happen."

"Hell, I'm patient. Go rob a bank. Let's say if you haven't paid by the end of the month, I start taking fingers. From her."

"Like hell," I said. "Let me tell you something, jackass. The wheels that your evil little piece-of-shit, spawn-of-Satan son had on his car when he ran Chris off the road are now in police possession. They had paint transfer from Chris's Mustang all over them. The chain of custody goes from Johnny, to your flambéed chop shop, to the cops. Despite your best efforts to shut this down, there will be another trial, I will be testifying, and your son will be going to jail. If you've got anything left to throw at me, then bring it on."

Empty static hissed over the connection.

"You just signed your death warrant." He said it simply, then hung up.

~~~

"You said *what* to him?" Allison's eyes were wide.
~~~

"He really pissed me off. I snapped." I didn't feel like repeating myself again. "Especially when he mentioned you."

"You think he's serious?" She wrapped her hands around her coffee cup and sat forward in the kitchen chair.

"Don't know. Probably. But the KPD detail will stay by the house until this all blows over. They're used to it."

"And when will that be?"

"I don't know, Allison."

"Sorry." She looked away. "I thought you were smarter than that."

"I know. I'm sorry."

"You might have put my parents in danger."

"And you." I felt awful. The coffee was lukewarm now. "How's your mom?"

Allison shrugged. "Upstairs asleep. Dad's been gone the last couple nights." She glanced sideways at me. "You can't stay with me every second."

I studied the scratches on the table top. Some of them were made by Chris. He'd been alive to make some of those scratches. Now he was gone.

And Allison might be next.

"Hey," she said.

I looked up. "What about moving out? How much do you have saved for a house now?"

"Not enough."

I swallowed hard. "You can stay with me."

She glanced at me, skeptical, then shook her head. "No." She rubbed her arms like she was chilled. "He said the end of the month. That's three weeks. Surely they'll arrest Johnny again before that, right?"

"I don't know. The FBI will be mad as hell if my outburst jeopardized their investigation. They'll have the final word on what happens, and when it's going to happen. Ken will help with KPD protection, but we might be on our own for a while."

Allison shook her head. She leaned back and stretched. "It's getting late."

"I don't want to leave you here alone."

"My dad would have a fit."

"I'll sleep on the floor."

"No, you won't." She saw me frown. "Look, nothing has to happen. We're adults."

I followed her upstairs.
Steve didn't come home that night.

~~~

We left the house at the same time the next morning. My car followed the path to the university, taking Neyland Drive along the river to the parking lot behind the football stadium. After parking and making sure I wasn't in anyone's field of view, I slipped the HK from my pocket. I buttoned out the magazine, then pulled back the slide and ejected the live round out of the chamber.

The Heckler & Koch USP pistols have a hammer mainspring lock on the inside of the magazine well that can make the pistols inoperable. This is what I did now, inserting the special key from my key ring into the lock and turning the catch. This blocked the hammer strut from compressing the mainspring and rendered the gun a non-shooting fancy paperweight. Then it went in the glovebox, locked as well, and the magazine and loose round went in the trunk.

The risk of carrying a firearm on campus was never justified by the benefit. There was no leeway on this policy. If I was caught with a gun on campus, I could kiss my doctorate here and at any other school goodbye. It was also highly unlikely that I would need it. Harrell sure as hell wouldn't know I was here. Just the same I slipped the ASP baton into the spot where the HK had been. I was licensed to carry the baton, and that would be a much reduced charge over a gun, if I ever had to use it.

It was a long walk to the huge steel and concrete football stadium that housed the engineering department. My coat wrapped tight around me, buffering the chilled October air. The hard copy of my dissertation was wedged under my arm.

The engineering department was right above the forensic anthropology department made famous by Dr. Bill Bass and Patricia Cornwell. There's no elevator in that part of the stadium building. I took the stairs two at a time to the fourth floor.

The entire department branched off of a shotgun hallway one hundred feet long. The door closest to my left was the main office for the secretarial staff. Past them was the
~~~

department head, and the doors further down were for faculty in descending rank. There were no doors on the right side, just a solid concrete block wall that separated the office area from the one-hundred-and-ten thousand seat football stadium.

The offices had originally been dormitory rooms for male students when the stadium had been built before the Second World War. Countless renovations since then had left the walls thick with glossy white paint that concealed a dozen shades of previous color beneath it. Each era of renovation could be traced to a layer of paint: battleship gray in the forties, utility green in the fifties, putrid yellow and light purple in the sixties, burnt orange in the seventies. Outdated two-prong electrical outlets were barely recognizable under the coatings.

The bathrooms were the worst part about the place. Ancient plumbing without fluid traps let sewer gas in through all the urinals. The smell was noxious in the winter and poisonous in the summer. Adding insult to injury was the lack of central air conditioning. If you were a first year grad student, you either bought your own air conditioner or you suffered. I'd purchased my own, thanks to my consulting work.

No one liked the department being located in the stadium. The faculty hated the steam heat and stairs. The graduate students hated the steam heat and the stairs and being forced out of their offices on football weekends. Weekends in graduate school were the time to get coursework and research done. Since nine-eleven, though, no one was allowed to be in any part of the stadium after five p.m. on Fridays through noon on the following Sunday. If you had work that required you to be on campus and in your office, tough nuts. It didn't matter that you paid eight grand per semester to go to school here. At six p.m. on the Friday of a football weekend, the cops came and changed all the building locks and ran dogs through the offices. The doors get taped shut when they leave. Evidently they use dogs trained to sniff out drugs as well as explosives, because the first time they did it there were a bunch of embarrassed faculty members, mostly in the anthropology department.

I sidestepped a cockroach the size of a Twinkie and walked quickly down the corridor. His door was closed. I knocked short and hard.

"Come in."

The knob squeaked loudly and I pushed the door open. "Hello, Dr. Peckem."

He looked up from his computer monitor. "Glad you could make it." He gestured to the chair in front of his desk.

I walked in further but didn't sit.

"Is that it?" he asked, looking at the Kinko's box in my hands.

I nodded.

"Let's see it, then." He swiveled in his chair and took it from my outstretched hands.

"It's not done yet," I said. "A few more chapters, plus a revision, and then whatever changes you and the committee recommend at the defense."

"*If* you pass the defense."

"Yes, sir."

I remained standing while he flipped through the pages. After a few minutes he grabbed a pen and made some notes on the front page, scrawling across the text. He ripped through the three-inch stack in about thirty minutes.

"Okay." He pulled the pages together and thumped them on his desk to shuffle them back together. "Marginally better than last time. You need to go back and expound on the places I marked. And you need a more thorough explanation on the biomechanical aspects of occupant cervical vertebrae in low acceleration events. I jotted down some references but you'll have to find them on your own."

"Thank you." I already had two hundred and sixty-three references, but it didn't matter. I'd have to track these down, too.

"And you need to get me an outline of the statistical analysis pronto. You're set to defend in six weeks. If you haven't incorporated the changes and performed a rigorous statistical analysis within two weeks, you will not make the deadline, and you won't graduate. Your committee needs at least two weeks to review the work before you defend it. Any shorter, and the questions get tougher."

"Yes, sir."

He turned back to his computer. That was my cue to get out. I placed the stack back in the box. "Thank you for your time."

He waved me out. I almost collided with one of the secretaries as I rushed down the hallway.

"Sorry, Shirley." I stopped and forced a smile.

"It's okay. Bad meeting?"

Now my smile was genuine. "No, it went great. Just more work to do."

"Hang in there. You'll make it." She shifted the papers in her arms.

"I'm trying." I turned to leave.

"Did that guy ever find you?" she asked.

"What guy?"

"Younger guy, short hair, slight limp. He was in here asking about you, said he was a former student. He wanted your address."

Panic struck me. "You didn't give it out?"

"No, no." She said it quickly. "Against policy. He said he'd see you around campus."

"When was this?"

"Yesterday." She must have noticed my demeanor. "You okay?"

"Yeah, yeah." Now my smile *really* was forced. "Thanks for the information."

"No problem. It'll work out." She gave me a knowing wink. If she only knew.

"I'm praying." I hit the door and bounded down the stairs.

~~~

The guy Shirley described didn't ring a bell. He might have been one of Johnny's crew. Or maybe he really was a former student. The impulse to call Allison swelled inside me. At the first landing I darted down the hallway of the anthropology department instead of going back out the way I'd come in. At the side exit door I whipped out my phone and called Allison.

"Listen, there's some guy looking for me at the university. It might be nothing, or it might be something."

"What do you want me to do?" No panic.

"Nothing yet. If it is them, they won't do anything while you're at work. Keep your eyes open and I'll meet you as soon as I get done here. If it turns out to be nothing I'll let you know."

I hurried out of the building. I cleared the glass doors and walked out underneath the giant concrete columns that
~~~

supported the skyboxes of the stadium. As I walked along the road I passed a few students with loaded backpacks walking to class. I glanced behind me out of habit. I froze.

Younger guy. Short hair. Slight limp. Open flannel shirt, t-shirt under it, blue jeans, maybe seventy feet back. I kept walking and stayed calm. He was blocking the path to my car. I didn't have much of a kingdom, but I'd trade it for my gun at this moment.

I crossed the road and entered the lower door of Estabrook Hall. This old building was a maze of hallways and partitioned rooms. My plan was to lose him long enough in here to make it out the top entrance and then book it to the nearest campus cop. There were blue emergency phones scattered all over campus, but if this was for real all they'd find is my body by the time they got there.

I rounded one corner and heard the door behind me open and shut. Footsteps shuffled on the tile. I made a right turn towards the bathrooms and then diverted to the courtyard door. I opened it quietly and dashed across the open space to the civil engineering lab in the basement. This early in the morning, no one was home anywhere.

I left the lab and went down another hallway. This should bring me to the double doors that led into the machine shop. I threaded my way down a dim corridor. Behind me was movement. Damn. He shouldn't have been able to keep up with me unless he knew the building. I risked a glance behind me and caught a shadow at the end of the doorway I'd just crossed through. My heart was pounding now, adrenaline beginning to dump in my system. If he had a gun, I was dead, caught in the fatal funnel of a hallway.

I hit the double doors. They were locked. I stepped back and pounded the hell out of the latch with my foot. They broke open and then I was through. Footsteps shuffling behind me. The exit across the room was too far away- he'd nail me as I ran for it.

I went back against the door. If he was a pro he'd clear the doorway first. He'd keep the gun tucked close in and the only thing I'd see is a muzzle flash. If he screws up and the gun muzzle comes out it's mine. Get the gun. Get the damn gun.

He shuffled cautiously up to the doorway.

C'mon, dammit.

He poked his head around and I slammed my fist against his face. He twisted at the last instant and I connected off center. I stepped forward, pushing into him. *Advance. Advance. Make him retreat. Assume he has a gun. Get the gun.*

His hands were empty. I kept my arms moving, punching and swinging, pushing him back in the doorway. His foot caught the edge and he went down, but not before he latched an arm onto mine. We went down together onto the hardwood floor.

He cursed as I landed on top of him. I drove my fist into his gut but he brought his left knee hard up into my side. Air left my lungs in a grunt. He connected again. I punched again. Then he rotated his body and jerked and I was off him and on my back. I scrabbled to my feet the same time he did. Blood ran from his nose. His arm shot out and clubbed me on the side of my head. I rolled with the blow and fell against the wall. He advanced. This wasn't looking good.

I rebounded off the wall and squared up with him. The smell of his sweat filled the close confines of the hallway. I feinted left with an extended left hand and jammed my right in my pocket and brought out the ASP, snapping it violently to the floor to extend the segments. His eyes got wide. I continued the motion in one fluid arc, swinging the baton between us like a sword. The weighted end whipped through the air. He dodged backward.

"This ends right here." I spit out the words, droplets of blood from my lips spraying toward him. The right side of my face throbbed. He'd landed some good blows. My side was killing me. I wanted to kill him.

"Jesus, man, I just want to talk." He said it while still crouched, eyes probing for a weakness.

"Cut the crap. I know Harrell sent you to kill me."

His brow furrowed. "Kill you? Dude, I'm disabled and unarmed. And I haven't seen Johnny since the crash happened. Are you nuts?"

His hands were still empty.

"So talk." I feinted again, shuffling my feet, trying to keep him off-balance. We parried each other in the dim light. I was angling for a killing blow. The weighted end of the ASP made tiny circles above my right shoulder.

"You're the guy helping the Camerons."

"Yeah." We shuffled some more. "Why the hell were you stalking me?"

"Military habit. I don't know who I can trust."

"Military?"

"Marines."

"Why the hell do you want to talk to me?"

"Because I was riding with Johnny when he ran Chris off the road."

He was slowing now. He backed up a few more feet. I advanced, keeping the distance close enough to hold the advantage.

"If you're lying I'll ram this baton so far up your ass it'll come out your throat."

"Try it, asshole," he wheezed. He stopped moving and fell back against the wall.

If he really was the passenger, he knew how that night had ended for Chris.

"You were with Johnny? In the Mustang?"

"Yeah."

"When did you get in the car?"

"At the last minute. While they were staging. Johnny didn't want anyone to see me riding with him."

That fit with no one else knowing he'd been there.

We glared at each other in the dim light. Now what?

One minute passed. Then two. Our breathing was loud.

"Follow me." I kept my eyes on him, shuffling backwards, moving as Rob had taught me. He followed, pushing against the wall, keeping his eyes locked on me. We exited the hallway into the civil engineering lab. I backed through the doorway carefully.

"No fast moves. Hands in view." Blood was dripping off my cheek. Blood was dripping off his chin.

I cleared the doorway but kept a measured distance between us. The open space of the lab gave us more room to move. We circled each other warily.

"So what the hell are you doing on campus?" I growled.

"I'm in school here."

"Thought you said you were military."

"I was. Then an IED blast took my leg off below the knee." He stopped moving and lifted the bottom of his right pant leg.

A narrow titanium cylinder extended out of the sneaker where his leg should have been.

"Son of a bitch. Sorry, man."

"Yeah." He dropped the cuff. "Can we knock this stupid shit off now?"

"You armed?"

"Just my knife. I could have gutted you with it if I'd wanted." The top of a folding tactical knife poked out from his left pocket.

"Is that a Benchmade?"

He nodded. "Yeah."

"Good knife." My own Benchmade was clipped in my left pocket, too. The knife stays in the left pocket in case your right hand gets trapped.

I rested the baton on my shoulder. The position looked casual but still allowed the alloy rod into action quickly. "So you just happened to be hanging around the department when I showed up?"

"Kind of. I have a class in Perkins Hall in a few minutes." He used the bottom of his flannel shirt to wipe the blood off his face

"When did you lose the leg?"

"Second week of September. I'd been deployed less than a week. Long story." He made his way to a plastic chair.

"Your left leg works fine." My side was still throbbing.

"Teach you to mess with a Marine."

We studied each other for a few minutes. I knelt and banged the end of the baton down onto the concrete. He winced at the noise, jerking slightly, as if each blow on the concrete were against his body. The long slender sections telescoped back into the handle. I slid it back in my pocket. "Why me?"

"Because we can help each other out. I can help you nail Johnny."

"Why not just go to the cops?"

"Because Chris wasn't the first person we killed." He looked me square in the eyes as he spoke.

"So what do you want me to do?"

"Negotiate. I testify against Johnny but they have to give me immunity for helping him with the first one." He cleared his throat and spit a bloody lump on the concrete.

"If you didn't get busted for the first one, why do you need immunity?"

"Once Johnny knows I'm involved, he'll cop me to the murder. And he's got the evidence to make sure I take the fall." He rubbed his side.

"So why get involved?" It still didn't make sense.

"Because I'll never be free, otherwise."

"Free from what?"

"Johnny. His dad. The life. Once they know I'm back, they'll collar me into working for them again. Doing bad things." He ran his hand through his hair. "I don't want to be their thug anymore. It was cool in high school. But after Chris got killed, I started having doubts. And then in Afghanistan...more bad things. Enough to last me a lifetime. I don't want to be a tough guy anymore."

"What happened in Afghanistan?"

"Hell." His demeanor changed. He moved his hand to his head.

I waited.

"I can't..." He stopped.

I pushed myself off the table. Something was on his conscience. I tried to take the edge out my voice. "So you want me to arrange immunity for you for a murder you allege you and Johnny committed- whenever the hell that would be- and in return you testify that Johnny intentionally killed Chris. Just need to get it straight."

"Pretty much."

"Who was the first?"

He rubbed his hand over his cropped hair. He glanced around the lab. "He was in school with us. Eddie Jarnagin. He pushed meth, Johnny didn't like the competition. I didn't think Johnny was going to kill him. I thought we were just going to scare him. Johnny made it look like a suicide. Johnny actually did it. It was dumb. We were dumb." He groaned and rubbed his head harder. "Johnny paid me a grand to help him set it up. In high school that's a damn fortune."

"You hung him from the goalpost," I said quietly.

He snapped his gaze back to me. "How'd you know that?"

"Never mind." I didn't mention Allison.

He ended up with his hands over his eyes, elbows on his knees, leaning forward in the chair. “Things change so fast.” The fight was gone from his voice.

His phone rang. He dug it out of his pocket, glanced at the number, then silenced it.

“You sent the text message to Allison. About being watched.”

He nodded again. “That was pure chance.”

“How’d you know they were watching her?”

“That’s where I bank.” He laughed. “I knew Allison through Chris, but she never knew me. I was leaving the bank when I saw Jake and Leroy in the car. It wasn’t hard to figure out what they were doing.”

Jake and Leroy. The bouncers. “How do you know them?”

“They’re Harrell’s chief enforcers. Everyone in Johnny’s crew knows them.”

We sat in silence.

“Come on.” I walked to the door. “Let’s grab some food at Ray’s place.”

He sat immobile for few seconds. He didn’t seem to hear me. Then he shivered slightly and dropped his hands. He rose from the chair and walked towards me. I held the door open and we walked back into the courtyard. The morning air numbed my face.

“You hit like a girl,” I said. It hurt to take a deep breath.

“So do you.” He held his side, wincing.

We trudged up the flight of stairs to the upper entrance of Estabrook. The few students we ran into gave us a wide berth. Then we were climbing the stairs to the Hill. We headed to the little café that Ray operated underneath South College. He was blind so he wouldn’t notice the blood, although other kids might. The cafe happened to be directly underneath Cathy’s office. I looked up as we approached. Her office light was on.

I selected two sandwiches and two soft drinks from the cooler. I walked up to the blind man behind the counter. “Two sandwiches and two Cokes, Ray.”

“Two sandwiches okay that’s five dollars and two Cokes makes it six even.”

“There’s a twenty in the bowl.”

His fingertips felt the ink and he nodded. "Twenty okay that's a ten and four ones." Practiced fingers grabbed the bills from beneath the counter and counted them into my hand.

The kid had taken a booth near the window. I slid into the opposite bench. "What's your name?"

"David."

"Got a last name?"

"Whitehead."

I moved the food and drink towards him. "David, can you testify that Johnny swerved into Chris intentionally?"

He nodded. He unwrapped the sandwich and bit into it. I waited.

"Was he trying to kill Chris?"

He stopped chewing. "Yeah." He rubbed his jaw.

"So what happened?"

David's eyes scanned the café. "Look, you've got to understand that Johnny doesn't screw around. If you piss him off, he will eventually get you. And he'll get you hard. Learned it from his dad." Another bite. "Johnny made Chris look like a fool over a girl. Chris couldn't fight him, nobody can fight Johnny, so he challenged him on the only terms he had a chance of winning."

"Racing."

"Yeah. Only Johnny never saw it as a race. To him, it was just an easy way to let everyone know he was the alpha dog. Taking Chris out was just a bonus." David popped open his can. "He modified his Mustang so he could beat Chris, but he didn't let anyone know it besides me and a few guys at the shop."

"Cheater nitrous and gears," I said.

He stopped chewing and looked at me. Wary. "How'd you know?"

"I inspected the car when it was at the dealership. I found the lines and brackets, and measured the rear axle ratio. Johnny could have beaten Chris that night. Fair and square."

"Yeah." David wiped his mouth. "Jesus, that was a fast car. But that's what Johnny wanted. Fast enough for a bad crash. Johnny's dad taught him how to knock the rear end of the other car if they were winning so that they'd lose control. That's why Johnny always wanted the inside lane. There was a lot of bullshit before the race. Usual trash talk. Then we got in the cars and you know the rest."

"Maybe. We'll get to that later." I popped open my own Coke. He finished off his sandwich.

I sat back in the booth. "Why were you even in the car if Johnny was going to pull this crap? It doesn't make sense."

He downed half the Coke. "I was the cameraman."

"What?"

"Johnny wanted to record the wreck. Like with Eddie." His eyes flashed up at mine. "He was gonna post the wreck on YouTube. That's why I had to sneak into the car. If Chris had seen me, he would have known something was up."

True. In a serious grudge race, a passenger was dead weight.

"Did Johnny say anything before he did it?"

"Did what?"

"Hit Chris's car."

"He said 'I'm killing this jamoke'. It's on the video." He eyed my sandwich. "You going to eat that?"

I pushed it towards him. He tore into it.

"So where's the tape?"

He shrugged. "Where's my immunity?"

"I can get it for you." I hoped I wasn't stretching the truth.

Then David paused chewing. His eyes lost focus.

"David?" I asked.

His eyes rolled back into his head, exposing the whites. A thin froth of Coke and saliva trailed from the corner of his mouth. And he fell sideways in the booth.

CHAPTER 16

I leaped from my side of the booth and rounded the table. My hip hit an adjacent table, spilling someone's drink.

"Damn, dude," the kid said. He scooted back from the edge.

I ignored him. David was on his side. I flipped him face down.

People were starting to notice. "Is he choking?" someone asked.

"No," I said. David's jaw was rigid. Small convulsions racked his body. I recognized the symptoms: seizure. From what?

Head injury? I didn't hit him *that* hard. Poison?

The student health clinic was over a half-mile away. Too far to carry him.

"What's going on?" Ray shouted from behind the counter. He began moving from behind it, his hands reaching out, feeling the fruit basket and the cash register. "Is someone hurt?"

"Don't know," I said. If it was a seizure, medical procedure said to keep him comfortable, wait it out. The problem was that David was the only person in the universe who could put Johnny away for killing Chris. He needed to stay alive for that. But my decision wasn't entirely altruistic. If David expired, so did the possibility of getting my consulting business back.

Get him to the clinic. Even if I had to carry him.

I pulled David out of the booth, keeping him face down. Compounding the danger was the food in his clenched mouth. That could damn well choke him to death. I bent low, pulled his legs toward me, then got his waist over my shoulder. We were about the same size, and I stood up steadily, cradling him on my shoulder in a fireman's carry.

I struggled to the exit. Kids parted like the Red Sea in front of Moses. One of them opened the door. “Thanks,” I huffed.

A few kids followed me outside. “I can get my car,” one volunteered.

“No time,” I said.

We were in the middle of campus. Waiting for an ambulance wasn’t an option. David had to stay face down. Need wheels. *Now.*

A university maintenance truck was parked just up the sidewalk. I shuffled toward it. The workers weren’t in sight.

It was a Ford Ranger with a regular cab. Yellow lights on the roof for safety when it was parked. They were off, as was the engine, but the keys were in the ignition.

I opened the door, put David’s feet on the bench seat, and shoved him in. His head would have to rest on my lap. I turned the key, revving the little four-cylinder to life. Then I hit the roof lights, put the truck in gear, and chirped rubber as we stormed to the clinic.

Traffic was backed up as we neared the intersection. I wasn’t waiting. I hit the horn, hopped the curb, and drove past the line of cars. At the stop sign I hit the horn again, cutting in between a row of cars held up by the traffic light. I avoided the light and went up the hill toward the Psychology building, then jerked the wheel left and cut towards the University Center.

I slowed for a throng of students in the street, leaning on the horn again. They scattered. I took the next right turn hard, fishtailing the truck in a screech of cheap rubber tires, then gunned the engine up the hill toward Hodges Library. Cars were stopped for the light there, too. I hit the horn again, slowed to a crawl, and inched out into the intersection. A turquoise Knoxville Area Transit bus squealed to a stop.

The clinic was about six hundred yards ahead of me. Problem was, there wasn’t a road leading to it in front of me. The intersection T’d off to the right and left, which would have forced me an extra mile to the main street on Cumberland or around the curve to the Music building. The area in front of me was a beautiful grassy quad that bordered the library, the dorms, and the social sciences complex.

David’s convulsions worsened.

Shortest path is a straight line.

I hit the horn and stomped the accelerator. This also had the unfortunate consequence of attracting the attention of a university cop in a Chevy Impala sitting in the turn lane as I blew in front of him. From the corner of my eye I caught a glimpse of coffee going out his window and his roof rack lighting up.

The truck bounced over the curb and launched into the grass. I weaved the Ford between the pedestrian posts and shot through the manicured greenway. The Chevy was just pulling onto the curb.

The little truck charged past the Clarence Brown theatre, breaking the quiet mid-day afternoon with a burst of drama. We went over a slight rise, truck fishtailing in the grass. The clinic came into view. I yanked the wheel to the left, cutting into the staff parking lot adjacent to the clinic. Almost there. The Chevy was several hundred yards behind me, siren screaming.

I slammed my foot on the brake. All four tires instantly locked up. No anti-lock brakes on this stripped work truck. The massive red brick wall of the clinic was coming up fast. Too fast. I gripped the wheel and turned it hard left. The truck swung around, then slid sideways to a stop inches from the brick.

I killed the engine and threw the transmission into park. Kicked open the door. David was heavier this time. Or I was weaker. I got him over my shoulder again and ran-stumbled to the clinic door.

~~~

"It's a seizure. Grand mal," the doctor said.

The cop had known it was an emergency as soon as he saw me carrying David. The guy ran me through the system, but when my deputy status came up, I was off the hook.

The doctor's name was Weisz. He held David's head in both hands, turning it gently in the exam room light. "Looks like he had a head injury." He looked back at me. "Did you guys get in a fight?"

"Long story," I said. "But I didn't do that to him."

"Might be when he lost the leg."

"It was." David's voice was soft.
~~~

He struggled to sit up. His prosthetic leg pushed against the paper covering the exam table. "That was a bad one." He coughed.

"How long have you had them?" Dr. Weisz asked.

David wiped his lips. "Since mid-July. They started after I lost the leg."

"I'd like to get an MRI," Weisz said.

David shook his head. "Already had a few. There's nothing to see. The VA docs said it was because of soft-tissue injury and post-traumatic stress disorder. PTSD."

"PTSD can cause seizures?" I asked.

Weisz nodded. "Under the right circumstances, yeah." He turned to David. "Were you in a confined area when the blast caught you?"

David nodded. "In a Humvee. IED came in."

Weisz's eyes grew wide. "And you survived?"

David nodded.

"How?" Weisz asked.

We both stared at David. The room was so quiet you could hear a fly fart.

David opened his mouth to speak. Then he stopped, shook his head.

Weisz looked at me. I shrugged.

"Immunity," David said.

~~~

The only person who could immunize David Whitehead was Dwayne Matthews, Anderson County District Attorney. Former Marine officer.

David had insisted on meeting with Matthews, but not in his office. Somewhere public, he said, where they couldn't change their mind and arrest him instead.

"Doesn't he want to bring an attorney?" Matthews asked me over the phone.

"He doesn't trust them," I said.

"He's a Marine?"

"Yes."

"Put him on the line."

I handed the phone to David.
~~~

Five minutes later. “We’ll go to his office,” David said. He handed my phone back.

~~~

No one said a word as we entered his office. Only after the clerk closed the door did Matthews speak.

“You just got back from Afghanistan?”

David nodded. “Yes, sir.”

“Hot as hell over there.”

“You were over there, too?” David looked at Matthews.

“Iraq. Gulf War One. We didn’t see near the shit that you guys did, especially in Fallujah.”

David nodded. “I wasn’t there, but yeah.”

“Heard it took a piece of you,” Matthews said.

David nodded again. “Yes, sir.”

“Soren said you know something about this crash. The one that killed Chris Cameron.”

David looked at the floor. Long pause. Searching for words.

Matthews studied him. “Son, either you’ve got something to say, or we’re all wasting our time.”

“Has anyone ever died for you?” David asked.

Matthews narrowed his eyes. “You mean, like Jesus?”

“No.” David grimaced. “You said you were over there. In the first one. Did you ever see someone die? Up close? Ever looked into someone’s eyes as they took a blast meant for you? Looked in their eyes and watched the life fade out of them?”

“No.” Matthews was unmoved. “So you did, and it gave you a change of heart? Is that it?”

I winced, but David didn’t react. “Maybe.” Then, “Yeah.”

He sat down in the chair opposite Matthew’s desk. “I’m different now. Different from what I used to be. Look, it didn’t happen all at once. How much do you want to hear?”

“All of it,” I said.

Matthews frowned. I didn’t care. The kid had done some bad things, and now he wanted redemption. He wouldn’t get it from me, but I was wanted to hear his story.

Matthews sat down. I retreated to the corner, near the door.

David leaned forward. “Landed in Afghanistan on July 12th. I was disappointed when they assigned me to running a security detail back and forth from the green zone to the
~~~

airport. Route Irish, they called it. Always a lot of suspense, but no action. Then it happened. Three of us in a Humvee. We were escorting some political dipshit to the airport. We had to stop for a minute because of a bad crash."

David rubbed his face. "There were a bunch of kids that ran up to the convoy. Some idiot opens the door to throw some candy out. IED comes in before he closes the door. Lands near our LT." David's voice dropped lower. "Dan Jacobsen was our lieutenant. He was riding with us. Wife, kid. Good guy. Not like me. He took the blast. The other two guys were killed, too. After I woke up in the hospital, I never said anything else about it."

"Why not?" Matthews's tone was rough.

"It was me that opened the door."

Heavy silence. It pounded my eardrums.

David paused again. He stood and walked over to Matthew's window. "That's when I learned what it was like to be on the outside."

"Outside of what?" Matthews asked.

"Of everything. Never felt that way before I got hurt. In high school, I was part of Johnny's crew. We were redneck thugs. We had power. Being part of Johnny's gang meant you had the run of whatever you wanted. Girls didn't turn us down for anything. If they did, we just took it anyway."

My hands clenched. My left eye developed a tic.

David kept going. "They knew better than to say anything, because Johnny would hurt them. Or get his dad to hurt their families. Never had to go through with it, the threat was enough. Johnny's dad is the king up there, which makes Johnny the prince. If you ran with Johnny, you ran with the big dogs."

David's mouth almost smiled at the memory.

"That's why I picked the Marines to get me out of Clinton. They're the toughest, baddest dudes in uniform. And I wanted to see some action. But after I got hurt...shit, things changed. Jesus, things changed."

He brought his hand to his face, rubbed his eyes.

"Lying in bed with my leg cut off, I learned what it was like to be weak. Never felt isolated before. On the outside. And all the time I was in bed after they cut me up, I couldn't sleep, couldn't eat. Just knew I'd never be the same. And then the seizures started. And I was lying there, thinking about how Dan had died, and then I thought about how Chris had died, and it hit me."

"You're the same as the insurgents who killed your lieutenant," I said.

"Yeah. But not now. Not anymore." David sat back down, using his arms to lower himself into the chair. His prosthetic leg kicked out. He reached down, brought it back in line.

"I don't want anything to do with Johnny, or his dad, or the life anymore. Not a damn thing."

"Everyone pays for their sins," Matthews said. "And you'll pay for yours. But you can walk away from that life right now."

"It's not that easy," David said. "

"Why not?" Matthews asked.

"Johnny's got some dirt on me. I helped him with the first kid he killed."

That got Matthew's attention. "Johnny's killed someone before? Why can't I just charge Johnny with the first murder?" he asked.

David shifted in the chair. He was uneasy. "It's, uh, complicated." He squirmed more, as if trying to be released from an invisible grip of something worse than Johnny.

Matthews shot me a glance. "The first one was taped, too?"

Now I was uneasy. "I haven't heard this part," I said to Matthews.

David's eyes were fixed on Matthew's desk. Silence ensued.

"Okay, look," David finally said. "Johnny was taping the first one. Understand?"

Matthews and I both looked at him. "No," we both said.

David muttered something under his breath. "I made the noose. I put it over Eddie's head. I put him on the chair. I bound his hands. How far do I have to go with this?"

"Are you saying *you* killed him?" Matthews asked. His tone betrayed his emotion.

"Hell, no, I didn't say that." David shook his head. "I didn't think Johnny was serious about killing him. I thought we were just going to scare him. Then Johnny kicked the chair away. Jesus, it was awful. Eddie dropped, but his neck didn't break all the way. He was kicking and making these gagging sounds. And Johnny was smiling the entire time. And he told me if I did something stupid I'd be next. That I'd be the one kicking and choking." He leaned forward in the chair. "He was using me to cover him. I was just too stupid to know it."

"Can you tell it's Johnny shooting the tape?" I asked.

He gave me the same look everyone else gives me when I'm being naïve. "No, you can't. I'm the only one in the shot. I didn't understand what he was doing to me until we watched the tape again. Then he told me if I ever cross him that I'd be going down for the murder, not him. I tried to get away. That's what the Corps was supposed to do. Get me out of this damned town." He slapped his prosthetic leg. "Now I'm back. And he'll just pull me in again as soon as he knows I'm here."

"You haven't made contact with him, have you?" I asked.

"No way. But it's a matter of time. And when he does find me, he'll be asking for more favors. And I won't be able to say no because of the damn tape."

"Jesus, this kid is evil," Matthews said.

"Learned it from his dad." David rubbed his face with his hand. "You guys do *not* understand who you're dealing with. I tried to tell him." He jerked a thumb at me.

"You were an accessory to murder. You're as guilty as he is, son." Matthew's voice was solemn.

"I didn't kill him!" David stood, kicked back the chair. It fell over, echoing on the wood floor.

This was going badly. "David, how old were you guys with the first one?" I kept my voice calm.

"Sixteen. Both of us."

I looked at Matthews. His desire for justice was admirable, even noble. But he had to understand. "And did the cops ever talk to you about the first one?"

"They talked to everyone, Johnny too."

My eyes went to Matthews. "Without this tape, would you even have a case?"

"We got him." He pointed at David.

"I'm doing the math, and here's what I see," I said. "A questionable juvenile accessory-murder charge on David or a winnable vehicular homicide case against Johnny."

"I'll damn sure get them both charged as adults for the murder." Matthew's eyes flashed anger at me. "You're not in the position to be deciding justice."

"No. And neither are you. That's for a jury. But do you remember what you told me after the first trial?"

Matthews looked away from me.

I didn't let up. "Let me remind you. 'It's not a justice system, it's a legal system.' Sound familiar?"

David was pacing behind me. "Are you guys going to help me or not?"

Matthews shifted his eyes to David. "You have to testify against him for the first murder, too, in addition to killing Chris Cameron. That's the only way I'll work it. That way he'll go away for a long time. Should make you feel better."

"Yes, sir."

Matthews pursed his lips and nodded. "David, I need to talk to Mr. Graves alone for a moment. You stay and fill out paperwork, then I play nice and let Mr. Graves take you out of here."

"Yes, sir." David bent down and rotated the chair upright, then quietly left the office. Once a Marine, always a Marine.

"What's up?" I moved after David to close the door.

"The Feds made the move on Bailey last night."

My jaw dropped. "How did it go?"

"Went fine. They nabbed him while he was on vacation out west. They're keeping it quiet for the time being. They coordinated through my office. A certain Mr. Kidd mentioned your name in passing. Said to keep you on a short leash until they finished with Harrell."

"They're going after him, too?"

Matthews nodded. "That's the impression I got. Kidd threatened to go after you just to keep you on ice until they finished their work here. I did my best to convince him otherwise because I need you out in the open for Johnny's hearing and the trial."

"Much appreciated."

"That's not all." His voice took an edge.

I sensed that I was about to be struck by a falling anvil. "There's more?"

"I received an anonymous tip a while ago that you had something to do with Palmer's death."

The blood in my body turned to ice. "I see. That wouldn't have come from James Harrell, would it?"

Matthews studied me. Then he nodded slowly.

"It did come from him?" I asked.

"Probably. But that's not why I'm nodding."

I met his gaze with my own. My face was hard. If he wanted to hit me with it, then fine.

"Palmer was dirty," I said.

Matthews nodded again. "That's what the tox screen showed. And his financial records. But he was also a cop."

"I'm a deputy."

Matthews frowned. "Don't give me that shit. You never had to pull over a speeding car full of potential criminals in the middle of the night, alone, with backup too far away to save your ass if things went bad."

Anger flashed in me, thawing the icy fear I'd just felt. "You embrace and protect evil just because it happened to belong to your tribe?" I tried to keep my voice steady.

"He was-"

"Evil," I finished for him. "He was human, and he made mistakes, but he ultimately embraced the dark side. And that's what you and I need to be united against."

"Life is more complicated than that, Soren."

"It is. But there is light and there is darkness. There's good and evil. I know which side I'm on. Do you?"

Matthews stared at me. "Yes. And that's why I looked into this anonymous tip."

Silence fell between us.

"And?" I asked. My hands were clenched, knuckles white.

"The GSR test on Palmer's hand showed that he fired the gun. It also showed traces of pepper spray on his finger. Non-departmental issue."

"Maybe he was out there to kill someone," I offered. "In a very bad and terrifying manner."

"Go on," Matthews said.

I shrugged. "And then he saw the error of his ways and couldn't bear to live anymore."

"Or maybe his potential victim was more dangerous than he assumed. And it was a legitimate case of self-defense."

"Maybe," I agreed.

"In which case, there's no need to pursue it further." Matthews fixed his gaze back on me. "Unless, of course, someone interferes with an FBI investigation. Then all hell would break loose."

I nodded. "Understood. Thanks for looking out for me."

"I'm looking out for myself, too." He pushed his chair back and stood up. "So don't screw this up. You might even be able to recover your career if things go right."

~~~

"So you're okay? No suspicious people hanging around here?" I scanned the lobby of the bank from the door of the office.

"Just you," Allison said. She walked over to a vertical file cabinet and pulled it open.

Guilty as charged. "Life is unbelievable sometimes." I turned back to her.

"What happened?"

"The guy I told you about this morning was the missing passenger from Johnny's car."

Allison spun to face me. "Who is it?"

"David Whitehead. Know him?"

Allison looked confused. "David Whitehead? He dropped out of school early to join the Marines." She paused. "That's why he wasn't in my yearbook. He was there that night?"

I nodded. "Came home before they shipped him out. Johnny chose him to ride along to film the crash. He knew David would be gone for a while after it went down."

"But now he's here?" Allison was incredulous.

"In the flesh, or what's left of it. He lost a leg after he got to Iraq. He's enrolled at the university, trying to go straight."

"He's as guilty as Johnny."

"We talked about it with the DA." I glanced behind her. "Is that fresh coffee?"

"What? Yes. What did David say?"

I pulled a styrofoam cup off the stack next the coffee machine. "He saw it all. That Johnny did it intentionally. Evidently he had a hand in killing the guy you told me about in high school, and now he'll testify in return for immunity on that. That's all I know right now."

"Son of a bitch. I knew it." Her jaw clenched. "And my dad was right. All along."

"The good news is that he'll testify."

"Where is he now?"

I paused. "You're not going to whack him, are you?"
~~~

"I'd be fine if it happened. After the trial."

"I don't know exactly where he is. He wouldn't even tell Matthews. He gave me his cell number and I dropped him off in Fort Sanders. He couldn't have walked far. More of a hobble, really."

"What about Johnny?" Allison handed me some sugar.

"Thanks." I tore the tops off the packets dumped them into the black liquid. "Matthews said they'd pick him up immediately."

"So what happens now?" she asked.

"Matthews will file the charges, Johnny will get arrested, and there will be another hearing."

"Like the last one?" She leaned against the counter. "Mom and dad can't endure that again. I'm not sure that I can, either."

"Include me in that count, too." I sipped the coffee. Sweet and black. I dropped my voice. "How are your parents?"

Allison looked away. "A mess. Dad comes home, gets drunk, tries to pick a fight with mom. Mom goes to Judith's house." She pushed her long, dark hair over her ear and glanced at me. "But this will help dad. He'll know he was right, and knowing that David is going to testify. It'll give him hope."

I frowned. "Allison, you can't tell him. Not yet."

"Why not?" Her words were sharp. Just like her father. "He needs to know."

"Allison, he can't keep it confidential. He'll tell someone, and then everything will fall apart."

"He won't. Not if I tell him." She focused on me. "Soren, he needs this."

"He'll tell the other kids. He hasn't been able to keep anything secret." I put the coffee down, moved back a few steps. "You know I'm right."

Anger flashed in her eyes. "My father isn't perfect. But he asked you for help, Soren. The least you can do is give it to him."

Her words hit me like a slap. I stared at her. "That hurts, Allison."

She looked away. "Maybe I'm doing it to you before you do it to me."

"Oh," I said. Then, "I see."

She covered her face.

I turned to leave.

"Soren," she said.

I paused in the doorway.

She exhaled, wiped away a tear. "I just want this to be over."

I didn't look at her. "It will be. Soon." Part of it already was.

My shoes echoed off the cold marble floor. As I left the bank, my phone rang. It was Matthews.

"Bad news," he said. "Johnny and his father are gone. We missed them."

~~~

A week flew by. Noon on Wednesday, late October, found me back in front of my laptop. I hammered the words out, flattening them on the screen of my laptop. The page number ticked over again: 507.

I'd run into some problems with the statistical analysis. My underlying data distributions weren't normally distributed. Not a critical error, but one that required time to resolve. And my rope was getting shorter and shorter. It was turning from a finish line into a noose.

My phone chimed. The number was unfamiliar.

"Soren? You there?"

"Steve?" I asked.

"It's me. We need to meet."

~~~

Twenty minutes later, a black Toyota Camry pulled into my driveway.

I pulled on my jacket and walked out to meet him. "That was quick," I said.

Steve powered the window down. He was wearing sunglasses and had a different cap on. It was pulled low over his head. "Aw, I need to make a stop in your neck of the woods, and I figured as long as I was up your way I'd get some advice." He sighed, looked at me through the dark lenses. "I ain't that smart, but you are."

I wasn't sure how to respond. Part of me wondered if it was about Allison. I stepped back, looked at the Camry. "New car?"

"No, it's from the Utility Board. We drive it on longer trips."

"You want to come in? Have some coffee?" I was certain that Allison had told him about David.

"Hate to decline, but I only got an hour or so. I'd be much obliged if you let me buy you lunch." He gestured to the passenger side.

I raised an eyebrow. "Is it about the case?"

Steve nodded. "It's about what you told me that night you were at my house, and I tried to give you money."

Damn it. Every hour mattered. I leaned in, took a whiff.

"I'm sober," Steve said. "I got to be back at work soon. It would mean a lot to me."

I walked around the car and dropped into the passenger seat.

~~~

We made small talk as he guided the car to the main road.

"Doing great. Ask me why." Steve glanced at me, smiling.

"Why?"

"Soren, I have turned a corner." He thumped his left hand down on the steering wheel for emphasis. "I know I've been difficult to deal with. Things just got so damn hard. But I've been thinking about what you said that night."

Relief flooded into me. "Steve, I'm so glad to hear you say that."

He nodded. "I can be handful to deal with. And it ain't no secret that I've got a temper. But what you said about my daughter, and my wife. You're right. They're everything I got. Everything I ever will have. I need to put them first."

We headed away from the lake, toward town. We turned down a back road, heading for an upscale end of town. Steve drove at a sedate pace. "There's something else. I know where Johnny is."

I snapped around to face him. "How?"

"I bribed one of his friends."

"Where is he?"

Steve glanced at me. "I can't tell you unless I know you won't tell Matthews or the cops. Not yet."

I almost laughed at the irony. A week ago I'd told Allison the same thing. "Steve, are you even sure they told you the truth?"
~~~

"I hope so. Cost me five grand."

"Did you tell the cops yet?" I leaned forward in the seat.

"Not exactly." He glanced back over at me. "That's what I wanted to talk to you about, too."

"Steve, what's to discuss? If you know where the Harrells are, then let's tell Matthews and get them picked up."

"Not the father," Steve said. "He's still hid real good."

I shrugged. "Johnny's better than no one. Let me call Matthews." I pulled my phone from my belt.

Steve reached over and grabbed it out of my hand. "Just hear me out. Please."

I tried to grab it back, but he powered the window down and tossed it out. The phone sailed away from us, down an embankment, and out of sight.

"Steve!" I shouted. "Damn it!"

"I'll buy you another one after we eat. Promise. Just listen."

I scowled at him. "It better be good. I don't want him to get away again."

"Hell, neither do I." Steve slowed down, then made a left turn into a subdivision. "Think it's tax deductible?"

"What?"

"The bribe."

"Steve, I have no idea. It doesn't matter. We need to get Matthews involved. Now."

"Son, Harrell already had one cop on his payroll. If there's another, and he gets wind of us, he'll disappear again. You're the only one I can trust. Now, like I said, you're the smartest person I know. Put that book-learnin' to work. So besides calling the police, what would you do?"

I shrugged. "Steve, you're giving me way too much credit. Trust me, I'm not that smart. And I'm definitely not a brilliant tactician." I waved my hands in a futile gesture. "Besides, it depends on where Johnny is."

Steve smiled. "No, you ain't getting it out of me that easy."

We drove past large houses with neat lawns, colored by fall. Steve headed to the back of the subdivision. He was looking at the house numbers now. He rolled the Camry into a long driveway, then parked near the front of the house. "This'll just take a minute." He started to get out, then motioned to me. "This is the wife of one of our board members. I hate being here alone, you know, just paranoid about sexual harassment, but if you don't mind, I'd sure appreciate it if you'd walk in there with me."

"Sure." I opened the door, circled around the front of the car. We walked up the sidewalk, onto the brick entry.

"There's another reason I ditched your phone," he said. "It gives you what Bill Clinton calls plausible deniability." He knocked on the door three times, then two. Footsteps sounded inside.

"Plausible deniability about what?" I asked.

Then Steve reached inside his shirt and pulled out a Colt 1911 .45 Automatic. "Helping me kill Johnny," he said.

CHAPTER 17

The door deadbolt clicked open. The latch on the handle moved down.

Oh, dear God.

Steve reared back and kicked the door in.

This isn't happening.

Steve exploded through the doorway. Raised his gun.

You bet your life it is.

Steve fired, but too soon. He jerked the trigger and the bullet missed its mark.

Glimpse of blond hair past Steve. It was Johnny, eyes open wide, in jeans and white t-shirt. And a revolver coming up fast.

Then a different shot. Booming, deeper. Magnum caliber. Another deep boom as it fired again.

Brick exploded near my face as the magnum slug went through the wall, just wide of Steve's head and inches from my face. Shards of brick peppered my cheek. I dashed to the side of the doorway, out of the line of fire. My hand shot into my pocket and pulled out the HK. I swung back around the edge of the doorway, bringing the pistol up, front sight acquired, tracking for a target. Tracking for Johnny.

Just as Steve came crashing back through.

He tumbled into me. My left arm went up on his back. My right hand moved out so I didn't inadvertently shoot Steve in the back.

Steve still had his Colt out. He was pulling the trigger. Again. Again.

Another magnum blast from the house, further away. Steve grunted.

Something shattered in the foyer.

I backpedaled wildly, but Steve had too much momentum. My heel caught on the edge of a brick paver and we went down hard. Steve fell back on me, still blasting.

"Goddammit!" Steve shouted. "He's getting away!"

My vision flickered as the force of Steve falling on me knocked the breath out of my lungs. "Uh," I croaked.

Steve slid off me. My chest heaved as I inhaled. The HK was still clenched in my hand, finger off the trigger.

"Soren! Soren!" Steve was shouting at me. "Don't let him run!"

The entryway was a mess, broken shards of glass and mirror all over the floor. I shook my head and stood up, thrusting the pistol out in front of me. Johnny had moved deeper in the house.

I glanced back at Steve. "You okay?"

He nodded vigorously. "Right behind you. My leg's messed up. Just get him. As long as he's free, Cathy and Allison ain't safe. That's what you made me realize."

"Steve, that's not what I meant-"

"Don't matter. That's what you made me see. Now get him."

"Steve, I'm not going into a damn house and flushing out Johnny. He's here, and we'll call-"

The sound of a garage door opener drifted from the side of the house. An engine roared.

Johnny's black Audi rounded the corner of the house. He passed Steve's Camry, braked, and muzzle flash erupted from the interior of the car.

I ducked inside the house. Steve rolled behind one of the porch columns.

Slugs slammed into the Camry. Two geysers of steam erupted from the hood and the front end drooped as the tire deflated.

I glanced at Steve. He pointed at Johnny.

Maybe it was for Chris. Or Allison. Or my career. Jesus, who knows. But I ran into the house.

The HK was tucked close to my waist so no one could grab it. My left hand was indexed close to my chest, ready to push out. I cleared the entry hallway, headed for the kitchen. Clear. I needed wheels. The garage was on the right. I stood opposite the hinge side of the door to the garage and yanked it open. The HK was in front of me, tracking. I fumbled on the wall for the light switch and opened the two garage doors still closed. Garage was clear. One car sat at the far end, in the third bay.

I had found James Harrell's personal Ferrari.

Johnny's Audi roared down the street.

It was a 550 Maranello, nearly identical to the same model as the one I'd destroyed at the club, only a little older and with a manual shifter instead of the F1 transmission. I ran to it, praying the keys were in it. And that it would start.

Yes on both counts.

The big V-12 snarled to life. My left hand gripped the steering wheel and my right hand pushed the chrome knob through the H-gate into first gear. I hit the throttle, slipped the clutch, and launched out of the garage.

I feathered the accelerator pedal and cranked the wheel around the corner of the house. I slowed for the transition out of the driveway, then floored the accelerator as the car straightened into the street.

The thrust of the car was delusional. Cold rear tires scrabbled for traction, lost it. I released the throttle enough for the Michelins to bite the asphalt. The end of the street was coming up fast. Johnny's Audi flashed between the houses ahead of me. I made up some speed at the next corner in time to see his taillights flash as he slid sideways out of the subdivision.

I upshifted on the next straight, sliding the long lever into second. Then it was hard on the brakes. The nose dropped and I turned the wheel again, guiding the car out of the subdivision and into the main road.

Hard on the gas again. The engine revved into a ferocious snarl. I shifted into third, then fourth, winding the engine out. I was already running at one-twenty. I upshifted again. My knuckles were white. If a car pulled out now, I wouldn't be able to stop in time.

Johnny's Audi was in the distance, pulling hard. The main highway was coming up, and that would be a straight shot of four-lane for miles. He was headed for the interstate. If he made it, he had a good chance of disappearing again.

The Ferrari closed the distance. Johnny made the turn onto the highway smoothly, cutting in front of a gold sedan. I downshifted as the turn came up, blipping the throttle and pulling the shifter back into fourth gear. Traffic was light, clear to merge. The Ferrari was pointed straight ahead and I floored the throttle again. The engine speed climbed to six thousand, then seven thousand, then near eight thousand RPM. I shifted into fifth, hit the gas and spun the engine up again and shifted into sixth. The speedometer was spinning too fast to read, but I knew the car could hit nearly 200 mph.

I twisted the headlight switch on and hit the hazard button. A small compact car veered in front of me. Hard on the brakes. I flashed my brights and laid on the horn. It didn't move and I was closing too fast, so I swerved into the shoulder. Pebbles slung into the wheelwells and into the traffic behind me.

Johnny was pushing the Audi hard, but it wasn't a match for the Ferrari. I was gaining fast. We were nearing the end of town, and traffic was sparse. The interstate was a few more miles away, and if he made it there, the speeds would climb into more lethal territory.

The road was open. The Ferrari was straining against the aerodynamic drag of the air. The speedometer was at one-fifty, then one-sixty. The Audi was getting larger. I was within fifty yards, close enough to make out his license plate. He had to see me.

Suddenly his Audi swerved to the left and he got on the brakes. *Crap*. I nailed my own brakes, but my reaction time was going to carry me past him. I downshifted, bumping redline, and the big Ferrari scrubbed off speed. My body moved forward, restrained completely by the seatbelt. The car shimmied right. I fought the wheel to keep it straight.

Johnny was twisting in the seat, trying to get his revolver lined up on me as I would go by. Twenty feet, then ten feet separated the cars when it became clear that I was going to stop before Johnny would. And then I knew how to make this end.

We'd both slowed to around seventy. The nose of the Ferrari was almost even with the Audi's rear bumper. Johnny got back on the throttle but I was ready for him. My foot pressed the accelerator into the carpet and the Ferrari darted forward, jumping up to his right rear wheel.

Time to PIT Johnny. Just like he'd done to Chris.

I re-gripped the steering wheel, moving my thumbs from the spokes, then jerked the wheel counter-clockwise. The left front fender of the Ferrari slammed into the right rear quarter panel of the Audi. The impact sent the rear end of the Audi skidding sideways, past Johnny's ability to recover it.

I moved my foot to the brake fast, but not before the Audi swung sideways in front of me. Johnny was fighting the wheel and raising the magnum toward me when the front of the Ferrari rammed the right side of the Audi. The airbag exploded in my face with a bang, throwing my hands off the wheel. The expanding nylon bag slapped my face hard.

The side airbag in the Audi also deployed. Johnny fired but the bullet went wild.

I shook my head and grabbed back on the steering wheel. My foot was stomping on the brake pedal, trying to press it through the floor. The airbag was deflating. Johnny's Audi stayed sideways. Sparks started spitting up from his left front wheel as the tire came off the rim. Just like it had done on Chris's Mustang.

A second later, the rims caught the pavement, and the car flipped over like a dying fish. It went airborne as it rolled on the driver's side, then slammed back to the road on its roof. Glass exploded from the car, small bits and fragments ticking against the windshield and hood of the Ferrari as I continued through his debris, still standing on the brake.

The Audi was still rolling and sliding, heading for the shoulder. It hit the grass and rolled again, this time coming to rest on its wheels. I continued through the detritus and dirt and slid to stop behind it.

The crash was horrific, sure. But Johnny was a healthy adult male, we were traveling slower than Chris had been during the race that killed him, and Johnny was driving a new car with the most advanced safety features money could buy. More importantly, he was desperate. All of the side curtain airbags in the Audi had deployed, making it impossible to see inside the car. If Johnny had buckled up, there was a great chance that he didn't just survive, but that he was still fully capable of escaping. Or pulling a trigger and killing me.

I hit the latch on the seatbelt. The HK was cradled in my right hand as I popped the door and got out quickly, keeping my eyes on the Audi. Still no movement. I moved forward, drawing near the quarter panel, trying to see inside the car between the deployed airbag curtains.

Inching forward more, HK held out, I drew even with the rear door, focusing on the front door.

The rear door banged open, slamming into my right wrist. My wrist went numb, my fingers lost their grip. The HK flew out of my hand. Johnny had kicked the door open and now he was sitting up, thrusting the magnum revolver in my direction.

I sidestepped as it went off. The blast from the muzzle flattened my shirt against my chest and nearly blinded me. I stepped in toward Johnny and pushed the gun away, clamping down on the cylinder like a vise with my tingling right hand. He was trying to pull the trigger again but I jammed my fingers in the flutes of the cylinder and it wouldn't turn. My left hand clamped down on his left wrist, the one with the gun, and I pulled it toward me while twisting the revolver violently to the outside.

Johnny's finger, stuck in the trigger guard, snapped like a dry stick.

He didn't let me have that for free.

His right hand jabbed toward my face, fingers clawing for my eyes. I angled my head away, maintaining a deathgrip on the revolver. His thumb crawled up my cheek, probing for my eye socket. I twisted my head back and bit down on the thenar eminence of his hand, at the base of his thumb, as hard as I could.

Johnny screamed. He brought his feet up and kicked hard, catching me in the gut. The kick pushed me back and I went ass over teakettle, still holding on to the revolver, until I hit the ground and the impact jarred it from my hand.

Something like jelly was caught in my teeth. Johnny's right hand was missing a chunk of skin. This was clear to me because Johnny had launched himself out of the car and was heading my way like an angry redneck heat-seeking missile.

I scrambled back and made it to one knee before he reached me. His foot lashed out, but he telegraphed the move like a soccer player, and as it connected to my chest I trapped his boot with my hands and launched myself backwards. Now Johnny went down hard, slapping his head on the ground.

Johnny rolled to his feet, and I did too. His right hand went to his pocket and grabbed a folding knife. He snapped the blade out and went into a crouch. I grabbed my own knife, flicking the razor-sharp blade open the same way, then switched it to my right hand, letting it lead the space between us.

"It's over," I said.

"Ain't," Johnny shot back. "Not 'till you're gutted like a hog."

He feinted, the thrust slicing the air between us. My knife was constantly moving back and forth, like the head of cobra, never pausing, always moving. The tip traced little frenetic zigzags in the air.

We circled each other. I was learning his timing. He was building up the courage to attack.

"Knife is a hard way to go, Johnny." His hands were trembling. Mine weren't.

"You're gonna find out," he hissed.

I sucked the loose flesh of his palm out of my teeth and spit it back to him. He roared and lunged. His knife sought me out, cutting the air. I parried, let him go past, and hammered the back of his bicep with my left fist as he went by. He carried through the movement and spun around, swinging his free hand at me, then stabbed his knife directly toward my throat.

My right hand was already up, moving toward the inside of his arm, knife blade forward. His knife hand shot toward me and I caught the inside of his forearm with my blade, forcing his arm outward, away from my neck. I pivoted my body and grabbed his wrist with my left hand. His momentum carried his arm and his body further toward me. My blade ran pierced his skin and sliced down his forearm, filleting his brachioradialis to his elbow.

All I did was stand there. Johnny's own movement carved the interior muscle off his arm.

He stopped. Inches from my face. His eyes went wide as he realized what had happened. I could see the veins in his eyes, the tiny pores oozing beads of sweat in his skin, which was turning whiter by the second, and a small patch of tiny freckles high on his cheek. I studied him like his mother probably had, seeing the details, observing them with her own eyes as she held him close. His breath reeked of peanut butter. His bottom row of teeth were slightly crooked. His left hand, index finger at an awkward angle, reached slowly out to my shoulder.

"Oh, Jesus. Sweet Jesus," he whispered.

I looked deep into his eyes, dilated black pupils surrounded by light blue irides.

And then I slashed downward with my blade, cutting deep into the elbow, slicing the ulnar collateral ligament completely off his arm.

His fingers opened, no longer working. His knife fell to the ground.

Rob had taught me that the next move was to thrust the blade underneath Johnny's armpit, through his rib cage, and into his lung, and keep doing it until Johnny was dead.

Instead, I reversed the knife, turning it to an icepick grip in my right hand, and tucked the point along the inside of my wrist. Then I brought it back up to Johnny's left side, along his rib cage. I curled my arm around him as if we were waltzing. My left hand still held his right wrist, but instead of fighting it, I was now supporting it.

"Stand up," I whispered. "Come on. Stand up."

His knees buckled. He started to sag.

"No, Johnny." I said it gently. "Stand up. We have to walk now."

Blood was pouring from his right arm. The brachioradialis muscle was hanging by the skin near his elbow. I let his wrist down and placed my palm under the muscle, squeezing it against the bones of his forearm.

~~~

Ken stood on the road and surveyed the damage. Deep gouges in the pavement marked the path of Johnny's Audi to its final resting place. The Audi was nearly unrecognizable. Every panel had been damaged during the rollover. The Ferrari was behind it, partly off the shoulder, cockeyed as it straddled the transition between asphalt and grass. The front bumper was smashed rearward into the leading edge of the hood. The left front fender was crumpled a little, and the left front wheel was trashed, but both doors were intact. The dark red metallic paint on the undamaged rear flanks reflected the sunshine, metallic flakes scattering the rays in every direction.

"Gosh, this was much better than letting law enforcement handle it. Good job."

"I didn't know it would end this way."
~~~

Ken gave me a skeptical look. "How'd it begin?"

"Steve called me, said he wanted to buy me lunch. He picked me up, threw my phone out the window, and then stopped at a house in town. Said it was for work. The door opens and Johnny's standing there with a revolver. Shots were fired. Then Johnny took off and disabled Steve's car. I ran inside and found the Ferrari. Here we are."

"Here we are." Ken pursed his lips. "You expect me to believe that it was a cosmic coincidence that Steve drove to where Johnny was hiding?"

I didn't say anything.

"Who shot first?" Ken asked.

"Well, it all happened so fast."

"Did you shoot?"

I looked him in the eye. "No."

"There won't be a shell casing or slug in the wall that matches your HK?"

"No."

Ken sighed deeply, then looked up at the blue sky. "I wonder why Johnny didn't disable the Ferrari."

We both turned to gaze at it. "Probably because he's afraid of his dad," I said. "And he might know where his dad is. The DA would appreciate that, right?"

Ken chuckled. "Sure. I'll do my best to convince him to let this slide. Trespassing, grand theft auto, reckless driving, and assault with a deadly weapon. Am I missing anything?"

"I meant well."

"I know."

"I never even heard the sirens," I said.

Ken looked at me. "Soren, you're a little spaced out. I think you're in shock."

"No." I stared down the road, watching the ambulance carrying Johnny disappear in the distance. "It was weird. I always thought I'd panic in a situation like that. Instead, I just got...calm."

"Situation like what?" Ken's brow furrowed.

"With the knives."

"You got lucky. And all that time you've been spending with that crazy Army buddy of yours probably saved your life."

He meant Rob. "Yeah," I said, running my hand through my hair. "I guess."

"You need to see a medic anyway. Come on." Ken didn't try to touch me, but he turned toward his cruiser. "I'll drive you to the Medical Center."

"I'm okay," I said.

"No, you're not. He got you in the leg."

I looked down. Blood matted the thigh of my pants. There wasn't any pain, though. My hands patted my leg, probing for a wound.

"It's not from me. I'm intact."

"Johnny's arm?" Ken asked.

"No," I said. "It's from Steve."

~~~

The whiteboard beckoned. The dry erase marker squeaked as I wrote out the familiar words.

Newton's Third Law: for every action, there is a reaction that is equal in magnitude and opposite in direction.

I stood back and surveyed the class. We'd started with twenty-six students. Now seventeen faces gazed back at me.

"You know the question," I said.

One of guys went first. He pointed to his book, open on the table in front of him. "This book is pushing down on the table, and there's a force pushing back up against the book."

"That's one example. Give me another," I said.

"Gosh, they're all over," a girl said. "My body in the chair, and the chair on the floor, and the floor on the building, and the building on the earth."

"And the rat in the cat in the house that Jack built," another kid said. Everyone laughed.

"Funny, but true," I smiled. "The point is that when one body exerts an action on another body, there is always a counter-action that is produced."

A few kids nodded. "Action and reaction," someone said.

"Yup. Now someone give me the metaphor for people. Like we did before." I capped the marker and set it on the tray.

"Well, if I hit someone, I'd expect them to hit me back," a Latino kid, Ramon, said. As soon as the words left his mouth,
~~~

one of his friends leaned over and popped him on the shoulder. Everyone laughed again.

"It's okay, jefe," the kid said to me. He rubbed his shoulder and smiled at his classmate. "I'll get you back when the professor's not around to save your sorry butt."

"Is that a delayed reaction?" his friend asked.

That made me laugh. "Great analogy. So remember how we apply it to life. Every time you push someone, expect them to push back."

My phone buzzed. I ignored it and kept teaching. A minute later it shivered madly again. I ignored it again. At the fourth time, Ramon interrupted me. "Dude, you better get that."

Murmurs of agreement flooded the room.

"Yeah, guess I should." I pulled out the phone, kept my eyes on the class. "Hello, this is Soren." And it better be good.

"Soren, it's Nicki." Breathless, strained. "Er, Jennifer. Johnny's dad is really angry. They're going after someone named David, and then you. Do something." Pure panic.

It caught me completely off guard. I wondered if it was the cocaine. But she'd said David's name. "Slow down. What's going on?"

"Johnny's dad. I just got to the club and they were all there. Johnny's dad and couple of Harrell's bouncers. The bouncers all had guns. Shitload of guns. All I heard was that they were going after some guy named David. Said he'd signed some kind of deal with the cops. I think he's one of Johnny's friends who was at the race that night."

Son of a bitch. "They're going after David? Right now?"

"Then you. You've got to do something."

The hell I do. The police need to do something. "Okay, okay. Are you in danger?"

The line went dead.

The class was frozen. "I knew it," said a kid at the back table.

"Knew what?" My mind was racing. We had twenty minutes of class left.

"You're one of those Russian sleeper agents." Nervous laughter.

"I wish it was that simple. Okay, do every third problem at the end of the chapter. Be ready to turn them in on Friday. Class dismissed."

They sat there, uncertain.

"Really, guys. You can stay, but I've got an emergency."

They didn't need to be told twice. The room was empty in less than a minute.

I called the number back but it went to Jennifer's voicemail. Crap. I dialed Allison next.

"Are you okay?" I asked.

"What is it now?" Slightly annoyed.

"I just got a call from Jennifer Cox. She said Johnny's dad is making a move against David."

"You're certain?"

"Don't know. Kind of weird. But I'm worried about you."

"What do you want me to do about it?"

"Stay in the bank, call Ken. Make sure you don't leave without the police escort. They'll do it. Get them to take you to the department. I'll meet you there after I get David."

"I thought you didn't know where he lived."

"I don't. I'm going to call him now. He can't be far from where I dropped him off." I packed up my book and lesson plan.

My car was in the staff lot outside the second floor entrance. I went down the stairs three at a time. Calling 911 was an option I didn't want to exercise yet. First, if Steve had been right about another dirty cop on Harrell's payroll, Harrell would almost certainly know that Jennifer was the leak. Then both she and David would be targeted. Second, if Jennifer was mistaken or lying, then crying wolf wasn't the way to endear the cavalry to come when they really were needed. I still had plenty of time to pick up David and get him somewhere safe. If Harrell's goons were leaving the club now it would take them a half-hour to get to the Fort Sanders neighborhood. I dialed David's number as I crossed the parking lot.

"Hello?" Cautious voice.

"David, it's me, Soren. We might have a serious situation developing."

"What, like dangerous?" Someone else's voice in the background.

"Are you alone? Are you okay?" I hit the button on the fob to open the trunk. I slid the loaded magazine and the single bullet that I'd extracted from the chamber into my right pocket, then slammed the decklid and got behind the wheel.

"Yeah. Fine. Studying chemistry at a friend's place. What's going on?"

"I got a call from Jennifer Cox-"

"Jennifer. Damn, I haven't seen her in forever. How is she?"

Not the best time for catching up. "She told me that Harrell's crew is on their way to see you." Jennifer had acted like she didn't know David. But David knew her. Strange. I unlocked the glovebox.

"Now?"

"That's what she said." My car roared to life and I backed out of the space.

"How the hell do they know where I am?"

"Don't know. Maybe they don't. But if it's all the same to you I'd like to pick you up and get you someplace safer. You know, filled with cops."

"I hate cops." He was walking now. His voice exhaled heavily with each step of his prosthetic leg.

"Look, I'm near Fort Sanders now. Near the university library. Where are you?"

"Hell if I know. Wait a second," he paused. "Laurel. And Sixteenth street."

"I'll be there in a minute." It was less than four blocks away, straight up the street. I turned north onto Sixteenth out of the lot next to the library. The stoplight at Cumberland gave me enough time to lean over and grab the HK from the glovebox. I jammed my left hand in my pocket, frantically grabbing at the key to unlock the gun. The light turned green and I hit the accelerator. Laurel was now three blocks away, at the crest of the hill. I scanned the sidewalk as I drove. No limping students. My car charged up the hill to the next light with every pound-foot of torque the engine had.

The light on Clinch a block before Laurel was red. I wasn't going to stop if there wasn't a cop around. Clinch was a one way street running west. I looked east, to my right. A solitary SUV had just pulled out far down the street, heading my way. I could make it. I glanced in the rear-view mirror.

And saw that Jennifer had played me for a fool.

There was a black '01 or '02 Ford F-150 two cars behind me. What really caught my attention were the three muscled and inked guys in the front seat. The two passengers had been at the strip club during my last visit. Jake and Leroy. I didn't recognize the driver. None of them were belted. They looked ready for action. They could easily tear me apart and then grab dinner without thinking twice.

They were following me to get to David.

Which meant Jennifer was on their side.

This was real.

Okay, this could be handled. I'd just lead them to my buddies at the City-County Building. My fingers found the gun key and yanked it out of my pocket. The HK was in my right hand. I turned it upside down, looking for the keyway.

Familiar movement at the crest of the hill. David was shuffling toward me. He was on my side of the street, coming down the sidewalk from Laurel. His shoulder drooped with a heavy backpack.

My heart skipped. *Don't wave.* He was still too far away to see my face, but he could identify my big, sparkling, candy-red German car sitting at the light two hundred feet in front of him.

He looked up as if he could hear my thoughts.

I froze, key in one hand and the gun in the other.

Don't wave.

He waved. And he started shuffling faster.

In the mirror one of the guys in the Ford pointed. Black gun muzzle in the cab.

The free fingers of my hands grabbed the wheel. I slammed my foot to the floor. Rubber chirped as I blew the red light. The driver of the SUV on Clinch skidded and swerved to avoid me as I launched in front of him. There was a brief horn blast and the SUV crashed into the car behind me. That bought me enough time to make it up to David. Cars parked along the street prevented me from getting to the curb. Just in front of him was a driveway leading behind an old church. I swerved into it. The car bounced onto the concrete entrance and the gun key fell from my fingers.

Double damn. It was a blind parking lot. No way out.

I opened my door. "Get in the car!"

The former Marine didn't hesitate. He shuffled faster and got to the handle of the passenger door behind me as the Ford swerved around the stopped cars and charged up the hill toward us.

There wasn't enough time to escape. And my HK was still locked.

David had the door open. I reached down under my legs, feeling around on the floor mat for the dropped key.

"I'm sorry. Sir? Sir?" There was an older gentleman standing at the bottom entrance of the church. He was walking towards me. "You can't park there. We have a Writer's Guild meeting..."

The first shots slammed into the passenger side of my car. The impacts thumped into the thick steel of the doors and zipped into the quarter panel. The key teased my fingertips. I snatched it up and held it tight in my fist.

Writer guy ran back in the church, waving his arms.

David threw himself and his backpack into the rear seat.

The Ford was charging up to us hard. I shifted the transmission into reverse. My car, an older Mercedes S-Class, was a German tank. That particular model of F-150 had performed poorly in government crash tests. Their delta-V might be lower, but the front of their truck would crumple like tinfoil. David and I would feel the seats push against our bodies. They'd be feeling the dashboard and windshield. Hard.

"Brace for impact!" I shouted. The HK went under my thigh. I slammed the gas pedal down and the car launched backwards out of the driveway. The shots were still coming, thumping into the trunk now. The rear window shattered, spilling shards down on David. Their engine roared louder and their truck surged forward. They must have thought we would try to run.

I hammered the gas pedal and aimed the rear of my car for the front of their truck. The distance between us closed in a flash.

The impact was ungodly. My body crushed into the leather seat. My head slammed into the padded headrest. The seatbelt strained across my pelvis, keeping me from launching into the headliner and snapping my neck. The noise deafened me. My vision went from black to red as the accelerative forces manhandled my body. Muffled bangs from the airbags in the Ford.

The Ford.

I shook my head and reached for the HK. It was gone. I spread my legs. There it was, on the floor mat. Score one for

Freud. My right hand lunged for it and my left hand unlocked it. I dropped the key and hit the seatbelt release. I twisted in the seat to get the magazine from my right front pocket, then slammed it in the mag well and chambered a round.

Shotgun blast into the rear decklid.

I turned around in the seat, leaning my chest against the seatback. My right hand had a deathgrip on the HK. I contorted my body to get both hands on the gun and point it out the broken rear window, over David's body lying in the rear seat.

Bad Ol' Leroy was leaning against the passenger door of the truck. Some kind of pump-action in his hands. He racked it again, slowly. He was hurt. Blood was smeared over his shaved head.

He wasn't them. But he'd do.

I brought the HK up. Front sight. My right finger dropped into the trigger guard. Front sight. Squeeze the trigger. Adrenaline made the front sight wobble. Or maybe it was my eyes. Leroy raised the shotgun.

The front sight was on the guy's center of mass as the trigger broke. The pistol recoiled in my hands. I didn't notice. He was still up. I fired again. And again.

He slumped forward. The shotgun clattered to the ground. Leroy was down.

Scan. Scan. I forced my eyes off him and scanned the front of the Ford. Jake had been in the middle. Now he was halfway through the windshield. He'd had the shotgun in front of him during the impact, and now the barrel and magazine tube poked out of his back. His open eyes were focused on infinity. His black cast, now meaningless.

The driver's side door was open. No driver.

My arms locked the HK in front of me. The front sight was in blurry view as my eyes searched the area around the Ford. I swiveled the gun with my gaze, keeping the front sight on whatever I looked at. I couldn't see all the way down the passenger side of the truck. The sides of the street were clear.

"You still with me?" I asked.

David groaned. "My ankle."

The impact had slammed the rear door closed. The problem was that both his feet had been in the way. The sharp rear door edge had cracked into his good ankle and then bounced partly open again. The angle of his foot and the blood told me he'd need serious help to walk. And there was still a guy with a gun around that was intent on killing us.

"It doesn't look too bad," I lied. "David?"

His eyes were fluttering. Seizure.

Nothing I could do about it now. I pulled back from the seat. The pistol went in my left hand. Without taking my eyes off the truck I reached behind me and pulled the door latch with my right hand. I kicked the door open. I shifted the pistol again and got out quickly. Backward shuffle to the front of my car. If the driver had a shotgun, more distance was in my favor. But I had to stay close enough to keep David alive.

Five rounds left in my gun. Eight in the spare mag in my rear pocket. One loose round in my front pocket. There were some loaded magazines hidden in my trunk, but the damage to my car made those impossible to access.

Everything was a threat. Movement down the street. Running student. Cars stopped at the intersection. My ears strained for sirens. Now would be a great time, guys. My arms were still locked out in front of me. My torso swiveled like a turret as I covered the Ford.

Shotgun blast from the rear of the Ford. Flash of movement at the corner of the truck. I squeezed the trigger twice, the heavy slugs banging through the glass of the cab and into the bed. I dropped to the asphalt. Under the car I could see black boots shuffling around the rear of the Ford back to the driver's side.

I crabbed to my right and poked the muzzle around the left front corner of my car. I triggered the last three rounds in the mag into the side of the bed the guy was trying to creep around. That made him hesitate. My slide locked back and I reached around for the spare in my left rear pocket. My left hand indexed the mag and slammed it home, then slapped the slide rearward and dropped it into battery.

Sirens now, far off. He moved.

I glanced under the car again. No boots. I looked up. Shotgun blast against the right side of my car. Plastic and glass peppered my face. He'd reversed course and was coming up on the passenger side of my car from the curb, using parked cars as cover. I stuck the HK around the right corner of my car and pulled the trigger. Again. Again. He was getting closer. I couldn't get a clear shot. Shotgun blast into the hood, too close, hot breath and fire. Pellets whizzed over my head. Then he started advancing from his cover to my car. Another shotgun blast. The front door window glass exploded in sharp shards. I scrabbled around the front of my car, back to the driver's side front fender.

As soon as the shooter could see into the rear seat, David would be dead. Another shotgun blast took out the rear door windows. All the glass in my car was shattered now. I moved quickly down the driver's side of my car, past the rear quarter-panel to the smashed front fender of the Ford. He wouldn't expect me to pop up from there.

This was it. My hands were a vise around the gun.

The guy neared the rear window opening.

I stood, front sight tracking.

The huge muzzle of the shotgun swung onto me.

A brightly-colored chemistry book whizzed out of the rear window opening like a Frisbee. The hardcover edge whacked the guy in the face, hard. He recoiled. The shotgun discharged.

I was firing. Not counting rounds, just dumping everything I had into him. After a couple trigger pulls I shifted my aim into his pericardial triangle. Then my slide was locked back, empty. I was still squeezing the trigger. The guy was down on the road. I jumped onto the trunk. Shards of glass scratched into the paint and my rear as I slid across the car. Then I was on the guy and kicking the shotgun away.

It didn't matter. He couldn't use it anymore.

"David! Talk to me!" I turned and yanked the right rear door open. More broken glass fell onto the street.

He was on his side. The seizure was past. His right hand had a calculus book ready to sling.

"Careful of the glass." Millions of tiny sharp edges glinted in the dying sunlight. "Did he get you? You hit?"

David shook his head. "Brace for impact? What kind of Battlestar Gallactica bullshit was that?"

Everyone's a critic. "Thanks for throwing the book at him." The only blood was on his ankle.

"Best use for the damn thing yet." David looked at his lower body. "The only good leg I had left." He tried to swing it around. Pain creased his face.

"Sue me." I stood up and looked down the street, past the Ford, for help.

The blast on my back punched me forward. Lead pellets tore my back to shreds. My body pitched against the quarter panel. My legs collapsed under me.

No. I got them all. No I didn't. Stupid.

The ground rushed up at me. My chin bounced off the wheel arch. My left arm extended to the pavement to break my fall but folded up useless as it hit. My left side was numb.

My right hand slammed the HK on the ground. I used it to push myself against the rear wheel of my car. The partially open rear door sheltered me for the moment. My head was spinning. David was trying to drag himself to the edge of the door. His hand reached for me.

Sirens were almost on us. I reached up and used the HK's front sight to snag the edge of the door. David's eyes met mine.

"Make sure you put the bastard away at the trial," I said.

David nodded. "Okay."

I pulled the door closed and my cover was gone.

A lone figure was standing at the crest of the hill.

James Harrell.

He glanced in the directions of the sirens. He held the shotgun out with one arm and jerked it up and down. The slide clacked back and forth. The sound was cold, hard, metallic. The spent cartridge hull bounced around his feet.

I dropped the HK on the ground, out of his sight. My right hand dug in my pocket for the single bullet that I'd extracted from the chamber earlier, when I'd gotten on campus and locked my gun in the trunk.

My last bullet.

Harrell could reach me. Hurt me. Hurt me bad.

I was losing strength fast. I'd be helpless soon. Before the sirens got here.

Harrell could hurt me like *they* did. Not for long. Long enough.

Not that. Anything but that.

Harrell approached warily, taking a few steps forward, then pausing. A black Cadillac idled on the street behind him.

The nickel-plated hollowpoint cartridge was in my hand. I propped the HK against my thigh and dropped the cartridge in the chamber. I picked the gun up carefully, keeping the muzzle pointed down. I'd always been taught not to drop the slide using my thumb. I tried to do it now but my thumb wouldn't make the motion. Fine motor skills don't work great when the heart rate is above one-sixty or so. Mine was way beyond that due to adrenaline and bleeding. My heart was beating faster to compensate for blood loss. It was a bad sign.

Harrell began walking towards us. "You hurt my boy," he shouted. "Look at all the shit you caused. If you'd just left my boy alone, none of this would have happened." He pointed at me. "Get ready for some pain. Some real bad pain." His free hand reached into his jacket, and it came out with a Ka-Bar knife. "I'm gonna fillet you like you did my son. And worse."

My breathing was becoming faster and deeper. My body was losing blood fast. I placed the rear sight block on the edge of my leather belt. Downward pressure with my arm made the slide go back. Crap. The slide wouldn't drop because the empty magazine was holding the slide lock up. I swept my fingers clumsily against the lever to drop the mag. It slid out and the cartridge almost did, too. I tilted the gun forward. The cartridge balanced precariously on the edge of the feed ramp, then eased back into the chamber. I rested the rear sight on my belt again. The downward pressure forced the slide back and this time the slide lock dropped into the frame. I pulled the rear sight off my belt and the slide went forward but the extractor hung up on the rim of the cartridge case.

Dear God. Give me a break. Please.

The extractor slipped over the cartridge rim and the slide went into battery. Divine intervention.

One shot to end it all.

"No, no, no..." I couldn't make my voice loud enough. The words rasped out of my dry mouth. Sudden thirst. Lowered blood volume activated my hypothalamus, pulling water from my tissue into my blood, trying to keep my body from dying. Terror fell on me like a cloak, a shroud, enveloping me. I looked toward Harrell.

And I saw *them*. The ones who hurt my sister and me. Standing up near Harrell. Heading for me.

No. No. They're dead. Tears flooded my eyes.

I raised the HK in my right hand. It was impossibly heavy. I was sitting in something wet. I glanced down. The road was bright red. My arterial blood.

End it.

I pushed the muzzle against the underside of my chin.

My finger slid into the trigger guard.

Save David. The words formed in my mind.

They're going to get me again. I swore never again.

Save David.

I can't.

Save David.

Tears of terror streamed down my face. With more effort than I had ever used before in my life, I let the gun fall from my skin.

I swung the pistol across my body. The front sight went in and out of focus.

The steps of precision shooting floated through my mind.

Position. Not the best.

Grip. I gripped the gun for shooting with one hand.

Breath control. I inhaled as deeply as I could. Knife pain stabbed my left side.

Sight alignment. The front sight wavered in the center of the rear sight notch. I held on Harrell's chest. He was between *them.* I moved the sights over, then back to Harrell. Oh, Jesus, if I only had enough bullets, I could get them all.

Harrell stopped about twenty yards away when he saw me raise my pistol. "I saw your slide lock back. You're out of bullets, son. And out of luck." He raised the shotgun. "Better safe, though."

Trigger squeeze. My finger took the slack out of the trigger. I exhaled halfway.

Remember to follow through.

The gun fired.

Harrell's knee blew apart. So much for precision shooting.

The bastard had grit. He fell heavily to the sidewalk but he kept his eyes on me the entire time. He didn't scream or yell. He pushed himself into a sitting position and raised the shotgun again. I put my arm over my face and brought my legs into a fetal position.

They were still there. Now both of them were smiling. The same sick grins from twenty-six years ago. Asking me how it felt. Telling me to like it.

This is how I end.

I prayed his aim was true. To finish it. I willed my heart to stop. Stop. Stop.

Three sharp blasts.

Nothing hit me. I looked up, blinked through the tears.

It was the Feds. The agent I'd called Jesus was running down the sidewalk, pistol extended out towards Harrell's supine body.

The bad ones were gone.

Paul was running to the Cadillac with his own pistol drawn.

Someone from the little church ran towards me. It was getting dark quickly. But the sun wasn't down yet. Strange.

The HK dropped out my hand.

"Hey, stay with me," a voice said.

"Jesus saved me," I croaked.

Then darkness came.

CHAPTER 18

Hanging. Darkness everywhere. Screaming shadows rushed at me. I raised my arms to fight them off. Ropes tied to my arms and wrists prevented me from extending punches. I couldn't land solid blows. All I could do was block and deflect their attacks.

I can't defend myself. My wrists pulled against the ropes. Pull harder. I can't defend myself.

They found me again.

My right arm came loose. I extended my fist at the next screaming shadow.

"Get his arm." Hurried words from far away.

The shadow caught my fist. I pushed until tears came. The thing overpowered me easily. "I can't defend myself." The words were clear in my mind but slurred to my ears.

"Defend against who? Against what?" Older woman's voice.

Darkness lightened to gray. I opened my eyes. My right wrist was being held by a stout nurse. A rivulet of blood snaked down my arm from the back of my hand.

"Be careful of the IV," she said, looking across my body. I turned my head. Another nurse was on my left side.

"Got it." The other nurse held up a bloody needle connected to a clear plastic tube. "I hate it when he does this." She twisted the needle out with gloved hands and dropped it in the biohazard container on the wall.

"You awake now?" the stout one asked me.

"Yes." The word stuck in my throat and I went into a coughing fit. She hovered a plastic cup of water in front of me. The straw poked my lips. I drank. It tasted of old vinyl.

"That's enough." She put the cup on the table. She helped the other nurse stick a new needle in the back of my hand. Purple bruises haloed other tiny holes dotted in the skin.

The other nurse walked to the door. "Does he have family waiting?"

"No, but there's an order to call someone from the police department. There was a police officer here hanging around here for a while. Even stayed overnight the day you came in."

"Big guy?" I asked.

"Huge," she replied.

That would be Ken. "How long have I been here?" My lips were chapped and cracked. My dissertation. The deadline.

"What?" Stout nurse turned back to me.

"How long. What day?"

"It's Monday. You came in here on Thursday evening."

"I need to go." I moved to sit up. My left side screamed. I laid back down.

The stout nurse chuckled. The other nurse came back in the room. "Attending's on her way."

"Where's my phone?" I craned my neck to look on the nightstand. Stout nurse walked over. Her ID badge said Marge. She picked up the black case and extended it out to me. I reached for it and she pulled it back. I hate that.

"No more thrashing and yanking out IVs. It's a pain in the ass."

"Okay, Marge." As if I had control over that.

She handed me the phone.

~~~

"You're awake." The voice came from a woman in the doorway.

She was leaning against the doorframe. Her white coat was open, showing a gray skirt and vested blouse underneath it. A thin fringe of black lace covered her cleavage. Dark red hair fell wavy, past her shoulders, framing her face and her cheekbones and the narrow black glasses perched on her nose. Green eyes sparkled behind the lenses.

The voice was measured, devoid of excitement, but with a hint of humor. It suggested experience of age and wisdom of
~~~

experience. She was probably a few years plus or minus forty, and she was the most beautiful woman I'd ever seen.

"Do you always watch people covertly?" I asked.

"Observation is part of my job," she said. "I get to do it as much as I want." She remained on the doorframe. She spaced the last words out for emphasis.

"You must be one of those doctors who observes from afar." I wasn't looking very dignified at the moment. Most of me wanted her to stay in the doorway. Part of me wanted her to come closer.

"Sometimes the patient prefers the distance." She tilted her head and studied me for a reaction.

My eyes widened, and I smiled involuntarily. "That's an interesting observation."

She nodded. "You're not implying I'm incorrect in my conclusion." She didn't ask it as a question. And she smiled again, seeming to enjoy my discomfort, but not in a malignant way. Almost playful, but not enough to let me judge her intent.

She was smart. Scratch that. She was intelligent.

I reached over to put my phone back on the nightstand. Pain pierced my left side and stabbed through my back. The phone hit the Formica surface and I laid back on the bed. "Any visitors?" I asked.

"A girl was here earlier. Allison. She left this for you." She held up an ArtForum magazine. "I took the liberty of reading it first." She tilted her head at me, as if contemplating an enigma. "Allison said you loved art. But your friend Ken said you were finishing a Ph.D. in engineering. Quite eclectic."

"Not just my friend. My best friend. I'd take a bullet for him."

She smiled. "You took a bullet for someone. You know you were shot?" she asked. She hadn't moved from the doorway.

"Yes. GSW to the left side of my back. Shotgun."

She nodded. "Double-ought. I saved a few of the pellets for you, if you want them. Some people do, others don't."

"I'll think about it. What else?"

"Several pellets penetrated the trapezius and supraspinatus. The trapezius..."

I interrupted her. "Is the superficial muscle that runs from my occipital bone to the lower thoracic vertebrae and then over to the scapula. Believe me, I know it's perforated because I can feel it. Where's most of the damage?"

"Superior and intermediate. Looks like he was aiming for your head. If he'd been closer, he would have made it."

I stared at the foot of the bed. It would have been over.

"That's not all," I said.

She waited until my focus came back to her. She shook her head. "No. The blast also fractured your clavicle. But what nearly killed you was a laceration to your subclavian artery. You were hemorrhaging out fast. Another ten minutes and you probably wouldn't have made it."

"Figured it was an artery. Saw the blood."

"In fact, if you had been a block further away, you might not have made it. Lucky for you that it happened so close to our ER." She studied me for a reaction.

I didn't have one to give her.

She started to say something, then stopped.

"Bad news?" I smiled. "Permanent impairment? What?"

"There's more," she said. "You also had six broken ribs. Two of them have evidence of a penetrating knife wound. Probably a deflated lung as well. But those healed up about thirty years ago. Along with the other scars."

My body stiffened. Hard to breathe. I sat up and turned to the nightstand, searching. Phone. Keys. Flashlight. Nothing else there.

I shifted on the bed and rolled to the other side. The bandages were tearing off my back. Nothing there.

"Stop it," she said.

On the floor. I leaned over the edge of the bed. Must be in my pants. Where were my pants? "Where are my goddamned pants?"

"Soren. Stop."

I threw the covers off my body. Some of the tubes got in the way. I grabbed the lines.

"*Stop it!*" she yelled.

I paused, clear plastic tubing bunched in my fist, ready to yank.

"It's not here." She dropped the ArtForum magazine on a chair and held out her hands. "Soren, the police took the gun."

No gun. That left my baton and my knife, plus the razor blade I kept in my shoe, and the ceramic blade in my wallet, and the spring-loaded steel pencil spike on the backside of my belt. One of those had to be here. I shifted my focus from her to the cabinets along the wall. A spare HK and four loaded magazines were hidden in the trunk of my car, but it would be a damn challenge to get it out because of the damage, and my car was probably at the police impound lot by now. All I needed was something sharp. Something that could be weaponized. I scanned the room.

"Not there, either." Her voice was steady. "Soren, you'll get them back. I promise. Just...stop."

I shifted back to her. She was calm. She'd stepped further into the room. A few tiny creases ran from the corners of her eyes. Not wrinkles, not yet. She probably obsessed over them like other women, but they were beautiful. Just like her eyes.

My body relaxed a little. Deep breath.

Something wet was running down my back. "I think my back is bleeding." I let go of the IV lines.

She walked over to the counter next to the sink and pulled on purple disposable gloves. Then she opened a cabinet and grabbed a box of gauze and tape.

"Lean forward," she said.

I did so.

She gently separated the back of the hospital gown. "You tore some sutures," she said. "But it's okay. I'll need to re-thread a few." She stood up. "Stay where you are. I'll be right back."

I didn't want to look at her. "Sorry."

"No, no," she said, working on the wounds. "I should apologize. I didn't expect that."

"I know." I rubbed my face. "It's not your fault."

She left the room. I watched the door, waiting. She came back with a small tray.

"This might sting." She prepped a syringe with lidocaine.

I nodded.

She worked in silence for several minutes.

I turned my head to look back at her. "I'm okay now."

She smiled, but her eyes were sad. "I think you're far from okay."

The needle pushed through the skin, a dull push, as if it were piercing leather. The monofilament tugged through the hole in the skin on my back.

"Any pain?" she asked. Soft words.

"No. The lidocaine is working."

"Two percent mix." She pushed through the other side. "We found several weapons on you. Plus a holster in your pocket."

I resisted the urge to shrug my shoulders. "Okay."

"I don't like weapons."

A moment passed. "I don't like them either." My voice was nearly a whisper. "But...if you knew...how it feels..."

She pushed the needle through the skin again. "I do," she said.

Silence.

I looked back at her. "Your turn."

She tugged the line. "At seventeen, a person I thought was a friend raped me. Then he panicked and tried to kill me by beating me with a piece of two by four. Left me for dead. But I didn't die."

I focused on the far corner of the room, unable to look at her. My lips pressed together hard, stifling the tears that welled in my eyes. "I'm sorry."

"It's okay."

"It's not. No one ever has the right to violate another person."

She leaned close to my ear. "Shh," she said. "You're contracting your muscles. Relax now."

I unclenched my fists.

She poked the needle into my skin again. "I refuse to live in fear." Her words were simple, plain, unapologetic.

Something caught in my throat. I coughed, eyes watering. She stopped.

"That wasn't from you," I said.

She paused. "I know."

More silence.

"I'm making progress," I said.

She tied off another stop. "Like how?"

I looked in her direction, but didn't meet her eyes. "I used to carry two guns."

Now she looked away, pursing her own lips. "I believe that was a significant decision for you."

"It was."

She pulled the line taut. "Almost done," she said.

The needle pushed through my skin once more, pulling the suture line with it.

~~~

"Where does the case stand?"

"The hearing is scheduled for next week," Ken said. "David's still willing to testify. You won't need to be there. Your report will be enough."

"Fine with me." The last place I wanted to be was in a courtroom. "I'll be there for the trial, though." I shifted my legs.

"That's still a long way off." Ken delicately grabbed the plastic cup of water in front of me. He tossed it down the sink and pulled a half liter bottle of water from his front pocket.

"Might be warm." He unscrewed the cap and stuck the straw in the opening.

"Thanks." I took the bottle and gulped down half of it. "Harrell?" I asked.

"Dead at the scene." Ken pulled a chair from the corner. "The Feds had control of the area by the time I made it over there. I talked with the guy who shot him. Said they'd been tasked with monitoring Harrell as a flight risk after they arrested Bailey."

"I never thought I'd appreciate government intervention in my life."

"The other agent pulled a girl out of Harrell's Cadillac. She was trying to hide a pound of cocaine in her purse."

That would be Jennifer.

"On a more serious note, Johnny went nuts when he found out his dad bought it. Right now we're keeping the story that it was only the Feds, but he'll eventually learn the truth about how it went down."

I nodded. "Even if he's locked up, it probably won't be safe for Allison and Steve and Cathy."

"Or you," Ken said. "After the stunt that you and Steve pulled, it's just a matter of time before Johnny takes over and decides it's time for a reckoning."

"What did the DA decide on Steve?"
~~~

"Dropped all charges." Ken stretched out. The plastic chair squeaked in protest. "Did the doc tell you when you'd be out of here?"

"Next week, if things keep improving." I looked over at him. "What's her name, anyway?"

Ken gave me a sly look. "Dr. Graves, do I detect something more than mere curiosity?"

"Not a doctor yet, Ken." My face flushed. "And I won't be unless I can get my laptop here. And my books."

"Got it covered," he said. He picked up my keys from the table.

"Did you guys impound my car?" I sipped the water again.

Ken nodded. "It's safe. But forget any ideas of rebuilding it."

"I was actually thinking of downsizing," I admitted. " But I'm still going to miss that old girl."

Ken stood up. "Don't buy anything yet. I'm working on something." He turned to leave. At the doorway, he looked back. "Her name is Laura."

~~~

I was ambulatory by the second week, out of the hospital the day after I was walking. Sleep became a fond memory as I pushed to get the dissertation done. The finished version was just short of six hundred pages.

My defense lasted four hours. At the end, I was asked to leave. My heart was pounding, dreading the outcome. Not daring to hope that I'd passed.

I paced outside the room, wondering what else I'd do if I failed.

My back ached.

Chairs scraped. The door handle turned. Dr. Peckem walked out.

"Congratulations, Doctor Graves." He offered his hand.

Stunned, I shook hands with him. "That's it?"

He smiled. It was the first time I'd ever seen him do it. "You did enough work for two dissertations. It was overkill. No one even questioned the decision."

Now I was speechless *and* stunned.

He dropped my hand and turned to leave. "Going out to celebrate?" he asked.
~~~

I shook my head. "Doctor's appointment. Stitches are coming out. I'm actually...uh... looking forward to seeing her."

Peckem smiled. "Tell her you're now a pair a' docs."

I laughed. "Will do, sir."

Then he paused, his hand on the railing of the stairs. "Try to remember to enjoy life a little while you're still young, Soren. I wish I had."

~~~

The relationship between Cathy and Steve worsened. Allison bought a house with her mom. I started looking for teaching jobs.

The pressure of school was gone. My dissertation was one of thousands packed on the shelves inside the university library.

I think about visiting it, but never do.

~~~

The trial was scheduled for December third.

Winter came early. Cold wind pushed on my body as I climbed the stairs to the courthouse. Normally expert witnesses don't sit through the entire trial. They show up before they're called to go on the stand and they leave the courthouse when they're done testifying. I would be staying for the duration of the proceedings.

The metal detectors at the entrance of the building were working fine this time. So were the ones outside the courtroom door.

The courthouse smelled like the old engineering buildings at the University. Thick humidity of steam heat made me sweat as I walked down the hallway.

There were more people in the courtroom than at the first hearing. It was the first time I'd been back in a courtroom since the last hearing. My stomach flipped and sweat broke out on my palms and forehead. The urge to turn and leave struck me hard. I pushed it aside and took a seat in the rearmost bench.

Judith and Allison flanked Cathy in the first bench. Steve was in the second bench, on the aisle. His leg was healing, but he'd have a limp the rest of his life.

Minutes ticked by. Allison glanced back and saw me and smiled. I waved covertly. I opened my laptop and double-checked my slides. My testimony would be the same as last time. I slid forward in the bench and leaned my head against the wood backrest. My shoulder would start aching after an hour or so. I hoped Matthews stuck to the script and called me first.

Matthews was at the right table, near the jury box. His paralegal was next to him. The damaged HRE wheel was on the floor next the paralegal.

I didn't recognize the attorney at the defense table. It wasn't Gaines. The likelihood of being paid probably vanished after Harrell's death, and so had Gaines and his paralegal.

Johnny was brought into the courtroom in handcuffs and an orange jumpsuit. He searched the visitor's benches as he was led to the defense table. His gaze settled on me. The bailiff pulled the chair out but Johnny wouldn't sit. He remained standing, eyes locked onto mine. The bailiff pushed down on Johnny's shoulder harder. Johnny shook him off. The new defense attorney leaned over and whispered something in Johnny's ear. Johnny lowered his face and sat down.

"All rise."

The judge walked in. Thomas Carroll. Relatively new to the bench. Matthews said he was honest.

The preliminaries were necessary but boring. Johnny pleaded not guilty. It wasn't a surprise. He'd rejected all the deals Matthews had offered before trial.

The attorneys made their opening arguments, words fired for effect, gauging the responses of the impassive jurors.

Matthews called my name.

Showtime. I stood carefully and carried my laptop with me to the stand. My eyes avoided Johnny but he fixed on me like a predator. Matthews reviewed my CV.

Same questions as before with one exception.

"And you were awarded your doctorate just a few months ago?"

"Yes. It was the culmination of years of hard work and peer-reviewed research into motor vehicle crashes." The words came out distant and impersonal.

The defense council made all the usual noises. The court recognized me as an expert in the field of motor vehicle crash reconstruction.

The images projected onto the wall from my laptop told the story. My words added details. This is where the victim's car braked. This is where the victim's car was struck by the other vehicle first. This is where the victim's car went off the road.

This is where the victim succumbed to his injuries.

The crash data from the 2017 Mustang was next. Here's the acceleration spike when the car struck the rear quarter-panel of the 1967 Mustang. Here's the acceleration spike from the front impact, when the '67 spun in front of the '17 and the driver couldn't brake fast enough to avoid tapping it.

The jury was nodding with my words. They seemed to understand.

"And were you able to find any physical evidence that linked the defendant's vehicle to the impact with the victim's vehicle?" Matthews crossed his arms.

"The police department confiscated a set of very rare and very expensive wheels from a business that the defendant's father owned. One of the wheels had damage to the aluminum rim consistent with this type of impact. There were flakes of paint on the wheels that were statistically identical to the paint samples obtained from the quarter-panel of the victim's car."

"And you have proof of this analysis?"

"Yes, sir." I handed Matthews the envelope containing the spectrographic results from Eric's testing. "The testing is certified by NIST on very expensive equipment at Oak Ridge National Laboratory."

"They take private work?"

"Occasionally, but the paperwork is a headache."

Matthews asked the results be admitted into evidence. Carroll granted the request.

"Is this the wheel those samples were taken from?" Matthews asked me. He walked over to the silver alloy. His paralegal scrambled over and propped it up.

"Yes, sir. And the samples were taken under police supervision."

"Your witness, Mr. Hackett."

The defense attorney scraped his chair back.

He was more aggressive than smart. He missed the opportunity to score a few points, and his attack on me turned off some jurors. A few of his questions tried to lure me to testify outside the bounds of my knowledge, but I held fast and told him I was only an expert in crash reconstruction. Not medicine. Not law. Not law enforcement.

Hackett attacked the chain of custody of the wheels. How can you, Dr. Graves, prove the wheels were on the defendant's vehicle at the time of the crash, when you never saw the wheels on Mr. Harrell's Mustang? Ever?

The wheels went from Johnny's car to his father's shop to police custody. The damage on the wheels is consistent with the kinematics of this crash. The paint embedded in the aluminum gouges prove it was on the left front wheel of the vehicle that struck the rear of the victim's car. My investigation alone can not prove that these wheels were on the defendant's car at the time of the crash. However, these photographs of the defendant's 2011 Mustang taken a few weeks prior to the crash and posted on his internet social website, show the wheels on his car. Then Matthews introduced them into evidence. The photos taken by the camera phone would be introduced later, during his direct on David.

I couldn't avoid seeing Johnny when Hackett wandered over to the defense table. Each time he did so, Johnny pointed his finger at me and dropped his thumb.

His final question: was it my opinion that the defendant intentionally swerved into the victim's car?

My answer: I can only establish that contact occurred between the vehicles. In this particular case I cannot establish which vehicle was intentionally steered into the other.

I ignored Johnny's stare as I left the witness stand. I slid back into the bench at the rear of the courtroom.

David was called after me. Matthews began his cross with the usual preliminary questions. Then it got interesting.

"Now, Mr. Whitehead, were you present at this racing event?"

"Yes, sir."

"Were you able to see the wheels on Johnny's Mustang?"

"Yes, sir."

"Was this one of them?" The paralegal scurried back over and propped up the wheel again.

"Yes, sir, that's one of them."

"In fact, you had a firsthand view of everything, didn't you?"

"Yes, sir. I was in the passenger seat of Johnny's Mustang." Whispers from the jury.

"And who was driving the vehicle you were in?" Matthews remained impassive.

"Johnny Harrell."

"Would you point him out, sir."

David's finger tracked to Johnny.

"Let the record reflect the witness identified Johnathan Earl Harrell."

Matthews continued. "Had you ever ridden with him during a drag race before?"

"No, sir."

"Why this time?"

"Johnny wanted someone to record it on video."

"Record what, exactly?"

David shifted. His hands fidgeted. "The crash." The jury remained impassive.

Matthews looked at the jury. "Johnny knew there was going to be a crash?"

David's eyes fixed on the wooden bar in front of him. "Yes, sir. That was the plan."

A few jurors looked over at Johnny.

Matthews stayed away from the blackmail. It would be poisonous to David's testimony. Johnny's attorney wouldn't want it brought out, either.

"Did Johnny say or do anything that made you believe his intention was to kill Mr. Cameron?"

David hesitated to answer. The courtroom hung on his pause. "He said he wanted to knock him loose just before the curve, after he was going fast enough to make it bad. I can't say that he knew he could kill him, but he wanted to."

"Why?" The question was on the juror's faces, but it was Matthew's voice.

David shrugged. "It was over a girl. And Chris and Johnny never got along."

Steve's cheeks were wet. It went deeper than that.

Matthews pressed on. "Describe in your own words what happened that night."

David glanced over at the judge. "Johnny stole Chris's girlfriend. Things got worse between them. Lots of trash talk, the usual bullsh-" He stopped before the word came out.

"Chris stood up to Johnny. Challenged Johnny to a drag race. Johnny told me that it'd be Chris's last. Johnny likes to record the bad stuff he does. He edits himself out and then posts it on YouTube. He told me I'd be the one recording the whole thing and I didn't argue. You don't argue with Johnny.

"We all showed up out there. It was late. Still hot. Chris showed up and it almost happened without the race. One of our crew pulled a baseball bat but Johnny said they'd settle it with the race. They argued forever about lengths and Johnny got his way. I had the camcorder and we got in the car. Johnny said he wanted everything on tape so I started recording. Johnny said he'd do it before the curve. Then it was on, and it happened fast. It's on the tape."

"We'll get to that in a moment," Matthews said. "Please continue."

"We took off. Johnny didn't have to shift 'cause it was an automatic. Johnny held back and let Chris gain on him. Then he got his car next to Chris's just before the curve. He jerked the wheel and we hit him like the other guy said." He gestured in my direction.

"It wasn't even that hard but Chris's car swung around in front of us. Johnny couldn't get on the brake fast enough and we hit his passenger door. We were kind of sliding together for a split second and then Johnny was on the brake and the other car was sliding away from us. Seemed like the other car would never stop rolling. I can't forget it."

"What happened after that?" Matthews leaned against the table.

"Johnny turned the car around and headed back to the start where everybody else was. He got out and told everyone that we had to wait to call the cops because they'd take his car if they came now. He said Chris was probably okay, but that he'd lose his car and he'd take it out on whoever made the call. Johnny said he'd call 911 as soon as he got back."

"Got back from where?"

"His dad's garage. He dropped his Mustang off, I helped him pull the wheels, and then Billy- one of his crew- took us back there in his Mitsubishi. Then he called the cops and that was it."

"So no one called 911 while you were gone?"

"No way. They were his friends, not Chris's. The garage wasn't far from the race, anyway. Especially the way Billy drives."

Matthews nodded. "Your Honor, we'd like to show the jury the video Mr. Whitehead filmed."

"Granted."

A television was wheeled in. The bailiff fiddled with the controls for a minute. The screen was turned to the jury and the judge but the sound carried into the benches. Muted roar. Engines revving. Muffled words, Johnny's voice. Screaming tires.

More roaring, quieter then louder as the transmissions shifted. Muffled tire screech. Impact. Shouted curse. Sliding tires, then metal sliding on asphalt, growing quieter. Silence.

"One hour for lunch," Carroll ordered. "This court will resume at one p.m."

It wouldn't be right to be seen with Allison or the Camerons, so I ate with Matthews. He was happy.

"I think we'll get it," he said. "Homicide with intent."

On the way back in I hit the men's room. Clanking pipes and a hissing radiator greeted me as I approached the urinal.

Metallic clacking noise. I glanced over at the line of stalls. Then a toilet flushed and one of the stall doors opened. Steve stepped out.

I flushed and turned around. "Hey, Steve."

He adjusted his suit jacket. "Hey, buddy."

We walked over to the sink. "You okay?" I asked. The automatic soap dispenser chugged.

He smiled. "Doing great." He waved at the towel dispenser. It whirred and he tore off the paper. "I think this is going to be a good day." He clapped me on the back. "You did great," he said. "And I'm glad you're with Allison."

I winced. My shoulder was still healing.

His enthusiasm was infectious. He looked better than I'd ever seen him. Maybe this is what it would take for him to come to peace.

Steve held the door open. As we neared the courtroom entrance, Judith intercepted me.

"You did great," she said. "This has been so hard on Cathy and Steve and Allison. You've really done so much for them. I wish there was some way I could thank you."

Steve walked ahead of me. I slowed to match Judith. "It's okay. Thanks for the kind words. I'll feel better after Johnny is locked up, though."

"Me too." She moved to my left and we walked down the hall. She bumped into a wastecan as we were talking.

"Clumsy me." She moved the can back against the wall. We walked down the hall to the courtroom doors. Steve disappeared inside the courtroom.

"Hold it." The officer by the metal detector in front of the door held his arm out.

"What?" Judith asked.

"Damn thing is on the blink again." He gestured at the metal frame we were about to walk through. The small row of LED lights on the side were off.

One officer searched through Judith's purse while the other retrieved a handheld wand from a nearby table. He swept the unit around us, blessing us with the magnetic loop, and waved us through. We walked into the courtroom.

"Wait a minute," Judith said. Most of the people had filed back in the courtroom already. She stepped close to me and gave me a hug. "No matter what happens, you did your part. You did good."

~~~

Hackett's cross couldn't repair the damage done to his case. He put Johnny on the stand for his direct.

Johnny's right arm didn't look right. He couldn't move it above his shoulder, and he asked the bailiff to help him into the witness box. He kept his eyes on me the entire time.

Hackett started his direct. It was all a mistake, Johnny said. He hadn't set out to kill Chris. They didn't get along. Not something to kill someone about. David had a beef against him. He was scared of losing his car. He didn't know Chris was hurt.

Johnny and Hackett were selling. The jury wasn't buying.

Matthews kept his cross short. He was ahead and he didn't want to screw it up.
~~~

Closing shots now. Matthews and Hackett went back over the case, each with their own spin. Red and orange light cascaded through the windows. The sun was low in the winter sky.

Carroll ordered deliberation. We filed into the hall. Judith and Cathy stayed in the pew. So did Steve. Ten minutes later we were back in the courtroom.

The jurors came back in and stepped into the jury box.

"Have you reached a verdict?" Carroll asked.

"We have," the foreperson said. She handed a piece of paper to the bailiff, who took it over to the judge.

"What say you in the matter of the State versus Johnathan Earl Harrell?"

"On the count of vehicular homicide, we the jury find the defendant guilty."

Dead silence.

I shifted in the pew. Something sharp poked me in the side. I fished around in the pocket of my jacket. My fingers closed on something small, cold, and metal. I pulled it out. It was the emblem I'd picked up off the ground and given to Judith, way back when we were out at the scene together, back when it all started. The little Mustang pony had been polished up brightly. It glinted in the courtroom lights, full and vibrant with life, the little muscles of the horse rippling with strength at full gallop.

I looked up towards Judith. She must have slipped it in my pocket when we hugged. She turned around in her seat and we locked eyes. She was crying but she smiled at me. It was a broken smile, melancholic and sad. Then she looked at Steve.

I followed her eyes. Steve shifted. I wouldn't have caught the motion but it was familiar to me. I'd witnessed it thousands of times, and done it many more myself. The right elbow swings up and to the rear as the right hand sweeps the front of the jacket back.

The noise from the bathroom stall.

Steve was a supervisor with the Utilities Board. He had access to any public building in Anderson County, including the courthouse.

He remained sitting but his hands came forward and up. The stainless steel slab sides of a Colt 1911 semi-automatic pistol poked into the aisle. Steve liked those old guns.

No. Damn it, no. I launched out of the bench.

The blasts rocked the courtroom. I lost count after four. A woman screamed. Steve was up and moving. I caught him broadside. We went down in a pile. My left shoulder slammed into the side of a bench. The pain was excruciating.

My right hand latched onto Steve's wrist. The gun went off again. Someone fell.

Steve was struggling. He was turning the gun on himself.

"Stop it! Stop this, damn it!" I was losing the battle. The muzzle turned up the wall and onto the ceiling, slowly pivoting to Steve's head

The bailiff was on me. A black duty boot cracked down on Steve's hand, mashing it and the gun into the floor. I was yanked up and tossed onto a bench.

Johnny was slumped over the table. The orange jumpsuit was slowly turning dark red.

"Dad!" Allison stepped over the back of the bench and tried to get to him. I caught her as she went by. She was crying hard, shaking. I pulled her to me. Cathy and Judith were still in their seats. They hadn't moved.

Judith met my eyes. She had known. She turned back to Cathy and pulled her sister close.

~~~

The failure of the metal detector was traced to a dead receptacle. The dead receptacle was traced to a magnetic switch that had been wired into the electrical wire that ran around the outside wall of the courtroom. If a strong magnet was placed near the switch, it disconnected, cutting the power in the wire. Nothing else had been plugged into the receptacle circuit that day.

The strong magnet was found inside one of the wastecans outside the courtroom. The wastecan had been pushed against the wall immediately before Steve had gone through the detector. It was premeditated. Steve admitted to setting the entire thing up in the weeks leading up to the trial. He said he'd acted alone.

I knew otherwise.
~~~

CHAPTER 19

"How's your dad doing?" I asked.

"Not good." Allison shivered and pulled her coat tighter. "He's got a good attorney, but they're going to put him in prison."

"I'll talk to Matthews. See if there's anything I can do."

"Thanks." Her breath frosted the air between us. "Judith knew about it, didn't she?"

"I think so."

Any doubt that remained about leaving, vanished.

"You don't have to go," I said.

Allison shook her head. "I can't stay here anymore. All I can think about is leaving."

We were standing on the porch of her parent's house. Where it had all started, four months ago.

Cathy had moved in with Judith. The house was up for sale. Allison was taking a job transfer to North Carolina. Not too far from her mom. Or Chris's grave.

She reached for my arm. I pulled her close, hugging her, not wanting to let go. Her tears were hot against my cheek.

"We can still be friends, can't we?" I spoke the words she had once asked me.

She nodded, wiping her eyes.

"If you ever need me, just call."

"I will. You can call me, too."

"Okay." My hand squeezed hers.

Early January snow blanketed the yard. The billowing white landscape looked like Chris's quilt.

They say not to look back. I couldn't help it.

Allison waved her hand in a small circle, then raised it to her face. The tears started harder this time. She turned quickly and opened the door to the kitchen.

My breath condensed in the air. Then I dropped into the seat of the rental car, hit the ignition, and left the driveway.

~~~

The smell of freshly-baked pizza hit me as I opened the door. Ken and Rob were at a table in the back.

Ken had a smile on his face larger than I'd ever seen. "What's up, doc?" he asked.

"How long have you been waiting to use that?" I shrugged out of my coat, wincing as it came off my left shoulder, then laid it on the back of the chair next to mine.

"Years," Ken said.

"You're next," I said to Rob.

"I'm working on it. First I need to eat." He tossed the menu on the table. "But before that happens, Ken has something to tell you."

I glanced at both of them. "What?"

"You didn't buy a car yet, right?" Ken asked.

"No, still got the rental."

"I've got one for you. But it needs some work." Ken was drawing it out, savoring the moment.

I knew what it was. I smiled, but I had to turn it down. "Ken, I need something newer than your father's Oldsmobile. It's your car. I'll help you fix it, but it's your dad's. And it always will be."

"That's not it," he said. "You doctors think you know everything."

Rob laughed. "That's true. I can't wait to be one."

I squeezed a lemon into the glass of water in front of me. "Okay, I give up. What is it? An old ambulance? A hearse? A tank? A Crown Vic like yours?"

Ken shook his head. He waited for me to finish.

"None of those." He sipped his water and leaned back in his chair. "Most confiscated vehicles have to be appraised and then go through a public auction. I talked with Matthews, and called in a few favors, and I'm in a position to make you an offer you can't refuse."
~~~

"One of the cars from the club?" I asked.

Ken shook his head again. "No. Those were all stolen. This one was legitimately owned. But you have to purchase it. I got the appraiser to value it as a loss, but it's still not cheap."

"Ken, I give up."

Rob popped Ken on the shoulder. "Just tell him."

Ken looked me in the eye. "Harrell's Ferrari."

The words hit me, left me momentarily dazed. "Ken, I can't afford that. They're probably asking fifty grand as it sits. It needs twenty grand in parts alone."

"I can't do anything about the parts, but the car is yours for fifteen thousand."

"Did you get a check from your insurance company for your Mercedes?" Rob asked me.

"Yes."

"How much?" Ken asked.

I looked at the table. "Ten thousand."

"Any idea where you might have some more money stashed?" Ken asked. His voice dripped with sarcasm.

I smiled at him. "Maybe."

"Dude," Rob said, smiling. "You can do this. Beg, borrow-"

Ken shot him a glance.

"But don't steal." Rob pointed at Ken. "It would make it difficult for him."

Ken nodded. "If you're going to do it, you need to jump on it. You could fix it, couldn't you?"

"No problem. Just takes time," I said. My phone rang.

"Graves," I answered.

"Is this Dr. Soren Graves?"

The title still sounded strange to my ears. "Yes. Can I help you?"

"My name is Nathan Edelstein, and I work for American General Insurance. Gerard Ripley from Liberty Mutual suggested I contact you. I understand you do accident reconstruction?"

"That's correct."

"You take cases that are, say, more unusual than others?"

"I guess I do."

"I have a crash that we'd like to have investigated. It's in Georgia, near Atlanta. How soon do could you meet with me about it?"

My schedule was empty, but I didn't say that. "I can fit you in sometime this week."

"We were hoping maybe a little sooner. We're willing to pay you a significant retainer if you could meet today."

"What kind of retainer did you have in mind?" I asked. Rob and Ken looked over at me.

"Ten thousand dollars," he said.

"I can do that. Where do you want to meet?"

He gave me a Buckhead address. I jotted it down.

"What time can we expect you?" Nathan asked.

"I'll be there by four. Anything I need to know beforehand?"

"Is it likely that a car could be wrecked and rebuilt multiple times?"

"How many?"

"We don't know yet."

"Sounds like insurance fraud." My stomach rumbled.

"That's what we're thinking. Only this time there's a complicating matter."

"What's that?"

"The last alleged crash had a dead passenger. And the owner disappeared after we gave him the check."

"Interesting," I said. "See you in a few hours."

I put my phone back in my pocket.

"Well?" Ken asked me.

I nodded, took a deep breath. "Okay. I'll take the car."

~~~

Laura McDonnell, Doctor of Medicine, closed her folder gently. "How's the pain?"

"You mean in the shoulder?" I asked.

She shrugged. "Wherever."

I nodded. "It's fine. Less every day."

She nodded, studying me, and nodded again, this time with a barely perceptible smile.

"How's yours?" I asked.

"Same." She turned and placed the folder on the counter. "It hurts a little less every morning I wake up."

I reached behind my back to grab the fabric of my shirt. Laura reached over and pulled the sleeve out. My arm slid down it. "Thanks."
~~~

"You're welcome. And thank you," she said.

I buttoned my shirt. "For what?"

"For leaving your gun in your car. At least, I'm assuming it's in your car. Unless you've reached a milestone and tossed it in the river."

I kept buttoning. "It's in the car." I fastened the last button and looked at her. "How could you tell?"

"There's an outline. Not very noticeable, but I know what to look for."

"Have you studied me that closely?"

She looked straight at me. "Yes."

I returned her gaze. "And what's your professional opinion?"

"I haven't reached one yet." She leaned closer. "But I'm cautiously optimistic." She stayed close for a moment, searching my eyes.

"Dr. McDonnell," I said, leaning toward her, "would you consider meeting me for coffee sometime?"

She broke into a genuine smile then. The tiny lines near her eyes lifted up, above her cheeks, radiant green eyes beaming. "Dr. Graves, I'd like that very much."

www.ingramcontent.com/pod-product-compliance
Lightning Source LLC
Chambersburg PA
CBHW051942240626
47153CB00005B/1594

* 9 7 8 1 7 3 2 9 9 6 5 3 3 *